continued .

D0451734

Because You Are Mine Series

BECAUSE YOU ARE MINE (ALSO AVAILABLE IN SERIAL FORMAT)
WHEN I'M WITH YOU (ALSO AVAILABLE IN SERIAL FORMAT)
BECAUSE WE BELONG
SINCE I SAW YOU

Titles by Beth Kery

WICKED BURN
DARING TIME
SWEET RESTRAINT
PARADISE RULES
RELEASE
EXPLOSIVE
THE AFFAIR (ALSO AVAILABLE IN SERIAL FORMAT)
GLIMMER

One Night of Passion Series

ADDICTED TO YOU (WRITING AS BETHANY KANE)
EXPOSED TO YOU
ONLY FOR YOU

One Night of Passion Specials

BOUND TO YOU
CAPTURED BY YOU

GLIMMER

BETH KERY

BERKLEY BOOKS, NEW YORK

THE BERKLEY PUBLISHING GROUP
Published by the Penguin Group
Penguin Group (USA) LLC
375 Hudson Street, New York, New York 10014

USA • Canada • UK • Ireland • Australia • New Zealand • India • South Africa • China

penguin.com

A Penguin Random House Company

This book is an original publication of The Berkley Publishing Group.

Library of Congress Cataloging-in-Publication Data

Kery, Beth.
Glimmer / Beth Kery. — Berkley trade paperback edition.
p. cm.
ISBN 978-0-425-27965-6 (paperback)
I. Title.
PS3611.E79G58 2015
813'.6—dc23
2014045338

PUBLISHING HISTORY
Berkley trade paperback edition / May 2015

PRINTED IN THE UNITED STATES OF AMERICA

10 9 8 7 6 5 4 3 2 1

Cover photograph of "Girl" © Maggie McCall / Trevillion Images;
"Hair" © GeorgeMPhotography / Shutterstock.
Cover design by George Long.
Text design by Kristin del Rosario.

ACKNOWLEDGMENTS

Many thanks to my editor, Leis Pederson, for her support of my story lines and my writing, and for keeping me on track. I owe a huge debt of gratitude to my husband, who struggles through and celebrates every book with me, and is a part of each of them as a result.

ONE

Alice Reed was used to hiding her nerves. She was used to hiding almost everything. Today was different though. She could have disguised her anxiety about her upcoming interview as easily as she could have ignored a provocative mathematical challenge.

"Don't worry about it. It'll be a piece of cake. Just focus on what you know. You're pretty damn awesome when you do that," Maggie Lopez said soothingly as she stood over Alice and gave her a friendly but critical once-over. Maggie was her graduate advisor at Arlington College's executive MBA program. After a series of initial screwups that now looked like serendipity, Alice rented the apartment above Maggie's garage. Most importantly, Maggie and Alice had become friends. She respected Maggie's opinion, so her anxiety ratcheted up even higher when she saw her mentor's slight frown as she stared down at her. A horrible thought hit her. She plopped her hand palm down on the top of her head.

"*Shit*. My roots. They're showing, aren't they? I forgot to color them. I got so caught up in running those numbers last night, I forgot about everything," she moaned as she flung herself out of her chair and rushed to the mirror mounted on the wall in Maggie's office. She was a decent athlete, but unaccustomed to wearing anything but combat boots, flip-flops, or tennis shoes. She nearly took a header in her new interview pumps.

Maggie sighed in amused exasperation behind her. "Only you

would forget an interview for a chance at the most coveted executive training program in the United States—the *world*—because of some inconsequential calculations."

Alice stared wide-eyed into the mirror. Her face looked especially pale due to her anxiety and the contrast between her short, near-black hair, navy suit, and lined dark blue eyes.

"You were the one who asked me to run those inconsequential numbers," Alice mumbled distractedly. She flattened the hair next to her part and peered furiously into the mirror, as if she held her reflection responsible for all her many shortcomings. Sure enough, there were the telltale glimmering, reddish-gold roots. "Fuck it," she muttered through her teeth. "This is a joke anyway. Durand has never sent a recruiter to Arlington College's MBA program before. Is this another example of famous Durand *charity*?" she demanded, rounding on Maggie.

Maggie had grown immune to her frowns and sharp tongue in the past two years, however. She knew damn well that Alice's bark was much worse than her bite.

Usually, anyway.

"Don't you dare put down this program," Maggie warned with a pointed finger and an ominous expression. "I happen to be extremely proud of it and everything we've accomplished in the past few years, thanks in large part to *your* brilliance, hard work, and groundbreaking research. Am I surprised Durand asked to recruit from our graduating class? *No. I'm not*," Maggie added with finality, when Alice gave her a half-hopeful, half-doubtful look. "The philanthropy and profit article sent shockwaves through the business community. Now stop feeling sorry for yourself," she said as she dropped into her desk chair, making the springs protest loudly.

Alice's pique deflated.

"I *am* proud of the P and P study," she said honestly, referring to the groundbreaking business article she and a few other grad students had published with Maggie as the lead researcher several months ago. "Did Sebastian Kehoe tell you he was coming to Arlington because of the study?" she asked. Kehoe was the vice president of human resources for Durand.

"No."

"Then why *is* he?" she grumbled.

Alice halfway wished Sebastian Kehoe had continued to ignore her little college. She performed best in solitude. It grated to have to sell herself to interviewers as if she were both a commodity *and* the pitchman for that commodity. To say she didn't interview well was a gargantuan understatement.

"Durand is coming because they're searching for talented, top-notch executives, I expect."

Alice snorted. "You told me to look at this interview as good experience for future interviews. Even *you* don't actually believe anyone at Arlington stands a chance with Durand."

"I don't know what I think, to be honest," Maggie said stiffly. She snapped several tissues out of a box and held them up for Alice to take. "Now wipe off some of that crap you insist on putting on your eyes. Comb your hair back from the part to hide the roots. Put on a little lipstick for once. And for God's sake, stiffen up the spine, Reed. I expect you to rise to the challenge, not wilt in the face of it."

Alice's spine *did* stiffen in reactionary anger for a few seconds before the truth of Maggie's words penetrated. Her mentor was right. As usual.

"I'll go to the bathroom to wash up a bit," Alice agreed in a subdued tone. "I have ten minutes before the interview starts."

"Good girl," Maggie said bracingly.

"*Alice,*" Maggie called sharply as Alice reached for her office door.

"Yeah?" Alice asked, looking over her shoulder. She went still when she saw the unusually somber expression on Maggie's face.

"There's been a little change of circumstances as far as your interview. Sebastian Kehoe became ill a few days ago and had to send someone else in his place."

A perverse, savage combination of disappointment, triumph, and relief swept through Alice. *So.* They'd sent some low-level stooge in Kehoe's place? Figured. She knew Durand would never take anyone in her graduating class as a serious contender for "Camp Durand." The four-week-long program on the shores of Lake Michigan was where the brightest and best business school graduates went every summer to show their stuff. Sixty percent of the Camp Durand counselors were chosen to become the highest-paid, most elite young executives in the world. Through a combination of team-building exercises, intense observation, and a highly reputable children's camp held on the lake, Durand culled the chosen few, ending up with the best of the best.

Those selected for Camp Durand were paid a hefty sum for their weeks of service, whether they went on to become permanently employed or not. Alice coveted that chunk of money, even if she didn't dare to hope she'd ever be offered a regular corporate position at the highly successful international company. She had student loans that would come due soon, and no solid job leads. Still . . . she was torn about being forced to prove herself to the slick, influential company.

"I *knew* Durand couldn't be serious about Arlington," Alice said.

Or me.

Maggie must have noticed the smirk Alice strained to hide. "They're so *unserious* about Arlington College that their chief executive officer is coming in place of Sebastian Kehoe," Maggie said.

Alice's hand fell from the knob of the door and thumped on her thigh.

"*What?*"

Suddenly, Maggie seemed to be having difficulty meeting her

stare. "Several Durand executives were on a business trip here in Chicago recently. When Kehoe got ill, Dylan Fall agreed to fill in for his remaining appointments." Maggie glanced at her warily. Or was it *worriedly*? "I . . . I didn't want to tell you because I thought you'd get more nervous, but I didn't want you to walk in unprepared, either," she said miserably.

A wave of queasiness hit her.

"Dylan Fall," Alice stated in a flat, incredulous tone. "You're telling me that in nine minutes, I'm going to be interviewed by the chief executive officer of Durand Enterprises?"

"That's right." Maggie's expression of stark compassion faded and was replaced by her game face. "This is the opportunity of a lifetime. I don't expect you to get a spot at Camp Durand, necessarily—that might be too much to hope for, all things considered. But you're a unique, smart girl, and you're kick-ass with numbers, and . . . well, you're the *best* Arlington has got. You're the best I've ever known," she added with a defiant look. "At the very least, you had *better* walk in there, hold your head up, and do Arlington College proud."

MAGGIE'S proclamation still rang in her head while Alice waited on hot coals in the waiting room of the dean of business's offices. The dean had apparently cheerfully vacated his office for Dylan Fall.

Of course.

Fall probably had people regularly lying across mud puddles so he could cross without soiling his designer shoes.

Maggie had been right to call her out earlier. Alice didn't stand a chance of getting into Camp Durand—let alone getting hired as an elite Durand executive. But that didn't mean she would cower. Alice had stood up to bastards and lowlifes that were a hundred times scarier than a suit like Dylan Fall.

She'd stood up and walked away, pride intact.

"He's ready for you," Nancy Jorgensen, the business department secretary twittered as she stuck her head around the corner of the door leading to a hallway. Alice stood, clutching her new vinyl portfolio and trying not to sway in her heels. She cast Nancy Jorgensen a dark glance. The middle-aged, typically gray little woman looked suspiciously flushed with color and excitement. She suspected she knew why: Dylan Fall. *Traitor,* Alice thought bitterly as she stalked past Nancy.

Just get this damn thing over with.

Instead of walking into the office Nancy specified, Alice charged. The door was lighter than she'd imagined from its formidable, oak-paneled appearance. She pushed at it too aggressively and it thumped against the wall inside the office. Alice started at the loud noise and froze on the threshold. The man sitting behind the large oak desk looked up and blinked.

"Is there a fire?" he asked quietly.

"No," Alice said, frowning, wary because she wasn't sure if he was kidding or not. Funny he had mentioned fire. She hadn't been this nervous since she'd locked herself in her bedroom and her uncle Tim had ignited some of her mother's meth-cooking chemicals in order to smoke her out of it. He hadn't succeeded, but he'd very nearly killed Alice—and himself—in the process.

Nancy closed the door behind her with a hushed click. Dylan Fall studied her while Alice's lungs burned for air.

He suddenly whipped off the glasses he wore and stood. Alice willed her ungainly limbs to move. He reached out his hand.

"Alice. Dylan Fall. I can't tell you what a pleasure it is to meet you," he said, his voice low with just a hint of gravel to it. Her spine flickered with heightened awareness at the sound.

"Thank you for taking the time to see me," she said, gripping his hand firmly and giving it a perfunctory pump. He held out his other hand in an elegant "please, sit" gesture and lowered into his seat. She sat in the leather chair before the large desk, feeling like her arms and legs were glaringly out of sync with her brain . . . worse, like she were a beggar supplicant at the polished altar of the god of wealth and power. She absolutely refused to be impressed or cowed by Dylan Fall.

You can refuse all you want. You are.

"I'm glad to have the opportunity to meet with you. From what I've gathered, much of the statistical brilliance from the philanthropy and profit article in the *Journal of Finance and Business* is owed to you," he said, picking up a pen and tapping it on the desk. He moved the pen in an absentminded fashion, running long fingers over the smooth metal cylinder, flipping it, and repeating the process.

Alice ripped her stare off the vision and focused on his face. Her heart had started to beat uncomfortably fast. He played with the pen in a distracted way, but his gaze on her was razor sharp. The thick drapes were drawn, blocking out the spring sunlight. The contrast of shadow and glowing lamplight made his strong jawline and near-black eyes appear even more dramatic. Enigmatic. She'd already known what to expect from his looks, or at least that's what she'd told herself. He had dark brown hair that was smooth, despite its thickness. It was longer in the front than in the back. He wore it combed back, the style suiting his business attire, even if it did look like it could be sexily disheveled in a heartbeat by a woman's delving fingers. A pair of lustrous, drilling eyes advertised loud and clear you better give Fall exactly what he wanted, or he'd freeze you to the spot. Dark lashes and slanting brows added to a sort of sexy gypsy-gone-corporate-pirate aura about him. His face was handsome, but in a rugged fashion—full of character and strength. He was far from being a pretty boy. There was something rough about him, despite the expensive suit and epic composure. The cleft in his chin only added to the sense of hard, chiseled male beauty.

The media loved him. She'd seen photos of him clean-shaven,

sexily scruffy, and even once with a beard and mustache. Currently, he wore a very thin, well-trimmed goatee. His skin wasn't pale, but he didn't look like the type of man who tanned as a matter of course, either. Alice imagined that, like her, he spent a lot of his time reading reports and squinting at numbers on a computer screen, or else sitting at the head of a boardroom table.

Durand Enterprises was well known for not only its strong philanthropic practices, but its financial robustness. Alice herself had suggested it right off the bat for their multifactorial, longitudinal study about the correlation between company philanthropy and profit. Alice had poured through journal and magazine articles, collecting relevant data on Durand, so she'd seen photos of Fall.

She'd stared at those photos a lot. So much so, in fact, that she'd started to think she was getting a little obsessed with the business mogul.

She was pretty unimpressed by men as a rule. She'd had to deal with her share of strutting, bullshitting, worthless, and dangerous males in her life. Good-looking men usually had even fewer redeeming qualities than the plain or ugly ones, in her opinion. The ugly ones had to compensate somehow in order to compete for women. She didn't usually blink twice when she met a hot guy, but Dylan Fall was the kind of rough-and-tumble gorgeous that had all sorts of involuntary chemical reactions sparking in her body.

At the moment, she damned him straight to hell for it. Didn't he possess an unfair amount of advantages as it was?

She straightened her spine and cleared her throat. "I was one of four research assistants on Dr. Lopez's project. We all did our share of research and running numbers."

His sliding fingers slowed on the pen. His gaze narrowed on her. "You're a team player, then?" he asked quietly.

"I'm just stating the truth."

"No. You're not."

Her chin went up. She almost immediately ducked her head when she felt how muscle and skin tightened, making her thrumming pulse probably more obvious to him, exposing her vulnerability.

"I spoke to Dr. Lopez about it in person before arriving here today," he said. "She says that most of the innovative statistical analyses run on the project were not only completed by you, but designed by you."

She couldn't think of what to say, so she just held his stare.

"You don't want to brag about your accomplishments?" he asked.

"Is that what you'd like? A little dog-and-pony show?"

His long fingers stilled, holding the silver pen mid-flip.

Shit.

Her cheeks flooded with heat. "I'm sorry. I didn't mean that," she said, flustered. "I'm just a little confused as to why Durand is here at Arlington College. We *all* are, to be honest. Did you come because of the article?"

"Does that surprise you?" he asked, tossing the pen on the blotter. "Durand was one of the main companies featured. You single-handedly vindicated our strong philanthropic principles using hard statistics to do it. I'm impressed," he said starkly. She swallowed thickly when he leaned forward, elbows on the desk, and met her stare. "Very."

"Did you need vindication?" she couldn't stop herself from asking.

He shrugged slightly and leaned back again, the action bringing her gaze downward to broad shoulders and a strong-looking chest. He knew how to wear a suit, that much was certain. Powerful. Elegantly dangerous. On Dylan Fall, a suit was transformed into the modern-day equivalent of a warrior's armor.

"Not really, no. Durand is a privately held company, as I'm sure you already know. There are no stockholders to whom I need to justify my actions."

"What about to other officers on the board?" she asked, curiosity trumping her anxiety.

His stare narrowed on her. "I was under the impression *I* was the one interviewing *you*."

"Sorry," she said quickly. Is that all she was going to do during this interview? Apologize? And was that a tiny smile tilting his mouth? Somehow, she'd rather it wasn't, as unsettling as she was finding this whole experience. She wasn't wilting, like Maggie had worried she would, but she *was* blowing this. Not by a slow burn, either.

More like death by blowtorch.

"I was just curious about Durand's reaction to the article," she backpedaled. "I worked on that project even in my sleep for fifteen months straight. It sort of gets into your blood."

"As someone who sleeps, drinks, and eats Durand, I'm inclined to understand completely," he said dryly. "Actually, Durand's philanthropic goals are built in to Alan Durand's—the company founder's—directives. Durand has a long tradition of community projects, people-building, and charitable programs. After completing the study, were you convinced it's a worthwhile goal for a company to have?"

"Sir?"

"Do you think most companies should include philanthropy in their operating directives?"

"The statistics certainly indicate they should."

"That's not what I asked."

She stared at her interlaced fingers lying on top of her folder. A small patch of perspiration wetted the vinyl. "If a company can increase its profits by doing good works for the community and its people, it seems like a win-win situation all around, doesn't it?"

She looked up at his dry laugh. "That's certainly a politically correct answer. Now give me an honest one, Alice. Do you think companies like Durand should continue with philanthropic community efforts?"

The silence stretched taut.

"Alice?" he prodded quietly.

"Of course. It's just . . ."

"What?"

"It's nothing." His dark brows slanted menacingly. "It's only . . . It seems . . ." *What the hell, you've already blown the interview anyway. Everyone knows you never stood a chance from the get-go.* "A little patronizing, that's all." She cringed a little when he went eerily still. "Aside from that, I think the answer is an obvious yes. I think large corporations should have charitable directives."

"Patronizing?" he asked, his quiet voice striking her as similar to the deep purr of a misleadingly calm lion. "Like Durand is grandstanding, you mean. Making itself look good in the public's eye for the sole purpose of selling widgets . . . or candy bars, soda, energy drinks, and chocolate milk, among other things, in Durand's case."

"All of the things your campers at Camp Durand—low-income urban youth from poverty-infested neighborhoods—consume," she couldn't stop herself from saying. Heat rushed into her cheeks.

She forced herself not to flinch under his boring stare, but her defiance definitely wavered. To call his eyes merely "deepest brown" or "almost black" vastly understated their impact. They shone like polished stones with fire in the depths. Somehow, his eyes managed to startle her on a constant basis instead of a quick rush.

"Do you consume those products, Alice?"

"Once in a while," she said with a shrug. In truth, she was a chocoholic. Durand Jingdots, Sweet Adelaides, and Salty Chocolate Caramels rated among her favorite guilty pleasures while sitting at her computer running numbers. Not that she'd confess that weakness to Dylan Fall. "Why?" she asked warily. "Is that a pre-requisite to be chosen for the Durand training program?"

"No," he said, picking up a piece of paper from his desk. Her heart raced. He was going to tell her any second the interview was over. *Let him.* The sooner she was done here, the better. He idly perused what she realized was her resume. "But I happen to know that Little Paradise—where you grew up—is one of the crime-infested, low-income urban areas you just described."

Her heart jumped uncomfortably against her sternum. She unglued her tongue from the top of her mouth.

"How did you know I grew up in Little Paradise?" she rasped, mortified that Dylan Fall, of all people, knew about the infamous place where she'd grown up—Little Paradise, the grossly inaptly named, sole remaining trailer park within the Chicago city limits; a grimy, mangy little community tainted by toxic-smelling fumes from the nearby factories of Gary, Indiana. The address wasn't on her resume. She wanted no part of Little Paradise. She'd used a local address ever since she'd left for college nearly six years ago.

"Dr. Lopez mentioned it," he said without batting an eye. "Are you ashamed of where you grew up?"

"No," she lied emphatically.

"Good," he said, dropping her resume to the desktop. "You shouldn't be."

He was probably only ten or so years older than her almost twenty-four years. She resented him for his air of experience and unflappable composure, despite his relative youth. What were the circumstances of him becoming CEO of Durand at such a young age? Wasn't he related to the company founder or something? She struggled to recall. It'd been extremely difficult to find personal details about both Alan Durand and Dylan Fall. She'd never found many details about Fall's meteoric rise in the powerful company.

It suddenly struck her full-force how out of place she was in the face of his polished, supreme confidence. He was no doubt amused by her gauche defensiveness and confusion.

"Are you going to ask me any relevant questions in regard to business, my interest in Durand, or my qualifications?" she asked through a tense jaw.

"I thought that's what I'd been doing." Her rigid expression didn't break. He exhaled. "Fine." He briskly put on the charcoal-gray glasses he'd been wearing and picked up some papers from the desk. He looked extremely sexy wearing those glasses.

Of course.

"I have some questions for you in regard to your research decisions on the philanthropy and profit research."

She began to relax slightly as he launched into a series of pointed queries regarding her statistical analysis. Alice knew mathematical models backward and forward. She was also a workaholic. In this arena, he couldn't fluster her. Even so, she sensed after a period of time that Fall not only understood the nuances of the statistics as well, if not better, than her, he was light-years ahead of her in knowledge about what her conclusions *meant* in the practical workings of the business world. She was envious of his knowledge, but also curious. Hungry. Tantalized by the glittering promise of power that those numbers might grant her when paired with knowledge and experience like Fall's.

After nearly an hour of intense question and answering, he tipped his forearm and glanced at his watch.

"You're a statistical trend spotter, aren't you?" he asked casually, referring to her ability to absorb data and quickly break it down into meaningful trends, spot anomalies, and even predict outcomes.

"I suppose you could call me that," Alice said.

"Are you a savant?"

"No," she denied tensely. The word *savant* labeled her as a freak. All she wanted was to go unnoticed. Freaks didn't blend in. "I just have a decent feel for numbers and what they mean."

"You have a *phenomenal* feel. A rare gift," he corrected, his deep voice making her spine prickle again in heightened awareness.

"I think you've informed me of just about everything I need to know," he suddenly said briskly, his gaze on the papers on the desk. Alice eased forward in her chair, recognizing the end of the interview. "I *was* wondering—were you interested specifically in Durand Enterprises before you began the philanthropy study?"

She shook her head. "No. I mean . . . I knew about it, of course. I was familiar with both its corporate success and philanthropic emphasis."

"Ah. I was under the impression from your advisor that you were the one who first suggested Durand for the study," he said.

"I might have been. I'm a business major," she said shrugging. "Durand Enterprises is one of the most successful businesses in the world."

He took off his glasses, his gaze on her sharp.

"Are there any questions you have for me?" he asked after a pause in which Alice had to force herself not to squirm.

"How many people will be chosen as Camp Durand counselors?"

"Fifteen. We try to keep the camper-to-counselor ratio as low as possible, while offering scholarships to as many of the kids as we can. New-participant numbers remain fairly steady, but the returning campers have to keep a clean legal record and pass several random drug tests if they have a history, in addition to maintaining an acceptable grade point average. As you probably already know, the camp focuses on junior high and high school-aged kids. Each counselor usually has around ten kids on his or her team."

"So only nine counselors make the cut to become a Durand manager," she reflected. "Do you honestly think that this setup— a summer camp on the shores of Lake Michigan for three weeks—

really gives Durand the information it needs to hire top-notch executives?" she asked skeptically. "It seems a little"—*silly*, she said in the privacy of her brain—"odd to expect business graduate students to have the necessary experience. We're not social workers or teachers. Or babysitters."

He flashed her a glance when she mumbled the last under her breath.

"You're not expected to be any of those. Well . . . maybe a teacher, but not in the classic sense. There are regular, experienced staff at Camp Durand—cabin and grounds supervisors around the clock. It's true, though, that the counselors play a crucial role in the camper's experience. The Durand counselors are, essentially, the face of leadership and support to each individual camper. We offer a weeklong training period to the counselors, so they know what to expect. That training program is similar to many management retreats utilized around the world by companies to hone leadership skills. But that's only the beginning. Then the kids arrive, and the challenge *really* begins. What's required to succeed as a counselor—and as a Durand executive—is a large measure of ingenuity, leadership, people skills, and humanity. Those are qualities we've been unable to measure adequately from a resume, recommendation letters—which are almost always glowing—and a few interviews. Camp Durand works for us, no matter how unconventional it may seem. It's worked for us for decades. The executive contestants are under nearly constant observation for four weeks: one week of training and the three weeks while the children are there. Their schedule is arduous. They're considered to be on the clock from seven thirty in the morning until nine p.m., when the night supervisory staff takes over for them. They're expected to work Saturdays until three, with only Sundays off. It's not enough to brag about qualities of leadership, planning, intelligence, innovation, salesmanship, compassion, determination, hard work, and courage: The counselors have to *demonstrate* those skills daily with a group of children, some of whom have been labeled as criminal, uncooperative, manipulative, lazy, or unreachable. It's a lot harder than it sounds at first blush," he said, his mild tone in direct contrast to his lancing stare.

"So Durand does it again. It combines philanthropy—no, it *uses* it—to optimize the bottom line."

His smile was closemouthed, slashing . . . *dangerous*.

"Yes, I understand. That's the way you would view it," he mused as if to himself, sounding not at all concerned by her pessimism as he leaned back in his chair. His stare on her made her feel like a wreck he was considering making into a project. It was a cold, sharp knife, that stare, so Alice couldn't figure out why it made her sweat so bad.

"Would you be adverse to accepting a position at such a seemingly mercenary organization?" he asked.

"No," she replied without pause.

His gleaming brows arched. "Ah. So you're a little mercenary yourself."

"I don't know about that. I'm not stupid, if that's what you mean."

He gave a gruff bark of laughter. "No one could accuse you of stupidity," he said with a swift glance at her paperwork spread across the desk. He stood abruptly. Alice jumped up like she'd been released after being held down on springs.

"This has been enlightening," he said briskly, holding out his hand. They shook. "We'll be making our decision on finalists for Camp Durand within the next two weeks. Chicago-area colleges and universities were Sebastian Kehoe's last stop on the recruitment tour. We'll be in contact."

"Right."

His eyes flashed. She grimaced. She hadn't meant to sound sarcastic, but recognized she had. Well, at least this fiasco was over with. Now she had all the valuable interviewing experience either she or Maggie could ever want for her. Everything after Dylan Fall would be trite. She had a future full of cakewalk interviews before she landed her new, realistic job.

Probably a boring, entry-level, menial one given the current job market.

She turned to go.

"Alice."

She came to an abrupt halt, pausing in the action of reaching for the door. She didn't care for the fact that she looked over her shoulder with a measure of eagerness. It was hard not to crave every glance she could get of Dylan Fall. Despite the fact that he intimidated her, he was one hell of a sight.

"I know a man—he's a member of the Durand board, in fact—who grew up in the Austin neighborhood on the west side of Chicago," Fall said. "Are you familiar with that neighborhood?"

She studied him narrowly, trying to see his angle and failing. "Yeah. It's one of the worst in the city."

"Worse than Little Paradise."

She barely repressed a snort. Mr. Slick, Gorgeous CEO in his immaculate Italian suit had a lot of nerve, presuming to know about Little Paradise. He noticed her flash of disdain, because his brows rose in a silent, pointed query.

"There's nothing worse than urban hillbillies, Mr. Fall," she explained with a small, apologetic smile. "I don't know how much you actually know about Little Paradise, but that's a pretty apt descriptor for who lives in the trailer park there. It's just that in our case, the 'hill' is a giant garbage dump."

She'd been trying to use levity. She must have only sounded flippant, though, because he looked very sober.

"My point is, Durand doesn't just offer philanthropy to needy kids to get publicity and prime photo ops, and then drop them off on the streets and forget about them. The man I'm speaking of rose through the ranks, starting as a Camp Durand camper when he was twelve years old. People-building isn't an empty philosophy at Durand. We want the best, no matter where the best comes from."

She realized belatedly she'd turned and was staring at him now full in the face. Searching. Suspicious.

Hopeful.

Against her will, her gaze flickered down over his snow-white tailored dress shirt and light blue silk tie. A vivid, shocking impression popped into her head of sliding her fingers beneath that crisp cotton and touching warm skin, her palm gliding against the ridges and hollows of bone and dense, lean muscle. Her gaze dropped to his hands.

Just the thought of his hands sliding across *her* skin made her lungs freeze.

I'll bet he could play me perfectly. He just looks *like he knows his way around a woman's body. He'd do things to me I've never even imagined.*

They were completely inappropriate thoughts, but that didn't halt her instinctive reaction. Need rushed through her like a shock to the flesh, leaving a trail of heat in its wake. Her thighs tightened, as if to contain that unexpected flash fire.

Maybe it was because her few former lovers suddenly seemed young and clumsy in comparison to Dylan Fall?

Her stare leapt guiltily to his face. His dark brows slanted dangerously, but he also looked a little . . . *startled?* His eyes flickered downward, just like hers had. She hunched her shoulders slightly at the web work of sensation that tingled the skin of her breasts, tightening her nipples against her bra.

The whole scoring, nonverbal exchange lasted all of three ephemeral seconds.

Her hand curled into a fist when she recognized she'd let her guard drop.

"I'm happy for your friend. But *I'm* not a charity project," she said.

"Neither was he."

She flinched slightly at the stinging authority of his reply. Dylan Fall was a little scary in that moment.

"We'll be in touch," he repeated, looking down at the desk in a preoccupied fashion, and she knew she'd imagined not only that spark of mutual lust, but his cold, clear anger at her pitiful display of insubordination.

TWO

The first thing Alice's gaze settled on when arriving at Camp Durand was the pale stone, ornate Victorian mansion looming above them. It stood perhaps a hundred and fifty feet from the edge of a craggy limestone bluff that dropped off dramatically to what Alice supposed would be a Lake Michigan beach. She couldn't tell for certain with all the surrounding trees and foliage blocking the view immediately in front of the slow-moving limousine in which she rode.

Her avid stare at the mansion was torn away by a flash of gleaming, tanned skin and flexing muscle. The object of her snagged attention was probably around six feet tall and had short wavy golden-brown hair. He was definitely an athlete, given that body. He was helping another young man suspend a large banner that read, *Welcome to Camp Durand. Welcome Home*, between two oak trees. The brisk Lake Michigan wind was giving the pair a challenge hanging the flapping sign. Alice guessed they were two other Camp Durand counselors.

Yes. You actually are part of their elite little group. This isn't a dream.

She had to keep reminding herself, but the trancelike quality of her consciousness only seemed to be amplifying since they'd pulled onto the long country road that led to the camp.

Within seconds of culminating her interview with Fall, she'd already abandoned all hope of getting a position at Camp Durand, let alone at Durand Enterprises itself. She'd shot above herself, but fortunately, she hadn't let her head get too caught up in the stars.

She'd moved on, interviewing for several stable, boring-sounding positions in the city. Maggie had been right about one thing: The encounter with Fall had turned her from a hopeless interviewee into an average one with better-than-average qualifications.

She'd survived Little Paradise and graduate school. She'd lived through an interview with Dylan Fall.

What else could rattle her?

When she'd gotten the call from Sebastian Kehoe two weeks ago, she'd been floored.

Kehoe hadn't said so, but given the lateness of the invitation call, she'd figured one of the counselors—one of the ones who actually *belonged* at Camp Durand—had backed out at the last moment.

"That's Thad Schaefer," Brooke Seifert said confidently from where she sat across from Alice, nodding at the gorgeous guy holding the sign. Alice sat alone on the long seat next to the window of the chauffeur-driven limo. Brooke Seifert and Tory Hastings, two other Camp Durand counselors, sat across from her, chatting about topics Alice knew nothing about. Which was the whole point: to shut Alice out.

This morning, Alice had taken the "L" out to O'Hare Airport to meet up with the limo driver and two other incoming Camp Durand counselors. Alice had almost immediately noticed Brooke and Tory's silent judgment when she introduced herself, the cool, slightly incredulous glances at her frayed jean shorts, T-shirt, combat boots, worn backpack, and army-surplus duffel bag. Which was fine by Alice. She'd already dismissed Tory and Brooke when the driver had mentioned their elite East Coast MBA programs and preppy, rich-girl names.

At the moment, however, all three of them shared something

in common. They were all drooling over the half-naked golden dude outside the window. Something about the proprietary quality of Brooke's tone just now implied she knew the guy personally.

"What kind of a name is *Thad*?" Alice mumbled, even though she didn't unglue her gaze from Thad for a second.

"It's short for Thaddeus, an old family name," Brooke snapped. "We went to school together at Yale," she said, her voice segueing to an intimate and slightly mischievous tone as she focused her attention on Tory, once again excluding Alice. Brooke had acquired Tory as a willing slave within two minutes of their meeting at the airport. Alice rolled her eyes, her gaze flickering back up to the stark mansion on the hill as if drawn by a magnet. She'd never seen a place with so many elaborate cornices, verandas, and towers. It looked so beautiful and *still* up there on the hill. Not that a house moved, of course. It was just that the trees and flowers swayed from the lake breeze and white clouds soared across the robin's-egg-blue sky, but the house itself remained impervious to the flutter of second-to-second everyday life, like it was enchanted . . . frozen in time.

"His family and mine go way back. Dad went to school with Judge Schaefer, Thad's dad," Brooke was saying to her new best friend forever, Tory.

"Who lives in the big house?" Alice asked.

Brooke made a muted sound of annoyance at the interruption of her story, but she must not have been able to stop herself from showing off her unique knowledge. "They call it Castle Durand around Morgantown," Brooke said, referring to the nearby Michigan town where Durand Enterprises' corporate headquarters and several manufacturing plants and warehouses were located. Durand employed more than fifty percent of Morgantown's population. "And Mr. Top Hot himself lives there, of course," Brooke said smugly as the car slowed.

Alice jerked around. *Mr. Top Hot* could only mean one man.

"Dylan Fall? Lives on the same grounds as the camp?"

"This property isn't just a *camp*. It's the Durand *estate*. It's not like he'll have campers traipsing through his drawing rooms or splashing around in his pool," Brooke said, scowling. "The estate is enormous. There are two golf courses, stables, several swimming pools, woods, a marina, miles of hiking trails, tennis courts, and gardens, and those are the *private* ones, not the ones designated for the camp. Although Fall very generously shares the stables, tennis courts, and one of the golf courses with the campers, from what I understand. My father played golf with some Durand managers here once at the executive course, and got a tour of the grounds," she added, turning to Tory.

"*We* get to go there . . . To the castle, I mean," Tory said. "Once in a while. There's a dinner up there on the night we finish our training, before the kids come, and there are other events scheduled up there as the weeks go on. It was on the agenda in our packets. So . . . what were you saying about Thad Schaefer?" Tory wondered.

Alice silently absorbed this unsettling news as the sedan swung into a parking lot and Brooke resumed her self-satisfied jabbering. She'd read about the events in the literature Sebastian Kehoe had sent. She'd thought the term *Castle Durand* was some kind of fancy term for the camp headquarters or something. She hadn't for a second imagined going to Dylan Fall's *house*.

"The Schaefers threw a big party for Thad and me when we heard the news," Brooke was saying. "It's the first time in Yale history that *two* of us were chosen from the School of Management for Camp Durand. Usually Durand only selects one. Thad and I hated competing for the spot. You can imagine how thrilled everyone was when we got the news we both got in."

Right. People celebrated across the known WASP world.

"*Two* of you," Tory said in awe. "I was the first to be picked from Brown in three years."

"They try to even things out among the big business grad schools and then leave room for . . . you know. Possible outliers and unique cases," Brooke explained patiently in a manner that set Alice to grinding her teeth.

"At least I'm unique," Alice said, shoving open the car door immediately when the car halted.

"Oh, you're *special* all right," she heard Brooke say behind her as Alice lunged onto the gravel lot. She slammed the door shut in order to halt the sound of choked laughter coming from within. Brooke and her minion would want the limo driver to open the door for them anyway.

The last two hours in the backseat of that car had been pure torture. It definitely didn't bode well for the next four weeks. Maybe this whole thing wasn't so much a dream as a nightmare.

She hauled her backpack onto her shoulder and gave the emerging driver a nod. He'd introduced himself earlier as Todd Barrett.

"I'll get all the bags and deliver them to the camp," Todd said in a friendly fashion, starting to move past her. He paused. "The cabins and dining hall are down that path, right over through the woods," he said, pointing. "If you want to have a look around, go on ahead. You can see the main lodge there through the trees."

"Okay, thanks," Alice muttered, embarrassed because something in his tone of voice told her he'd noticed her "outsider" status with Brooke and Tory during the drive, and felt sorry for her.

The banner hangers had risen on their stepladders. As Alice slowly approached them, a strong gust of lake wind suddenly jolted the dark-haired guy on his ladder and whipped the sign out of his grip. The vinyl material plastered against his chest and face. He made a muffled sound of distressed surprise and faltered on the stepladder, blinded. The hand that held the hammer flailed in the air as he grabbed for a solid grip with the other. Alice dropped her backpack, ran, and flew up the first three steps of the stepladder, grasping him at the waist.

"Whoa, hold still. I've got you," she said. When he'd steadied on his feet, she reached and helped him peel the sign off his face. He looked around at her with thankful, startled dark eyes.

"You okay, Dave?" someone called.

Alice glanced aside and saw the guy they'd been leching over in the limo running up to them, the other end of the flapping banner and a hammer in his hands. Dave seemed to have gained his balance. She let go of him and stepped back down onto the ground.

"That's a *frickin'* strong wind," Dave said disbelievingly, following her down the stepladder.

"Maybe you guys should hang it in the direction of the wind," Alice suggested delicately, pointing between two alternate trees. "I know the kids won't see it when they first arrive next week, but they will as they walk toward the cabins."

Thad laughed. "The brains of the outfit," he said, hitching a thumb at Alice. "I guess Harvard taught *you* everything but basic common sense," he told Dave.

"You were marching in the same asshat parade. I was just doing what Sebastian told us to do. It was supposed to be a welcome for the counselors, too, but Sebastian and his crew didn't get it up in time," Dave said, firming his hold on the end of the madly flapping banner. Then he smiled, and Alice realized he was really very handsome in a quiet, reserved, smart-guy fashion. "So . . . *welcome*. And thanks, by the way," he said to Alice, stretching out his hand. "Dave Epstein. And that's Thad Schaefer."

"Alice Reed," she said, shaking Dave's hand first.

"You move fast," Thad told her as they exchanged a handshake. "I like that it in a woman."

Dave snorted. Alice rolled her eyes and smiled, because Thad Schaefer had clearly been teasing. He had a tattoo of a leaping shark on his biceps and a smear of dirt on a bulging pectoral muscle. His green eyes were warm and friendly on her face. She didn't *think* he was a male clone of Brooke, or at least that was her first impression.

"Seriously," Thad said as she dropped her hand from his. "I like fast people in general. At least while I'm here I do. Sebastian put me in charge of football, swimming, and sailing. Do you want to help me coach football? You're a Durand counselor, right? You three are the last to get here. We've been waiting for you," he said, nodding in the direction of the sedan. The driver was removing their luggage from the trunk, and Brooke and Tory were milling around, glancing in their direction, Tory holding back her long windblown blond hair from her face.

"Hey. I thought *I* was going to coach football with you," Dave said, scowling.

"That was before I saw her," Thad replied.

Dave made a subtle "I see your point" shrug. Alice laughed. She couldn't help but be flattered. Thad hadn't said it in a gross, lecherous fashion. He'd sounded honest and down to earth, and just plain nice. The two men seemed completely at ease with each other, and their comfortable bubble seemed to expand somehow to include her. It was just what she needed after sitting in the backseat with Brooke gnawing at her nerves for hours.

"Still, no fair recruiting her before anyone else gets a chance," Dave persisted. "Are you any good at archery?"

"I don't know," Alice said. "I've got a pretty good aim with a rock though."

"Do we want to know why?" Thad laughed.

"Probably not."

He had a dimple in his right cheek and a great smile.

"I'm nothing great at football, but I like running. And oh . . . *yeah*, I am a Durand counselor," she said dubiously, checking off Thad's earlier queries.

"You sound a little uncertain about that," Thad said.

"I feel a little old to be a camp counselor, I guess. It's a unique setup they have going on here," she said.

"If you call being under the microscope during an almost fourteen-hour workday a unique setup," Dave said quietly. She shared a glance of silent understanding with him. Durand employees would be watching them constantly while they were there, observing how they reacted to stress, tallying who rose to challenges and who failed.

"Well, I plan to have some fun while I'm here," Thad said. Dave gave him a skeptical look. "There's nothing to say I can't work hard and have fun, too," Thad reasoned.

"Spoken like a true-blue Durand executive," Dave replied with amused sarcasm.

"I'm just a little nervous about the kid factor," Alice admitted honestly. "I'm not so sure what being a Durand exec has to do with babysitting."

"Maybe the question should be: What does being a Durand exec have in common with being a prison guard or probation officer?" Dave said. "I hope I don't sound too pessimistic for saying that, but Sebastian Kehoe told Thad and me firsthand a few minutes ago that quite a few of our sweet little future protégés have multiple past arrest records."

"He was probably exaggerating to make a point," Thad said with a shrug.

"I don't think so," Alice replied. She felt Thad's gaze go sharp on her, but didn't flinch in returning his glance. She herself had a couple petty arrests on her record, both acquired before she was seventeen. Police prowled Little Paradise constantly. Alice could never claim to have been an angel growing up, but neither could most kids. It was just that in Little Paradise, you had a damn good chance at being caught at something suspicious. She'd been squeaky clean since moving to Chicago and earning her under-graduate and graduate degrees. But it was kind of hard to live in Little Paradise—it was sort of challenging to be Sissy Reed's daughter—and not have *any* run-ins with the law. She imagined it was a similar scenario for a majority of the kids who would be arriving by the busload from Chicago and Detroit in a week's time.

She broke Thad's stare when Tory and Brooke drew near. Brooke squealed Thad's name and flew into his arms, her fingertips brushing over dense shoulder and back muscles. Alice noticed with grim amusement that her hug was a hell of a lot more enthusiastic than Thad's perfunctory one. But in all fairness, maybe that was because he was holding a flapping sign and a hammer at the same time.

Thad and Brooke made introductions.

"Dave Epstein," Brooke mused a moment later as she shook Dave's hand. "Didn't you go to high school at Choate Rosemary Hall with Thad?"

"Yeah. On *most* days, that is . . . when Thad wasn't skipping class and fishing around the Thimble Islands in his dad's boat or sleeping off a hangover," Dave gibed with a half grin.

Thad looked like he was going to defend himself, but then just shrugged. "If it wasn't for Dave riding me constantly in high school to study, I'd probably have ended up as a fisherman instead of being here with all of you guys. Forget that. I'd just be a bum in a boat," Thad amended, his eyes gleaming humorously as he glanced at Alice. "I *suck* at catching fish."

Alice laughed.

"As if," Brooke said, automatically dismissing Thad's joking modesty. She glared briefly at Alice, and then gave Dave a sidelong, assessing glance before she swung her attention back wholesale to Thad. Alice wasn't surprised to learn that she wasn't the only one Brooke found wanting. Even Tory had seemingly become invisible with Thad present.

"Here comes Sebastian Kehoe," Dave told Tory and her quietly under his breath after they'd chatted for a few more minutes.

Alice glanced in the direction Dave was looking, curious and a little anxious to meet Durand's vice president of human resources. Kehoe's position was so significant to the company that he actually sat on the Durand board—another example of Durand's almost obsessive commitment to hiring and developing top-notch managers. The other counselors would have met Kehoe during their interviews. Alice was the exception. Yet another reason she felt like she was beginning two steps behind the starting line.

Sebastian Kehoe was her boss for the next four weeks. If she didn't pass muster with him, there was no way she'd ever be considered for a position at Durand. Kehoe's salt-and-pepper hair placed him in his early fifties, but he appeared younger because of a relatively unlined face, a tall, lanky frame, expensive-looking outdoor clothing, and a vigorous spring to his step. He gave the impression of being fit and energetic, but in a neat, meticulous kind of way. Alice figured he was the type to never waver from his high-protein, low-carb diet and daily, ritualistic workouts.

"Brooke, Tory, wonderful to see you. Welcome to Camp Durand," Kehoe called, stepping up and shaking hands. "And this must be Alice Reed."

"Yes, sir, it's nice to finally meet you in person," Alice said, shaking his hand. She'd only spoken on the phone with him briefly, when he'd called to offer her a position at Camp Durand.

"I'm looking forward to getting to know you better," Kehoe said in a friendly fashion, but Alice noticed his assessing, curious glance. "It's unprecedented for me to not be more familiar with the recruits. Mr. Fall spoke so highly of you, though, I knew you'd fit right in."

His words seemed to vibrate and swirl in the gusty air that surrounded all of them, perhaps because the opposite of Kehoe's statement seemed glaringly obvious to everyone, including Alice.

"You know Dylan Fall?" Thad asked her, amazement edging his tone.

"No," Alice assured quickly. She gave Kehoe an anxious

glance. Kehoe's gaze was on her bare legs, but quickly leapt up to her face. *He's trying to figure out why in the hell Fall vouched for you.* A spike of irritation went through her when she realized Kehoe thought it might have to do with her legs . . . or any other part of her body aside from her brain. "I mean, yes," she fumbled. "Mr. Fall interviewed me for the Camp Durand position."

Dave whistled softly, as if impressed. Brooke looked mutinous.

"Call me Sebastian, please, Alice," Kehoe said a little sharply. Had he noticed Dave's whistle and Thad's awed tone at the mention of Dylan Fall? Alice had the impression their unguarded admiration for Fall annoyed him. "And you and I will have plenty of opportunity to get to know one another here. All of us will. By the end of training and camp itself, you'll know each other as well as your closest friends and even some family members. Maybe better. The cohort of Camp Durand managers we hire every year remain close-knit for lifetimes, all because of what happens here on this shore and in these woods," Kehoe said.

Alice forced her face into a polite, interested expression. Somehow, when Kehoe talked about Camp Durand, it reminded her of the processing for a cult. Dylan Fall may have been infuriatingly confident, but he'd never given her *that* particular impression of Camp Durand or Durand Enterprises. Fall was too blatantly individual to ever be remotely considered a company drone.

"Are you two having trouble with the sign?" Kehoe asked.

"Only because we were hanging it against the wind. Alice was kind enough to point out our idiocy and told us to hang it in an east-west direction," Thad said, seeming to find his own stupidity on the subject funny. Alice liked him even better for it.

"The wind has been unusually bad since yesterday," Kehoe conceded. "That's why we hadn't gotten the banner up for your arrivals. There'll be plenty of time to hang it this week before the kids get here. We always put the welcome sign between those two trees, so that the campers can see it from the second they arrive. It's a Camp Durand tradition," Kehoe said, trumping Alice's banner hanging advice single-handedly. *Like it matters,* she told herself disgustedly. She really needed to get over the idea that she didn't belong there. She had the qualifications and she'd been hired for the job, fair and square. And perhaps most importantly, starting today she was being paid a heretofore-unimagined amount of money.

For that salary and the possibility of an even larger one in the future, she could get over a lot.

Thad and Dave started to roll up the vinyl banner. Alice stepped forward to assist by taking the hammers they both clutched.

"Let's get up to the lodge so that I can make introductions and we can have lunch. The ten other counselors are waiting for us. We have a lot of business to attend to this afternoon: getting to know one another, a tour of the camp, orientation to the training schedule, a general overview of our camp philosophy and how our classes and activities demonstrate it," Kehoe said, as if ticking off a mental list. "Hopefully you've already gotten a good understanding of all that from the packet of literature I've sent, but now you'll begin to see the principles put into practice. Ten Durand managers usually volunteer every year to assist me here. We have an unprecedented twelve this year, though. We find it helps to refresh employees about Durand's origins and philanthropic directives," Kehoe explained as Dave tucked the rolled banner beneath his arm and Thad shrugged on his shirt.

Alice glanced at Dave and read the wry message in his dark eyes.

And it never hurts to have extra Durand staff to spy on us, of course.

She suppressed a small smile, guessing his thought.

"Plus, we need to do cabin assignments. The counselors pick their roommates randomly," Kehoe said as he started down the path and they fell into step surrounding him. "I think you'll be pleased with the cabins, by the way. Mr. Fall had all of them renovated last fall. Even the camper team cabins are extremely luxurious."

Alice listened, observing everyone closely as Tory asked how the children and counselors were assigned to teams.

"The returning campers are assigned to their old team color. As for the newcomers, after observing all of you this week during your counselor training, and studying our staff child psychologist's assessments about each camper's strengths and challenges, myself and the other managers will designate the teams later this week," Kehoe said briskly, leading them to the clearing that was in front of a handsome, modern, mountain-style lodge building. "Mr. Fall himself will be giving you your list of campers and file folders, as well as designating your team color at the dinner up at the castle on the last night of your training."

Alice knew from the literature she'd received that the teams engaged in a friendly competition that culminated at the end of camp. Every child and team was rewarded and commended for something meaningful without exception, but the awarding of the Camp Durand Team Championship trophy was a special event. Each team could acquire points that were either earned straight out—say, by the winning of a competition or achievement of some team goal—or they might gain merit points awarded by Kehoe and/or other managers based on individual character growth and excellence.

She would have thought the whole thing sounded a little too rigid and militaristic for her liking if it weren't for the photos she'd seen of kids of various ages grinning away while they played water polo, piloted sailboats, rode on horseback, or painted on easels set up on the white sand beach. The informational packet Kehoe had sent her had made one theme crystal clear: The Durand counselors were expected to give these kids the time of their lives. Whatever happened at Camp Durand had to be wonderful, because the experience was meant to expand the impoverished children's horizons, to encourage them to hunger for more, to *expect* good things of themselves, other people, and life in general.

An organization with that primary goal couldn't be so bad, could it?

She felt a tickle on her right cheek and turned to see Brooke studying her as they walked up the lodge steps, her eyelids narrowed. Alice straightened her spine and cast her eyes forward. Might as well face it. Brooke Seifert was going to do her damndest to make sure that Alice was one of the first counselors to be checked off the Durand employee list.

And out of pure stubbornness, Alice was just as determined to see Brooke fail in that task.

"Just out of curiosity, what's the dress for the dinner at the castle, Sebastian?" Brooke asked.

"Semiformal attire."

Brooke shot a triumphant glance at Alice as they all started to file through the lodge's front doors. Despite her determination, Alice felt herself wilting. Brooke had *known* she wouldn't have anything "semiformal" in her grubby duffel bag.

Certainly not one thing suitable to wear to the prince's castle perched atop the hill.

THE weeklong training flew by in a flurry of activities, challenges, and meetings. Every counselor was expected to complete every activity in which they'd lead the campers. In addition, they had to then learn how to instruct the campers in the various tasks safely and with psychological acumen.

Alice excelled in almost anything that involved strategy, physical strength, thinking out of the box, mental and physical endurance, and most aspects of teamwork. She knew right away—and

realized with a sinking feeling that Sebastian Kehoe and the various managers recognized, too—that she had significant challenges
when it came to basic knowledge of some activities, such as nutri-
tion and cooking class, public speaking, or artistic expression.

And her most gaping shortcoming? Trust of her peers. Trust in
any of the Camp Durand process. Part of her loved being in the
gorgeous outdoor setting, testing her personal strength, playing
games, and bonding with some of her fellow counselors.

Another part remained observant, but aloof. Wary. She got
along especially well with Dave Epstein because they had that quality in common. Thad became another quick friend, but Thad was
just too nice of a guy to ever be as cynical and vaguely amused as
she and Dave were by the whole process. Thad never hesitated to
throw himself into the thick of things. He also never wavered on
his stated plan on that first day to have fun. Alice envied and
respected his ever-present drive, optimism, and energy.

Alice thought for certain they were going to send her home on
the afternoon she was paired up with Brooke Seifert on a steep
and treacherous zip line challenge. Why someone would ever want
to leave the solid ground and zoom over the canopy of the forest
while suspended on a thin wire, Alice couldn't fathom.

In the same fashion as the campers would be handled, the
counselors were paired up according to their experience. Brooke
had zip-lined several times, so she was labeled the "expert." She
had the task of coaching and reassuring Alice, who was a designated
"novice."

Alice wasn't just a novice though. What she *was*, was deathly
afraid of heights.

As a very young child, she'd taken a bad fall and woken up in
the hospital. She didn't remember the accident—or anything at all
before waking in that hospital bed. Nevertheless, ever since then,
her stomach and brain had minds of their own when her feet went
too far off the ground. Of course, she'd withheld all of that from

Sebastian Kehoe when he'd asked them some pre-activity questions.

If thirteen-year-old campers could finish the zip line task, *she* could.

But *Brooke* reassure her? What a joke. She'd muscle through the task on her own, thank you very much.

Despite her determination, she'd been stiff with anxiety and dizzy by the time they climbed to the way-too-skinny forty-five-foot-tall wooden platform suspended over the woods. She'd held her own, though. Until . . .

"Look at that," Brooke said under her breath while Jessica Moder, their assigned Durand manager, had turned away to adjust their equipment. Alice instinctively glanced where Brooke pointed, vertigo hitting her like a tidal wave when she stared directly down at the forest floor. Far below, she blurrily registered Sebastian Kehoe talking tensely and gesticulating to a tall Durand manager with a military-style haircut and a face like it was carved from a rock. A cold sweat broke over Alice. The canopy of leaves blurred in her vision, and she barely managed to jerk her gaze off the horrible drop to the forest floor.

"That manager, Sal Rigo, is a creep," Brooke muttered under her breath. "It looks like Kehoe is giving him hell for always slinking off from his assigned post. He deserves it." Brooke turned to smile brightly at Jessica, who now was approaching them with a harness.

"I was telling Alice that I was a little nervous the first time around, but once I was airborne, it was too fantastic," Brooke told Jessica enthusiastically. Her chattiness diverted Jessica from noticing Alice's pallor and struggle to keep down the contents of her lunch, but that was just happenstance. Alice knew perfectly well Brooke had tricked her. She'd been an idiot to listen to her and look down over the edge of the platform.

Alice went first, Brooke's saccharine reassurances for her safety bouncing right off her. What did she care about Brooke or her stupid platitudes when she was harnessed to this death contraption?

"Are you ready, Alice?" Jessica asked gently.

"As I'll ever be," Alice replied grimly. She held her breath.

Then she was sailing past the lush green treetops, her stomach seemingly left behind with Jessica and Brooke on the platform. A yawning vacuum had taken its place in her gut. She was positive she was going to drop to her death at any moment, but hated that prospect less than the idea of showing weakness in front of Brooke or any of the Durand managers.

She vaguely recognized Thad Schaefer's smiling face at the next platform, but was too blank with terror to put a name to the other people waiting for her with outstretched arms.

They helped her unharness, but Alice was having trouble decoding the enthusiastic, encouraging comments people were making. The only thing she was sure of in a muzzy sort of way was that the task was done, and she'd survived. All she wanted now was to be alone. No one seemed to realize that her legs were barely holding her up and the edges of her vision were black. She didn't really come back to herself even partially until she was back on the ground.

"Alice?" she heard Thad call out to her as she hurried down the trail in the general direction of the cabins.

"I'm going to head back to the cabin and take a shower before dinner," Alice called back to him where he stood on the bottom steps of the platform. Thad nodded, but from the look on his face, he was a little suspicious. She waved in a friendly, reassuring fashion and resumed walking.

She was desperate to get away from them, as wild to be alone as an injured animal.

Five minutes later, Thad found her off the main trail in a small clearing in the woods, throwing up at the base of an oak tree.

Or *finishing* throwing up, anyway. By the time she felt his hand on her back, and she looked around, startled, almost everything in her stomach was long gone.

"Oh God," she mumbled miserably when she saw him standing there, his brows slanted, his green eyes concerned. She wiped her mouth and straightened, stalking hastily away from the tree and heading aimlessly into the forest. Where could she go in this god-forsaken place where she could be fucking *alone*? Couldn't she even throw up without a Durand manager nearby tallying the contents of her stomach in a notebook, or worse yet, a gorgeous guy watching every disgusting moment?

"Alice," Thad said tensely from behind her.

She just kept walking, barely keeping her head above a dizzying sea of mortification. Unfortunately, she was moving too fast for her rubbery legs and dazed state.

"Wait, Alice," Thad implored, and she could tell by the proximity of his voice and the crunch of the brush under his feet he was jogging to reach her. He grabbed her hand. She whipped around at the physical restraint, ready to lay into him. He was closer than she thought. He slammed into her, and Alice's legs buckled.

She fell hard on her butt in the tall grass.

For a few seconds, she just sat there, the meadow flowers and grass tickling her bare legs, the shock of the impact vibrating her brain.

"God, I'm sorry," Thad said, dropping down on his knees heavily in the grass next to her. He touched her back. "Alice? Are you okay?"

She brought him into focus. Strangely, the harsh shock of the fall had cleared her head. His burnished blond hair glistened in the sunlight. His already deep tan had grown a shade or two darker being outdoors almost constantly for the past few days. He looked like a young, golden nature god with the lush, verdant foliage surrounding him. He squinted at her worriedly, turning his green eyes into emerald slits.

"Of course I'm not okay," she said irritably. "I just fell on my ass. Hard. And didn't anyone ever tell you it was rude to watch someone throwing up?"

"I'm sorry. I was looking for you and I just happened to come upon you while—Alice, are you going to be okay?"

The full extent of his worry fully penetrated her awareness. She grimaced. "Yes. I'm fine," she mumbled. "Aside from the fact that I could have done without you seeing that."

He slumped onto the ground next to her, his thigh near her hip, his arm planted behind her. She looked at him warily. The clearing where they sat was cast in part sunlight, part shade from the surrounding trees. He flipped open a button on one of the pockets on his longish cargo shorts and silently handed her a bottle of water.

"Thanks," she said earnestly after she'd rinsed out her mouth and taken several swallows. He took back the bottle and capped it when she'd finished.

"What made you throw up?" he asked simply.

She stared at her bent knees and distractedly picked at a piece of grass. "The zip line. I'm scared shitless of heights," she replied succinctly. When he didn't reply, she glanced at his face. He looked bemused.

"What's wrong?" she asked a little defensively. "Lots of people are afraid of heights."

He shook his head. "Nothing. It's just . . . You seemed fine when we unhooked you from the harness."

"Why'd you follow me, then?"

He quirked his eyebrows. "Not because I thought you were sick. I was just trying to get you alone."

"Oh," she said softly after a stunned moment. She studied her knee intently.

"Have you always been afraid of heights?" he asked her. The

hairs on her nape and arm stood on end. His voice sounded closer, like he'd leaned in.

"For as long as I can remember. It's my first memory, waking up in a hospital when I was really little. Apparently I'd fallen off the ladder of an abandoned water tower in my neighborhood."

"So you must not have always been afraid."

She glanced at him uncertainly.

"Little Alice wanted to climb. She wasn't afraid."

"I don't know anything about Little Alice. I only know heights are my worst nightmare. Actually, *falling* is," Alice corrected with a wry look, her stare locked in his. He returned her smile. He reached up and pushed her bangs off her forehead. The leaves on the trees flickered, dappling his face and shoulders with moving light and shadow.

"You're pretty amazing, you know that?" he murmured.

"No idea why you'd say that. Do you think I have some unique talent for hurling?" Her words made it all come back to her in graphic detail, how he'd watched it all. Her stomach squirmed. She turned her head away from him, self-conscious of his closeness when she'd just been sick. He laughed, and suddenly he was looping his arm around her waist and shifting in the grass behind her. He pulled slightly and her back fell against his chest.

"I mean you're amazing because you did that zip line and you were so afraid and sick, and none of us even guessed. Relax," he said gently when she stiffened and tried to move away from his casual embrace.

"Thad, I just got sick. I don't want to . . ." She faded off uncomfortably. She wasn't sure if she *wanted to* even if she *hadn't* just gotten sick.

"I know," he said. "I'm not coming on to you. But it's nice out here. Just sit with me for a minute until you feel better, and then we'll walk back to camp. Do you want some more water?" he asked, holding up the bottle.

She didn't, but she took the water anyway, glad for something to do with her hands. After a minute or two, when Thad didn't try anything, she did start to feel a little better. They started to talk about their past experiences and their impressions of Camp Durand so far.

It wasn't so bad, sitting in a sun-dappled glade in the woods without a damn Durand manager anywhere in sight, relaxing into Thad Schaefer's embrace.

IT'D been the only time she'd been paired up with Brooke during their training, although they had to put up with each other for several team challenges. They hadn't killed each other yet, but their mutual dislike had started to approach genuine hatred after a week of enforced contact.

Or at least on Alice's part, it had.

Alice was patient. Brooke may think she'd remain unscathed after that zip line incident, but she was wrong.

ALICE had been positive she'd get Brooke as a roommate when they first arrived. It'd be *just* like fate to shaft her in that way.

Bizarrely, fate had sent Alice a fairy godsister instead.

She came in the form of a fellow counselor: a beautiful, fun-loving, exceptionally smart young Indian-British woman who had been educated at Oxford. Her name was Kuvira Sarin—Kuvi for short. Kuvi possessed a killer accent and a suitcase full of brightly colored tops and shorts, darling swimsuits, fluttering beach cover-ups, awesome strappy sandals, and bangles that looked amazing on her smooth, caramel-colored arms. She was funny and warm and fearless in equal measure, and Alice felt truly blessed to have her as a roommate.

On the last evening of their weeklong training, she and Kuvi entered their cabin, tired out from the rigorous activities of the day, but anticipatory, too. Tonight was the dinner and team flag selection at Castle Durand.

Tonight, Alice would see Dylan Fall again.

As she and Kuvi entered their cabin, Alice was reminded again of just how lucky they were. It was one of the most luxurious suites Alice had ever seen, let alone stayed in—although she kept that bit of information to herself. It featured two queen-sized beds, a large bathroom with a compact washer/dryer, a large sitting area, and a comfortable outdoor terrace that overlooked a white sand beach and the Great Lake. When she and Kuvi had first entered their cabin a week ago, Alice had immediately gone for the bed that faced both the front door and the patio entrance to the terrace. She always needed to be in a position to see all the entrances to a room while she was in bed.

Force of habit.

Presently both she and Kuvi collapsed on their beds, sighing in comfort at the cool air-conditioned suite and the slow release of tight, sore muscles. Today they'd completed the wall-climbing challenge—another activity Alice had been dreading. Thanks to Thad's easygoing leadership, however, the fifteen counselors soared through the challenge. Of course, it helped that Thad was aware of her vulnerability when it came to heights. She didn't think he'd told anyone about her weakness, but he did little things as he'd strategized the team wall climb that made her think he was being sensitive to her irrational fear. At least for the wall climb, her anxiety only lasted for the brief up and down, and was quickly relieved.

Training was finished, and Alice had come through, if not with flying colors, at least without any scars on her record.

"Done," Kuvi sighed happily.

"Yeah. Now for the hard part," Alice said, rolling her head on the bedspread and giving Kuvi a grin.

"Do you want to shower first?" Kuvi asked. Alice suppressed

an increasingly familiar sinking feeling. She and Kuvi had already discussed the fact that they'd need to shower immediately and get dressed if they wanted to be on time for the meet-up before the dinner at the castle.

"No, you go ahead," Alice said, sitting up and looking at her closet, forlorn as she imagined the uninspiring contents.

When Alice walked out of the bathroom after her shower forty-five minutes later, Kuvi looked around as she fastened an earring. Kuvi looked very pretty in a high-low fuchsia dress that hung in the back to her calves, and then rose in the front to show her knees. Alice's cheeks heated when she saw Kuvi's gaze drop over the sundress she wore.

"I didn't bring anything for a cocktail party," Alice said, sounding a little sharper than she'd intended.

"I *know*, I didn't bring much either. They didn't tell us we'd need to dress up. It's a *camp*, for Christ's sake," Kuvi said, her disgusted, mildly outraged tone applying a bandage to Alice's acute discomfort. "Is that the only dress you brought?" Kuvi asked her matter-of-factly.

"It was between this and a purple one like it," Alice said, shifting uncomfortably on her bare feet. Thus far, her lack of nice clothing hadn't been an issue. All the counselors wore some combination of shorts, T-shirts, swimsuits, tennis shoes, and hiking boots. Alice lived in clothes like that, so she'd felt like she'd fit in just fine. Thanks to Brooke's pointed query about the attire for the Castle Durand party, however, Alice knew what to expect for tonight.

She'd had all week to dread this moment.

"I'd loan you one of mine, but . . ." Kuvi shrugged, glancing significantly at Alice's figure and then hers. Alice was long-limbed, slender and tall for a woman, while Kuvi was short with lush, feminine curves.

"What size shoe are you?" Kuvi asked, studying Alice's bare feet narrowly.

"An eight."

"Perfect. You know that dress isn't bad at all, and that orange is great for your coloring," she said, studying Alice closely. "Take off the tube top, though," she said, referring to the stretchy white top she wore under the dress. "We're trying to send that dress up the fancy scale, not down."

"But—"

"Trust me," Kuvi said, the manic gleam of a challenge entering her hazel eyes. Alice was reminded, as she had been several times that week, that she didn't ever want to be on Kuvi Sarin's opposing team. Kuvi opened her top drawer briskly.

"The women in my family are known for their skin," Kuvi said distractedly as she rooted around for something. "But your skin might beat us all. It's so smooth, and it's turning even a prettier color as you get tan. You must have an Indian in your white-girl family tree. Maybe we're far distant relatives," Kuvi joked as she extracted a large plastic bag filled with costume jewelry.

"You don't want to be remotely related to my family, trust me."

Kuvi grinned. "Okay. Off with the tube top."

The halter dress was a little lower cut than Alice preferred, thus the reason she usually wore a tube top under it. The cut was decent by most standards, but Alice was a little conservative when it came to that sort of thing. Once again, her past experience from Little Paradise intervened on present-day life. If a girl went around wearing anything remotely suggestive in Little Paradise, it was an open invitation to trouble. Taking off the tube top wasn't as bad as she feared, though. The neckline revealed just the hint of the valley between the swells of her breasts and exposed her upper back.

"You're built," Kuvi said frankly when Alice walked out of the bathroom after removing the tube top from beneath the dress and refastening the halter. "You should have heard what Thad said when he first saw you in a bathing suit."

Alice nearly demanded "What?" but then stopped herself at

the last minute. She wasn't so sure she wanted to know what Thad had said.

Which was weird. Why wouldn't she want to hear about a gorgeous, smart, sweet guy like Thad Schaefer saying something lecherous about her? He hadn't tried anything with Alice since that day he'd held her in the woods, but it wasn't because he wasn't interested. Alice would have to be an idiot not to notice the heat in his eyes every time they were together.

"What do you usually do, *bind* those things?" Kuvi asked baldly, staring unabashedly at Alice's breasts.

"I wear sports bras a lot," Alice said, willing the air-conditioning to cool her hot face. "I'd prefer to keep them out of the limelight," she said, waving in the general vicinity of her chest.

Kuvi smirked. "I hear you. Men already don't take us seriously enough, especially in the business world. Don't worry. The dress doesn't make your boobs look huge or anything. It just suggests."

Kuvi proceeded to confidently costume her in a pair of dangly gold earrings, which showed off nicely next to her near-black hair and tan. "No necklace necessary given your gorgeous neck, chest, shoulders, and back," Kuvi said in a stern, matter-of-fact assessment before shoving several gold bangles and one purple bangle on her wrist.

She pulled a pair of golden sandals with ankle straps out of her closet and held them up excitedly. The shoes were unapologetically sexy, their purpose solely decorative versus practical—like jewelry for the feet. They looked like something a harem girl might wear. Alice finally balked.

"I can't wear those, Kuvi."

Kuvi peered at the shoes critically. "Yeah, you're right. You have too much substance for these froufrou things," she agreed, tossing the sandals heedlessly back in the closet.

"I'll just wear these?" Alice asked hopefully, holding up a pair of inexpensive, neutral-colored flats she owned. Kuvi nodded encouragingly. She really *was* nice. "Are you sure you don't mind about me borrowing the jewelry?" Alice asked doubtfully, fingering an earring a moment later.

"Mind? It's *fun*," Kuvi insisted. "You look gorgeous."

Alice didn't agree, either about the fun or how she looked, but she didn't want to ruin Kuvi's apparent good time. She appreciated her roommate's efforts, but the glamorization of Alice Reed could only go so far without descending into the ridiculous.

SHE and Kuvi walked out into a clear warm summer evening. A good chunk of their total party of twenty-eight people had already arrived at the assigned spot in front of the main lodge when they strolled up to meet them. Being a social butterfly, Kuvi immediately fell into animated conversation with Thad, Dave, and a pretty, quiet young woman from Stanford University named Lacey Sherwood. Lacey and Alice were both runners. Lacey had competed in track in college, but Alice just jogged for exercise. They'd run together a few early mornings this week, though, and found they were compatible, both for the exercise and the company.

"You guys both look great," Thad told Kuvi and her when they approached. His gaze was warm on her—Alice—though. He looked pretty amazing himself, wearing a light blue button-down, charcoal-gray suit, and narrow black tie. She really was out of her league, Alice thought. He'd packed *that* suit to come to a summer camp?

It's not just any summer camp, stupid. It's a retreat and training ground for the best executives in the world, and that's precisely what Thad looks like.

Lacey was almost as quiet as Alice as they all chatted, not because she was a loner like Alice, but because she was shy. Alice caught Thad staring at her bare shoulders, arms, and breasts a few times, which was sort of unsettling, but was also nice. She felt glaringly out of place for the event. Having a gorgeous guy openly admire her certainly helped ease her discomfort. For a few minutes, Alice actually started to feel like maybe her nervousness all week about this event had been for nothing.

Until Brooke and Tory walked up, anyway. Naturally, Brooke had pulled Tory's name during the roommate selection. Luck always favored women like them.

Brooke looked sophisticated and chic in a white dress that snuggly hugged her fit figure and flared in pleats to just above her knees. The color set off her golden tan and shoulder-length brown hair. Alice had no doubt that the earrings and watch she wore glittered with real diamonds. She was the epitome of tasteful elegance and money. Tory looked almost as magazine-cover worthy in a floaty silver-gray chiffon number.

Alice's cotton sundress and borrowed costume jewelry suddenly seemed especially tacky in comparison. The thought irritated her. The warmth and generosity of Kuvi's loan of the jewelry was worth a thousand times Brooke's diamonds.

"Don't you two look . . . *colorful*," Brooke said dubiously after she greeted Alice and Kuvi. Then she turned her complete attention to Thad and Dave.

"I just overheard Kehoe saying it was too nice of a night to drive the vans up to the castle. We'll see who's laughing when Brooke has to walk up that steep bluff wearing those heels," Kuvi whispered to Alice under her breath, her voice brimming with suppressed laughter.

Kuvi was right. Alice did get a flash of amused vindication looking over her shoulder and seeing Tory and Brooke trudging up the very steep road in their spiked heels several minutes later. She turned back around, determined to ignore Brooke for the rest of the night.

The road they trekked up was lined with gorgeous hydrangea and rose bushes. The tallest spires and towers of the castle poked over the crest of the hill in front of them. The mansion slowly rose above the horizon as they walked toward it, like it was floating.

She was about to enter Dylan Fall's home.

THREE

The guest entrance faced opposite the Great Lake, although Alice caught a glimpse of the shimmering blue water through a grove of trees as they approached. They crossed a drive that circled around for front-door drop-off. The group gathered on and around the steps. Sebastian Kehoe authoritatively rapped on the pair of massive carved wood doors using a brass doorknocker. When he dropped his hand, Alice realized the large ornate door-knocker was in the shape of a knight in armor. She started when Kehoe suddenly reached up and used the brass sword to rap on the shield again, the sound jarring her.

"You okay?" Kuvi asked under her breath from beside her.

"Yeah," Alice assured with a swift, reassuring smile. Luckily, no one else seemed to notice her flash of nerves.

She held her breath at the sound of someone moving inside the house. A woman in her mid to late thirties opened one of the doors wearing a wide smile. Alice exhaled shakily in relief. She'd been expecting Fall right off the bat.

"Louise," Sebastian said familiarly, taking her hands between his. "I hope we aren't giving you too much trouble tonight," he said as Louise beckoned them inside.

"No trouble for me. You know how Marie is with these things. I just stay out of the *generalissimo's* way," Louise joked as their large party trooped into a huge light-filled entry hall.

Louise had a very compact, neat figure and was dressed with

casual professionalism in a pair of black pants, a fashionable belted cotton blouse, and ballet flats. Who was she? Was she related to Fall somehow? Alice glanced around curiously, seeing graceful archways that led to various parts of the house, carved teak paneling, museum-quality oil landscapes, stunning flower arrangements on gleaming tables, and a sweeping grand staircase. Soft evening light emanated from a circular bank of oversized windows at the landing of the stairs. Above them, a crystal chandelier hovered, looking like a giant suspended crown waiting patiently for its wearer. It was a given that *Alice* would be in awe of the surroundings, but even Brooke and Tory looked impressed.

Who *was* Louise? Alice recalled that Dylan Fall was single. Maybe his marital status had altered since she'd done her research?

"Welcome all of you," Louise called out after they'd all entered and someone shut the front door. "Mr. Fall will be receiving you on the terrace. Follow me, please."

She and Kuvi brought up the rear. Dozens of leather soles and high heels on the wood floors and oriental carpets created a hollow, hushed tramping sound that echoed off the walls and high arched ceiling. Once again, Alice had the strange, fanciful sensation that the beautiful house was alive. Watchful.

Waiting.

She repressed a shiver.

"Who do you think she is?" Alice whispered furtively to Kuvi.

"Who?" Kuvi whispered back, hazel eyes wide.

"That woman?" Kuvi blinked when she nodded in the direction of Louise.

"The cook or maid? Or a housekeeper maybe?" Kuvi replied with a dubious shrug.

"Oh," Alice mumbled, feeling stupid for thinking Louise was somehow related to Fall. What did *she* know about this sort of world?

A gong sounded, the tone sweet and clear. Alice's feet faltered, but Kuvi kept walking. The mass of men and women moved ahead of her. Something caught her eye to the right, a flash of jewel-colored light. She craned to see into the room off the hallway.

Had the sweet, mysterious gonging sound come from in there?

Her feet didn't make a sound on the oriental carpet when she entered. She stared down the length of a silent, still room—the dining room, no doubt, given the highly polished fifteen-foot-long mahogany table surrounded by chairs and a massive china cabinet that looked to be filled with porcelain and silver treasures. She saw what had caught her eye: a circular-shaped alcove made entirely of glass that took up the entire end of the room. At the top of the clear windows were several stained glass panes. She caught a glimpse of the tops of lush trees and swaying flowers, and then the shimmering, sea-like Great Lake in the distance. The sun was setting, sending its rays through the stained glass. Translucent beams of ephemeral, jewel-colored light penetrated the thick shadows all the way at the back of the room.

Everything was hushed and still.

Alice held her breath so as not to break the spell.

She took another step into the stunning room, then another, drawn to the windows and how they changed light into elusive, slanting jewel bars she knew would slip right through her seeking fingers.

She held out her hand.

"Alice," a man said sharply.

Alice froze, her eyes going wide in alarm, her limbs beginning to tingle. She'd recognized that deep, slightly rough voice.

She spun around. Dylan Fall stood in the entryway to the dining room, his face rigid as he pinned her with his stare.

"What the hell are you doing in here?" he demanded tensely.

"I heard a gong and wondered what it was, and then I saw the view and . . ." She faltered in her pressured explanation when she soaked in his appearance, the vivid, striking reality of him standing there in the entryway. He looked very tall and intimidating and just . . .

Plain *amazing*.

He wore a pair of tan summer-weight trousers that had been perfectly tailored for his long legs, trim hips, and flat abdomen. The first few buttons of his white shirt were left unfastened. His sport coat was a darker shade of brown with subtle tan striping woven in the fabric. The expensive, stylish clothing fit him with a careless, sexy ease. Dylan Fall wore the clothes, not the other way around. That much was crystal clear. She yanked her gaze off the appealing expanse of his broad chest—he looked like he could more than hold his own in a rugby match, despite the fashionable clothing. He was long and lean, but powerful.

She focused on his face. Unlike when she'd seen him for the interview, he was clean-shaven. She started when she noticed the blazing quality of his eyes.

"Alice?" he said again, this time very quietly, his gaze narrowing on her.

"The gong . . ." she muttered again stupidly.

"You couldn't have heard a gong."

His words struck her like a lash. It took a moment for his meaning to settle in.

"What did you *think* I was doing in here?" she asked in a choked voice, recognizing his cold anger at last. "That I snuck in to steal the silver?"

He blinked at her returned flash of anger. A hard, masklike expression stole over his face. "Of course not. I just saw you moving around in here while I passed. It took me off guard." He stepped toward her. She searched his expression desperately, but saw no evidence of the fierce emotion she'd witnessed in his eyes just seconds ago. Here was the utterly in-control man she recalled from her interview.

"Would you like to see it?"

"See *what*?" she asked with flat-out suspicion.

His stern, sexy mouth flickered with amusement. He waved at the far end of the room. "The view you spoke of just now," he replied calmly.

She glanced back and saw the windowed alcove, seeing the picturesque tableau as if for the first time.

Her mouth dropped open. What had she been thinking, leaving the group to wander around this house alone? *His* house. She felt a warm pressure on her bent elbow and suddenly she was walking next to Dylan Fall as he guided her, her numb legs seemingly moving of their own volition. Instead of leading her over to the windowed sunny alcove, he directed her to the far side of the room and a sideboard. Still touching her arm lightly, he used his other hand to remove the stopper from a decanter and pour a finger of amber-colored liquid into a crystal highball glass.

"Drink it," he said.

She stared down at the glass, and then at him dubiously.

"I don't drink hard liquor. That'll kick my ass," she said bluntly, considering for the first time the possibility that Dylan Fall was a tad *off*.

The thought didn't diminish his blatant attractiveness in the slightest; especially when he gave a soft, hoarse bark of laughter. White teeth shone against his shadowed face. There it was, that flash of the dangerous marauder beneath his polished exterior, the sexy outcast transformed into the most confident of insiders.

Get a grip, she scolded herself, but she couldn't prevent that squeeze of her heart in her chest.

He raised the glass and tipped a portion of the golden liquid between his lips. His strong throat convulsed as he swallowed.

"Good thing I do," he muttered before he set down the unfinished drink on a silver tray with a muted crash. Then he was leading her down the length of the dining room. They came to a halt, standing side by side in the sun-filled alcove. He didn't move his hand from her arm. It burned not only her skin, but her consciousness. She awkwardly straightened her elbow, and his fingers fell away. The air-conditioning in here must be cranked. His hand had been warm and steadying against her strangely chilled skin.

"Have you ever seen anything like that?" he asked quietly next to her.

She glanced dazedly up at him. His masculinity was so potent it was tangible. He eclipsed her entire vision. How tall *was* he? Six foot three, maybe? His bold male features and short sideburns created such a clean, striking profile. The dark irises, lashes, and lowered eyebrows looked especially defined next to the whites of his eyes as he peered out the window. She followed suit, staring blindly out the panes of glass.

Slowly, the vision in front of her resolved.

Her Camp Durand peers and Kehoe's staff milled around a stone terrace featuring a splashing fountain. She and Fall were looking down on them from a higher floor. A colorful, meticulously maintained palette of gardens surrounded the terrace. Two formally dressed waiters were passing among the main group with flutes of champagne on trays. Everyone was admiring the gardens and view, talking and laughing. Over to the left, several white-jacketed caterers were setting up an elaborate serving table. Kuvi's puzzled face leapt out at her from the others as she scanned the large terrace. Clearly, her roommate was the only one who had missed Alice.

There was a wide path that led through a vibrant green yard to a waist-high, pale stone wall in the distance. There would be a drastic craggy drop-off to the lake on the other side of that boundary, Alice knew. She numbly recognized Thad, Brooke, and Tory standing at the wall.

"Alice?"

She blinked, belatedly recalling Fall's question.

"No. I've never seen anything like it. You don't see views like that in Little Paradise," she replied through a sandpapery throat. Maybe she should have taken that drink after all.

"No," he agreed. She sensed his stare on her cheek. "But Little Paradise hasn't been your whole world, has it?"

"No. Thank God," she mumbled under her breath. "Not since I went to college."

"And before Little Paradise?"

She shrugged. "Nothing. I lived in that garbage dump until I escaped for college."

"I see." She looked over at him. He was watching her steadily. A strange feeling overcame her, like a door was opening in her chest. She had a bizarre yet shockingly strong urge to sink deeper into his dark gleaming eyes . . . to feel his arms close around her.

What the hell was wrong with her?

"Alice? Is everything okay?"

"Yeah," she said through rubbery lips, forcing her gaze out the window again. Her heart began to roar so loud in her ears she wondered if he heard it.

"I was glad to hear you accepted the position at Camp Durand. I wasn't entirely certain what to expect as far as an answer," he said neutrally.

She grimaced slightly, grasping for steady mental footing. "Not too shocking, after that interview, I suppose." He didn't respond. "I was just as surprised to get the offer," she admitted after a moment, feeling strangled by the oppressive silence of the house that surrounded them.

By the man.

It was all so strange.

"I *did* hear a gong sound," she defended suddenly— *stubbornly*—as if to push back the haze encroaching on her, the strange, unnameable emotion that approached panic.

"Yes. I just realized what it was you must have heard. I think Marie was responsible. My cook is a bit of a tyrant. I mean that in the fondest sense of the word," he assured dryly with a sideways glance at her. Alice gave him a shaky smile, relieved by the news. Maybe she wasn't crazy after all? "Marie occasionally uses an antique gong she found here in the house to alert the catering staff she has something she wants done immediately. She has those poor people hopping around like nervous rabbits. I hadn't realized you could hear it from here, but that must be the culprit."

"Oh . . . it really did sound like it came from this room."

"An old house like this can play tricks on the senses."

"I'm sorry for—"

"There's no harm done. I hope," he added quietly. There it was again, that brief flash of a killer smile. "And *I'm* sorry. For snapping at you."

She swallowed thickly. Through the window, she saw Kuvi cross the distance of the terrace and say something pointedly to Dave Epstein. Dave scanned the crowded terrace from his greater height and shook his head.

"I should get out there. I think my roommate is wondering where I went," Alice said, starting to back away.

"Wait a moment."

She blinked in surprise at his low, clipped command. Goose bumps rose on her arms. He looked a little embarrassed by his tense declaration. It was strange, to see him off balance—Dylan Fall. He cleared his throat.

"Have you spent a good summer thus far?" he asked.

"Spiffing." She was confused as to why Dylan Fall was singling her out for garden-party talk before they even got to the garden. Perversely, she didn't want to play along.

He gave her a dark glance. "Do you always have to be sarcastic?"

"I wasn't being sarcastic," she lied.

His gaze scored her. He wasn't going to be sidetracked. She sighed and began ticking off her boring, very unsophisticated activities this summer. "I signed on with a temporary maid service to help pay the bills now that my student loans are coming due. Maggie was on sabbatical in Mexico, so I babysat her Irish setter, Doby. He had a bad case of fleas and threw a huge fit when I dragged him to the vet. He nearly broke my wrist, he freaked out so bad in the waiting room."

She gave him a "well, are you satisfied?" glance, but he was impervious.

"You and Maggie are close, then?"

"Yeah. I live in an apartment over her garage," Alice replied stiffly, suddenly thinking of an issue that had been niggling at her. "I asked Maggie why she told you about me growing up in Little Paradise. She swore she never did."

He had the decency to look vaguely embarrassed.

"Why did you say that? And how *did* you know where I'd grown up?" she demanded.

He frowned as he stared out at the Great Lake. He looked hard and intimidating, and for a second, she couldn't believe her cockiness in berating him.

"We did a basic security screening on some of the more desirable candidates for Camp Durand," he said after a pause. He glanced at her and saw her offended expression. "It helps us to narrow down the contestant pool. You can't really blame us, can you? You'll be working with children, after all."

Her defiance flickered out. "I guess not," she said. "Still, no one likes having someone pry into their private life without permission. Would you?"

"You gave permission in the original paperwork you signed when you applied for the position." He scowled slightly. "And no. I didn't like it when it happened to me, either. One of the consequences of the job, I suppose."

A smile curved her mouth at a thought. "Did *you* have anything to hide?"

"Plenty."

She glanced at him in surprise. She hadn't expected him to say that. Movement and color caught her eye out on the terrace. A Durand manager's peach-colored skirt billowed in a gust of wind.

"Aren't you worried you should be out there?" she asked.

"Not particularly," he said, his gravelly voice causing the skin of her cheek and ear to tingle in awareness. "I just received an unpublished quarterly report for Durand. I got caught up in looking at it just now. That's why I was running behind and wasn't there to greet you all," he said.

She raised her eyebrows expectantly when he paused.

"I was wondering if you would consider taking a look at it as well, along with our last quarterly and a few annuals. To see if you spot any significant trends. I admire that knack for numbers you have. There's no hurry, though. I know you need to get settled in, and your kids are coming tomorrow. You aren't obligated," he added when she didn't respond immediately.

"Sure. I'd be happy to," she said once she'd gotten over her surprise at his request. The idea of losing herself in numbers—of escaping all this strangeness and surrounding herself with the familiar—sounded *very* reassuring at that moment. She perked up a little, as if she was finally rising out of the strange oppression that had come upon her since she first entered this house.

He nodded, seeming satisfied by her response. "Thanks. I guess we better go make a showing at the party," he said, not seeming very excited about that fact. "Shall we?"

Much to her dismay and bewilderment, he fell into step beside her, as if he planned to escort her. Alice couldn't think of anything to say to stop him. She couldn't tell him what to do in his home and at his dinner party. They walked through the quiet house together, and down a flight of stairs. When they reached a large, high-tech family/media room at the back of the house, she hesitated.

"This way," he said, touching her bare upper arm again, obviously misunderstanding her uncertainty.

He unlatched one of many French doors and guided her through the opening. His fingertips lightly touched her bare back, stealing her focus. Suddenly, the entire Durand party was right there in front of her, several of them turning at the sound of the door opening, their attention snagged when they noticed Fall's tall, singular form emerge from the house. Alice's cheeks flamed in embarrassment as their host walked down the steps to greet them, his hand only falling away from her back when they reached the bottom step.

ALICE endured the group's curious, puzzled glances at her entrance with Fall, but inside, she was boiling over in mortification. *Damn him.* Alice longed to stay under the radar. Dylan Fall had thrust her into the limelight, just by standing next to her in all his powerful male glory. As soon as Fall approached Sebastian Kehoe and shook his hand in greeting, Alice faded back from his side and hurried toward Kuvi, ducking her head in an attempt to avoid attention.

"How did you end up with Mr. Top Hot?" Kuvi asked her a moment later as they stood at the fringes of the crowd, her hushed voice vibrating with amusement.

"I wasn't *with* him. I . . . I had to use the bathroom, and when I came out, he was there, so he showed me the way," she said, flustered. In Little Paradise, Alice had become an accomplished, stone-faced liar. Why was she losing the skill now?

She noticed Brooke watching her from where she stood at the back of the terrace. Alice turned her back deliberately to her. "And don't call him that . . . that *stupid* name," she hissed at Kuvi, her embarrassment now choking her. "That's what Brooke calls him."

"Really? That's what Dave called Fall when he was joking

earlier," Kuvi said unconcernedly, taking a sip of her champagne and glancing past Alice's shoulder. Given Kuvi's prurient interest, Alice had a pretty good idea who she was staring at. "Personally, I think it's an excellent description. Bloody hell, that man is smoking. Those eyes. That hair. That *body*. And he was *touching* you."

"Stop it, Kuvi," Alice implored shakily under her breath. *"Please."*

Kuvi's gaze flickered to Alice's face and her smile faded. She nodded toward a bar that had been set up near five round tables surrounded by chairs. "Let's get a *real* drink, shall we?" she suggested.

FALL'S tyrant *generalissimo* cook, Marie, did a fantastic job of directing the campaign of their dinner. Alice relaxed a little as they ate a chilled cucumber soup followed by perfectly cooked salmon, potato croquettes, a frisée salad, and finally a delectable chocolate cheesecake, all served in the midst of the idyllic garden setting. Thankfully, she sat at the table farthest away from the head one, where Fall sat with Kehoe and many of the Durand executives. Thad, Dave, and Kuvi were good company, even with Brooke there. Brooke went everywhere Thad did, and Tory trailed Brooke in turn. In all fairness, Brooke was okay during dinner, occasionally including everyone at the table in her conversation. And whenever Brooke's attention was focused exclusively on Thad or Dave, Tory was actually pretty nice.

During coffee and dessert, Fall stood and gave an unscripted, engaging, and surprisingly funny little speech about what he'd learned from his experience as a Camp Durand counselor. Everyone listened to him with a rapt, spellbound focus.

He's good, Alice admitted to herself. In the photos she'd seen of him—and in her own experience—he usually came off as intimidating and rapier sharp. In reality, he could be warm and charming and even a little self-deprecating. It only made him more magnetically attractive, Alice acknowledged. Clearly she wasn't the only one who thought so. Kuvi made eye contact with her after Fall finished his speech and waved her hand subtly in the vicinity of her chest as if cooling down the flames. Alice grinned.

A Durand executive hastened to Fall's side, placing a wooden box in front of him. Another manager placed a stack of colored folders and a tall but battered-looking trophy next to the box. There was a black flag with gold diamonds on it tied just below the brass figure on top, which was a depiction of several hands clasped together.

"Oh, right," Fall said, arching his dark brows in amusement. "Time for the sacred Selection of the Colors Ceremony." He picked up the beat-up trophy and considered it fondly. "The Diamond Team won last year's overall competition. The Team Championship trophy will be passed on for safekeeping to the counselor chosen as the Diamond Team leader tonight. In a time-honored tradition, the members of the Diamond Team will then hold the trophy throughout the three weeks of camp, until a new team is designated as the winner on the final night. Now, the Red Team—that was *my* team—has a long history of heart-stopping Camp Durand victories and innovative strategies—which have occasionally been *viciously* maligned as underhanded . . ." A few amiable hisses and boos emanated from the managers' table. Fall faked being offended at the sounds, but then chuckled. Alice's heart palpitated uncomfortably at the easy, rich sound and the flash of white teeth on his handsome face. "I'm entirely impartial about the Camp Durand Team Championship, of course. The team competition is a minimal focus here. A passing spectacle," he said, setting down the trophy with a small smile, his hand lingering on the base. "But whoever *does* get the red flag, I need to immediately speak with you in private when we finish here about potential strategies . . . I mean, about whether or not you enjoyed the dessert tonight," he rushed to correct.

Alice joined in the laughter. She'd already gathered that despite Sebastian Kehoe's attempts to downplay the importance of the Team Championship trophy, it was a major deal, not only among the counselors and campers every year, but some of the Durand executives. There were thousands of Durand managers around the globe, but the select few chosen from Camp Durand had a reputation for being the best and brightest. If an attending manager had originally been a counselor, he or she took pride in that fact, *and* in his or her original Camp Durand team. Fall was just joking about the unspoken obvious.

"I see Sebastian is sending some eye darts my way, so I assure you all that I'm kidding," Fall said wryly as he untied the diamond flag from the trophy and shoved it into a hole in the wooden box. "We actually take the rules very seriously for the kids' sake, so *please* don't use me as an excuse to break any." He picked up the first groups of files, beginning the flag selection.

A moment later, he drew the coveted diamond flag for Kuvi. Alice's roommate returned to the table beaming a moment later, carrying the trophy, her campers' informational packets, and flag.

Fall called Alice's name a few minutes later. She stood and walked to the head table like everyone else had to receive the files for her assigned campers and her flag. Fall reached into the flag box.

Somehow, she wasn't surprised when he withdrew the strip of red cloth and handed it to her. Her uncanny knowledge didn't stop her heart from thumping like crazy in her chest, however, especially when she saw that gleam in Fall's eyes as he handed her the team flag.

"Well, imagine that," she heard someone say very quietly as Alice started to return to her seat to polite applause. She glanced sideways, and saw Sebastian Kehoe watching her through a narrowed gaze.

FOUR

That night, Alice had a seemingly comical, but in reality, terrifying dream that she was being chased around the main lodge of the camp by a ten-foot-tall knight wearing thick brass armor who poked at her aggressively from behind with a sharp sword. All of the other Durand counselors were calmly watching this abuse, wholly unconcerned by her plight.

Alice had no doubt the knight wanted to kill her.

The knight jabbed at the back of her head. Pain sliced through her, and she awoke with a muffled shout.

She immediately recognized her surroundings due to the starlight glow reflecting off the white beach and emanating into the cabin from the patio doors. She guiltily glanced over to see if she'd wakened Kuvi with her yell, sighing in relief when she saw her roommate's form remained unmoving.

Her heart still racing, she swung her legs off the bed and stood. Thanks to the scary dream, perspiration had gathered between her breasts and on her nape. A glowing digital clock on her bedside table told her it was 4:52 a.m. Morning. The kids would be arriving at around noon today, according to Kehoe. She must be a lot more nervous about the idea of whether or not she had what it took in her to lead the band of kids . . . or the ability to show the executives even a glimmer of the innovative leadership potential prized by Durand.

Her stomach fluttering with nerves, she knelt in front of her closet, blindly fumbling for her tennis shoes.

She knew from experience a brisk jog would help ease her rampant anxiety. If she didn't get ahold of herself, she was going to spin out of control and ruin everything before the first day of camp even came to an end.

She shrugged on an exercise bra, but otherwise just left on the shorts and tank top she'd worn to bed. No one else would be up this early. No one would see her.

She'd jogged with Lacey Sherwood during several early mornings this week, but always after dawn broke. It was still dark when she softly closed and locked the cabin door and jogged down the front steps. Lampposts set along the path helped her to navigate as she settled into a comfortable jogging pace. She wound her way through the silent dark cabins and headed toward the beach.

Her body warming and loosening from the brisk exercise, she admired the moon-bathed pale coastline as she ran. She breathed in the cool morning air, the hushed sound of the waves whisking on the shore soothing her. Slowly, a calm seeped over her as she ran along the damp sand.

In her mind's eye, she saw the pieces of paper with her campers' names, ages, cities of origin, histories, and assessments provided by a child psychologist listed on it. She'd memorized almost every word in those files before she'd fallen asleep last night. She was worried Kehoe and his team had assigned her the most challenging campers. Kuvi's campers' descriptions hadn't seemed half so intimidating as Alice's.

Multiple prior arrests for drug possession, breaking and entering, and assault before age fifteen . . . Post-traumatic stress disorder following the witnessing of her mother's murder . . . six unsuccessful foster home placements, where he was typically removed after multiple incidents of running away . . . victim of bullying and physical aggression by peers resulting in multiple injuries and hospitalizations . . . parental neglect reported by school's social worker after investigations into child's home life

*revealed that the child is left alone for extended periods of time
with inadequate nutritious food or necessary supervision, resulting in the child being dangerously overweight, diabetic, and non-
compliant with treatment.*

Those descriptions, and others as well, paraded through her
head. The histories weren't as shocking or unfamiliar to Alice as they
were to most of her peers. That fact worried Alice even more. Just
because she'd grown up in Little Paradise, she wasn't prepared to
help kids like this. In fact, she was starting to worry her own experience with deprivation, neglect, and constant threat had left her even
less capable of assisting in comparison to her fellow counselors.

She turned back toward camp after twenty minutes on the
beach. To her right, she spied a path that disappeared into the
thick woods. It led to the tennis courts and stables, she knew. This
particular part of the trail wasn't lit with lampposts, but the faint
glow of dawn had started to lighten the eastern sky over the
woods. Morning was here. She aimed for the path, knowing it
would lead her back to camp.

Despite the dim light of dawn visible on the shore, however,
she soon discovered the surrounding trees made it almost pitch
black in the woods. Only the paleness of the pavement below her
feet guided her. She became hyperaware of the sound of her tapping tennis shoes on the path and her even but escalated breathing.

Another noise entered her ears. She turned her head, her feet
faltering slightly on the path.

The source of the sound eluded her. She resumed her former
pace. She'd thought she'd heard another footfall aside from her
own. It'd been her imagination—or more likely, her own heartbeat
thumping in her ears.

Nevertheless, she quickened her pace, some instinct goading
her. She thought the stables were just yards ahead. Weren't there
path lights around there? She didn't ride, like many of her fellow
counselors did, so she wasn't certain.

The darkness seemed to crowd her, the shadows to encroach. A close, suffocating feeling pressed on her throat and chest.

Again, she heard a steady tread, slightly off-tempo from her own.

She stopped abruptly and spun around. Her heart jumped in her throat when the footsteps continued, clearer now that she stood still.

"Who is it?" she yelled into the black forest.

The footfalls ceased abruptly. A shiver snaked beneath her heated skin. The entire forest fell silent. She started when she thought she saw something white flicker in the shadows just at the farthest fringes of her vision.

"Who's back there?" Alice demanded, anger and panic edging her tone. The white figure remained still. And quiet.

Or *wait* . . . was it slowly, silently soaring closer?

Terror shot through her veins. She turned and began to run again, still staring over her shoulder. *Yes.* Something pale was gliding through the darkness toward her. Whoever it was wasn't answering her, and therefore wasn't friendly.

It didn't even look human.

She immediately quashed the disturbing thought. She started to sprint.

"Shit," she muttered under her breath when she heard the footsteps behind her increase in tempo as well. Yes, it was definitely human. Somehow, the knowledge didn't help. She was being chased.

He's going to kill me.

Stop it! she shouted at herself mentally, recognizing the irrationality of not only her thought, but her bizarre certainty that it was *true.*

She saw some lights ahead through the trees. *Thank God.* As she took a curve, she also spotted the outline of a building. Even though she'd expressed a firm lack of interest in horseback riding, she recognized the stables. The footsteps behind her grew louder. Her pursuer was getting closer. He was faster than her . . . stronger. Panic rose in her like a heavy, smothering blanket, weighting her muscles and lungs.

Her breath grew ragged. A stitch started to pierce her side. She made a split-second decision and left the path. If she tried to make the camp, whoever was behind her would eventually catch up . . . and who knew what he had in mind? Whatever it was, it wasn't good. If she reached the stables, she could possibly barricade herself inside.

The glow of a dim outdoor lamp next to the stable entrance guided her. Panicked, she glanced behind her and saw the murky figure follow her off the path. It *was* a man . . . wasn't it? Only the movement of a pale shirt or garment was clear in the dark gray gloom.

She reached the building and fumbled around wildly for a door. She cried out in desperate relief when the knob twisted— she'd feared it would be locked. If only she *could* lock it once she got inside. Otherwise, she'd be trapped. The door swung open at her shove.

She ran directly into something large and solid. Someone grabbed her shoulders. She screamed.

"Shhh," a man said, sounding alarmed. "It's okay. Stop it, I'm not going to hurt you," he said sharply when she instinctively pushed away from him, slapping and then punching at his chest.

"Let *go* of me, damn it," she seethed.

He grunted and cursed when she landed an uppercut just below the sternum. There was a clicking sound. A light blazed into her eyes.

"Alice?"

She blinked, disoriented.

"Dylan—" she muttered hoarsely, too shocked upon seeing his hovering face to realize she'd called him by his first name.

He stared down at her, his hands still cupping her shoulders firmly. His dark brows were bunched in alarmed consternation.

"What is it? What's wrong?"

It took her jumbled brain a moment to take in the fact that he'd grabbed her from the front, not behind. He'd been *inside* the building when she flung open the door. She looked over her shoulder, panting, searching the shadows, and seeing nothing but a thick dark gray gloom. "Someone was following me through the woods . . . chasing me."

"Who?"

She gave him an exasperated glance. "I don't know, he wasn't being polite and answering my questions while he ran me down," she ground out. She stared at his chest. He was wearing a black T-shirt, jeans, and black boots. "It wasn't you," she stated, as if affirming that fact to herself. Dylan's face and body were strikingly solid and strong and *comforting*, but panic still hazed her consciousness. She wasn't sure why, exactly. Alice had been chased through the grimy streets of Little Paradise untold times and seldom had felt this level of primal fear. "He was wearing a white shirt, not a black one . . . I *think* . . ." She faded off, registering Fall's fierce stare. She hesitated. Was he silently doubting her?

"What are you doing out in the woods at this hour?" he asked.

"Jogging," she said, bristling at his question. "What are *you* doing down here?"

"I ride Kar Kalim most mornings at dawn," he said distractedly, his narrowed stare trained out the opened door. His gaze flickered down to her confused expression. "My horse," he added.

"He was *chasing* me, and he wouldn't answer me when I asked who it was," she insisted succinctly.

He nodded decisively and slammed the stable door behind her. "I believe you. Come on," he said, urging her farther into the room. For the first time, Alice realized they stood in a sort of open area that had saddles, bits, bridles, and ropes hanging everywhere. She inhaled the scent of hay and animals. The odor wasn't unpleasant, necessarily, but for some reason, nausea flickered in her belly.

Several pitchforks leaned against one wall. In the distance, she saw a long row of four-foot-high wooden doors and the silhouettes of horses' heads arching over the top of them.

"But he's still *out* there," she exclaimed, glancing behind her at the closed door. Dylan didn't understand at all; he couldn't seem to grasp the level of primitive fear that had flooded into her veins out there in those dark woods.

"I know," Dylan said firmly, guiding her over to a closed door. He opened it. "I'm going to take care of it." He flipped on a light. She realized it was some sort of office. The barn smell wasn't so strong in here. An old wooden desk sat in the center of it, a computer, stacks of papers, folders, and notebooks on top of it. There was a sagging brown couch on the right wall. Raincoats and hats hung on a rack, while several pairs of rubber boots were lined up beneath them.

"It's the stable manager, Gordon Schneider's, office. He doesn't arrive at work until seven," Dylan explained. When she just continued to look over her shoulder, fearful the man on the path was about to burst in on them, Dylan touched her jaw, gently but firmly. She stared up into his face, her attention finally fully snagged.

"I'm not going to let anyone hurt you, Alice. Do you understand?"

She nodded, holding her breath because he didn't move. His skin remained in contact with hers.

"There are two locks on this door, do you see?" he said after a lung-burning moment. He swung the wood door to show her. "This is a solid oak door, and no one is going to get past that dead bolt."

"Okay," she said, her voice shaky with relief. He really *did* believe her. His hand fell away from her face. "Wait, where are you going?" she demanded shrilly when he started to move away.

"To see who's out there. Lock the door after me," he said. He did a double take, wincing slightly as he stared at her face. "Alice," he said sharply. "Everything is going to be fine. Lock the door after me, do you understand?"

"*No,*" she breathed out through bared teeth. "If you walk out of this room, I swear to God I'll *kill* you, Dylan Fall." She heaved on the door, shutting it with a bang. She lunged past his tall form and slammed the dead bolt home before she twisted the second door lock. Her back thumped against the door. She gasped for air.

"Alice—"

"You're not leaving me."

It took a second or two for the rapid clicking sound to enter her awareness. It was coming from inside her own head. Her teeth were chattering uncontrollably.

"Christ," he muttered. He stepped toward her, worry tightening his features, but Alice was already lurching at him. She flung herself gracelessly against his chest, her cheek bumping and settling just below a solid pectoral muscle. She didn't understand what was happening. What was that black cloud of fear that hovered just at the edge of vision, threatening to blind her? Strangle her. The fact that she couldn't name that shadow made it even more frightening.

Her arms squeezed Dylan's waist, and the threatening shadow slinked away slightly. Then Dylan's arms were surrounding her, and he was pulling her tight against his body. The heavy weight on her chest and throat lifted, granting her air. She inhaled choppily.

"*Alice,*" he muttered thickly, sounding a little undone.

"Don't leave me," she repeated, despising the crack in her voice. She felt his fingers move in her hair and his hand cup the back of her head. His touch urged her to move. She tilted her head back, seeing his face hovering over her. His gaze moved over her face searchingly, landing on her neck. She felt the throb of her exposed pulse. Heat swept through her at his heavy-lidded stare.

"I'm not going to leave you."

His fierce, quiet declaration sent an electric spark through her, mixing with her fear and anxiety. Something flickered and then flamed high inside her, and whatever it was made her inchoate fear and uncertainty scurry into the darkest places of her consciousness. She felt Dylan stir against her and realized it was *desire* that had scattered the shadows.

Pure, raw, powerful lust.

Suddenly everything made sense: that strange, thrilling intensity in his eyes when Dylan looked at her, his electric touch on her skin, and her confused but powerful reaction to that touch.

Dylan Fall *wanted* her. And in that moment, Alice had never wanted or needed anything more than him.

Without thinking, driven by the too recent memory of her fear and the shock of her own sudden, unmasked need, she pressed closer to him, her stare narrowing on his hard mouth. Her hand flew to the back of his neck, her fingers burrowing into his thick hair. It felt even better than she'd imagined it would. She went on her tiptoes and urged him to her. He lowered his head slightly. Her lips brushed against his.

"No, Alice," he said, but the same mouth that denied her softened ever so slightly. She plucked at his lips, and although he remained mostly still, she felt the leap of tension in his hard body and the slight give in his mouth. His cock hardened even more where it was pressed against her lower belly, the sensation enflaming her. She pressed tighter, her breasts crushing against his lower chest, but still, he wouldn't participate fully in her kiss. Irritated and aroused, she bit softly at his lower lip, forcing his mouth to open.

"Don't leave. *Stay* here with me," she hissed, her whispered words and her unspoken invitation shocking to her own ears. She slicked her tongue along the seam of his mouth. He uttered a curse, but his tongue came with it.

Abruptly, she was at the core of a hot fire. In a split second, she'd gone from the safe periphery to the center of the inferno, and Fall was consuming her.

He sealed their mouths, molding her lips to his. His tongue penetrated her, sweeping, seeking, owning. His opened hand slid along her hip and cupped one of her ass cheeks, pushing her to him at the same moment he flexed slightly, sliding his erection against her straining body. He leaned down over her, bending his knees slightly, finding the prime angle of penetration for his kiss. He fucked her mouth unapologetically with his tongue while his mouth applied a demanding, precise suction that seemed to pull at her very core. His lips moved, too, molding her to him, shaping their flesh.

It was delicious and heady. *He* was. He smelled like spice and clean outdoor air and sex. He tasted like heaven. She strained to keep up with his demanding kiss, tangling her tongue with his wildly. Alice gripped his neck and waist tighter, dizzied and over-whelmed by the sudden fierce blast of his hunger.

His big hand slid under her running shorts and underwear, and he was molding her bare ass to his palm. She felt his cock leap against her, the weight and density of his erection maddening her. When he tore his mouth from hers, she strained for him, seeking with her lips. Long fingers delved beneath her panties, searching between her thighs. His fingertip touched her sex. She started like an electrical shock had gone through her.

He held her stare and slowly penetrated her with his forefinger.

She gasped raggedly, sagging against his solid body.

"Is this what you think you want?" he grated out, his mouth hard, his face rigid.

He sent his finger high, withdrew, and then slid it high again. She bit her lip in anguished arousal, lost in his eyes.

"Yes," she gasped.

"You're tight and hot. And wet," he added with a slight snarl as he finger-fucked her. "This *is* what you need, isn't it?"

The intimacy of what was happening overwhelmed her. Her forehead fell against his chest, her mouth hanging open. She couldn't respond. Pleasure and pressure swamped her, fueled by her strange, chaotic emotional state. He backed up slightly, one hand at her back, the other piercing her body, firm and fast. His movement caused her to bend slightly at the waist, improving the angle of his penetration. She *was* wet. The sound of him moving deliberately and forcefully in her lubricated sex reached her ears. He must have heard it, too, because he growled, the sound feral and thrilling. Suddenly, his hand was gone and he was pushing her toward the desk. Her bottom hit the wood surface, loudly jolting the legs back an inch on the bare floor. He lifted her slightly, setting her ass at the edge of the desk. His hands slid beneath her T-shirt.

"You're not the only one who needs something, Alice."

Her heart started to drum loudly in her ears at his low, tense declaration. She wanted him like crazy in that moment, but a Dylan Fall gripped by lust was an awesome, intimidating experience. In her few former sexual relationships, she'd often hesitated in the midst of lovemaking, unsure of what she wanted, second-guessing whether she was giving too much of herself away, or too little. She had offered herself to Fall. But there was no doubt that now that he'd accepted, he would set the pace. He expected her to give herself wholesale. *That* was how things were done with him.

She read the message in his eyes right now. Clearly, what he wanted was no small taste.

She was blinded for an instant as he jerked her damp T-shirt over her head. She assisted him, whipping her arms through the sleeves, spinning just as furiously in the twist of raw animal lust as him. The embarrassing realization that she was hot and perspiring from her run and being chased flickered across her awareness, but then it was gone, evaporated in an instant by the heat they generated. Besides, sweat somehow seemed appropriate in this wild, desperate, impulsive scenario. Then his fingers were sliding against her perspiration-damp skin beneath her tight jogging bra. He lifted the binding material over her breasts. His actions weren't rough, but they *were* precise and forceful. One second, she was wearing the bra, and the next, her breasts bounced softly free from the restricting garment. He flung the twisted fabric heedlessly in the direction of her T-shirt. He paused. Her nipples prickled and tightened at their exposure to the cool air and his hot unwavering stare.

"Jesus," he muttered, his nostrils flaring slightly. He wore a strange expression of mixed awe and rabid male hunger. His warm hands skimmed up her sides, lightly bracketing her breasts. The easy slide of his skin against hers reminded her again of her sweatiness, but this time it only aroused, as if her perspiration was a prime conductor for all the electricity leaping between them. She cut off a moan at what she saw on his face as he cupped her and held up her breasts for his avid inspection. He pinched at the nipples slightly, plumping them following their constriction in the tight bra.

"Dylan," she said shakily, the tension building inside her unbearable. Cutting.

"It's okay. I'm just amazed," she thought she heard him say through the roar in her ears. "You're larger than I thought you'd be. You hide yourself. I knew you'd be beautiful but . . . not like this." His thumbs whisked over her nipples and they tightened almost painfully. He glanced up at her. She bit her lip when she saw the gleam of humor mixing with the arousal in his eyes. "You're a goddess disguised as a bad-girl math geek, Alice Reed." Again, his thumbs whisked over the sensitive nipples, coaxing them to stiff peaks. Her sex thrilled and tightened at his touch, like she was an instrument and he was plucking her strings knowingly. Her flesh sang. She whimpered, but what she wanted to do was scream.

"Don't tease me," she insisted hoarsely as he watched her reaction like a hawk while he played with her, and she watched him in turn.

"No. Not now," he agreed, his amusement once again replaced by his rapier-sharp focus.

She held her breath in sharp anticipation as he moved his hands to her back. "I've got you," he urged, and she realized he wanted her to arch for him . . . display herself for his consumption. The thought made liquid surge at her core. Her back curved and she leaned into his hold. "That's right," he praised, taking her partial weight with his hands and lowering her torso a few inches. He stepped into her, forcing her thighs to part for him. He flexed his hips, grinding his erection against her pelvis and lower belly. Without pause, his dark head lowered and he took a breast into his warm mouth.

He was greedy from the first. She'd known he would be. She cried out when he applied a firm suck and laved the nipple vigorously with his tongue. He must taste her sweat. Her desire. Hot forbidden pleasure spiked through her. She loved it. She stared at the vision of his dark head hovering over the thrusting pale mound of her breast, his mouth latched to the tip, his firm lips clamped around her. His cheeks hollowed out slightly as he drew on her.

It was the most erotic vision she'd ever seen in her life.

Helpless in the clutches of sexual heat like she'd never before experienced, she circled her hips, pressing her sex against the root of his cock. Wild. Frantic. Still supporting her with one hand, he fondled her other breast, shaping the mound to his palm. She loved the way he held her in his hand so possessively almost as much as the way he sucked her so surely. He made a rough sound in his throat, the vibrations penetrating her, thrilling her.

He lifted his head, switching to the other breast without pause. Using his hand, he plumped her for his mouth, sucking the nipple into his humid heat. His focused lust was palpable. It was too much, the pleasure so precise it bordered on pain. Alice squirmed in anguished arousal. She put her hands on the desk behind her, heedlessly scattering a few papers across the desk and onto the floor, using her hold for added pressure to grind against him. The sensation of the shape and fullness of his cock behind his clothing only amplified her frenzy.

He lightly brought down his palm on her naked thigh.

Her eyes popped wide at the slapping sound of skin against skin. It hadn't hurt, but it'd been a mild remonstrance. She forced her writhing to still. *The beast is feasting, and he doesn't want to be disturbed.* Even her humorous thought sent her into a deeper trance of lust.

Of forgetfulness.

Now that she was supporting herself, he used both of his hands to hold up her breasts, pushing them together. It was a lewd, blatant display of ripe sexuality. The mounds were pale compared to his hands and her tanned arms, chest, and shoulders. Her nipples were usually a delicate pink color, but the one that wasn't in his ravening mouth at the moment was reddened, damp, and pebbled from his attentions. He ran his thumb over it while he greedily sucked, and Alice keened, twisting her hips against his cock. She was no better than an animal in heat in that moment.

Worse, because she had no excuse for her wantonness.

The next thing she knew, he was lifting her off the desk and turning her. She was growing used to the way he handled her. It wasn't rough, by any means, but he never hesitated for a second in positioning her precisely how he wanted her. The combination of his single-mindedness and exacting strength was a potent aphrodisiac.

"What are you doing, squirming around like that, little girl?" he demanded roughly near her ear, a hint of dark amusement in his tone. His mouth moved on her neck. He bit gently on the shell of her ear and she cried out. She backed against him, finding what she wanted, grinding her ass against his cock. He was a full, delightful package, so primal, flagrant . . . *male.* She bared her teeth, desperate to rid him of the jeans and feel him, hot and hard, skin to skin. She reached around, her hand finding him, grasping the dense column through his jeans.

He groaned roughly and grabbed her hand. He placed it on the desk in front of her.

"Both hands on the desk," he ordered. "Bend over."

She did what he demanded, acquiescent because she felt him shift behind her and the movement of his hands between their straining bodies. He was freeing his cock.

He was going to give her what she wanted.

She looked over her shoulder, panting, hungry for the vision of him. Her own body blocked it, however. She saw his hands moving hastily between his thighs, unfastening his jeans. She turned around, reaching for him single-mindedly.

A surprised, stupid-sounding yelp popped out of her throat when she was suddenly spinning around again, and Dylan was placing her hands on the desk.

"Bend over," he repeated, low and succinct near her ear. She complied, only because following his demand was a quicker method to attain her ultimate goal. Then his thumbs were hooking the waistband of her running shorts and panties. He jerked them downward in a perfunctory motion to her knees. The garments fell to her ankles.

"Step out of them," he commanded gruffly.

She kicked aside her shorts and underwear, now nude save some bootie socks and her running shoes. He placed a hand on her lower back and pressed, urging her to bend over more. The head of his cock brushed against her ass. She moaned, heat rushing through her at the sensation of the bulbous smooth head and the sheer weight of his arousal. He held her hips and flexed. The long, thick shaft slid against her perspiration-damp naked skin. His rough groan fused with hers.

"Is that what you wanted?" he asked in a tight, feral tone as he continued to glide his taut, naked cock back and forth against her ass.

"Yes. Yes," she assured, clamping her eyelids shut, overwhelmed by the raw intensity of the moment. Her hand rose from the desk and she began to reach behind her hip, craving the feeling of his cock in her hand. He was faster than her, though. He grabbed her wrist and placed it gently back on the desk.

"Keep your hands there, damn it. I'm about to burst for you," he bit out roughly. Breathing raggedly, she followed his direction. He stroked her hip and ass. "Your skin is so soft. Such a beautiful color," he said, as if forcing all the tension out of his tone. The heavy shaft of his cock thumped into the crack of her ass. He cupped the cheeks, molding the flesh around the shaft and sawed his hips back and forth. His groan sounded like it tore at his throat.

"You're so sweet. I don't know what the hell is happening here," she heard him say thickly as he continued to pulse his cock in the furrow of her ass, "but you're impossible to resist, Alice."

FIVE

She made a desperate soughing sound, sensation flooding her. She was spinning out of control.

He thrust and squeezed her ass tighter against his cock. Then his hands were gone, and she made a muffled sound of bemusement.

"It's okay," he murmured from behind her. "Condom."

He left his cock throbbing next to her ass, the sensation taunting her. She heard the sound of the condom package ripping. She bit her lip to cut off a sharp cry. The anticipation was killing her. It only grew worse when he rolled on the condom while his cock was still burning her skin. She felt his hand slide down the shaft, and then the hard, thick crown pressing against her slit. He pulled back one buttock, opening her further to him. He pressed. She gasped, her eyes springing wide as he slowly entered her body. He must have interpreted her loud exhale as a sign of discomfort, because he paused.

"Shhh," he quieted, one hand making a soothing gesture at her hip while the other one cupped her ass and kept her in place for his possession. He pulsed his hips back and forth gently. Her flesh began to melt around him.

"That's right," he muttered, flexing until she gritted her teeth at the pressure and pleasure. He was patient, but firm, in gaining entrance. Determined. Again, she had that vivid impression that once Dylan Fall started something, he never wavered.

She was glad. So glad.

"You're so tight. So *wet*," she heard him say as if through a tunnel.

"Oh God," she cried out in high-pitched disbelief as he slowly, but surely, slid into her to the hilt. He held her against him, not letting her move. She felt his balls press against her outer tissues. Her breath stuck in her lungs. He stretched her, filled her. He was in her pussy, but he overwhelmed her mind . . . her very being.

Dylan pushed everything else away.

Yes. This is what she needed. Nothing else existed but him in that moment—Dylan and this frothing, volatile need.

He began to move his hips in a taut, fluid, rapid pumping motion. He groaned harshly. Alice's mouth fell open in disbelieving pleasure. What was he *doing* to her? She'd had sex before, but she'd never experienced *this*. The friction was unbearable. Savage. Sweet. His pelvis slapped against her ass as he pumped harder. Air popped out of her lungs.

"Oh Jesus," she gasped, her eyelids clenching tight. He held her hips and buttocks firmly in his hands, tilting her pelvis upward slightly, serving her to his pillaging cock. He was ruthless. She gripped the desk tighter, stiffening her arms to brace herself for the impact of him. He continued to fuck her fast and furious using that strong, rhythmic, slightly circular motion of his hips. She rocked back and forth as they crashed together. She pushed back against him, the ache in her mounting. Swelling. The sound of their slapping skin filled her ears.

God, the man knew how to fuck.

"You feel good, baby. Too good," he rasped from behind her. "Sweet, hot little pussy. It's going to be hard to go slow with you," he grated out, his tempo never breaking. He thrust deep and groaned. "Maybe impossible," he added, sounding angry at his conclusion.

Heat flooded her cheeks and her sex at his illicit words. The friction he built was unbearable. She lost all sense of time or purpose as he took her by storm. The chaotic brew of emotion and lust reached a boiling point, his pounding cock sending her over the edge . . .

Breaking her.

She shattered in orgasm.

"Fuck," she heard him mutter. Climax spiked through her flesh, shaking her, and he was lifting her to an almost upright position, her back still slightly tilted forward, his cock lodged high in her. He filled his hands with her breasts and bent his knees. He drove his cock into her in short, powerful jabs. He growled, deep and harsh. Alice's world quaked. She was a single vibrating nerve of pleasure, her sole purpose to burn. Another wave of climax tore through her as he took his fill of her in that position, pushing her down on his thrusting cock with his hold on her even as he bucked his hips, plunging into her.

He grunted in what sounded like pure frustration.

"I can't last. You're too hot, Alice. Hands back on the desk."

She reached for the edge of the desk blindly, bending over. Her breasts still held fast in his hands, he pumped forcefully. He sank into her and stayed, pressing his testicles tightly against her outer sex. His cock swelled and jerked in her channel. She cried out, anguished by the sensation. His groan started out low. He gripped her breasts tighter, and the groan grew louder, rougher, the harsh, tearing sound filling her ears.

He was coming. His cock filled her so completely that she felt the spasms in his flesh as he emptied himself, the sensation powerful, fierce, and yet somehow sweet. Poignant.

Their ragged breathing twined in the still room. Alice's head had fallen forward. Her short sweat-dampened hair was plastered against her forehead, neck, and cheeks. She lifted her head, and his hand moved on one of her breasts, his taut hold gentling. A fingertip feathered her nipple. She stifled a cry of dawning misery.

Of renewed arousal.

What did you just do?

"Quiet," he breathed out, gently touching her nipple again, circling the crown with his fingertip. Had he heard the trapped cry in her throat? "It's going to be okay," he said. She wasn't sure she believed him, but his touch felt so good. She wasn't ready to come to terms yet with what she'd just done.

You jumped on Durand's biggest boss, all because you got as freaked out as a child by a distant figure in the woods. You're not a little girl. You're a grown woman in excellent physical condition. You've been known to occasionally make your worthless uncles and their loser friends squeal in desperate pain.

Had there *really* been someone behind her? Suddenly, the whole memory seemed surreal, like she'd been pursued by a nightmare.

A phantom.

Dylan opened his hands at the stretch of skin above her breasts, just below her shoulders, and lifted her several inches, pushing her against him. Her back was plastered to the front of him, his cock still skewering her. His hand slid back down over her breasts. He lifted them, cradling them with his palms. He gently pinched her sensitive nipples. She moaned softly, her clit twinging with arousal. One big hand skimmed down her bare belly, lightly caressing her damp skin, making her shiver. He touched her outer sex.

"Dylan . . ." she protested shakily. She quivered when he slid his forefinger between her labia. He rubbed her lubricated clit. How had he known tension still lingered in her flesh? Here again, he knew precisely what he was doing. "Oh," she ground out, her body tightening. *Christ, it feels good.*

"It's okay," he rasped from behind her. "It's going to be okay. Trust me, Alice."

She moaned. What the hell was she doing here? Not just in Dylan's arms with his cock embedded in her and his hand working its magic between her thighs . . . *here* at Camp Durand. Did she actually think she could ever be accepted?

He'd asked her to trust him, but Alice didn't trust easily . . . if at all. It didn't matter. Dylan was trumping everything, including fear and doubt. Isn't that why she'd so uncharacteristically, brazenly seduced him?

She was shaking again in climax beneath his sure hand in under a minute, compounding her sins . . .

Unable to do anything in the moment but submit to the glory of it.

SHE realized with a sinking sensation that while she was nude, save for her socks and shoes, Dylan was almost fully dressed. It seemed to symbolize their whole encounter, Alice realized as she scuttled for her discarded clothing a few minutes later. Alice had been caught red-handed in the midst of her naked vulnerability, while Dylan had exposed only what was required to silence her panicked frenzy.

He'd wrapped up the condom and disposed of it, then tucked himself back into his jeans before she even had a chance to untwist her shorts and panties. She kept her face lowered to hide her red cheeks—to prevent him from seeing her shame—but after a moment, she felt his stare on her like a brand on her skin nevertheless. She started to step into her panties, but her vulnerability overwhelmed her.

"Turn away," she said angrily.

"What?"

His slightly stunned tone made her grit her teeth. Her eyelids stung with humiliation.

"Turn away while I dress. *Please*," she grated out, barely tamped down emotion constricting her throat.

His hissed curse made her heart jump, but then she heard the subtle sound of his boots on the wood floor. She glanced up hopefully. He'd turned, although something about the stiffness of his back told her loud and clear he wasn't happy with her request and might change his mind at any moment. She dressed like she thought it was a race event in a Camp Durand competition. By the time she was finished, her breath was coming in jagged pants just like it was after she'd climaxed so thunderously just moments ago.

Twice.

"Are you done?" he asked, and she could tell by the heavy sarcasm in his tone he was pissed.

She straightened and lifted her chin. *You flew across the forest suspended by a skinny little wire, certain you were going to die at any second. You can look Dylan Fall in the face.*

"Yes."

He turned around.

In that moment, she would have gladly chosen to zip line straight off the Sears Tower and plunge to the earth instead of meeting his lancing stare.

"I don't know why I did"—she swallowed thickly, finding it hard to name what she'd just done with Dylan—"*that*," she said, waving lamely at the desk.

"I know." He paused, and then nodded once as if he'd come to some decision. "I want you to come to my house tonight."

She made an incredulous sound of disbelief and laughed. "Why?"

He met her stare and shrugged slightly, his bland expression saying, *Isn't it obvious?*

"Are you crazy?" she sputtered.

"No," he said grimly, turning toward her. "Are you?"

"No!"

"So this is all par for the course for you?" he asked, arching a dark brow inquisitively and glancing at the desk, where Alice had just been screwing him like her life depended on it moments ago. A wave of humiliation swept through her, fury hot on its heel.

"What if it is *par for the course* for me? What business of it is yours? Just because I fucked you once doesn't mean I want to make it a habit. Screw this," she mumbled hotly, stalking toward the door. She jammed back the dead bolt forcefully. She hoped her chaser was still out there, because she'd kick his ass for getting her into this situation.

Ghost pursuer or not.

"Alice."

She paused in her flight, hating her automatic reaction to Dylan saying her name. Still, she remained with her back to him. Defiant, but . . .

Listening.

"I know that you're feeling out of sorts. Overwhelmed, being here at Camp Durand."

Her heartbeat started to throb in her ears. "Because I don't belong here, you mean?" she snapped.

"No. Because you're afraid you don't belong here. But you *do.* Alice, look at me."

He spoke very quietly, but there was steel in his tone. She found herself turning and looking over her shoulder, unable to continue looking away, just like that first time during her interview. He hadn't moved, but meeting his stare made him seem to zoom closer in her consciousness, like a weird camera lens effect.

"Do you remember how I told you about that man on the Durand board? The one who grew up in the Austin neighborhood in Chicago?"

She nodded warily. He made a subtle gesture with his hand in the direction of his abdomen.

She spun around fully.

"You were talking about yourself?" she asked numbly.

He nodded.

Her mouth fell open in disbelief. "*You.* You came here as a camper when you were twelve years old?"

"It saved my life," he said with absolute certainty. "If it weren't for Camp Durand, I'd be dead or rotting in a prison cell right now."

She just stared. Her brain couldn't seem to absorb the news. Smooth, intimidating, supremely confident Dylan Fall had once been described in a camper packet like the one she'd received last night? Her imaginings about that piratical, ruthless edge to him had a basis. What had that long-ago assessment said? *Teachers have noted flashes of pure brilliance interspersed with belligerence and uncooperativeness, frequent school absences and tardiness, aggression and frequent fighting.*

She imagined the words, of course. Still, the description somehow fit his independence and that blade hinted at just beneath the polished sophistication, that vague, but ever-present idea that if you didn't give him exactly what he wanted, you just might end up pinned against the wall, staring helplessly into Fall's shining dark eyes and feeling the carefully concealed razor edge of his personality firsthand.

Alice certainly understood that edge all too well now, although not in the aggressive sense. The sexual one.

"So you see, I have more than a glimmer of understanding of what you're experiencing here," he said. "You feel like an outsider. Part of you is sure that at any moment, someone is going to discover the truth about you, and kick you out on your ass."

"You think we're *alike?*" she asked with sarcastic incredulity. "You think you know me because you were a little kid at Camp Durand? I'm not a twelve-year-old child."

"*I'm* not either," he bit out, the sizzling thread of anger in his tone making the tiny hairs on the back of her neck stand up on end. For a moment, neither of them spoke while Dylan seemed to master his flash of anger.

"I'm a thirty-four-year-old man who is the leader of one of the most successful, profitable companies in the world. My everyday decisions affect thousands of Durand employees and their families across the globe. But there isn't a day that goes by that I don't have some distant thought—no matter how brief—that someone isn't going to expose me for what I am, and kick me straight back to the gutter where I belong."

The silence throbbed in her ears. She couldn't draw breath.

After a tense few seconds, he exhaled and shook his head as if to clear it.

"Leave your cabin at exactly nine thirty tonight and head toward the stables. Your duties will be finished by nine, and the night staff will take over supervision of the kids. The counselors are free to do what they want after that. Make up a story to your roommate and leave your cabin."

"I don't understand," Alice said honestly. "Why *should* I?"

"Because you need something to ground you while you're here. You're overwhelmed. You're second-guessing yourself constantly. I see it on your face."

She made a sound of self-disgust. Was she *that* transparent? "Nobody else seems to think so," she said in her defense, thinking of Thad saying he'd never guessed she was sick following the zip-line challenge.

"Nobody else probably can read you like I can," he said with a silky calmness that infuriated her. "I told you. We have something in common. Are you really going to try to convince me that you haven't been overwhelmed being here?"

She clenched her teeth and raised her chin.

"That's what I thought," he said when she refused to confirm or deny it. "You'll come to the house. I want you there."

"For sex," she stated more than asked, her voice flat with amazement at his gargantuan presumption.

"You could come to study the Durand reports, like I asked you to last night. Or you could come to talk. Or you could come and get what you just got in this office. Many times over, if I have my say about it," he added with a hard glance that sent a thrill through her. He paused. "Are you scared right now, Alice?"

"No," she bit out honestly.

"Right. You're pissed. You're *worked up*," he emphasized, taking a step toward her. "But you're *not* scared." He shrugged slightly in a "well, then?" gesture. "I'll leave what we do during the night up to you."

"I'm not traipsing around in these woods at night by myself after what happened out there," she said, pointing in the general direction of the woods.

"Good. I don't want you wandering around by yourself until I get a handle on what happened. Stick with your friends, staff, and the kids in the meantime. Don't wander off." He noticed her expression and guessed at her amazement. "I'll be *waiting* for you when you leave your cabin tonight. I'll make sure no one sees us. This is between you and me, and I expect you to keep it that way," he said with a hard, pointed glance. "But I'll be there. In the woods. Head toward the stables. I'll join you just as soon as you're out of anyone's vision. I'm *not* going to let anything happen to you."

She swallowed thickly at his forceful repetition of what he'd said earlier.

"So . . . you . . . you saw him, too?" she asked hoarsely, pointing toward the woods. Her flash of hope mortified her. She dropped her stare furtively, worried he'd notice it. "You believe me about the man chasing me?"

"Of course I do."

Her gaze shot to his at his utter confidence.

"You *did* see him?"

He shook his head slowly. "I didn't *have* to see him. Maybe you don't think we're alike, but I can guess at one thing we probably have in common, given our backgrounds. We don't spook easily. One look at your face out there just now," he said, nodding in the direction of the stable entrance, "and I knew for sure you were convinced the devil was on your heels."

The ensuing silence was deafening.

"I'm not agreeing to come," she said.

"You'll come. Head toward the stables, and I'll meet up with you on the path."

He stepped toward her, impervious to her dazed state, and finished unlocking the door.

THE whole experience—the person chasing her through the woods, the scorching sexual escapade with Fall, and his subsequent outrageous proposal that she continue carrying on with him—left her in a strange state indeed.

She'd heard people who were in a state of shock could operate on automatic mode, going through the motions of survival without really being aware of what they were doing or how they were doing it. As Alice waited for the arrival of the buses filled with campers that brilliant summer day, she figured that's what was happening to her. True, this morning had been earth shattering and totally unbelievable. But with her mind and spirit focused elsewhere, it was also kind of hard to work herself into the feverish anxiety she'd been in when she'd awakened this morning, before she'd jogged on the beach . . .

Before Fall.

She couldn't stop replaying those taut, intensely erotic moments with him. She'd grow hot and restless at the most inopportune times. It all seemed dreamlike in the vivid bright light of day. Then she'd feel the tenderness between her thighs, the slight, strangely pleasant ache that was her constant reminder. Her sex still felt primed, like the desire she'd experienced had been so great, it needed hours or days to fully dissipate.

It'd been real. *He* had. Their mutual desire was tangible still.

She blinked, coming out of her torrid memories when she noticed Thad watching her. They were standing next to each other, awaiting the arrival of the busloads of campers.

"You certainly are calm about all this," Thad observed. "As usual."

"Is that how I look?" she asked with a small laugh. "If that's the impression I'm giving, I really am a much better actress than I thought."

Or I'm a hell of a lot more shell-shocked.

"I think it's more than acting," Thad said very quietly, as if he didn't want his voice to carry to anyone else in the crowd of people waiting. The Camp Durand staff was all there, waiting at the edge of the forest: counselors, the Durand managers, and various other employees hired every year for camp: a cook, a nurse, a tennis instructor, two lifeguards, night supervisors, a janitor, a man who worked in the small boat marina, and even Gordon Schneider, the stables manager. A flash of heated embarrassment had gone through her when someone had introduced her to Schneider a few minutes ago, and she recalled what she'd been doing against the man's desk early this morning.

The counselors wore their team flag like a scarf in various conspicuous places so that the arriving campers could identify them easily—Alice, like most of the other counselors, had her red flag tied around her neck, but Thad wore his orange one around a golden muscular biceps. Kuvi jauntily displayed her diamond flag on her head, tied like a pirate's scarf, and was pulling off the look adorably.

Alice glanced at Thad sideways. "What do you mean?" she asked him in a hushed tone.

"Don't you ever get ruffled?" Thad murmured, his voice barely audible above the chattering, excited crowd surrounding them. "You're like Patton heading into battle."

She shook her head. "Like I've told you before, I'm an actress and didn't know it, then. Shame they don't have theater as one of the activities around here. I'm scared stiff about being a miserable failure with these kids. With Camp Durand in general."

"You told me while we were in the woods the other day that you came from a similar background as a lot of the campers," Thad said. A wave of regret swept through Alice. She shouldn't have told him about her childhood during their amiable interlude in the forest. She'd revealed too much. What if he mentioned it to Tory or Brooke, and the news somehow reached the Durand managers or Kehoe? Maybe it wouldn't matter. Look at where Dylan Fall had come from, after all? She still couldn't believe *that* revelation.

Still, her impulsive confession to Thad made her feel uncomfortably exposed.

"Won't that commonality in your background make it easier for them to relate to you?" Thad continued. He stared at the still empty road ahead of them. "If I were those kids, I'd resent someone like me."

"Someone like you?" Alice wondered.

He shrugged, as if trying to minimize what he was saying. "Someone who doesn't know crap about what they have to go through every day of their life. Why should they listen to some privileged white guy from Greenwich, Connecticut?" he joked, but she heard the hint of worry in his tone.

A minor shock went through her. Gorgeous, utterly confident, natural born leader Thad Schaefer was worried about *failing?* At *this*, an outdoor leadership retreat, the likes of which he'd probably attend and excel at no matter what type of executive position he ended up taking?

She suddenly saw Dylan's gleaming eyes and heard his quiet voice echoing in her head as he described why Durand utilized the camp to select its executives every year. *Then the kids arrive, and the challenge really begins . . . It's not enough for counselors to brag about qualities of leadership, planning, intelligence, innovation, salesmanship, compassion, determination, hard work, and courage: they have to* demonstrate *those skills daily with a group*

of children, some of whom have been labeled as criminal, unco-
operative, manipulative, lazy, or unreachable. It's a lot harder
than it sounds at first blush.

Of course Dylan had been one hundred percent right. Thad
recognized that, just like Alice did now, even if she hadn't at the
time Dylan said it. Compassion went through her as she studied
Thad's profile.

"I think they'll listen to you," she said quietly. "Because *you'll*
listen to them. It might take a bit for them to warm up to you, but
when they do, they're going to understand how lucky they are to
have gotten you as a counselor."

Thad gave her a surprised glance. He looked pleased. Out of
the corner of her eye, Alice saw movement and a yellow school bus
entered her vision.

"They're here," she said, her heartbeat giving a flutter.

"Do you really think that? About the kids being lucky?" Thad
asked her as the crowd around them started to whoop and clap in
excitement.

"Sure I do," she told him as they began to walk up en masse
to greet the kids. A sideways glance told her Thad was still watching her. "You managed to make a fan out of me, didn't you?" she
laughed. "And trust me . . . that's no easy feat," she added, rolling
her eyes.

"Alice Reed is a believer?" he murmured. "Okay. Then bring
'em on. I can take anything now," he said, his gaze beyond warm
on Alice's face.

Alice experienced a sinking feeling. Was she leading Thad on? She
genuinely did like him, so maybe not? What sane woman wouldn't
be euphoric over the idea of someone like Thad favoring her?

So why did she feel like something was missing when it came
to Thad?

The bizarre, compelling experience at the stable was eclipsing
everything, confusing her.

Dylan Fall was.

His very presence was like some kind of powerful magnet on her awareness. On her body.

Something told her that the pull would only grow stronger as the hours of the day passed. By the time their proposed meeting approached, Alice worried she'd be unable to resist him.

SIX

Sebastian Kehoe wanted them to launch into their regular schedule immediately upon the first day in order to get the kids accustomed to it as quickly as possible. Since their mandatory planned activities and workshops all took place in the morning, however, that left lunch and then free time in the afternoon. Free time wasn't necessarily a free-for-all, though. Every day of the week had several scheduled activities, such as football, baseball, competitive swimming, kayaking, horseback riding, archery, sailboating, gardening, hiking, woodcraft, or an art class. The camp counselors led these activities. The kids could choose to do one activity or several, or just swim and socialize with friends, although they were required to do at least four free time activities every week in order to prevent *too* much languishing and goofing off on the lovely white shore beach.

Alice learned quickly, however, after spending time with her new charges, that languishing wasn't much of a threat at Camp Durand. The kids looked forward to the afternoon activities because they were loosely structured and fun. Plus, there was the added benefit of an opportunity to gain points for one's team by an athletic win, artistic expression, or individual skill in the gardens, in art class, or on horseback. The rumor of the reputation of the team trophy had apparently already spread on the first day. The kids liked the idea of racking up points for their team.

Thankfully, five of her ten charges were "experts," meaning

they were returning to Camp Durand—some of them for third or
fourth times. This meant that they usually were more on top of
things than Alice. Her experts relished guiding the less experienced kids—and Alice especially. She didn't mind their eager
instruction. She was thankful for their knowledge, because that
first day was pretty hectic.

The range of sizes, strengths, and vulnerabilities on the Red
Team was huge. The first to diligently seek her out upon arrival
was a clean-cut sixteen-year-old boy named Noble Darian, who
went by Noble D or "D." Noble D was as serious as a minister.
Later, he solemnly told Alice a minister is exactly what he planned
to become following his education at a Baptist college, where he'd
already received a basketball scholarship. Alice already knew from
reading Noble D's history that he'd grown up in a Detroit war
zone and had responded to the stress of the shooting death of his
oldest brother by becoming the male figure of the family at age
ten. No psychologist needed to tell Alice what the challenge was
with D. It was to give him permission to let go of the responsibility and burden of watching out for everyone else for a short period
of time and just be a kid.

Terrance Brown was on a different end of the spectrum, every
bit as physically imposing as Noble D, not only in the vertical
direction but the horizontal one as well. He wore a perennial grin,
because he was always trying to make someone laugh with his bag
full of off-color jokes or, even more often, because he'd just pulled
a fast one and was waiting for you to find out about it the hard
way. Alice knew from his records that the fun-loving fifteen-year-
old was dangerously overweight and diabetic. With little parental
supervision and a troubled home life, Terrance self-soothed with
a diet of fast food, chips, and candy. He observed everything about
people and was smart as a whip when it came to social interactions
and body language. He possessed a silver tongue and was, at
times, as sweet and generous a kid as Alice had ever met. Alice

thought that if Terrance could harness some of his charm and social acumen, he would make a fine lawyer, salesman, or politician. She couldn't help but like Terrance almost immediately, even if she wasn't fooled for a second by his innocent faces and ever-ready jokester act.

There was Jill Sanchez, a withdrawn, painfully thin thirteen-year-old who reminded Alice of a lost baby deer in headlights when she got off the bus, standing in the parking lot alone and dazed-looking. Jill had hardly spoken since witnessing the shooting of her mother last winter, although she'd previously been a bright and outgoing student at Grover Cleveland Middle School.

And then there was Judith Arnold, a pretty, athletic, but angry seventeen-year-old who was reportedly quite brilliant when she put her mind to things, but was too busy snarling and being uncooperative with the world to ever show it. Unlike many of her fellow campers, Judith came from a comfortable middle-class home—or at least that's how things stood presently. It hadn't always been so rosy for Judith. Apparently, Judith's mother had determinedly struggled against poverty and single-handedly fought to make a better world for her daughter and herself. Mrs. Arnold, who raised Judith alone, had been dead set against her daughter attending Camp Durand. Somehow, Judith had successfully convinced her mother otherwise.

The interesting question for Alice was why Judith had been so determined to come, given her obvious condescending attitude about the camp. Judith possessed the air of being above her peers . . . above *everyone* at Camp Durand, for that matter. The fact that she was pretty, smart, and confident only added to the impression of her loftiness and disdain toward the rest of them. Alice thought Judith might be her biggest personal challenge at Camp Durand. The girl could be a straight-up bitch when she put her mind to it, easily pricking Alice's own defensiveness, uncertainties, and temper. Unfortunately, Judith seemed to take an instant strong dislike to Alice, which meant that she was doing her sneering-bitch act way too much for Alice's comfort.

The Red Team was on the roster that first night for dinner duty along with the Blue Team, which meant that Alice and her ten kids helped Mira, the camp cook, prepare and serve all one hundred and fifty-three campers and the Camp Durand staff. It was their first real team effort, because the kids had chosen to do various things that afternoon after lunch and settling in at their team cabin.

All in all, Alice thought they'd pulled things off pretty well. There was one anxious moment. Jill Sanchez was scared to tears while serving hamburgers and grilled chicken to a group of boisterous teenagers from the Purple Team who were shouting rude questions at her and then not giving her the time or patience necessary to reply. Before Alice could get on-site to interfere, Judith leapt into the fray, soundly putting the lead instigator in his place. Judith led away a cowering Jill. As a consequence, the older girl acquired a small silent shadow that trailed her everywhere.

Alice was glad she'd observed the episode from a distance. The counselors were expected to choose a student leader for their team after five days of observation, utilizing their best judgment not just for the individual leader but the entire team. Noble D was the obvious choice, and had been the Red Team student leader for the past two years. Alice was taking a wait-and-see attitude, however, to watch how things unfolded. She was hesitant to heap more responsibility on D than was required, no matter how much the kid deserved the position.

By that evening, Alice was exhausted but very satisfied with how her first day with the kids had gone. A few of the kids had warmed up to her. Most were polite but cautious. Alice understood and respected that, though.

She would have been the same way.

The campers had their own team cabin. It was large, with one side housing the girls' bedrooms, the other with the boys'. In the middle was a large common room, where they'd hold several small group sessions throughout camp and the kids could relax, play games, and watch television after the evening activity. The cabin and individual suites were as large and every bit as luxurious and well-appointed as Alice and Kuvi's. Alice was a little envious of the campers, to be able to spend a teenage summer in such an idyllic place.

Alice entered the common room at around eight thirty that evening, finding most of her kids lounging around and talking, many of the younger ones looking tired after a long day of travel, sunshine, swimming, and the waning excitement of their first day. Crystal Dean, a Morgantown resident and junior high school teacher who had worked as a night cabin supervisor at Camp Durand for six years, was there a little early for her shift.

"You're welcome to go if you like," Crystal told Alice brightly, looking up from the game of crazy eights she was playing with Matt Dinorio and Rochelle Phelps. "I've got everything under control here. These kids won't have any problem settling in to sleep tonight," she added with a grin as Rochelle gave a wide yawn.

"No, Alice!" Terrance Brown called out from the sofa where he was watching television. He picked up the remote and shut it off. "You've got to stay for some ghost stories," he said, grinning excitedly.

Alice gave him a droll look. Matt Dinorio and Justin Arun, two Red Team experts, had been explaining at dinner how they made a bonfire sometimes and told ghost stories while at camp. Terrance, who had never been to a camp, had acted like the whole idea was hilarious. He was obviously secretly interested, though.

"We can't light a campfire in here," Alice said.

"Why not?" he joked. Matt shot him a dirty look and told Terrance to shut up.

"No, seriously, I want to!" Terrance insisted, unswayed. He pointed at the modern gas fireplace that was safely behind a pane of glass. "We'll dim the lights and turn that on."

"Yeah," several of the kids enthused, some of the older kids acting like it was beneath them, but they'd endure it because it'd be worth a laugh.

Alice checked her watch. She'd been highly aware of the clock ticking away the minutes until she was supposed to meet Dylan all day. Now that the time was drawing near, and her anxiety and uncertainty were growing, she thought it might be helpful to have a distraction at the present moment.

"Okay," she conceded. "But nothing too scary. We don't want any nightmares," she warned, as Terrance moved faster than she would have thought was possible given his size, standing and starting to turn down the lamps.

"No offensive language or gore, that's the rule," Crystal called out as the other drowsy kids seemed to reanimate, laughing and helping Terrance turn down the lights. Terrance flipped on the switch for the fireplace, and the common room was bathed in shadow and the glow from the fire. "And if anyone has any nightmares, no more ghost stories," Crystal warned.

"Don't any of you midgets mention it if you have a nightmare," Terrance warned a couple of the middle school kids before he bounced back on the couch.

"That's not the point, Terrance," Noble D remonstrated before Alice could.

"Who's going first?" Terrance asked, ignoring D.

"I'll go," Justin Arun said. Alice sat down on the sectional couch, interested and warmed by the fact that Justin had volunteered first. Justin had a speech impediment due to a cleft palette. Even though he'd had a surgical repair, he still had residual problems with speech. She knew from his history that when he'd first come to Camp Durand two years ago, he'd hardly spoken at all, far too used to bullying and beatings to put himself at risk. Currently, Justin spoke loudly and without any evidence of shyness despite a slight lingering lisp and a nasal quality to his speech. Justin had blossomed at Camp Durand during the past two summers. His mother and teachers attributed his improvement to the weeks spent here at camp.

Alice was impressed.

Justin told Resurrection Mary highlights, the urban legend about the pale teenage girl who hitched rides with unsuspecting males requesting they take her "home," only to have them drop her off at Resurrection Cemetery and then disappear.

"That one is *real*," Terrance said with a dramatic, somber glance at fourteen-year-old Angela Knox, who sat next to him. The girl's eyes widened.

"Really?" Angela squeaked.

"*No*. Terrance, give it a rest," Judith said scornfully, gliding into the room. Alice had noticed she'd kept separate from the others ever since they arrived at the cabin. "You guys are telling ghost stories? Lame," she muttered under her breath, sitting and hoisting long legs onto the arm of the upholstered chair.

"I don't know if there's any truth to Resurrection Mary," Matt Dinorio piped up. "But I can tell you one ghost story about Camp Durand that's real."

"*Not* that one about the mother who haunts the woods and the castle because her baby was killed in there, and she wanders around looking for her," Justin Arun said disgustedly, rolling his eyes.

"Yeah, that's just a story Jackson Jones made up two years ago because he said something white was chasing him in the woods," Noble D said.

"Chasing him in the woods?" Alice asked with an amused tone, despite the goose bumps that popped up along her arms.

"Jackson Jones is full of it," Noble D said, shaking his head dismissively. "He was a camper here for three years. He went to Ohio State to learn how to be a writer like Stephen King or something, but Jones doesn't need classes to know how to spin some..."

"Bullshit," Judith said succinctly when Noble D faded off. She rolled her eyes. "Can't you even say the *word*, preacher boy?" she asked Noble pointedly. Alice noticed that D's eyes flashed with anger at the girl, and then quickly turned warm as his stare fixed on her face.

"No, I'm telling you, it's true," Matt insisted excitedly. "I told one of my teachers about it after I heard the story last year, and Mr. Glyer said he *did* remember something about that happening years ago, right *here* at Camp Durand. It was all over the news. Mr. Glyer wasn't talking about a ghost, he just meant a kid really *was* snatched and killed here."

"A kid was killed at Camp Durand?" Rochelle repeated shakily.

"No camper has ever been killed or died at Camp Durand! That's ridiculous," Crystal said suddenly with an air of sharp finality. "The worst thing that's ever happened to a kid here is a bad case of poison ivy."

"Isn't anyone going to tell Hook Man?" Alice asked, referring to the classic scary campfire story. Something about Crystal's tone of voice had warned her it was definitely time to change the subject.

SHE left the Red Team cabin at around five after nine, stepping into a warm night. The wind off the lake gently rustled in the surrounding trees, making a sighing sound. Otherwise, everything was hushed. Kuvi's and her cabin was only fifty feet or so down the path. She could see the light on inside through the screen door. Kuvi was back already. In the distance, she noticed Dave Epstein walking out of the Gold Team cabin. He started in the direction of his cabin, glanced around, saw Alice, and waved. He paused, like he was considering coming in her direction. Before he could, Alice waved back and immediately headed in the opposite direction from him, toward her cabin. Her heart started to race in her chest.

You're going to meet Dylan, aren't you? You're going to meet him at nine thirty. That's why you didn't want to delay by talking to Dave.

What do you actually hope to gain by fooling around with the CEO of Durand? You're going to end up disgraced and booted from the management recruitment process, all for a few good fucks?

A *few* incredible *fucks*, another voice in her head argued.

But it wasn't just that. It wasn't because Dylan had had her shaking with pleasure in a way she'd never experienced with another guy. It was *him*.

She craved to be with him up there in that lonely castle. She wasn't sure what being with him again would be like, exactly, but she was so curious . . . so *hungry* to find out.

"You're obsessed," she muttered under her breath scathingly as she quickly mounted the steps to her and Kuvi's cabin. Before she opened the screen door, she glanced back into the dark woods where the path lights couldn't penetrate.

Was he back there already? Watching? Waiting? For the second time that night, her arms roughened with goose bumps. She'd never admit it to her kids, but these woods *were* eerie.

At night, the Durand estate seemed to transform into a different place.

Kuvi was half reclining on the couch in their seating area, drinking a Diet Coke and watching television. They chatted about the ups and downs of their first day with the kids for a few minutes before Alice went to her dresser and pulled out some fresh shorts and a top.

"I'm going to take a quick shower and go out for a bit," she said, averting her eyes from Kuvi.

"Out? Where?" Kuvi asked, sitting up and looking interested.

"Just to . . ." Alice shrugged uncomfortably. "Meet someone."

"Oh, I get it," Kuvi said, grinning knowingly. "You're meeting up with Thad."

"No—"

"It's okay," Kuvi insisted, giving her a conspiratorial glance. "I see the way he looks at you. Your secret is safe. Not that you need to keep it a secret, of course. They've made it clear our time is our own after nine p.m." She collapsed back on the sofa. "And God knows we deserve every minute of it, as hard as they work us."

Alice opened her mouth to correct her roommate—she didn't like telling Kuvi a lie, even if she hadn't actually *said* anything. Kuvi had just assumed. In the end, she left Kuvi to watch *Law & Order* and hurried into the bathroom.

How could she be honest with Kuvi about something she wasn't even fully admitting to herself? Besides, Kuvi would probably try to convince her that fooling around with Dylan Fall was extremely unwise. Alice didn't need to hear that from an outside source. She already *knew* she was being impulsive and stupid. What's worse, she was acting out of character.

All that knowledge didn't stop her from walking out the cabin door at nine thirty sharp, her breath choppy from mounting excitement.

SEVEN

She immediately left behind the network of paths leading to the staff and team cabins and took the more remote trail to the stables. There were lampposts for the first hundred feet or so, but then they ran out. Alice realized nervously that no one would ride in the pitch darkness, so there wasn't as great a need to light up this path.

She left the last lamppost behind and entered the shadows. A gust of wind off the lake made the tree branches creak as they swayed. She peered into the woods to the right of her. Had she just heard the crunch of footsteps on the earthen floor?

"Alice, it's Dylan."

He said it very quietly before he touched her back. She jumped, despite the fact that he'd warned her. He'd approached her silently from the left of the path, when she'd been straining to see his shadow to the right.

"Sorry," Dylan said quietly, no doubt feeling her jump with his hand on her back. She looked up, squinting. She could barely make out his tall opaque shadow against the murky, sinuous, moving backdrop of the swaying tree branches. His hand moved across her back and transferred to her arm. His fingertips slid down the sensitive skin of her inner elbow. She shivered in anxiety, but a heavy, pleasurable feeling throbbed in her sex.

The forbidden tryst excited her. *He* did.

"Okay?" he asked, his hand enfolding hers.

"Yeah," she whispered.

"Just follow me, then. There's a trail that leads up to the house from one of the horse paths. I take it all the time to ride Kar Kalim, but you have to know it's there to find it. It's hidden. I'll turn on a flashlight when we get on the trail. The foliage is thick there. No one will see us or the light."

She didn't reply. Something about his hushed tone, the dark night and the trees sighing and creaking around them seemed to emphasize the illicit quality of the whole thing. As she followed Dylan on the path, guided by his warm, firm hold on her hand, she felt as if they were committing a crime together, stealthily moving toward their target, two outlaws bound together by their secret plan. There was a wild, desperate sense of committing the outlandish, but also an intoxicating thrill to the whole thing.

"We're going to leave the path here. It'll be uphill," he said quietly at one point. She put out her foot, but paused, hesitating to leave the paved trail. The pressure of his hand on hers increased. She stepped, feeling soft cut grass beneath her canvas tennis shoes. Her tread was unobstructed by weeds. "It's a horse trail," he said in a low, hushed tone, and she knew he'd read her hesitation in leaving the known path behind.

"I don't know how you're doing it," she whispered a moment later, referring to his silent navigation in the darkness. "It's pitch black out here."

"I've walked around at night for years out here," she thought she heard him say.

"You mean when you come down to ride your horse at dawn?" she asked.

"Then. Other times, too. I walk when I can't sleep," came his low, rough voice in the darkness.

"And that's a lot?" she whispered.

"That's a lot."

She swallowed thickly at something she heard in his tone, but couldn't quite identify.

After walking on the soft ground for a few minutes, Dylan paused. She heard the sound of brushing leaves and the snap of a twig.

"Press up behind me," he muttered. "Put your face up next to my back and follow me closely."

"Why?"

"Because we're at the woods that hide the path to the side of the house. I'm going to push aside the brush and branches, but you're likely to get scratched if you go in without something blocking your face."

"Okay," she agreed, her heart pounding in her ears. He let go of her hand and she reached out, her fingers touching cotton. She made a sweeping motion with both hands, charting the territory of him. A sharp thrill went through her. She touched his wide back just beneath his shoulder blades. Her hands lowered down the taper to his waist. She gripped him.

"Step into me, Alice."

She shut her eyes—she couldn't see a damn thing, anyway—and pressed her cheek against his back. For a stretched second, he didn't move. She was utterly blind, but he felt so solid and strong beneath her palms and her cheek. She inhaled, catching the scent of his freshly laundered shirt and just the hint of the spice of his aftershave. Without thinking, her hands slid around to the front of him, and she pressed her face fully to him, nose against his spine. She breathed him in . . . absorbed him. Sexual arousal swelled in her, warm and heady.

He'd gone very still at her touch. The chemistry between them was electric, and unprecedented in Alice's experience.

He hissed her name into the darkness. He caressed the outer part of her hand where she clasped him. She pressed closer, her lower belly curving around his butt. He was wearing jeans. She could feel the pocket seams making an imprint against her skin, and beneath the denim, the dense muscle of his ass. Suddenly, he was gripping her hands, lifting her tight hold on him. A flash of embarrassment went through her.

He hadn't wanted her to squeeze him *that* tight.

His body shifted against hers, and she was plastered against him again, this time to the front. A hand opened at her lower back. His fingers moved beneath her chin. He applied pressure, and her face tilted up. His mouth seized hers, his kiss firm and warm and hungry . . . such a forbidden, sweet solace in the darkness.

Such a delicious drug. She thought she'd imagined the intoxication of his kiss, but if anything, she'd underplayed it. All of her anxieties about this madness in which she was willingly participating evaporated under Dylan's molding, hungry lips.

She moaned softly as his tongue pierced her lips, and his kiss grew fiercer. Hotter. His hand slid down over her ass, cupping the curve. He urged her closer yet, pressing her fast against him. She felt a slight shock go through his body at their contact. It thrilled her, that she had the power to sexually charge him like he was igniting her . . . bringing her to life . . .

Revealing a part of her she didn't know existed.

He ripped his mouth off her a moment later, his warm, ragged breath striking her heated cheeks.

"I don't know what it is about you," he said in a quiet rough voice. "You take me from zero to a hundred in a second flat."

Alice opened her mouth to speak, but his fingers had found their way beneath her shorts and he was stroking the tender skin where her thigh and buttock met. He caressed the lower curve of her ass and she felt his cock leap against her. She firmed her hands on his shoulders and slid her body higher on him, going up on her tiptoes, her mouth seeking him out.

"Uh-uh." He popped the ass cheek he'd been fondling with his palm. She made a little squeaking sound of surprise.

"If you keep it up, I'm going to have you right here in these woods," he muttered.

"Maybe that's where I want it," she breathed out.

"No. Not again," he said, his lips brushing against hers as he spoke quietly, but firmly. "I'll have you next in my bed. I'm going to learn you tonight. I'm going to find all the sweet spots on your beautiful body," he promised darkly, biting gently at her lower lip. "I want to see your face so I know when I've found them. I want to watch you coming."

He grabbed her wrists gently and drew her hands off his shoulders. His little speech had left Alice mute. He'd made his decision. It would be foolish to argue. He turned around, one hand behind him touching her lower back, urging her behind him. Alice blinked, willing the wild surge of lust that had gone through her at his words to fade so that she could attend to the task.

"Stay close," he said.

She put her hands against his back and followed him blindly into the thick brush, holding her breath because she was trusting him so completely in the darkness.

She'd made her decision, too, and it was firm . . . although she couldn't comprehend precisely why.

THEY left the woods on a side lawn that sloped to the castle. He led her around the back to the terrace, where they entered using the same French doors Dylan had led her out of to join the party. Had that just been last night? she wondered in amazement as she watched Dylan key in a password to an electronic security system once they were inside. He took her hand and led her through the sophisticated media room.

It seemed impossible that a little over twenty-four hours ago, her heart had been pounding at the unfamiliar, unexpected touch of his fingertips on her bare skin, and now she was hastening after him as he led her to bed. The house was hushed and sparsely lit as she followed him into the great hall, hurrying to keep up with his long stride.

"Is there anyone else here in the house?" she asked.

"No. Louise, Marie, and Carlos—the groundskeeper—are day staff."

In the great hall, the stunning crystal chandelier had been set to a very dim setting. She stared up at it, the exquisitely cut shards of glass blurring slightly in her vision.

"Dylan," she said in a strangled voice.

He glanced back at her face and came to a halt. He turned to her, stepping closer, and brushed his knuckles against her cheek softly.

"What?" he asked tensely.

She struggled to find words for what she was experiencing. He lowered his head.

"Do you want to change your mind?"

"No. It's not that."

"Then what is it, little girl?" he murmured. She shivered when he called her that. Alice was tall for a woman, and strong, even if she didn't feel large next to Dylan. He dropped a kiss on the top of her head.

"It's just . . ." She swallowed thickly, because she'd just inhaled his scent, and his nearness was making her unformed thoughts even less substantial. "It's all so strange," she whispered, reaching up to touch him beneath the sleeve of his T-shirt. His skin was smooth and thick, his biceps hard as a stone.

"You think it's strange? That I want you?"

"Yeah," she admitted. But it was more than that, and she thought Dylan suspected that, too. Her attraction to him was just as unprecedented and . . . charged.

He leaned over slightly and met her stare. "I wish I could help clear things up for you. It's not normal operating procedure for me, either. I've never slept with an employee of Durand. I could get in trouble for doing this. I could be censured. Maybe I ought to be fired."

"You're the boss," she whispered.

She searched his face. He looked very grim. Why *was* he doing this? Why was he taking a risk like this, for *her*?

And yet, she had the strangest feeling he did understand her disoriented bewilderment, even shared in it to some degree. She recalled vividly that startled look on his usually controlled expression when that powerful charge of lust had sparked between them at her interview. He, too, was swept away by something he hadn't expected and didn't fully comprehend. There was something bigger than her going on, something bigger than him.

He looked so beautiful to her in that moment, his rugged face cast in shadow and the golden glow from the chandelier, his dark eyes gleaming as he stared at her with a strange mixture of watchfulness and unguarded heat. She placed her hands on his chest and pressed, the solidity of him, the sheer male strength, grounding her.

"You can help me," she said, her voice firmer. "Take me to bed, like you said. Make me forget everything else."

His face went hard. He ran his knuckles along her jaw. "I don't want you to forget me, Alice."

Her eyes widened in slight surprise at his fierceness. "As if I'd ever forget *you*." She thought she could lighten his somber mood with a smile and her hands stroking his chest, but it didn't work.

"I want to ask you something important before we go any further," he said.

"Okay."

"You had it pretty rough growing up."

"It was no picnic," she agreed dubiously.

His nostrils flared slightly, and she saw the hard gleam in his eye. "Were you . . . safe there? In Little Paradise?"

"Safe?"

He nodded, his expression grim.

"No, of course not," she said with a disbelieving bark of laughter. What was he getting at? She noticed his intensity deepen and sighed. "My mother cooked and sold meth. Do you know what that entails? Our mobile home stunk of chemicals. We were constantly at risk of fire or an explosion. I slept with the windows open in my bedroom, even in subzero temperatures, so that I could get decent ventilation from the toxic air. Thank God for electric blankets. Whenever Sissy was in jail—or once, prison for two years straight—my uncle Al was in charge, both of me and my mom's 'business.' That wasn't bad, though. Al was better than Sissy. Uncle Al did a better job than Sissy in keeping his brothers and their degenerate friends and customers away from me. But Sissy wasn't in jail the majority of the time. Unfortunately."

"What about your father?"

"Dead." She was accomplished at this particular lie.

"How many brothers did your mom have?" Dylan asked.

"Seven. My mom was the only girl. I only knew five of her brothers, though. Chuck was in prison for as long as I can remember. Rourke died of a drug overdose when he was twenty-four. Why are you asking me about this now?"

"Were you hurt? In any way?"

"What?"

He closed his eyes briefly and looked away, although he continued to stroke her shoulders and upper arms. She had the strangest impression he was trying to soothe her. It helped. A little, anyway, although it didn't lessen her bewilderment.

"I'm sorry," he said starkly after a moment. "I'm only asking because I know what it can be like for a child in a rough neighborhood. A rough family." He met her stare. "You're always straightforward with me, so I'll be the same with you. I'll want to bind you sometimes during sex, Alice. Tie you up while I make love to

you. Give you pleasure. Challenge you, a little. I'm not talking
about anything serious, if you don't want it. And it'll always be
up to you. I'm just trying to be up front about it, because I don't
want to hold your wrists or something while we're in the thick of
things, and have it be . . . bad for you."

Her mouth dropped open as understanding permeated. This
was a first for her. She wasn't intimidated necessarily by what he'd
said. She wasn't a sexual libertine, by any means, but she was okay
with people doing whatever felt right to them, as long as no one
got hurt and it was consensual. In *theory*, it seemed fine anyway,
but she was ignorant as far as practice. She suddenly felt like a
bumbling foreigner in a strange land.

Which, face it, you feel like most of the time around Dylan.

She thought of his dominant, confident manner of touching
and handling her in the stables. He'd moved her around not
roughly, but knowingly. She'd *loved* it. It took a few seconds for
what he was *really* getting at to register. Her lungs came unstuck.
She exhaled heavily.

"You're worried I've been abused?" she asked shakily.

She saw the muscle in his jaw flicker with tension.

"Have you been?"

She shook her head. "Not sexually. Is that what you're asking?"

His hands tightened on her arms. "In *any* way," he bit out.

She snorted. "No. But I think a mental health professional
might have a different definition for abuse than I do. For the most
part, I was ignored. I was perfectly fine. Everyone just thought I
was Sissy's weird, nerdy little girl. I had my own room, which I
guarded like a fortress. While I was at school, I booby-trapped it
from intruders. My room used to be Sissy's room and was the best
in the trailer. I took it over while she was in jail once, and installed
the dead bolts myself. I was twelve when she came back. She made
the loudest fuss you've ever heard when I refused to get out of that
room, but eventually she gave up. Uncle Al thought it was funny,

even if he did hate her yowling. I'd set her stuff up nicely in the room that used to be mine, and it was just easier for her to crash in there, and let it all go. After a while, I think she actually forgot the big bedroom used to be hers. Meth puts a few holes in the brain," Alice recalled, laughing bitterly until she noticed Dylan's sober expression. She sighed. "The answer is no. I didn't consider myself abused. I *don't*," she emphasized when there was no relent to his boring stare. "Sissy was meaner than my uncles, especially when she was high or sick, which was most of the time. I avoided all of them, although Uncle Al could be okay at times. But the back of their hand came a lot easier to the Reeds than using words to ask for what they wanted. The Reeds are fluent in sign language." She jokingly gestured flicking her hand in a smacking gesture.

She couldn't read his expression as he watched himself lightly massaging her shoulders. For a stretched moment, he didn't speak.

"I'm sorry," he finally said.

"Don't be," she replied stiffly. "They hardly ever caught me. I owe my quick reflexes and ability to take care of myself to Sissy and the Reed brothers. I could dodge a fist or a palm quicker than a fly by the time I was seven, and as for taking care of myself—better me than them. I did all right."

"No. You did fantastic," he growled softly. His gaze moved over her face. He must have noticed her defensive expression. He shook his head. "Jesus, you're prickly. I'm *not* feeling sorry for you. I can relate. I just thought it was better to know for certain."

"What about you?" she asked.

"What about me?"

"Were you abused? Is that why you like to tie up women? Did someone tie *you* up or something?"

His face went blank. He exhaled sharply after a moment. "I guess I deserved that," he muttered under his breath. "No. I was just telling you some of my sexual preferences. They aren't related to anything from my past. I was never sexually abused. But who knows where this stuff really comes from? I just didn't want my preferences to . . ."

"Damage me? It's okay," she said. She started to suspect she might have an idea from where this all was originating. "I'm not going to shrivel up on you or curl into a hysterical ball, *despite* how you saw me in the stables this morning. That guy in the woods just freaked me out. I'm *not* usually like that," she assured with a hard glare.

He rolled his eyes. Guilt slinked through her. She had no doubt she tried him at times with her defensiveness. She just couldn't seem to control her reaction sometimes. Her defensive armor was practically hardwired in her brain.

"I don't think you're hysterical. I'm just trying to be clear about some basics, that's all."

"I don't know if I'll like what you're talking about or not. I've never . . ." She faded off, her face scrunching up as she tried to imagine it: being tied up or restrained while Dylan made love to her. She wasn't sure the idea sat well with her. Or *part* of it didn't. The part about Dylan touching and pleasuring her, that part was great. She wouldn't have any control, though.

But you loved it, the way he dominated you in the stables.

"I only want to make you feel good, Alice. If it doesn't feel good or right, just say so." Heat rushed through her. Having Dylan roughly murmur those words with that hot gleam in his eyes? Well . . . *that* sat with her just fantastically.

She nodded in agreement.

"One other thing," he said quietly. "I'll use a condom with you, if that's what you want. I'm healthy, though. I haven't been seeing anyone for the past two—no, not since April eighteenth, in fact. Over three months," he added, his brows knitting together as he reconsidered. "And I just had my yearly physical."

He knew the *exact* date? That didn't bode well, Alice thought. Whoever he'd been in a relationship with must have meant something to him, to have abstained all this time from sex. Surely celibacy wasn't a natural state for a man like Dylan. She swallowed thickly, trying to bring her ping-ponging thoughts under control.

"I haven't been in a relationship since I was in undergrad . . . if you want to call it that," she mumbled, her cheeks coloring at how lame that sounded. Numbers had been Alice's lover for the past two years in graduate school. Lovely, safe, predictable numbers. Dylan was the opposite of predictable, but at least he was trying to be honest from the first. "I just had a complete physical when I had the drug screening done for this job at Camp Durand. I'm healthy. And I'm on the pill."

He nodded. "There. That's out of the way. It wasn't so bad, was it?"

She returned his small smile. He was right to have brought it up. She wasn't so thrilled about what he'd said about him restraining her sometimes, but she wasn't afraid, either. And she was curious.

Maybe she was too far gone, her attraction to him an unbreakable, compelling restraint in and of itself.

He caressed the skin at her nape with blunt fingertips and cupped her neck. Reacting on instinct, she lifted her face, and his mouth was on hers, his lips moving hungrily, forcefully . . . and again, she felt that thrilling edge to his lust.

His arms went around her, and her feet left the ground.

"Why are you smiling?" he asked her gruffly a moment later as he mounted the stairs, Alice in his arms.

"It's just . . ." she glanced around at the elegant, sweeping grand staircase and back at his face. "I can't believe this is happening."

"It's happening all right."

"I feel a little like Scarlett O'Hara. I always wondered what Rhett did to her when he got her behind locked doors," she said distractedly.

He looked somber as he kept his gaze trained at the top of the stairs. Determined. "Now you'll be the one behind the locked door. No more wondering," he said, and Alice's heart paused before it surged, resuming its race.

She strained to look around a moment later when he shoved open a wood paneled door with his foot and threaded her body through the opening. It was a large, handsomely decorated bedroom. The bed was right in front of her, while to the left was a sumptuous living area situated around a carved mahogany fireplace. Alice noticed two crystal chandeliers as Dylan spun and kicked the door shut behind them. The chandeliers were stunning, one at the foot of the four-poster bed hovering over a long gold damask bench, one over the luxurious sitting area before the fireplace. The sumptuous crystal stood in direct contrast to the beige, dark blue, and gold décor, the masculine bold prints on the fabrics, and the hearty suede accents in the rest of the suite. Over the bed was a handsome painting of a black horse.

"Lock it, Alice."

His low, rough voice brought her out of her rapt admiration of his private domain. She leaned down, twisting the brass knob on the door.

Locking them in. Sealing her fate.

He held her stare as he carried her over to the bed. He laid her against a mound of silk and suede pillows.

"This room is amazing," she croaked as one of his hands slid down her bare leg. He unceremoniously whipped off her canvas slip-on tennis shoes and tossed them onto the floor. Her eyes widened when he just as casually slid his fingers beneath the waistband of her canvas shorts and unfastened the top button.

"Thanks. It's newly decorated. I just moved in a few weeks ago," he said as he lowered the zipper of her shorts. He sat down on the edge of the bed.

"But . . . I thought you'd lived at the castle for a while," she managed in an unnaturally high voice as he tugged her shorts down over her hips. He drew them off her bare feet, and the garment went the same way as her shoes.

"I've lived in this house for six years," he said, his attention on her bare legs. He stroked her calf with his palm, his fingers caressing the back of her knee. Alice shivered. He glanced at her face. "I just switched suites, that's all," he said, continuing to watch her closely as he skimmed his fingertips across the sensitive patch of skin. He really had incredible hands. Big. Warm. Knowing. She felt herself growing damp at his touch in combination with his focused stare. He had the look of a man who was anticipating a feast, and Alice was it.

"Why did you switch suites?" she whispered numbly. The daily life of a gorgeous bachelor tycoon seemed inexplicable to her.

He shrugged and his hand trailed up her leg. He experimented, palming the muscle first, then sliding his fingertips against the skin between her slightly parted thighs. Her clit twinged with arousal at his nearness, her flesh prickling beneath his touch.

"I wanted a change," he said idly, watching his hand stroke her. Alice stared, too. It was impossible to look away. "I like the view better in this room."

She cleared her throat, liking the view very much herself at the moment. He continued to stroke her inner thigh, as if he enjoyed the sensation. Her skin color had deepened to a golden peach color. Despite the fact that he didn't look as if he'd spent as much time in the sun as she had for the past few weeks, his hand was still darker than her thigh.

"And so you just had a whole new suite redecorated? Everything in here *is* new, isn't it?" she asked, glancing around.

"A lot of it, yes," he said, meeting her stare. He moved his hand, boldly cupping her sex through her cotton panties. She gasped softly in surprise. He began to move his hand in a subtle circular motion. "I suppose you think that means I'm spoiled?" he asked calmly.

"I . . . *No*," she said in a choked voice. She wasn't *thinking* much of anything.

His heavy-lidded stare lowered to her mouth, his hand continuing to stimulate her sex in a knowing, possessive manner that was making it hard for her to draw a full breath of air. He pressed.

"Mmm," he murmured, sounding pleased. "You're getting warm. And wet."

Arousal tore through her. As if to prove his point, his massaging hand moved across her belly as their gazes clung. She felt the subtle humidity on her skin. Her abdomen muscles leapt. His touch set her nerves alight, creating a webwork of prickling pleasure. Her nipples pinched tight. His gaze flickered downward to her chest, as if he'd known precisely what reaction his touch was having on her.

"I'm going to finish undressing you," he said, his voice a rough, rich seduction.

She nodded, her tongue suddenly feeling very thick as a strange combination of languor and sexual arousal weighted and warmed her muscles.

He slid his hand under her cotton shirt over her belly button, his fingers gliding over her ribs. The shirt bunched around his forearm. His fingers moved over the catch at the front of her bra and she felt the elastic give. Then he was scooping the shirt beneath her armpits and lifting it. Alice instinctively put up her arms, and he whipped the shirt off her. When she lowered her arms, she looked downward, stunned. Knowing what was coming tonight with Dylan, she'd worn a regular bra, not the restraining exercise bras she usually favored. The cups of her bra slid across her breasts, exposing her nipples.

"Smooth," she joked through a tight throat, referring to how he'd bared her with a few effortless, quick moves.

He flashed her a quick grin, but his gaze was steady on her as he pulled back on the cups of her bra and she lifted her arms one at a time, freeing herself from the straps. She lay back on the mattress. He cupped her breasts gently, and his small smile faded.

"I kept thinking of you all day. It wasn't my imagination. You really are exquisite. It's not that common, for a woman as slender as you to have breasts like this . . . to have such sensitive nipples," he murmured. She wasn't so sure she liked the idea of him being such a breast expert, but her body seemed less discerning. Her nipples tightened even more, as if to prove his point. He gave a small smile and swept his hands downward, his thumbs still on the underside of her breasts, his fingers bracketing her rib cage. He paused, holding her firmly. It felt so good when she inhaled choppily to feel the security of his hold.

His smile turned tender, and he met her dazed stare. "I can feel your heartbeat."

"Dylan," she mouthed. She reached for him. He turned his face and kissed the underside of one of her forearms when she grasped his head. Liquid heat surged at her sex at the simple, profoundly erotic gesture. He gathered her arms and placed her wrists gently above her head on the mound of pillows.

"Keep them there," he said. His tone was gentle, but there was a glint in his eyes that told her he meant business. She frowned, but nodded. His hands slid beneath her panties, drawing them down her legs and off her. He palmed the inside of the thigh closest to him and spread her several inches.

"Is it one of your 'sexual preferences'? To remain dressed while the woman is completely naked?" she asked, still scowling a little despite the electrical effect of Dylan's fixed stare between her thighs.

"Not particularly, no," he said distractedly. "But right now, I want to play with you. I told you I wanted to watch you come."

EIGHT

She felt heat rush into her cheeks. *Play* with her? Her brain didn't like the sound of that, but her body reacted as if it possessed a different mind than the one in her head. She had a sudden urge to place her hands between her thighs to stanch the ache there.

She glanced aside when suede fabric brushed her hip. He'd just pulled down a pillow from beneath the mound of them at the head of his bed. Her brows drew together in puzzlement when she saw it wasn't a typical small, decorative pillow. It was nearly two feet wide and wedge-shaped, one end about ten to twelve inches thick, the other only a few inches wide. "Lift your bottom and back a little," he directed. She followed the urging of his hand and directions uncertainly. He slid the thin end of the pillow beneath her, pushing until it rested at her middle back. Because of the wedge shape of the soft cushion, her hips had rolled back and were suspended above the rest of her body. Dylan gently pushed back her knees toward her chest.

Her ass was curved at the edge of the high part of the wedge. Her buttocks and the back of her thighs were completely exposed, her legs suspended in the air.

"Now stretch your arms back over your head, Alice," he said, his voice sounding a little rougher than before. Tense. Did he like seeing her like this? she wondered dazedly as she straightened her arms. The possibility struck her as strange, and yet excited her, too. It was an awkward position, because she hadn't been in it before—unless she counted the exercise pose where one rolled one's legs and feet over the head to stretch. But this was only partially that pose. With the wedge raising her hips and ass, her legs bent toward her chest. The soles of her feet felt strangely naked and vulnerable, suspended in the air the way they were. Thanks to the soft, but firm suede wedge pillow propping up her hips, it might have been an unusual pose, but it *was* comfortable.

If one could call this mounting feeling of vulnerability and arousal *comfortable*.

"There. Are you okay?" he asked, running one hand along the back of one suspended leg. He reached between calf and thigh, and stroked the back of her knee. A shiver tore through her.

"Yes," she admitted in a choked voice. He was studying her face, his hand wedged beneath her bent knee, rubbing that patch of sensitive skin there. He grimaced and suddenly pushed aside some of the pillows where her head and shoulders rested. Her spine straightened and her head fell onto the mattress. "There. Is that better?" he asked. She nodded, too overwhelmed to speak. "Good. Now reach for the headboard," he instructed. "Stretch your torso tight. Your nerves will be more sensitive that way."

Oh *God*. It must be true, because as she straightened and tensed her arms above her head, he stroked the back of her arms, and the side of her ribs and her breasts. She couldn't control the shudder of pleasure that went through her.

"Why are you making me do this?" she asked breathlessly, because he was awakening her body with his hands, stroking her like he was slowly building a fire in her flesh. He caressed one breast lightly, his fingertips feathering her nipple, while his other hand stroked her sensitive, exposed side. She had a wild, savage urge to beg him to grasp the mounds in his molding, demanding hands like he had in the stable earlier, to treat her not roughly but

firmly. Thoroughly. Then he opened his large hand along the back
of her thigh, and he was parting her legs. He palmed a buttock.

"Because I like having you at my mercy," he replied.

Her stare darted to his, her mouth opening to ask him what
kind of answer that was. His fingertips touched her outer sex, and
he was deftly penetrating her pussy with his finger.

A cry flew past her lips instead of a protest.

"Nice and warm and wet. God, you're soft," he muttered
darkly as he watched himself pierce her. She winced, pressing back
with her hips to increase the pressure. He still sat at the edge of
the bed, one knee bent and resting on the mattress, his torso
twisted slightly. Alice realized hazily she was displayed like some
kind of sexual buffet for him, pussy and ass in the air, her legs
suspended and spread . . .

Naked, wet, and willing.

She bit her lip to stifle a moan at the volatile yet strangely
arousing thought.

"You look incredibly beautiful, Alice," he said, and she had
the odd impression that he wasn't just speaking of her physical
beauty as his hot stare ran over her. He was talking about her
pose . . . her nudity . . . her availability to him. Her pussy tightened in longing, undone by the thought.

"Oh yeah," he grated out, thrusting his finger faster in and out
of her. He'd felt her tighten in desire. "You feel so good."

He edged closer to her on the bed, his knee bumping against
the wedge pillow where she lay. One hand still moving between
her legs, he opened the other over her lower belly. She wore a one-
piece bathing suit to swim at camp. Her stomach and breasts were
paler than the rest of her. Alice glanced down, spellbound by the
sensation of his warm hand and the vision of it spread against that
vulnerable expanse of pale skin. He caressed her and she trembled
beneath him.

"You're so sweet," he praised thickly, pumping his finger in and out of her channel more forcefully. With the hand on her belly, he reached, parting her labia. He groaned, deep and rough. Alice's head fell back on the mattress, undone by the vision of his male hunger as he stared at her exposed outer sex.

"Why do you color your hair?" he asked her tensely.

She was dizzy with arousal. She couldn't compute his question. "I *don't*," she said thickly, thinking he'd meant she dyed her pubic hair. Her entire awareness was on what he was doing to her pussy, and she couldn't think far past that territory.

"I mean on your head, Alice," she heard him say with strained amusement. Distantly, she realized he knew her dark hair color wasn't natural, because of the light brown, strawberry-tinted hair between her thighs.

"Never mind. I know. It's because you want to blend in, isn't it?" he asked. He rubbed the tip of his forefinger in the cleft of her labia, stimulating her clit, and she completely lost the ability to focus on conversation.

She moaned uncontrollably. She was wet between her labia, too. Burning. He applied a firm pressure against her lubricated clit, pressing and sliding and agitating until she felt a scream rising in her throat. At the same time, his knuckles bumped gently against her outer sex as he fucked her harder with his finger. She lay there, hating her helplessness and loving it at once, burning . . . about to reach a flashpoint at any moment.

"Are you going to come for me?" she heard Dylan say. She opened her heavy eyelids only to see him staring at her face. Her lips felt puffy and sensitive. Her cheeks must be bright red.

"Yes," she managed shakily.

A small snarl shaped his mouth. He pushed his finger into her faster, his other forefinger stirring her clit vigorously in the juicy cleft of her labia. She sizzled. The undersides of her suspended feet burned. Her toes curled inward.

"Dylan."

His name still burning her tongue and lips, she tilted her chin back and ignited. He pushed another finger into her. She shook in pleasure. He grunted, low and rough, and finger-fucked her hard while she came. A high-pitched wail entered her awareness, and she realized it was her own pleasure she heard like a siren pounding in her head. At the realization, she choked it off, mortified.

"Don't hold back," he grated out harshly. He stirred her clit faster and thrust forcefully with his fingers. Her scream broke free from her throat.

"That's right," she thought she heard him snarl as a fresh shudder rippled through her.

She came back to herself when he nipped at her lower lip. She opened her eyes, still panting, to see Dylan's mouth hovering over hers. He looked quite fierce. "Don't hold back from me, Alice. I'll want my due. Always," he said, before he seized her mouth with his.

His kiss was almost angry . . . certainly all consuming. She moaned into his mouth, both overwhelmed by the strength of his lust and hungry for it at once. He probed her mouth, making it clear his intent to plant himself deeply in her. When he sealed their kiss roughly a moment later, she was craning up for more of him. But he was pushing himself up onto his knees. She blinked at the vision of him. She hadn't even realized he'd straddled and come down over her while she recovered from her shattering climax. His longish bangs were sexily mussed and his eyes narrowed. His jean-covered thighs looked long and strong as he knelt there. Her stare froze at his crotch. Things looked very full there.

"Don't look at me like that, Alice."

She blinked and met his gaze. "I wanted to play with you more, but you're making it hard." He slid his hand against his erection and grimaced. "Jesus," he muttered, his gaze stuck between her thighs. He'd spread her thighs further when he'd come down over her just now, making room for his body. He put his hands on her hips. "Let's just turn you over," he said, his voice a rough caress. Alice turned at his urging, her breathing still choppy, her flesh still torpid and tingling from orgasm. Her belly came down on the soft suede slant of the wedge, her ass at the edge. "Now reach again with your arms," he said from behind her, and she felt his hand glide down the stretch between her shoulder and elbow, urging her to straighten. She pressed her hot cheek to the soft duvet and panted, anxious anticipation and arousal rising in her again. "There. I want your arms to stay like that," he said quietly from behind her. The heavy fullness behind his fly brushed fleetingly against her raised, bare ass, scattering her thoughts. Then he was sweeping his hand from her upper arm and down the length of her back. She shivered in pleasure when he stroked and then cupped a buttock.

"Beautiful," he murmured thickly. "You've got a gorgeous ass."

She made a shaky sound of arousal as he took both cheeks in his big hands and massaged her lewdly.

"I want to see you," she voiced her most fervent wish at that moment. He hadn't let her see and touch him in the stables. He wasn't allowing it again. Her need started to cut at her.

He parted her ass cheeks. Alice whimpered at the sudden exposure, her muscles tightening. She couldn't see him, but she felt his stare on her, scoring her.

He groaned roughly and got off the bed.

Alice lifted her cheek, wild to know what he was doing. He stood at the side of the bed and ripped at the button fly of his jeans. He whipped off his shirt in one fluid, sinuous motion. She went very still, staring at the lean, ridged expanse of his taut abdomen and wide chest. He was beautiful. Powerful. So male, it made her ache to look at him. There was a fair amount of dark hair on his chest, but not *too* much. She could perfectly see the delineation of hard muscle and his small, erect nipples. His ribs and abdomen made a tapestry of ridges of bone and muscle along with smooth stretches of skin. Her brows furrowed when she saw two small white scars on his right side below his ribs, one slightly larger than the other. Surgery scars, maybe? The jaggedness of them argued against it. Concern fractured her arousal slightly. But she didn't ask. She didn't like it when people noticed her invisible scars, so she instinctively stilled her tongue about his visible ones.

Those small imperfections only seemed to highlight the appeal of everything else, a tiny vulnerability in a sea of masculine strength. A thin trail of dark silky hair led from just below his bellybutton, transecting a taut belly and disappearing elusively into the V of his partially unbuttoned fly.

God, what she wanted to do to him.

Then he knelt and she was deprived of the elusive mouthwatering vision as he jerked at the laces on his hiking boots. But an entire new fascinating landscape of his muscular shoulders and back was revealed to her. She felt that pull she always experienced around him, that inner tug to draw closer.

"Dylan," she muttered, starting to rise up and edge off the wedged pillow toward him.

He glanced up, his eyes seeming to glow in his shadowed face.

"Stay there, Alice," he said firmly. "Don't move."

She paused, biting her lip.

He stood, the vision of him dominating her vision. She felt strangely helpless lying there naked with her bottom sticking up in the air and her thighs parted, but intensely aroused as well. Something about waiting for him—anticipating what was coming next—spiked her lust.

He kicked off his boots and shucked off his socks quickly. His face looked hard and tight as he ripped at the remaining buttons of his fly and hooked his thumbs into both his jeans and white underwear at once. He pulled forward on the waistband of his boxer briefs, and his heavy erection fell free. Alice's breath stuck at the brief electrical glimpse, but then he was bending and force-fully shucking the rest of his clothes off his legs.

Finally, he stood before her, naked.

Once, Alice would have thought it rude just to gape in open-mouthed wonder at a man, but all the rules seemed to go out the door with Dylan. Besides, she loved the way he ate her up with his unguarded male hunger. Why shouldn't she reciprocate? Any-way . . . there wasn't really any other way to react to the sight of Dylan naked and aroused.

"Is this what you wanted to see?" he asked her quietly.

Her breath caught and fresh heat rushed into her cheeks and sex when he took his cock into his hand and rubbed it slowly. He was heavy with arousal, the shaft suspended between strong thighs. The head was smooth and succulent looking, flaring from the tip to a defined ridge beneath the crown. The shaft was thick and straight, his testicles round and shaved.

"Yes," she whispered, caught in a spell of pure lust. She'd known he was formidable and flagrant from his possession in the stables, but the vision of him left her breathless. Her mouth watered. She swept her tongue along her lower lip to gather the extra moisture.

"Alice," he said tightly.

She blinked, her gaze darting to his face. She quailed a little inwardly, he looked so intimidating at that moment. He took a step and jerked open a bedside table drawer. He withdrew what she recognized as a condom, and then he was clambering on the bed behind her, six feet and several inches of hard primed male. She lifted her head and strained to look around, desperate for the sight of him.

He opened his hand along her hip and rubbed her ass. "Put your head back on the mattress," he said.

"But—"

"Alice. Please. I want you to feel, not see."

"Why?" burst exasperatedly out of her throat. His other hand was on her now, sliding up the length of her back. She exhaled in pleasure as he stroked her, her argument forgotten. Her burning cheek sank against the cool duvet.

"You're incredible," he rumbled behind her. He kneaded her shoulder muscles and a buttock at once. He palmed her ass so possessively that he lifted her flesh. She could feel the cool air strike the wetness between her thighs. "Dylan, please," she whispered hoarsely.

"Be patient. I'm enjoying touching you," he said. She bit her lip upon hearing the edge to his tone. He would take things at his own pace, whether she liked it or not. She *did* like it, though. Too much. He held her hips with both hands and paused, and again that overwhelming sense of arousal and . . . something else. What was it she was feeling?

It just felt so good, so grounding and *right* to be held by his hands.

A choked sound left her throat. "Shhh," he soothed, his hands moving along the side of her ribs. With her hands stretched above her, the skin was pulled very taut. She shivered in pleasure every time he touched her there, like a plucked harp string. "I can feel you tremble. Does this feel good?" he asked, now stroking the side of her ribs.

"You know it does," she mumbled.

"And this?" he ran his thumb down her spine. Her eyelids clamped shut. She quaked and cried out at the pleasurable sensation of his short, blunt-tipped nail scraping her backbone.

"Yes," she gasped.

He continued down her lower back. Her eyelids sprang open when he ran his thumb very lightly along the crack of her ass. Then, without warning, he palmed her entire outer sex and thrust his middle finger into her sheath. He moved his hand in a subtle circular motion, stimulating her sensitive lips and her clit.

"And this?"

"God, yes," she hissed.

"I think I'd like to watch you come again. You need to get comfortable with trusting me. With letting go."

He slid his finger high into her, and then removed it from her pussy. With his other fingers, he parted her labia and slid the well-lubricated middle finger against her clit. Alice moaned uncontrollably. Again, she started to burn. She was so helpless lying there, a raw, undefended bundle of nerves. All she could do was throb and feel and give in to it. The sound of him moving rigorously in her sex reached her ears. How embarrassing. She was drenched. She moaned louder, unable to stop herself.

"God, it's going to feel so fucking good inside you," he said from behind her, his tone lust-bitten. Dark. He wasn't unaffected by all this, despite his dominance and insistence upon setting the pace. She lost all sense of time as he stroked her. Her fingers clawed at the duvet. The soles of her feet grew hot. He stirred her masterfully . . . relentlessly, and she felt herself cresting. She strained for it, craved it.

She broke, shuddering in release.

"Yeah. Give me that," she heard him snarl through the roar in her ears. She felt him part her, widening her slit. As always, his actions struck her as matter-of-factly masterful, as if he knew his way around her body better than she did. He pressed the steely head of his cock at her entrance.

She screamed as he entered her. She was still climaxing. It was too much pressure, too much pleasure. He held her hips in place and drove into her, grunting savagely. Her eyes sprang wide and she clawed at the sheets. Because of the wedge pillow and her elevated hips, he was striking her at an angle she'd never before experienced. Because of his size, he was piercing her deeper than she'd ever known. He began to thrust with that stunning, sinuous glide of his hips.

She inhaled raggedly for oxygen, and then screamed anew.

He set a wicked pace. She gripped the bedding as the storm that was Dylan rocked her. She had no other choice but to take it, and she was glad for it, pleased that he overwhelmed her senses and made thinking an utter impossibility. She didn't want to think about how helpless she was when she was with him, how vulnerable. The suede pillow beneath her was soft, but her body was set against the grain of the fabric. That—and more importantly, Dylan's tight hold on her hips and ass—made her completely immobile as he thrust into her powerfully again and again.

"Tight, hot little pussy," he grated out from behind her. He slowed. She whimpered when she felt the long thick shaft nearly leave her, but then he thrust again, deep. He groaned roughly, and repeated the stroke. She realized he was watching himself pierce her. She began to bob her hips subtly, tempting him to resume his former pace. He lifted his hand and popped a buttock firmly. She gasped and stilled, panting. Expectant. He drew his cock nearly out of her again and thrust deep, grinding his balls against her outer sex. She tightened around him, moaning feverishly.

"Such a temptation, aren't you?" he growled from behind her. He popped her bottom again. It wasn't a hard stroke, but it drove her mad. She writhed in an agony of pleasure, her muscles straining tight.

"Again," she said, only half aware of what she was saying . . . of what she begged for.

He slapped her ass again. She squeezed him tight and twisted her hips ever so slightly. She was transformed by lust, becoming a shameless, writhing creature.

"Jesus," he groaned, his tone tight. Angry. Wild. He planted his fists on either side of her head and the pillow, bracing himself over her. He began fucking her again wholesale. The wood headboard clacked against the wall, the sound blending with that of her roaring heart and their slapping flesh. "If you dish it out, you've got to be prepared to take it," Dylan bit out from above her.

"Harder," she goaded him, defiant even while he rattled her with his stark possession. "I can take it. I can take *you*."

"Then you will," he grunted and lifted one hand from the mattress. He slapped the side of her buttock as he rode her hard. He pummeled her senses. She felt his cock lurch viciously in her channel, felt him swell impossibly huge.

She clutched the bedding mindlessly. He gave a low ominous growl and planted his fist back on the mattress.

Ruthless to the last, he fucked her while he came.

He slowed and then went still, his cock embedded fully in her. His breathing above her head was harsh and uneven. She lay there listening to it, relishing the evidence of his pleasure.

"You're going to kill me, Alice," he accused after a moment.

"Not if you kill me first."

He gave a harsh bark of laugher. His strong forearm moved away from where she could see it in front of her face. She whimpered when he withdrew his cock. Her tissues stung a little. She started to turn over, but he stopped her by grasping her ass. His finger slid into the juicy cleft of her labia, rubbing her gently but firmly.

"I couldn't wait for you, thanks to your teasing," he said dryly as he stroked her clit. "But you've got one more orgasm in you."

Her mouth fell open in disbelief. As it turned out, he was right. She was starting to realize Dylan always was.

NINE

He went from deep sleep to a groggy wakefulness. A feeling of vague dissatisfaction lingered in his consciousness. What had wakened him? His bedroom was dark. His arms were both extended, as if he'd been holding something. If a woman was in his bed—which was often enough—it was for sex. He slept alone, even with someone else in his bed. He didn't protest at the idea of a woman sleeping over, but in Dylan's case, that didn't mean snuggling and spooning all night long. If a woman had other ideas about that, she soon realized her mistake and either accommodated his preferences or didn't return.

But he had the distinct impression that he'd *wanted* whatever had been in his arms tonight very much. And now they were empty.

Alice.

The memory of their fevered, wild joining last night flashed across his brain. She'd turned him into a savage yet again, he recalled with an amused sense of grim acceptance. She wasn't like anyone he'd slept with before, but then . . . that was stating the obvious.

He'd fallen into a deep sleep with her pressed against him, the weight of her against his chest, her scent filling his nose, her smooth, round ass nestled against his groin. The sensation had been both arousing and relaxing at once. It was a relief, the weight of her reassuring, the scent of her only adding to the reality of her. Before he'd drifted off, he'd acknowledged she'd beckon him soon from sleep, the delight of her naked, supple body pressed against him too difficult to resist.

Now he'd awakened, but the object of his desire was gone.

He sat up in bed.

"Alice?" he called tensely. The room was very dark, but he could see that the door to the bathroom was partially open. No light shone through. She wasn't in there. She'd disappeared. The idea of Alice wandering around the house alone set alarms blaring in his head.

Shit.

He sprang up from the bed, reaching for his discarded jeans on the floor and hauling them on, nearly tripping in his haste. A cold sweat broke out on his skin.

A cry pierced the silence—an alarming confirmation of his worries. He lunged for the door.

ALICE awoke to a woman calling out in a singsong voice. Her heart jumped, sending her into instant wakefulness.

Again, that plaintive call. Despite the melodious quality, the sound made her skin crawl with dread. She sat up partially, propping herself on her elbow, panicked. Where was the door? Where *was* she?

It wasn't the dim, shadowed vision of the large bedroom suite that eventually oriented her. It was the heat and the hardness of the man who lay behind her. He was on his side, his arm draped around her waist possessively. Electrical memories of what he'd done to her in this very bed barraged her mind. She was curled into his body, and it felt wonderful. A lingering sense of unreality prevailed despite her comfort, the uneasy disbelief that she'd just spent a night of wild, uninhibited sex in Dylan Fall's bed, that the gorgeous, influential CEO of Durand was interested in her, when he could have any woman.

Yet for a split second, all she wanted to do was cuddle against his length again, to glory in his solid male strength, to forget everything else—

The amorphous voice again pierced her awareness. What was it saying? Was it a name? It sounded like a word being repeated, but it remained indistinct. If Alice had to guess, she'd have said it was possibly a two-syllable word.

For a moment, all was silent. Had it really been a voice? She knew that old buildings and houses often fooled people. Ancient pipes and ventilation, settling and creaking floors could be misinterpreted as cries or footsteps. Maybe the sound was that of a trapped animal?

"Dylan," she whispered.

He remained unmoving. Her hesitance in waking him for such a stupid reason had hushed her, never really giving full voice to her fear and uncertainty. She slowly started to lie down again, craving Dylan's heat and the security of his embrace. Before she could settle, she heard the cry again, the sound raising bumps along her forearms.

Carefully, she eased Dylan's arm off her waist and rolled off the large bed. Separated from his heat, she shivered. One thing that must not be ancient in the castle: the air-conditioning. She found her discarded shorts and top in the darkness and rapidly dressed. A glowing digital clock across the room informed her it was 3:19 a.m. She'd asked Dylan to set his cell phone alarm for five a.m., plenty of time for her to sneak down to her cabin unnoticed.

Still plenty of time to set her doubts to rest about the sound she'd heard and climb back into bed with Dylan.

His bedroom door shut behind her with a muted click. Like the rest of the house, the hallway was large and dramatic, with gleaming mahogany wainscoting, arched ceilings, elegant ivory, dark blue, and gold wallpaper, and several ornate carved doors to the right and left of her. A few dim wall sconces lighted it. She turned in the opposite direction of the grand staircase.

All was quiet now, except for the pounding of her heart in her ears.

She was being stupid. She should go back to bed and the haven of Dylan's arms.

Just to the end of the hallway, that's as far as she'd go. She could make out a large gold mirror set above a gleaming wooden chest with drawers. The sconces' dim lighting didn't fully penetrate the shadows here. She touched the smooth surface of the console, grounding herself. Her reflection looked indistinct and ghostlike in the dark mirror.

The woman called out to the left of her, louder this time. Alice whipped her head around and gripped tighter at the edge of the chest, the shivers rippling beneath her skin feeling like dread itself taking weight. It *definitely* was a woman. And this time, she'd heard the warmth of her tone, a sort of light, playful quality, like a mother speaking to her baby or a small child.

She wasn't sure she'd ever felt her heart beating this fast, as if the organ itself recognized some primal, atavistic fear that her brain couldn't comprehend.

She realized she was staring into dark empty space, not a wall. The hallway branched off here to another portion of the house. Unlike the main hallway, though, it wasn't lit. She peered, trying to penetrate the thick shadows with her vision, the skin of her arms tight and prickling with goose bumps. Her feet moved, even though she hadn't told them to. She found herself continuing, gripped by a bizarre mixture of fear and . . .

Longing?

A figure rushed across the hallway ten feet ahead of her. A woman. Alice cried out, startled more than frightened. She had the brief impression of shoulder-length brown hair and a pretty, striking face. The woman's clothing was less distinct—a pale, luminous dress, she thought—but one thing flashed clear in Alice's eyes as the woman reached for a doorknob: a stunning gold fili-greed bracelet that looked like delicate interlaced vines and leaves.

No sooner was the vision there than it was gone.

Alice stood there, shocked, not believing her own senses. There wasn't a patch of her skin that wasn't tight and tingling. There had been no sound of a door opening and closing, the woman had just been there one moment, and gone the next.

Bullshit, her rational brain inserted itself.

She rushed into the darkness, pausing when she thought she'd reached the location where she'd seen the woman in the hall.

"Hello?" she called loudly, hating the high-pitched, panicked quality of her voice. Hands outstretched, she sought blindly in the darkness. She patted desperately against the surface of the wall, feeling only the texture of wallpaper and the top of the wainscot-ing, but then—

Her hands traced the outline of the wood frame of a door. Yes. There *had* been a door. That's where the woman had vanished to.

How is it that you saw her so clearly, though? It's pitch dark in here.

She continued to feel frantically for the knob, her hands search-ing, ignoring the warning, logical voice in her head. She needed to get in that room and see that woman. *Now.*

Light flooded the hallway. She gasped in shock.

"Alice?"

She stared in the direction of the voice, one of her hands in a clawing position on the wood paneling of the door, the other grip-ping a brass knob. Dylan stood just past the chest of drawers at the intersection of the hallway, wearing his jeans, the top buttons still unfastened. His fingers touched a light switch.

Oh God. He's looking at me like I'm crazy.

"I heard something," she said hollowly. She lowered her hands from the door. "A . . . woman calling out something. And then just now, I saw—" She halted, realizing how odd she sounded. Dylan was her mirror. He looked increasingly tense and alarmed.

Maybe even a little horror-struck?

She gripped her hands together tightly to stop them from shaking. Unable to continue meeting Dylan's stare, she looked at the door. Her fingers itched to touch the cool knob again.

"Alice, come here."

She swallowed thickly at the sound of his voice and looked around. He was walking toward her. He looked beautiful and solid, his lustrous hair sexily sleep-mussed, the shadow of whiskers on his jaw. Had she really been pressed against that hard, ripped torso just minutes ago? Why had she ever left?

"She's in there," she mumbled, reaching for the door again, perversely drawn to it.

Dylan caught her wrist abruptly. She gasped and looked up at his inscrutable face.

"*Who's* in there?"

"A woman. I saw her. She disappeared into there," she insisted, nodding toward the door.

"There's no woman in there," he said, dark brows slanting ominously.

She felt a sweat break out on her skin. "But I *saw* her."

"Alice, there's no one else in this house but us."

She jerked on her wrist, but he held it fast. "Just let me look in the room then, damn it! I saw a woman. Maybe it was your cook or your housekeeper or something," she reasoned, even though she'd seen both Louise and Marie, and neither woman remotely resembled the fair, elegant woman wearing the pale dress. She lunged toward the door, determined to see for herself, but Dylan pulled her into his arms, halting her. She stared up at him, stunned.

"Alice, there is no woman in this house but you," he said succinctly. "That's an empty bedroom that hasn't been used in ages.

I don't want you going in it. There's a caved-in floorboard in there.
It's dangerous. I'm having someone coming next week to fix it."

"Are you calling me crazy? I saw a woman!" she said, anger
entering her tone. Confusion. Fear.

"No. It's just—"

She sensed him holding back. "What? What is it? Dylan?"

He closed his eyes briefly. Jesus. She really was giving him more
than he bargained for.

"There's no one in this house but us," he finally repeated
grimly.

"So I saw a ghost?" she asked sarcastically.

He frowned down at her, his sleek brows slanted. "Of
course not."

She caught his scent—spice, lingering soap . . . sex. Her body
flickered with awareness, despite her desperation to understand
what was happening.

"Do you believe in them? Ghosts, I mean?" she asked shakily,
her gaze sticking on the vision of his strong, bare chest. He stood
so close. He was so touchable, no matter how intimidating he
seemed to her at times.

"No. And you strike me as much too practical and rational to
believe in them."

"I *don't* believe in them," she said quickly. Despite her assur-
ance, however, she turned her face back toward the door, as if it
had some kind of magnetic pull on her consciousness. He caught
her chin with two long fingers and gently urged her to look at him.
His gaze narrowed on her, turning his eyes into gleaming cres-
cents. His hands moved on her upper arms, molding the muscle
gently. Her attention was caught.

"Isn't it more likely that you were disoriented being in these
unfamiliar surroundings, and that you got up and were still half
asleep?"

"You mean I was sleepwalking?" she asked.

"Isn't that more plausible than seeing a ghost?"

Her mouth hung open. She stared past his muscular arm down the hallway. It certainly all looked ordinary, if luxurious, in the bright lights Dylan had turned on. She couldn't think of what to say. Since she didn't believe in ghosts, she *must* have been dreaming. She'd never sleepwalked before, but she *had* been having especially vivid nightmares since coming to Camp Durand.

But no. It'd been all *too* real.

"Alice?"

She focused on his face because her world had started to swirl. He touched the side of her neck and cradled her chin in his palm. It was a possessive, grounding gesture. Nice. She shivered and stepped closer to his body.

"You must think I'm crazy," she muttered, seeking his heat. "*I'm* starting to think it."

"No. It's like I said. I think you're disoriented and overwhelmed being here. It's understandable."

"If I was somebody else, it would be understandable. I don't *do* things like this," she insisted. "And I've been having the weirdest dreams since I came here."

"What about?"

She shook her head in frustration. "Stupid things. Being chased. Feeling like someone . . ." *Wants to kill me,* she finished in her head, recognizing how melodramatic she'd sound saying it.

He caressed her cheek with his thumb and she looked up at him uncertainly. "You're okay now. But this is what I've been trying to tell you," he said quietly. "Entering this world can make you feel like you *are* a different person."

"You keep saying you're not feeling sorry for me," she whispered. "But I don't believe you, Dylan."

His gaze narrowed. "You should. And because I understand what you're experiencing doesn't equate to feeling sorry for you."

"Are you telling me that you saw imaginary people when you

came to Camp Durand? You don't *understand* me seeing that woman," she said bitterly. *Why are you always making a fool of yourself in front of him?* He was the one man she'd actually condescend to try to impress, and all she could do was act like an idiot or a crazy woman.

His thumb caressed her lower lip. Electricity flickered across her nerves at the touch. He firmly raised her chin, refusing to let her duck to hide her embarrassment and confusion.

"I understand better than you think," he said gruffly before he leaned his head closer.

"What do you mean—"

He shook his head grimly, but it was the fixed, hungry stare on her mouth that really silenced her. Her breath hitched, and suddenly his mouth was covering hers. It swept over her in a rush, the overwhelming, intimidating, compelling reality of Dylan Fall. Who had time to worry about insubstantial ghosts when *he* was here?

He pulled her closer, bending his arms to seal her to him tight. Her breasts crushed against his ribs. Her fingers flexed, the tips sinking into dense pectorals. Suddenly, her face was pressed against his chest, inhaling his scent, her lips moving, her tongue slicking against his skin. A profound need to drown herself in him overwhelmed her. He felt so good, so uncompromisingly solid. She twisted her face slightly, loving the slight abrasion of his chest hairs on her lips and cheek, the warm smoothness of his skin, the dense muscle beneath. Her fingers ran along the side of him, awed at his rigid strength. His skin roughened at her touch, and he palmed the back of her head. She delved her hands beneath his jeans and rubbed the tops of hard smooth buttocks. She quickened in excitement. He nudged her slightly, silently encouraging her, and her lips found a tight, hard nipple. She moaned, suddenly feeling fevered, and laved it with her tongue. His cock jumped against her.

"You look so hungry," he muttered thickly, the proximity of his voice telling her he was watching her. "Are you really that hungry, little girl?"

"For you," she muttered. "Yes."

She applied suction to his stiffening nipple, running her tongue over the puckering disc. He gave a restrained, gruff moan. Her hands moved around his hips. One hand dipped into his partially opened fly as she scraped at his nipple with her front teeth. She'd show him just how hungry she was.

He groaned roughly, the kneading hands at her back lowering. He bent his knees. His hands spread on her hips and ass.

Then he was lifting her, his mouth fastening on hers. It felt *so* good. Alice encircled him with her arms at his shoulders and with her legs at his hips. His kiss was deep and drugging.

He broke their kiss roughly a moment later and began to stride down the hallway. He stared at her with a furious focus. His lust had the effect of sunlight on a nightmare. The dark hallway and the door, the calling voice and the woman, all were forgotten.

IT'D be convenient to say that his concern for Alice Reed was what motivated him to touch her. If he possessed her, he could control what happened to her. He could keep her—and in turn, a part of himself—safe and inviolate. They had more in common than she understood.

But all of that rationale would have been a lie.

He wanted her, plain and simple. He hadn't been prepared for her beauty. She was lovely and scarred and defiant of those scars, and twice as beautiful because of her rebellion. She was vulnerable, and she was strong because she knew her weakness and had built up a commensurate defenses.

He was going to have to break her . . . break through those walls. He needed her trust.

She stared at him now as he soared down the hallway toward his bed, intent on ravishment. Amazingly, she didn't seem to understand the spell she could cast with her eyes. They were large and magnificent, a unique and seductive dark blue color. But it was what he read in her eyes that made him hunger. Right now, he saw the uncertainty and mutiny he'd witnessed in them from the first. Now, something else was there, though, something as harsh as an electrical shock and teeth-grindingly erotic. Lust shone there. Need. She was young, and struck him as largely inexperienced when it came to sex, but she was honest about what she wanted. She was passionate, fierce . . . even wild when aroused.

Miraculously, her past hadn't managed to spoil that freshness in her.

He lunged into the bedroom and kicked the door shut with a loud bang, never taking his eyes off her. Her lips were full and reddened from their former lovemaking and his kisses. There in the hallway, he'd wanted to derail her confusion and fear, but he'd become lost in his own hunger, a victim to his own machinations. He loved her mouth, and wanted to spend hours plucking at it, coaxing it, feeling her sighs run across his lips . . . ravaging it.

He bent, setting her at the edge of the bed. She remained in a seated position. Her smoky eyes lowered over him as he stood before her, his cock throbbing between his thighs. When her stare settled on the outline of his erection, he gritted his teeth. A vivid fantasy popped into his head of sliding his straining cock between her flushed lips, looking down into her eyes as he slid along her tongue— those eyes that belonged both to an innocent and a seductress.

Nevertheless, he moved his hand at the same moment that she reached for his cock, halting her. They'd had the same fantasy at the same moment—he'd read it in her eyes—and their mutual understanding strangely both aroused and intimidated. The need to take control swelled in him. He leaned over her, gently taking her other wrist and placing her hands behind her.

"Let me touch you." He flinched slightly at her softly rasped words.

"You are, beautiful. With your eyes. And it's more than enough," he said, grimly going about the task of unbuttoning her shirt. Thankfully, she hadn't put on her bra when she took her little nighttime stroll. His muscles tightening in anticipation, he parted the fabric of her cotton shirt, baring her breasts. Her smooth skin looked flawless and golden in the lamplight, her large nipples a dusky pink.

God, she was a fucking dream. He wanted to eat her alive.

Lust tore at him from the inside, demanding its due. For a moment, it blinded him. He sank to his knees before her.

He placed his hands on her rib cage, lifting slightly. She arched for him. So sweet, so generous in allowing him to consume her. He leaned down and took a nipple into his mouth, drawing on her with single-minded lust.

He wasn't gentle. He was hungry, sucking sweet, responsive flesh, maddened by her large stiffening nipple and ripe firm curves. Filling his hands with her, he feasted while her soft cries and surprised-sounding gasps filled his ears. He held her breasts while he moved his mouth between each tempting crest, drowning in the bounty of her, every taste making him crave more.

Her nails scraped against his scalp, and a measure of reason returned. He slid his lips over her stiffened nipple regretfully, his tongue lingering for a moment. He stood. She looked dazed and startled by his abrupt movement, but he couldn't think of what to say to reassure her. His need boiled inside him. It'd threatened to spill over at her desperate touch.

Without a word, he walked over to his bureau and opened a drawer. Her midnight eyes grew huge when he returned a moment later, carrying a pair of black leather padded handcuffs.

"You're having difficulty keeping your hands where I ask you to put them," he stated the obvious, attempting a small smile. It didn't work. His muscles were too tense with need to relax into levity in that moment. She looked so tempting sitting there, her eyes shining with trepidation and lust, her breasts lush and vulnerable, flushed from his feasting. "Take off your shirt and move up on the bed. Lie down," he directed. "Put your head on the pillows. The restraint will make things easier for you."

"Easier for me, or for you?" she asked, the familiar Alice-wariness back in her eyes. Despite her suspicion, she twisted out of her shirt and slid along the sheets, lying back with her head on the pillows.

"Easier for both of us," he replied, coming onto the mattress on his knees. He felt her gaze on him as he gathered her wrists and inserted them into the cuffs.

"You're very . . . efficient at that," she said. "I suppose you've had a lot of practice?"

He gave her a wry glance before he reached behind the pillows and the mattress and withdrew a strap that was fixed to the bed frame. "Do you really want to know?" he asked quietly as he gently moved her arms over her head, trying his damnedest to ignore the way the movement raised her round, thrusting breasts. The fullness of them in contrast with her narrow, finely made rib cage drove him nuts. He quickly attached her cuffs to the strap. She immediately pulled on her restraint, testing it.

He'd expect nothing less of her.

"You've tied me to this bed," she said, not accusatorily, necessarily. If anything, she sounded a little stunned.

"I want you to hold still," he said as he began to unbutton her shorts with grim determination.

"You want me to hold still while you do *what*?" she asked. He glanced up swiftly at the note of panic in her tone.

"While I take my fill," he said simply. Her mouth fell open.

"I'll keep you safe, Alice. You have to trust me to do that. If I'm ever too forceful with you, just tell me to stop. Do you understand?"

She nodded slowly.

"Good," he said, turning his attention to the task of peeling her shorts and underwear off her hips and long legs. The vision of the way she'd looked out there in the hallway—so disoriented and afraid—leapt into his mind's eye.

You say you'll keep her safe, but do you really have any idea what you're doing?

His good friend and onetime mentor Sidney Gates had looked worried when Dylan had admitted—very briefly—that he and Alice had become intimate. That concerned expression had cut to the heart of him. Had Sidney been worried about Alice?

Or about him?

Everything was at stake. He couldn't fail in this. He *wouldn't*.

He stared down at Alice's naked, bound body.

"Why are you so serious?" she whispered. He glanced up and saw the almost awed expression on her face.

"There's nothing more serious than this."

He slid his hands beneath her hips, his fingers delving into the firm flesh of her ass. He leaned down over her sex, tilting his head slightly, catching her heady scent in his nostrils. The impact of her fragrance was instantaneous. His cock lurched viciously. His mouth watered. He felt her sleek, toned muscles tense in his hands, and knew she was anticipating the moment as much as he was. He nuzzled the soft light auburn curls over her cleft. Her sex was still swollen and damp from their former lovemaking. He'd ridden her hard. She'd come just as hard. His cock ached at the mere memory.

He'd take her hard again. Soon. Very soon.

He kissed her labia, applying a firm, indirect pressure on her clit. She moaned shakily and shifted her hips.

"Hold still," he demanded. He opened her thighs wider.

His tongue parted her folds in a firm, questing caress.

He was distantly gratified when he heard her ragged moan, but mostly, he was spellbound by his task. He laved her clit. Her abundant cream coated his tongue. She was exquisite. Intoxicated by her taste, he used one of his hands to part her labia. He circled and played with her nerve-packed flesh for a while, thoroughly enjoying her soft cries and helpless whimpers.

The need to feast overcame him. He refused to be denied. She couldn't distract him with her touch, bound as she was, but she twisted her hips when her pleasure grew too intense. He opened one hand over her hip, holding her down onto the mattress. He stabbed at her clit with a stiffened tongue before he soothed her with a gliding caress, ruthless in extracting his due.

"Oh no. Oh *yes*. God, you're killing me," she moaned emphatically a moment later.

His eyelids opened heavily and his gaze flickered up to her face when her words registered in his lust-drunk brain.

Jesus.

She was so beautiful. Her naked torso had taken on a gleam from a light coat of perspiration. Her full breasts heaved as she panted, the nipples stiff from arousal. Her cheeks were vividly pink, her lips flushed and puffy. It beckoned him, her mouth. He longed to pierce it with tongue and cock.

Her dark eyes were wild.

Yes. *This* expression on her face was so much better than the fear he'd seen as she'd stood in that hallway minutes ago.

Her lower lip trembled as he inserted two thick fingers into her creamy pussy. He held her stare.

"Stop fighting it, beautiful. Give in," he directed.

Her moan was rough and anguished, as if he asked too much. She twisted her head, pressing her flushed cheek into the pillow. But he was determined. For several seconds Dylan just stared at her flagrantly pink, glistening sex, letting his hunger build as he thrust into her clasping, muscular channel. Finally, unable to resist any longer, he tilted his head and covered her outer sex with his mouth. He couldn't disguise his greed. She keened loudly as he took her clit captive in his mouth, sucking her tautly and whipping the kernel of flesh with a stiff tongue.

Slippery juices and heat surrounded his fucking fingers. She cried out sharply, the sound striking him like an incredulous question. It crazed him, that sound, the sure knowledge that she was responding to his demanding touch.

He twisted his wrist, corkscrewing his fingers into her tight channel. He sucked her clit between his teeth. The walls of her sex clamp him tighter. She screamed as orgasm hit her.

He replaced his mouth with his finger, giving her what she needed to continue coming powerfully. Nothing could stop him from taking what *he* wanted as well. She was soaked. He slid one hand beneath a smooth thigh, rolling her hips back forcefully on the bed and parting her wider. He dove between her legs, his tongue immediately plunging into her pussy, driving deep and hard.

Pure decadence, to dip into her warm honey. A vicious sense of triumph spiked through him when she made a strangled sound and then screamed full throttle yet again.

If he didn't watch himself, he'd lose himself to her. He could die happy like this, with the taste of her on his tongue, and with her juices running down his throat. He'd never known a woman to get this wet. She was so responsive. Mindless with lust and acting purely on instinct, he ran his finger below his piercing tongue, spreading her juices along her ass cheeks and perineum. Her cream had already gathered in the crevice of her bottom.

He lightly caressed her tiny, puckered asshole. He felt her muscles stiffen. His cock raged, but he knew he'd let his lust get the best of him at that moment. Something about her taste and wholesale responsiveness, which stood in stark contrast to her hallmark wariness, turned him into an animal. It *meant* something to him, her unguarded reaction.

He withdrew his tongue and finger and kissed her damp mound.

"Sorry," he muttered thickly, rising up over her.

He wasn't really, but he knew he'd shocked her with that intimate touch. It was too soon, to expose her to the full extent of his greed.

Her expression as she looked up at him undid him. He gritted his teeth together and reached for the bedside drawer and a condom. She looked vaguely bemused and thoroughly ravished and . . .

Delicious.

He felt her eyes on him as he stood and shucked off his jeans, then rolled on the condom. He crawled back onto the bed, straddling her.

"You don't have to be sorry," she said through soft pants. "It felt so good. I loved it."

"Jesus," he muttered under his breath, straddling her bound body.

"What?"

He palmed his heavy cock from below and guided himself to her entrance. "How can you be such a smart-ass and so sweet at once?" he asked tensely. He glanced down and paused in his haste to get inside of her. The downy hair between her thighs was dark with moisture.

"I'm not sweet," she hissed.

Unable to resist, he worked his cockhead along the creamy seam of her labia. She moaned shakily. Wetness coated his knuckles and gathered on the thin condom. Her pussy was a man's dream come true.

"Oh *yes,* you are," he groaned, before he repositioned himself, flexed his hips, and drove into her. Her clamping heat made his eyes roll back in his head. She made a squeaking sound and pulled on her restraints, baring her teeth. He planted his fists in the mattress and thrust, sinking into her to the balls. She gave a sharp cry and lifted her head, scraping her teeth against his ribs. He grunted at her show of animalistic hunger, withdrawing and sinking again, setting a wicked pace from the first.

"Do you want to bite me, Alice? Do you want to bite me while I fuck your little pussy?" he taunted her as he pounded into her, and the headboard began to rock against the wall. It was so good, having her there, helpless and hungry, bound beneath him while he plunged into her sweet heat.

"Yes," she gasped, before she took a bite out of his side. His skin roughened in heightened arousal. She licked at the abraded skin with a warm tongue, as if in apology. Even in the midst of rabid lust, he marveled at the stark reality of her.

His spine tingled. His muscles strained when he drove into her hard, and she bit him again.

"You're going to pay for that," he growled.

She *did*, before he was done with her that night.

Dylan thought he might have paid even more, given her demonstration of such sweet savagery.

TEN

The sound of Dylan's phone alarm going off awakened her from a deep, drugging sleep. She'd only passed out just less than an hour ago, unraveled and sublimely satiated from Dylan's lovemaking.

Dylan had handed her his phone upon her request before they'd drifted off. She tapped the screen, turning off the alarm. She blinked, lying there immobile for a moment as memories of the bizarre, incredible night washed over her. Turning her chin, she peered into the darkness. Dylan had pulled her into his arms after he'd released her from the restraints. He didn't move now, obviously still asleep. She thought of the world outside of the mansion: an alternate universe, a world to which she needed to return.

For the second time that night, she eased out of Dylan's arms.

One large warm hand suddenly gripped her hip as she tried to slide off the mattress.

"Alice?"

"Yeah?"

"Weren't you going to wake me?"

"What?" she asked, confused by the steel in his tone. He sounded very awake and alert for someone who had just seemed fast asleep . . . for someone who'd had little rest because he'd been making her scream in pleasure all night. "I thought you should just sleep—"

"Are you forgetting that I don't want you to wander around

this property alone?" His hand left her hip and she heard movement and the rustling of sheets. "I'll walk you back every
morning."

"*Every* morning?" she asked dubiously.

"Yeah. You'll come back. Tonight. And the night after that.
Right?" he said, his tone implying this was going to be a regular
practice. Despite her uncertainty and doubt, she melted a little at
the sound of his sexy sleep-roughened voice emanating from the
darkness. She longed to cuddle back against him . . . to forget that
other world . . . to trust what was happening between them. But
then again—

"Don't you think we're being stupid?" she blurted out.

"No," he said, his voice firmer. "I won't be able to rest, knowing you're sleeping so close and yet separate. Will you?"

She paused, her mouth hanging open as his words painted a
picture in her head of tossing and turning in her bed in the cabin.
Tortured.

Burning.

"No," she whispered after a moment.

"There you have it. Getting some decent sleep isn't stupid. Not
accepting the obvious is." She blinked when he switched on the
bedside lamp. He looked *good*. He leaned on one elbow, his back
to her, but had twisted his torso around to pin her with his stare.
The sheet rode low on his trim hips. His broad well-muscled back
beckoned her. She wanted to muss his smooth sexy hair even more
than lovemaking and sleep had. "I want you to remember what I
said. About not wandering off by yourself," he repeated.

"So the ghosts don't get me?" she asked, using sarcasm to
defray the alarmingly strong desire she experienced at that
moment. She dragged her gaze off the vision of him and stood next
to the bed. Her determination was halfhearted at best. She cast
him a sideways, covetous glance. His stare lowered over her naked
body, making her skin prickle.

"There are much worse things on earth than a ghost," he said grimly after a moment, turning away and throwing the sheet off of his naked body.

THAT afternoon, she and Thad fell in step side by side as they vacated the field behind the stables that was used for football and soccer. The kids had rushed ahead of them along the wooded trail toward their cabins to wash up for dinner. She and Thad had stayed behind to gather up the equipment and scrimmage vests.

"You were being modest about your skills. As usual," Thad teased her, referring to Alice's sixty-yard run for a touchdown just minutes ago.

"It was pure survival. Judith Arnold looked like she was going to mow me down. I think she considered it a rare opportunity to flatten me without getting into trouble."

"We were playing touch football," Thad said.

"I doubt that'd stop Judith," Alice muttered under her breath. She noticed Thad's sideways glance. "The girl hates me, plain and simple."

"Weren't you the one who suggested it'd take a while for them to get to know us? Trust us?" Thad asked.

"Yeah. I guess you're right," Alice admitted as they walked off the field slowly. She didn't know about Thad, but she was exhausted after the first full day of camp.

After a total of only three or four hours of sleep in Dylan's bed. At least the sleep she'd gotten had been deep and solid.

Getting some decent sleep isn't stupid. Not accepting the obvious is.

Graphic memories of being in his arms, of moments of intense intimate pleasure swamped her brain. It felt odd having those memories, as if they belonged to another person's experience. Yet at the same time . . . she'd never felt anything so deeply. So personally.

Her body heated of its own accord at the vivid memories. An ache mounted between her thighs. Something rose in her, a powerful craving like she'd never before known. It alarmed her, but she couldn't deny it.

Despite a head full of uncertainties, she couldn't wait to see Dylan again tonight.

When a brisk wind came off the lake, she turned her face into it, hoping to cool her flushed cheeks.

"You okay?" Thad asked her.

She glanced at him in feigned surprise. "Yeah."

"Good first day?" he asked.

"Yeah. It was great, actually," Alice said after a few seconds of reflection. She was telling the truth. The kids had been sweeter, fresher, and more excited to be there than she'd realized they would be. The opportunity for supportive, stress-free fun in such an idyllic setting, the removal of all the usual difficult obstacles from their life, seemed to peel back a lot of their armor. "For the most part, it was really special," she admitted to Thad.

"You shouldn't let Judith worry you. She'll come around. And the other kids are already warming up to you. Even mine," he said, referring to the kids from the Orange Team who had been playing football with them. Alice noticed his smile and grinned back. Unlike her, Thad looked even more appealing when he'd worked and played hard all day. His golden hair was sticking up in spikes and darkened from sweat. His gray T-shirt clung to his toned torso, emphasizing his taut muscles.

"You're the one reassuring me now. I can see why. You've found your stride," she said as they entered the woods. "You're fantastic with kids. You should be a teacher."

He looked startled at her off-the-cuff statement, but she'd only been telling the truth as it struck her. He was a natural with kids, warm and funny but authoritative. Easy to follow.

"Sorry," she said, perplexed by his slightly stunned expression.

"It's okay," he said, hitching the equipment bag higher on his shoulder. "It's just . . ."

"What?" Alice asked, sensing his disquiet.

"I've thought about it before," he said. He glanced at her uneasily. "Being a teacher. A coach, too. I thought about that even more than being a fisherman," he added jokingly.

Even in the shaded woods, she saw his face deepen in color at his admission.

"Why *don't* you?" she asked in a rush. "You'd be so good at it."

His smile looked a little strained. He shook his head.

"What?" she prodded, confused.

"It's not what Schaefers do."

"*Schaefers?* Like your mom and dad, you mean? Your aunts and uncles and cousins?" She already knew Thad was an only child. "What does it matter what *they* do? We're talking about you."

He shook his head again. "I went to school for business. A Yale MBA isn't cheap, you know. I can't just trash it all on a whim."

"The idea of being a teacher is a whim? Is that you talking? Or your dad?" she asked slowly.

His green eyes flashed at her. Alice bowed her head, recognizing she'd come on too strong. As usual. Neither of them spoke for a stretched moment. Birds twittered in the trees and the leaves rustled in the gentle wind. A thought occurred to her and she gave a bark of laughter.

"What?" he asked.

"It's weird," she said impulsively. "I've been thinking of myself as the loser here." She noticed his dark scowl and flagging step and knew she'd misspoken again. "Not that I *am*—or *you* are—or anything. I'm just talking about irrational insecurities. Because I didn't grow up like you or Brooke or Dave did, I've been feeling like I'm constantly running uphill while you guys fly effortlessly. But all of those advantages I've been thinking you guys had over me . . . they can just as easily be disadvantages, too. Right?" she asked desperately, searching his expression. It took her a second to realize they'd stopped and were facing each other.

"Yeah. You're right," he said soberly after a moment. "You have no idea how hard it is to live up to my father's expectations. It's like some kind of impossible dream, one I know I'll never succeed at, but can't seem to help trying to make reality anyway. It's like a habit I can't quit."

Compassion swept through her. Her lips twitched into a smile and she resumed walking. "At least now you know. That it's a disadvantage, I mean—your concern about doing what your parents want when it comes to the idea of being a teacher. It's better to realize what you're fighting, isn't it? To know what's holding you back instead of . . ."

She shrugged, fading off. He looked at her inquiringly.

"Just accepting it," she finished.

"I'll never be a teacher, Alice."

"Yeah, well . . . I never thought Durand would look at me twice as a potential executive. Life is a funny thing," she said, trying to lighten his mood.

I never thought Dylan Fall would look at me twice, either. Yeah. Damn *funny thing, life.*

She tamped down the thought, focusing on Thad. She felt guilty for making him so serious all of a sudden. A little sad. How horrible, to want to do one thing with your life, but doing something else because it was expected of you. Sissy and her uncles had no expectations or aspirations for Alice whatsoever. She'd never realized that was a kind of freedom until now.

Thad's expression darkened as he peered ahead of them fixedly. Her concern swelled.

"Did you know that Durand did security screenings on us even

before the interview? Even before we were hired as counselors?"
she blurted out, eager to change the topic . . . to erase his unchar-
acteristic oppression.

He frowned. "I don't think that's legal, is it?"

"I don't know, but they did it," she said with grim finality.

"How do you know?" Thad asked.

She shifted the mesh bag of vests she carried, buying some time
while she thought up a viable explanation.

"From something Maggie, my grad school advisor, told me,"
she said vaguely. Poor Maggie. She was being used as the scape-
goat not only for Dylan's lies, but her own.

Thad grunted and shrugged. "Durand can be a little Machia-
vellian. The corporate world can be. I guess I'm not shocked."

"You mean you think the company is manipulative? Dishon-
est?" she asked, concerned.

"No. Not really," he admitted. "Just ruthless. Highly *discerning*. That's no surprise, surely. Lots of big businesses are. *Fall*
certainly is."

"You think Dylan Fall is ruthless?"

"Well . . . like I said. Highly discerning. I didn't mean it in a
bad way, Alice. He's a legend in the business world, a fine example
of capitalism at work. It's the American way, right? I would have
thought you didn't mind, when it comes to Fall."

"What's that supposed to mean?" Alice demanded.

"Nothing," Thad said, his casual shrug and sharp stare at
odds. "It just seems like you two are on the same wavelength.
You're the only one who was hired by the CEO personally. And
you two seemed—friendly at the castle dinner."

"Because he showed me how to get from the bathroom to the
party, we're suddenly best friends?" she scoffed uneasily. "I hardly
know anything about him."

"Then you aren't so different from the rest of us," Thad said.

"How *did* he become CEO of Durand at such a young age?"

Alice couldn't stop herself from asking, despite Thad's reply. Surely someone with Thad's affluent upbringing and background had some inside information—more than *she* would, anyway. Thad's pace slowed, and he eventually stopped. So did she. The edge of the forest was just feet ahead, a distant cabin roof coming into view. Maybe Thad thought they shouldn't have this conversation about Fall in the open air near the camp?

"I *thought* he was related to the founder and owner, Alan Durand. Or his wife," Thad said.

Alice nodded. That had been her vague impression, too. "It's funny, but there isn't much backstory available about Durand or Fall. I had to do a lot of research for the philanthropy and profit article we wrote, but the details about Fall's rise are murky. But you sound certain Fall *isn't* related to the Durands?" she probed.

Thad gave her an amused, knowing glance. "I guess not. According to Kehoe, the Durands didn't have a family heir."

"What else did Kehoe say about Fall?" Alice asked slowly. She'd remained cautious in her dealings with the vice president of human resources. He always seemed friendly enough to her, but she sensed his sharp observance, his continued vague suspicion about her presence at Camp Durand. He suspected something about Dylan's insistence upon hiring her. Perhaps she felt a little guilty in her dealings with Kehoe, too. She really had "taken up" with Dylan Fall, after all, and confirmed all Kehoe's suspicions. A flickering of doubt went through her at her promise to meet Fall again tonight, despite her overwhelming desire to do so.

Had Dylan just hired her because he was so attracted to her? And why hadn't she been dwelling on that disturbing thought all day?

Because you've been too busy melting at the memories of him . . . craving more of him.

She pushed the volatile thoughts aside.

"Dave mentioned something on the first day that we were here about Fall being a Durand relative," Thad explained in a muted tone. "He wasn't saying it to Kehoe, but Kehoe overheard him . . . and he made a point of correcting Dave. A *major* point."

"What'd Kehoe say?"

Thad threw a cautionary glance toward the camp. "Kehoe sort of barked out from across the main lodge meeting room that Dylan was no relative to Alan Durand or his wife. It sort of flustered Dave, because Kehoe was so sharp. Dave said he'd thought he'd read Fall was a relative somewhere, and Kehoe snapped at him again. *Us*, actually. All of us sitting there. He said that it was time we all learned that sometimes, people got into positions not because of what they knew, but *who* they knew . . . and he said that Fall had one sure talent: how to ingratiate himself with the powers that be," Thad said in a hushed, confidential tone.

"The Durands?" Alice whispered, her heart starting to pound in her ears.

Thad nodded.

"But haven't Alan Durand and his wife been dead for years?" she asked. "If what Kehoe said was true, Fall would have had to be a kid when he 'ingratiated' himself with the couple," she mumbled, thinking furiously. Had Dylan become a favorite of the Durands when he was a teenage camper at their charitable organization? She hadn't told anyone—even Thad or Kuvi—what Fall had told her about being a vulnerable child at Camp Durand. She didn't think it was her place to expose what he'd told her in private.

Or maybe Fall's vulnerability about his past felt a lot like her own, and she'd protected it instinctively.

"I'm not sure when they passed away exactly, or how Fall knew them," Thad said quietly. "But I think Alan Durand lived longer than his wife, even though he was supposed to be weak and a sort of invalid for years. He certainly left his stamp on his company, though. Fall is hamstrung in his daily operations as CEO by the detailed operatives and the extensive trust document that rules all of Durand's finances."

"But I understood that Fall actually owns a good portion of Durand shares."

"But not the majority," Thad said. "The majority is held by the trust."

Alice mulled this over as Thad glanced toward the camp. "Here comes Dave," he said, frowning slightly.

"Oh . . . yeah," Alice said distractedly, resuming walking.

"Alice."

She paused and looked back at Thad. His expression was serious again.

"Thanks. For those things you said. I really have been accepting it as a given that my parents' expectations for my life are more important than mine. I'm not saying I'm going to change my plans—this opportunity with Durand is too good to pass up—but it helped to hear you say that. To realize I have a choice. You're really easy to talk to," he said quietly.

She smiled and shrugged, embarrassed. "Sometimes, it just helps to hear yourself say it out loud."

What would Kuvi or Dave or Thad say if she told them about how she'd spent last night? She scowled slightly at the judgey-sounding voice in her head. Still—there was no doubt about it. Her impulsivity when it came to Dylan Fall—her oddly intense obsession with him—could crash down on her at any moment given these circumstances. Most people would question Fall's ethics in sleeping with her in this situation. They'd certainly question her judgment. What if Kehoe found out? She was being stupid. She was letting her guard down, something Alice just didn't do.

But for some reason, it felt nothing but *right* when Dylan touched her—

"I'd like to be able to talk with you more," Thad said, interrupting her thoughts and taking a step toward her. Alice's heart jumped. "Alone. In private," he added tensely.

"I thought you guys got lost in the woods," Dave said dryly, approaching them. Alice took a step back. "Our teams have dinner duty," he reminded Thad. "If you want to shower first, you better now."

"Yeah. Okay," Thad said distractedly, dragging his gaze off Alice's face. "See you later," he told her pointedly before he jogged toward his cabin.

"Do you want me to take that stuff?" Dave asked her in a friendly fashion, waving at the scrimmage vests. "The equipment storage is close to our cabin."

"That's okay, but thanks. I can do it."

Dave tilted his head in the direction Thad had just taken. "Sorry for barging in on you two," he said quietly. "I figured Thad had forgotten about dinner duty. He tends to forget about a lot of things when you're around," he said with a smile.

"It's not a problem at all," she assured, eager to correct his misunderstanding. "We were just talking."

Dave's look was a little too knowing for her liking. "Kuvi mentioned you being away from your cabin last night." Alice's stomach dropped. "Don't worry," Dave said quickly, obviously interpreting her alarmed expression. "Kuvi and I can keep a secret. It was just by chance that we realized we were both in the same situation. That's the only reason we talked about it."

"*What* situation?" Alice asked numbly, confused.

"We're the roommates who have roommates that are . . ." Dave rolled his hand in a circular motion as if he wasn't going to condescend to state the obvious. Alice wished he would write it down for her, because she had no idea what he was talking about. "*I* was the one who mentioned it to Kuvi first—about Thad being away most of the night from our cabin. Then she told me about you, and it all made sense. Kuvi normally wouldn't have said anything, if we hadn't had that in common. And don't worry," he mimed locking his lips together and flinging away the key. "Your secret is safe. I approve of Thad's taste—for once. Like I said, privacy is a rare commodity around here. We've got to help each other protect it, right?"

"Dave, I don't think you—"

Someone shouted Dave's name. He turned and waved. "Gotta go. See you at dinner," he said, jogging down the path and leaving Alice utterly bewildered how to proceed with this new complication in her life.

THAT night, Alice talked the kids into a fun game of Pictionary despite Terrance's insistence that they tell more ghost stories. Given what had happened to her last night at the castle, she thought she'd heard enough ghost stories for now. Crystal had worried about the kids having nightmares. Little had she known that *she'd* be the one waking up in the midst of a nightmare, she thought with self-disgust. Somewhere in the midst of the rowdy game of Pictionary, Alice fortified herself and made a decision.

She wasn't going to meet Dylan tonight in the woods. She was overwhelmed by everything that was happening to her.

What she needed was some time and space to figure it all out.

Her decision left an uncomfortable ache in the vicinity of her chest as she left the Red Team's cabin that night. Muted pink and lavender light still clung in the western sky. She immediately spied Thad and Brooke standing at an intersection in one of the camp paths. Thad looked around as Alice closed the screen door behind her, as if he'd been expecting her. He took a half step back, and Brooke took a full step toward him, her gaze fixed on his face. She spoke quietly. For once, Brooke didn't look like a bitch. Maybe it was a trick of the fading light, but instead, she looked anxious. Thad turned back to her and said something Alice couldn't hear.

Feeling like an intruder, Alice hastened in the direction of her cabin. She felt jumpy and vaguely nauseated. Dylan would be waiting for her in the woods in half an hour. It pained her, to think of him waiting there alone.

Her body felt itchy. Restless. She wasn't sure she could ever rest, remembering their lovemaking last night, reliving the things he'd done to her . . . the things she'd loved, knowing every second she was depriving herself of all that.

Great. It'd taken her nearly twenty-four years to discover she was a nymphomaniac.

She recalled all too well that strange incident in the castle's hallway, too.

A nymphomaniac who's prone to nightmares—

"Alice."

She braced herself at the sound of tapping tennis shoes on the path and Thad's voice. She turned. Behind Thad's shoulder, she saw Brooke watching them. At Alice's stare, Brooke spun around and walked in the opposite direction on the path.

"Hey," Thad said, coming to a stop a few feet away. He grinned. "I was waiting for you to come out."

"And Brooke was waiting for you?" Alice asked with a small smile.

Where had *Thad spent last night? It's none of your business,* she chided herself. It wasn't like she didn't have some secrets of her own. Besides, knowing Thad, he'd snuck out on one of the fishing boats and fallen asleep while the waves rocked him. She'd come to learn he loved boating and the water. He hadn't been kidding that first day about considering becoming a fisherman.

Thad shrugged, looking vaguely embarrassed. *And* very handsome in a pair of jeans and a white sports shirt that set off his even tan and green eyes.

"She wants something that isn't real," Thad said, nodding in the direction where Brooke had just stood.

"You mean the blue-blood scion of the Schaefer dynasty?"

"Yeah. Unlike you, she doesn't seem to realize that identity is phony."

"I don't think it's phony," Alice protested. "You're as much of a gentleman aristocrat as anyone I've ever met."

He laughed and touched her arm with light fingertips. She swallowed uneasily and glanced away. Things would be so much easier if she was crazily attracted to Thad, and not the CEO of Durand Enterprises.

"Do you want to take a walk?"

"Where?" Alice asked, glancing uneasily in the direction of the woods where she'd told Dylan she'd meet him at nine thirty. The woods had already fallen dark. Surely he wasn't in there yet.

Thad looked vaguely bemused by her pointed question.

"I don't know. On the beach?" he asked.

"Yeah. Okay," Alice said stepping away from his touch. Thad was nice and sweet, but she liked him as a friend. If it weren't for Dylan dominating her thoughts, maybe there would have been a chance. *Maybe.* But it was time she put a halt to Thad's romantic interests, before things got out of hand, and she ruined their friendship for good. Alice didn't want to lead him on, especially when she was so emotionally confused.

They headed for the beach, in the opposite direction of the thick woods. Would Dylan be angry at her for not showing up? Worried? Well she couldn't help that. Both of them knew they were behaving irresponsibly by giving in to this thing between them.

"Whoa, wait up," Thad joked when she hit the beach. "What's the hurry?"

"Nothing. Sorry." She'd been scurrying to get away from her cabin and the woods—out of potential sight of Dylan. She noticed Thad's vaguely puzzled glance in the dying light. "What?" she asked.

"Nothing. You've just seemed a little . . . preoccupied all day," he said, falling into step beside her.

"Oh. I guess I have been. A little," she said slowly, staring out at the crimson-streaked sky over the shimmering lake. The day had died in a glorious sunset.

"Are you going to leave me in suspense?" Thad asked amusedly when she didn't elaborate.

She threw him a small smile. "Do you believe in ghosts?" she asked flippantly after a short silence, interrupted only by the waves caressing the beach in a silken rhythm.

"Yeah, and vampires, too, but I have my doubts about werewolves and goblins." He laughed and she gave him a sharp glance. His humor faded.

"Are you *serious*?" he asked, his brows slanting in what she recognized as concern. For her sanity, no doubt.

"Never mind," she mumbled.

"No, Alice . . ." He reached out and touched her upper arm, but she just shook her head, embarrassed, and kept walking. His hand fell away.

"It's not a big deal. I just had a bad nightmare last night, that's all," she said, her tone assuring him it wasn't important. "What would you think about transferring Terrance to the offensive line? He could do some major blocking if we taught him how to use his heft to his advantage."

Thad paused for a moment at her abrupt change of topic to football, but eventually joined in the safe conversation. After a while, they fell silent, neither of them speaking as they progressed along the shoreline and darkness fell over them.

Her heart gave a little leap of dread when he put his hand on her upper arm again, but this time, she paused. Best to get this over with.

"I'm sorry for shutting you down like that. Earlier," she heard him say, his voice sounding close under the cloak of darkness. "I didn't realize you were serious."

"It's okay. It must have sounded odd. I don't believe in ghosts, either. Not really."

He laughed softly. "It must have been a hell of a nightmare for you to bring it up." His hand tightened on her arm and she felt his heat. There was a half-moon. Between its light, the reflection in the water, and starshine, she could see when Thad's head dipped toward her face. "Talk to me, Alice," he murmured. His breath brushed against the skin of her cheeks. Her heart started to drum in her ears. His head lowered more. She felt his lips brush against her temple. The scent of his aftershave tickled her nose. She made a muffled sound of distress and stepped back.

"Don't, Thad," she said.

He was still touching her arm. She hadn't stepped back as far as she'd thought.

"Why not? You're not involved with anyone, right?"

"No, it's not that," she insisted, recalling how she'd told him during their training week that she didn't have a boyfriend.

"Because you must have caught on by now—almost every other Camp Durand counselor certainly has—that I'm kind of crazy about you," he muttered, his tone warm and wry, like he was a little amused and embarrassed by his feelings. By his honesty.

"I . . . Thank you. That's so sweet," she began softly. She stiffened when she saw movement behind Thad's shoulder.

"Hello."

Thad's hand dropped away at the man's voice. He spun around.

"Who is it?" Thad asked tensely. But Alice already knew who it was. No one else possessed that tall, formidable outline.

"Fall," the looming shadow said. "It's Thad Schaefer, isn't it?"

"Oh . . . yeah. Sorry, we didn't hear you come up. Out for a walk, too, sir?"

Alice had to hand it to Thad. He'd recovered remarkably well, given the circumstances.

"Yes. I'm sorry to disturb you and—"

Dylan's words hung in the humid night air expectantly. She sensed Thad hesitate in saying her name, like he didn't want to expose her unnecessarily. As if Dylan wouldn't get his answer one way or another.

As if he didn't already *have* the answer.

Irritation spiked through her chaotic state.

"It's Alice," she replied, unable to hide the edge to her tone. She didn't *want* to disguise her agitation at Dylan at that moment. She didn't appreciate him spying on her. "Alice Reed," she added darkly, hoping Fall felt her glare at his shadow.

"Yes. I remember," came his hoarse, vaguely amused voice from the darkness. "The head of the Red Team, right?"

"Right," she said through gritted teeth.

"It's a nice night for a walk," Dylan said, his light tone making her grind the enamel off her back teeth. "Nicer by the beach than in the woods. I guess that's why you two picked it."

She clamped her teeth tighter, hearing his veiled message. His barely disguised anger.

"The breeze is nice," Thad agreed.

"I have to be getting back," Alice said abruptly. The frothing tension of the moment was just too much for her. Let Thad and Dylan enjoy the *nice* night together. She'd had enough.

"Uh—" Thad began.

"I'll see you tomorrow, Thad. Thanks for the walk," she said not unkindly before she lunged onto the sand toward the tree line.

"Alice—" Thad called out, but he stopped himself with a frustrated sound. He probably thought she wanted to escape because she didn't want Fall to suspect she'd been fraternizing with another employee, even though there were no hard-and-fast rules about dating that she'd ever read in her packet. Her blood felt like it was steaming in her veins as she headed for the wooded path, her anger and longing and confusion a volatile brew.

This time when she plunged into the dark woods and heard the firm, quick step behind her, she knew damn well it was a flesh-and-blood man, not a phantom. She flew around when he halted her flight by a firm grip on her upper arm, the front of her body coming into contact with his solid length.

"Stop it," she muttered, landing a fist in the middle of his chest.

"Why are you always hitting me?" Dylan hissed. Despite his hushed tone, he sounded just as irritated at her as she was at him.

"Because you deserve it," she spat, her choppy breath mingling with his in the opaque darkness. "Why did you have to follow me? Can't you take a hint?"

"No. Spell it out for me," he seethed. She couldn't see him in the darkness, but somehow knew he was snarling. He stepped closer. Her pulse leapt at her throat as her skin began to tingle at the contact.

"You know we shouldn't keep doing this, Dylan," she whispered between clenched teeth.

"So you thought you'd take up with pretty boy instead?"

"No. Jesus, I wasn't *taking up* with him! We were walking."

"I want you to stay away from that kid."

"*What?*" she sputtered, finding it difficult to keep her voice muted in her fury. "He's a year older than me, not a kid! He's my friend. And at least he wanted to do something with me other than take me to bed," she stated fiercely.

"That's not what it looked like to me," Dylan replied dryly.

"I was in the process of . . . Oh, forget it. Why should I explain myself to you?" she said scathingly.

"Stay away from him. Take your walks with someone else. I don't know enough about Schaefer."

She blinked at the cold. What a weird thing to say. "You're crazy."

"Maybe," he replied grimly. "But not about this." His hand tightened on her arm and he brought her closer. Her breasts pressed against his ribs, her lower belly against his crotch. She placed her hands palm down against his chest. Instead of pushing him away, however, she just absorbed the sensation of him: the hard muscle, the strong beat of his heart. She sighed in frustration, resisting an almost overwhelming urge to plant her face beneath her hands and inhale his scent. "But maybe you're right about one thing," he said.

She started in surprise. "One thing?" she asked derisively. "I can't *wait* to hear which one."

"I haven't taken you anywhere nice. Anywhere . . . romantic, where we can talk and get to know each other better."

That gave her pause. "You want to *talk* to me?"

"Yes," he replied, ignoring her confused sarcasm.

"And be *romantic*?"

"Spare me the sarcasm, Alice. I'll be the first to admit I'm not an expert on the topic, so there's no need to patronize."

"I'm *not* patronizing you." She gyrated her hips slightly, pressing tighter against him. "I thought you just wanted to fuck me."

She felt his cock swell at her purposefully crude taunt. The air surrounding them suddenly felt too thick to breathe.

"I *do* want to fuck you," he grated out. Triumph spiked through her at the anger in his tone. She'd gotten to him. For once. His hand skimmed down her spine, his fingers playing at the top curve of her ass. Alice trembled in excitement.

"Among other things," he continued more evenly, as if he'd gotten ahold of himself in the interim. "We'll drive down the coast on Saturday night. I know of somewhere nice, and the owner will be discreet about our presence there. That'll give us some time together. I have to travel tomorrow, but I'll be back in plenty of time for that," he mused, and Alice knew she hadn't derailed his infuriating confidence. Trying to ignore his low rough voice and his hand caressing her back and ass was only making her more enthralled by the second. "Now. Are you going to tell me why you were avoiding me?" he asked. His warm breath brushed against her upturned lips, and she felt something give within her. Soften.

"Don't you think it's obvious?" she asked. "We shouldn't be

doing this. You could get in trouble with the board. I could be sent away from Camp Durand. And I *need* this job, Dylan."

For a moment, he didn't speak. She held her breath, wondering what he was thinking. His mind seemed so impenetrable to her at times. Her breath hitched when he cradled the side of her head with his spread hand. His thumb rubbed against her temple, the slightly rough pad sending prickles of pleasure beneath her skin.

"No one is going to send you away from Durand because of this. You have my word on that."

"And you? What about *you*, and your job?"

"Are you taking care of me?" he growled, sounding dangerous and vaguely amused at once. "Do me a favor, and don't do it by taking romantic walks on the beach with Thad Schaefer."

"I'm serious, Dylan!"

"So am I. I'm the largest shareholder and the CEO of Durand. No one is going to send me away, either. Maybe the situation isn't ideal—"

She snorted, but he ignored her.

"—but that's not going to keep me from you, Alice."

She went entirely still, his words affecting her whether she liked it or not. Her chin tilted back. She couldn't have said whether she kissed him or he kissed her, but their lips were suddenly sliding together, nibbling and plucking in the darkness. Electrical charges seemed to zip beneath her skin, setting her to full, blooming life.

"I've decided," Dylan said next to her lips a moment later. "You're going to spend the nights with me."

"Don't be . . . such a . . . tyrant," she hissed, her mouth closing and making a sandwich of his lower lip. He gave a soft grunt.

"Don't be such a rebel. Especially when you don't even know what the hell you're rebelling against."

"You expect me to change my nature for you?" she challenged softly, sandwiching his lip again, this time with her teeth. She felt him harden next to her belly at the rough caress. Arousal stabbed at her.

"No," he said, bending down over her. He grabbed her ass with both hands and sealed their bodies even tighter. Alice arched her back, bowing into him, her body responding of its own accord to his touch. Naturally. "As long as you don't expect me to change, either," he said before his mouth settled on hers, firm and forceful. Possessive.

Her body went hot and liquid beneath that kiss.

"Are you going to keep resisting me, Alice?" he asked her seconds later against her lips while he molded her ass cheeks to his palms. Damn him. He knew perfectly well what he'd done to her with that kiss.

"Maybe," she whispered edgily.

"Then I might just have to punish you."

Her body quickened before she even fully understood what he'd said. It was the mere tone of his seductive threat that had done it; the warm hint of humor and, just beneath it, the thrill of steel that was like knuckles tracing her spine or the quick sting of skin against skin.

"Are you afraid?" he asked. Perhaps he'd noticed the hitch in her breath.

"No," she said honestly. Fear wasn't what she was experiencing, being pressed up against him as night enfolded them and he rubbed her ass lasciviously. Their hushed, prickly banter was akin to potent foreplay. "But do you really think that'd work?" she persisted mockingly.

He slid one hand down the skin of her bare arm while he cupped a buttock firmly. His hand enfolded hers. She shivered. "Oh, it'll work," he said, and she knew he'd felt her reaction.

"I'll still be a smart-ass," she assured.

"Changing you isn't the purpose of a little punishment," he

said, and she heard the smile in his voice, the one that reminded her of a pirate.

Her heart started to race. His sexy threat caused any number of erotic scenarios to pop into her head, each of which left her anxious and breathless. Still . . . she couldn't allow him to push her around like this. Just because she wanted him like crazy didn't mean she trusted him. How could she trust him, when she didn't even trust herself?

"I'm not going to the castle tonight," she said shakily.

"Yes, you are," he corrected.

Her heart throbbed at that. There it was again. That extra jolt of excitement that went through her when she and Dylan were together in the darkness, that charged spike of the forbidden.

"All right," she conceded breathlessly after a moment. "I'll come."

"Yes, you *will*," he growled quietly, kissing the corner of her mouth, his tone leaving no doubt about how he expected her to *come*. Excitement rushed her at the thought, but she forced herself to ease back from his embrace slightly.

"To look at the Durand reports, like you asked," she clarified.

She felt him stiffen. Was it her imagination, or did the chirping birds and crickets in the surrounding forest all go quiet? Dylan was one of those rare men whose moods could potentially alter the atmosphere, at least in her opinion. She waited anxiously.

"Fine," he said after a moment. "If that's what you'd like."

"That's what I'd like," she lied.

She heard his muted, derisive snort.

He took her hand, and once again she was following his sure tread in the pitch dark.

ELEVEN

Dylan moved on the bed, straightening a long leg and inadvertently pulling down the white sheet to his waist as he did so.

The sound of soft sheets hissing against naked skin fractured Alice's already fragile attention. She leaned forward in the chair and cast a cautious glance in his direction, using the winged back to shield her curiosity. He was turned away from her, fast asleep. Once they'd reached the castle, she'd insisted on setting herself up to examine the reports in the sitting area versus in bed.

On the dark, tense trip up to the castle, she'd considered insisting that Dylan let her study the reports in an empty office or den somewhere. By the time they'd entered the dark mansion, however, she'd changed her mind. The brooding house drew her in many ways, but there was another side to her fascination with it—a darker side. She hated admitting it to herself, but Dylan's big house scared her. At night, it stood watchful and somehow secretive, perched atop the bluff above the camp and draped in shadow. When she'd entered earlier, hand in hand with Dylan, a hushed sense of expectancy seemed to cloak the hallways and far-off darkened rooms. The heavy pressing sensation tightened Alice's chest and made her jumpy.

Only Dylan's presence scattered the inchoate shadows. She didn't want to be alone in some far-off study while Dylan lay in his bed.

With the exception of Dylan's movement just now, every time she'd warily glanced around the wing of the luxurious chair before, he had been utterly still. It miffed her a little, that he'd fallen asleep so easily, given her restlessness. She scowled as she set down the computer he'd given her to use on the coffee table. She input some numbers from the report into a calculator and jotted down some notes.

The sheet and comforter had pooled around his waist. His back was beautiful, smooth skin gloving defined powerful muscles. She kept tracing the sexy slant from wide chest and back down to a narrow waist. Despite his bangs being longish, the hair at his nape was cut in a sharp line. Concise. She experienced an overwhelming urge to press her nose to that spot, to slick her tongue along his hairline while she inhaled his male scent and mussed the longer hair on top with her greedy fingers.

Arousal prickled her clit. Her nipples chafed against the cups of her bra. She distractedly pressed her fingertips to her warm cheeks and then her lips, scraping the overly sensitive skin with her fingernail. Pleasure rippled through her. She shifted uneasily in the chair, pressing down on the cushion with her hips to get friction on the growing ache at her core.

Time dragged by tortuously slow. For short periods she focused on her task, but she was far less efficient than usual. The ache between her thighs mounted until it was impossible to ignore. Increasingly desperate, she dropped her pen on the seat cushion and moved her hand on her thigh, sliding it upward toward her sex.

Realizing belatedly what she was doing, she straightened the quarterly report in her lap, rattling the pages and lassoing her fraying attention.

It didn't work.

Earlier, Dylan had walked out of the bathroom wearing only a pair of dark blue cotton pajama bottoms. His image was burned in her mind's eye. Alice had tried to look away from the intimidatingly awesome sight of him, but had failed. He'd stalked around the foot of the bed, his dark gaze trained on her.

"Are you sure you don't need anything else?" he'd asked her, nodding significantly at the glass of Diet Dr Pepper and a package of opened Jingdots sitting on the table next to her along with the pile of Durand reports, a notebook, and a calculator. Alice had been thrilled to see a large glass jar filled with the addictive candies sitting on the countertop in the massive kitchen.

She'd yanked her gaze off the compelling vision of his ridged, taut abdomen and defined oblique muscles disappearing beneath the waistband of his pajama bottoms. She'd shaken her head.

"No. I have everything I need right here."

What a fucking liar you're becoming.

He'd paused by the corner bedpost. She looked down at the report in her lap fixedly.

"Stubbornness can be a good thing, Alice. But it's not *always* a virtue."

Her pulse had leapt at her throat, his low gravelly growl tickling her ear. She'd kept her gaze on the report, exhibiting said questionable virtue in spades. He'd climbed into bed without another word, shutting off the bedside lamp and lying down with his back turned toward her.

She'd squinted at the page determinedly, but it was no good.

If she really wanted to get anything done, what she needed was for Dylan Fall to be miles away. Having him in bed just feet away wearing nothing but a thin pair of cotton pajama bottoms that left little to the imagination—well, that was doing nothing for her usual concise ability to focus on the numbers.

To think rationally in general.

In fact, his presence in that bed was a powerful magnet to her attention, not to mention her libido. Her sex felt overly sensitive. Hot. The snug material of her jean shorts seemed to tug at her awareness, stimulating her sex unintentionally.

She leaned forward warily and spied around the wing of the chair. He was still turned away from her, as unmoving as a statue.

She touched herself through her jean shorts, biting her lower lip at the pressure. Things felt very humid between her thighs. She rubbed up and down over her clit with her fingertip, pressing firmly, bucking her hips forward slightly. Sensation pulsed through her, delicious and forbidden, and yet strangely insufficient at once. Frustrated, she slid her forefinger beneath the frayed edge of her shorts and touched the edge of her panties. Her finger slipped beneath the elastic.

She was juicy.

She surrendered for a moment to pleasure.

The sound of Dylan moving on the bed penetrated her consciousness. She jerked her hand like she'd been burned, her wrist thumping against the arm of the chair. Guiltily, she scurried for her pen, ducking behind the wing back for cover. For a tense moment, she was afraid to look toward the bed. She stared at the numbers on the page blindly, her heart pounding out a wild rhythm in her ears. She was acutely aware of the dampness of her finger spreading on the pen she clutched.

"Come here."

She blinked in shock, sure she'd imagined his gravelly command. Her charging heart seemed to pause. Warily, she peered around the chair. He'd turned over in bed, and was facing her. The bed was cast in shadow, but she saw his eyes gleaming from beneath heavy lids. She swallowed convulsively.

"I'm . . . I'm not finished yet," she muttered lamely.

"Yes, you are. With that. Come here," he repeated.

Moving very slowly, she set down the report and stood. She placed the pen she gripped onto the table and started to walk toward the bed. He remained unmoving. His gaze on her was hawklike. Electric. Feeling self-conscious in the spotlight of his attention, she slid her hands against the back of her jean shorts, wiping away her juices.

"Don't," he said sharply, sitting up slightly, leaning on his elbow.

"Don't *what*?" she wondered, her knee bumping against the side of the bed.

He reached for her right wrist. *Oh no.* He held her hand in front of his face. She held her breath as he peered at her fingers with narrowed eyes. *Thank God*, she'd wiped most of the evidence of her arousal on her shorts. Her finger glistened a little still, but it might have been from her soda can or perspiration.

"What are you doing?" she mumbled, pulling on her hand. Instead of freeing her, he lifted her fingers to his face.

To his nose. He inhaled. She froze. He met her stare, and her eyes went wide at what she saw. He looked very hard in that moment. Feral, but fierce. Focused.

"I don't appreciate that, Alice," he said, his quiet tone striking her as ominous. She shivered.

"Appreciate *what*?" she sidestepped.

"I don't appreciate you insinuating you don't need to be touched—that you can do without sex tonight—when it's obvious you're lying."

"It's not obvious—" She gasped loudly, stunned. He'd opened his lips and inserted her finger into his mouth. He laved the skin with a warm tongue, sucking slightly . . . searching. Something pulled like a fishhook at her very core. Heat rushed through her.

"There's nothing more obvious than that," he said with a significant glance after he'd slid her finger out of his mouth. Alice just stared at him, speechless. He looked beyond hungry.

"Take off your clothes," he said.

"Why?" she whispered stupidly. His manner tonight excited her almost unbearably, but she was wary as well.

"Because I'm going to spank you for being so stubborn," he said. His hard mouth flickered. "Then I'm going to make you scream in pleasure because you're so stubborn. Now go on," he urged. "Take off your clothes. I want to watch."

She might have been able to resist if his mouth hadn't softened with humor. *Or* if his face hadn't gone all rigid and forbidding once again when he said he wanted to watch while she undressed. He wasn't really as intimidating as she sometimes imagined. It was lust that made him seem so hard at times.

And he did want her. *Bad*. It was written all over his face and in every line of his coiled muscles in that moment. The knowledge empowered her. She wanted him just as bad. It was an awesome, scary thing, when you looked unblinkingly into the face of desire.

She slid out of the canvas shoes she was wearing and unfastened the top button of her shorts.

"I don't want to be spanked," she said as her fingers lowered. Even the indirect pressure of her fingers sent her sex to tingling.

"We'll see," he said enigmatically, his seductive gaze following the path of her fingers. Her fingers reached the lowest button. "Touch yourself again. Like you did over there in the chair."

She paused. "You were spying," she accused.

"I was watching you work," he replied without a trace of guilt. "When I saw you touch yourself, it was just an added benefit. Do it now. While I'm watching," he demanded tensely. His fixed stare between her thighs seemed to have weight. She moved her fingers over her damp underwear, stimulating her labia and clit. God, she was wet. They moaned in unison. Suddenly, his hand was on her wrist again and he was lifting her hand to his mouth. He sucked her first two fingers into his warm mouth. She watched him suck and tongue her, trembling in the face of his hot greed.

A moment later, her fingers popped out of his mouth and he pushed her hand back between her legs. He pressed her damp fingers between the opened fly of her shorts. He moved his arm, maneuvering her in an up-and-down action, forcing her to touch herself. No, not forcing her. She was quite cooperative. His added pressure and guidance made her more stringent than she would have been normally, that's all. She quaked, it felt so good. His eyes seemed to blaze as he watched himself manipulate her. Then he let go. She kept at it, though, rubbing her pussy rigorously between her opened fly, giving him exactly what he'd asked for, giving herself what she needed.

"Yeah, that's right," he said thickly, his face hovering close to her thighs. "That's mine to watch, Alice," he breathed out.

She wanted to disagree with him, but something about the almost worshipful way he watched her as she masturbated stilled her tongue. Besides, his blatant possessiveness at that moment turned her on. Maybe there were different shades of the truth when it came to a desire this powerful.

"For now it is," she agreed, slipping her fingers beneath the waistband of her underwear and dipping her fingers into abundant cream. In that moment, it pleased her to say it. Her pleasure *was* his. She stirred in her juicy sex, biting her lip to stifle a rough moan. Dylan didn't bother censoring himself. He groaned harshly and placed a large hand on her ass, pushing her to him. He jerked her panties down roughly and pressed his face between her thighs. His tongue slid between her stroking fingers. She cried out shakily at the sensation of his tongue burrowing between her labia and laving her clit firmly. She moved aside her hand, instinctively bowing down to his obvious mastery at the task. Shivers of distilled pleasure convulsed her body.

It all happened so fast. So completely. One moment, she'd half-resisted him.

The next, she was his to do with whatever he wanted.

He covered her outer sex and applied that suction that made her eyes cross while he agitated her clit with his tongue. Her fingers sank into his thick hair, mussing it wantonly. She lost herself for a blissful moment, lost herself to him . . .

She cried out when he lifted his head from between her thighs. He used his fingers to part her labia, and for a lung-burning second, he just stared between her thighs while she looked down at him. He hadn't brought her off with his firm, lashing tongue, but he'd come close. So close. Alice came close, too.

To begging.

Before she could, he dropped his hands and scooted up in the bed to a seated position, his abdomen muscles flexing. She just stood there, dazed and strung tight as a vibrating wire.

"Take off the rest of your clothes and come down in my lap," he said as he tossed a few pillows behind him and leaned back.

A protest rose to her tongue, but she stilled it as she looked down over his body. His arousal was flagrant and awesome, tenting the thin cotton of his pajama bottoms. She could clearly see the shape of the slightly tapered, fat cockhead through the material. Her mouth went dry, her protest evaporating.

It's nothing serious. It's just sex. Just playing around. You're almost twenty-four years old, isn't this the time of your life you're supposed to be having a little fun? It all would have sounded great in her head if another voice wasn't insisting at the same time that Dylan Fall was the exact opposite of a meaningless joy ride; more like riding a rocket into uncharted portions of the galaxy.

She cleared her throat, jerking her gaze off his erection and began to strip off her clothes. When she finally peeled her bra off her breasts, he held out his hands to her. She went.

She had a sketchy idea of what he wanted. He wanted her to lie in his lap so that he could spank her. Her cheeks flamed at the idea as she came down on the mattress on her knees and lowered over his hard thighs. His hand on her waist urged her higher. She halted and bit her lip at the sensation of the crown of his erect cock brushing against her belly. The thin material of his pajama bottoms felt very insubstantial, their mere presence a tease of his nakedness. His hand curved around a bare buttock.

"Come all the way down," he urged, guiding her with his hand. When she'd finally settled, her breasts were on the outside of one of his hard thighs, her bottom draped over the edge of the other, and his cock was burning a swath of her skin along her belly and between her ribs. Her awareness of his cock throbbing against her was so acute, she held her breath.

"Relax," he said, caressing her hip, ass, and thigh.

"That's easy for you to say," she muttered.

He paused in caressing her bottom. His stroking hand had been very distracting.

"You've never been spanked before?"

"No, not like this" she sputtered, frowning. "Just, you know . . ."

"What?" he asked.

"Last night."

"Oh, right," he said, and she could hear the smile in his voice. He resumed caressing her. "That wasn't the same thing. That was in the heat of the moment. This will be more deliberate, do you understand?"

His patient tone, his hand stroking her bare skin and the feeling of his erection pulsing against her belly were all making it hard for her to focus. "You don't need to make it sound like I'm a stupid schoolgirl or something. Not everyone is into kink like you."

He snorted with laughter. She craned around to see his face.

"What?" she demanded.

He shook his head, forcing his smile to fade when he saw her outraged uncertainty.

"Easy, Alice." Something swelled tight in her chest as their gazes held. His fingers lowered, tickling the tender skin just between her thighs and near her sex. Her brittle defenses shattered. She sagged against his hard thighs and awesome erection.

"I didn't mean to laugh," he said quietly. "You're just so . . ."

"What?"

"Prickly. Sweet." He forced her thighs to part with a gentle, pressing fist. She gasped as he penetrated her slick slit with his finger. His facial muscles went rigid. "It's true that I want to fuck you pretty much 24-7," he said as he pushed his finger in and out of her and she bit her lip at the pressure. "It's true that I want to do any number of *kinky* things to you, as you put it. But that doesn't mean that I don't care about you," he told her pointedly, his finger still moving between her thighs.

"You don't even know me," she whispered hoarsely, her gaze held captive by his.

"I know more than you think. And what I don't know, I'm going to discover."

"Dylan," she said heatedly because he withdrew his finger and rubbed the extra lubrication into her outer sex with rigorous precision.

"You're soaking wet." She moaned shakily, speechless in the face of her desire. Her clit burned deliciously under his finger. His mouth went hard. He lifted his hand and gently pushed at the back of her head, urging her forehead to the soft sheets. "When your mouth isn't killing me, your eyes are," he stated harshly. "Keep your head down while I spank you."

For once, she had no response. She bit her lip in wretched excitement as he caressed her bare ass, leaving a trail of her juices with his finger. He lifted his hand and swatted the bottom curve of both her buttocks.

She moaned uncontrollably at the sharp crack of skin against skin and the brisk impact. His cock leapt against her, sending her excitement up another notch. His spank stung, but quickly transformed to an arousing burn. She squirmed in his lap, agitated and aroused. He placed one hand at the base of her spine, stilling her ass, and spanked her three times in taut succession.

"Stop squirming." A thrill went through her at his harsh, desire-bitten tone. She stilled with effort. His cock throbbed beneath her. Her bottom burned. His big hand rubbed the tingling skin. She couldn't muffle her moan of arousal.

"Was it too hard? Because you have to tell me if it was, and I'll attenuate."

She merely shook her head, rolling her forehead on the mattress. He ceased stroking her ass for a moment. She almost could feel his focused attention on her.

"You liked it?"

His low voice curled around her like a caress. She made a sound of assent. It was all she could do, biting her lip as hard as she was. It was humiliating to lie in his lap naked like this, exposed and vulnerable while he spanked her bottom. And yet, she'd never been more excited in her life. He lifted his hand. Her blood raced like a flash flood in her veins. Her sex and ass muscles clenched.

He popped her ass several more times with a cupped palm. When she couldn't stop herself from squirming against his raging erection, he grabbed one ass cheek and squeezed it tight before peppering the captive flesh with spanks.

"Stay still, Alice," he insisted. He paused, rubbing the globe of punished flesh as if to soothe the sting. It only frothed her excitement more.

"I can't," she wailed.

He delved his fingers into the short hair at the back of her head and forced her to turn her head. In her peripheral vision, she saw him studying her profile narrowly. "Am I hurting you?" he demanded.

"No. I mean . . . it stings a little, but . . ."

"*What?*"

"Don't stop," she begged shakily.

He either grunted or cursed, she wasn't sure which. She never figured it out, either, because his hand was falling, cracking her ass several times, making her burn. Everywhere.

Oh God, what was wrong with her? She'd grown feverish. How could she possibly *like* this so much?

Distantly, she realized he'd stopped spanking her, although he rubbed her ass with his free hand. She heard the bedside drawer open as if he'd jerked it tautly.

"What are you doing?" she asked shakily.

"Giving you what you deserve."

Her eyes sprang wide at his grim response. What did she deserve? Something worse than his hand, perhaps? A paddle or whip? Alarmed and curious, she lifted her head and started to twist around. Despite her flash of anxiety, she was also highly aware of the slight dampness at a spot on her upper belly. He was so aroused, so hard, that his desire was seeping through the fabric of his pajama bottoms. She had a sudden urge to gaze down at him, and started to raise herself.

"Put your head *down*, Alice," Dylan told her. Something about the edge to his tone made her follow his command. Then he was sliding his left hand between their pressing bodies.

"Oh . . . Jesus," she cried out when he pressed against her clit, and it began to buzz. "What the hell—"

"It's a vibrator. Come, Alice," he demanded, before he began spanking her ass again.

She wasn't really sure what happened next, except for that she short-circuited as pleasure swamped her. Her orgasm was almost harsh it was so powerful. She came thunderously to the cracking sound of his palm against her ass and the sensation of his cock throbbing furiously beneath her.

He thrust his finger high into her. The vibrator continued to buzz her clit ruthlessly. She cried out as another wave of orgasm shuddered through her. She was vaguely aware of him talking.

"Yeah, that's right. I can feel you," he rasped. "You come so hard, don't you?"

Alice guessed so, because she almost blacked out in the seconds that followed. She came back to herself at a loud cracking sound. The sting on her bottom in tandem with wracking shudders of pleasure was delicious. Forbidden.

"Again," she whispered, shameless at the center of the fire. He gave her what she wanted, smacking her ass briskly as she finished climaxing. He rubbed and molded her buttocks into his palm as her pleasure waned. She sagged into his lap, spent by the force of her orgasm.

It'd felt so good, she realized dazedly. So good, she suspected she should be worried. She pressed her flushed forehead and cheeks into the soft sheets.

"God, I'm as much of a pervert as you are," she moaned. Her mouth twitched at his low, delicious laughter.

"No. You have a way to go before you get there," he said. He pressed gently down on the middle of her back and lifted his hips, grinding his cock against her. Her eyes flew open, her satiation breaking at the reminder of his full, furious continued arousal. "I think I'll show you."

"Show me what?" she muttered, turning her head. He'd removed the hand that was holding the vibrator from between her thighs.

"What a degenerate I really am."

She smiled, both wary and excited. She loved the hint of humor combined with the stern edge she so often heard in his tone. Did he know, somehow, that if it weren't for that gentle amusement, she might rebel at his authority over her senses?

"Okay," she agreed.

"Lift up and scoot back just a little," he said tautly.

She pushed up several inches from his lap, bracing herself on her elbows and knees. She saw a quick flash of movement beneath her. Her eyes went wide. He'd just lowered his pajama bottoms below his testicles. His cock lay along his pelvis and taut belly. The thick head glistened with pre-ejaculate. Her fingers itched to touch him. Her mouth watered.

He reached up and cupped her suspended breasts in both his hands, his thumb and forefinger tracing her nipples, rubbing them. She moaned. He continued to mold one breast and tease the nipple with one hand. The other dropped to his cock. He lifted the staff until it was at a right angle from his body.

"Your breasts haunt me." A thrill of sensation went through her when she heard how tight his voice was with arousal. He fisted his big cock, stroking himself. The sound and sight and feeling of Dylan nearly breaking with need was an addiction she'd never known or imagined. "I'll be in a meeting or on an important phone call, and I close my eyes and see them. Give me something else that'll torture me to remember, Alice. Let me feel them around me."

She acted on instinct, lowering again, this time with her breasts in the center of his lap. She pressed the flesh against his erection, pushing the thick column in the valley between her breasts. His guttural groan sounded so sweet in her ears. She craved seeing him just a fraction as undone as he made her. His hand fell away.

Later, when she recalled what she did next, a wave of heat and embarrassment would rush over her.

She used her hand as one point of pressure and his taut abdomen as the other, squeezing his cock between her breasts. She lifted and writhed in his lap, stroking his cock with her flesh, letting him take his pleasure. He began to shift his hips up and down subtly in a fucking motion, and that thrilled her, too.

When he put the vibrator back on her clit, and started to talk dirty to her—*I'm going to spank you harder this time for being so good, Alice. You're so firm and soft, and I'm so fucking hard for you. That's right. Faster. You're so gorgeous when you're hungry. Touch your nipple. Pinch it*—she lost all vestiges of control or propriety. His cock poked out between the crevice of her squeezing breasts and she leaned down and sucked the succulent head into her mouth. His taste soaked onto her tongue.

She grew even greedier.

She cried out, her sexual trance breaking, at the sound of Dylan cursing harshly and pulling her off him. His cockhead made a popping sound as it leapt from her lips, she'd been sucking him so hard.

"Come here," he said. "Sit up."

She blinked. Was he angry? No, she realized breathlessly as he guided her with his hands until she straddled his lap. He dropped one hand and reached for the opened bedside drawer, his gaze moving from her face to her heaving breasts. He withdrew a condom.

She studied his rigid face a moment later as he held up his cock to enter her. He was nearly as rabid with lust as she was, by the looks of things. She gave a shaky, helpless moan as his cock pierced her slit. He was huge with need, and this was a new position for them. The pressure was intense.

"Shhh," he rasped, holding a portion of her weight with his hands at her waist. He lifted her, and she followed his lead, rising over him. He jerked her back onto his cock with a lewd slap of flesh. Alice gripped his shoulders and shuddered. "Things might start out deliberate with you, but they turn to"—he moaned loudly as they repeated the taut stroke in unison, and again, their straining bodies crashed together—"fucking madness in about two seconds flat," he grated out between clenched teeth.

His large hands lowered to her hips, his fingers delving into the flesh of her ass. Alice had hardly paid attention to what he said, because he was lifting and then grinding her down on him again, and her cry was mixing with his harsh grunt. Pleasure swamped her from every direction. He'd set a faster pace, a ruthless one. She rose and fell over him as he built a delicious friction in her. He looked beyond beautiful to her in that moment, his torso muscles drawn taut and defined, his arms bunched tight. She leaned down and took a gentle bite of an edible-looking shoulder muscle.

He swatted a buttock and then gripped it, driving her down on him. She hugged him desperately, like he was a life preserver and she was in fear of drowning. She pressed her aching breasts against his chest and writhed against him. Time seemed to go still, and yet they moved together, faster and faster, harder and harder. There was something wrong. A pressure was building in her that was beyond the need for sexual release, twining with her arousal and pulling so tight it felt like it squeezed at her heart.

"*Help me*, Dylan," she moaned feverishly.

"God bless it," he hissed, and she heard the fierce anguish in his tone. His hold tightened on her hips and ass, and his muscles swelled impossibly hard. He pounded her down on him, and she was tossed in a sea of pleasure and pressure. She felt his thumb on her clit, pressing and sliding. Lifting her cheek off his chest, she screamed and bucked her hips against his hand. Orgasm slammed into her.

Her eyes sprang wide at the sensation of his cock swelling in her while she shuddered in bliss. He jerked her down against him, nailing her to his lap as he started to come. Through her haze of pleasure, she saw him watching her with a tight, glittering gaze, a slight snarl shaping his mouth. A muscle leapt in his rigid cheek. She felt his cock convulse deep inside her. With a hand at the back of her head, he pushed her down until their foreheads touched.

"I'll always give you what you want, Alice. Always."

The words sounded like they'd been ripped out of his throat. *No*, Alice thought wildly as he moved her over him again, withdrawing and sinking and making her gasp.

Surely she was mistaken, but his words sounded like they'd come from someplace even deeper.

TWELVE

Alice's brain was confused. She couldn't figure out why she kept cherishing those strange, wild, emotional moments making love with Dylan and, at the same time, cringed in anxiety when she found herself indulging in the experiences and the memories so completely.

"I think I'm going crazy," she said quietly, her lips feathering Dylan's skin. They'd turned out the light and set the alarm. He lay on his back with his arms surrounding her, and she on her side pressed against him, her cheek resting on his chest. His idly caressing fingers on her shoulder slowed.

"Why do you say that?"

"Because I can't figure it out."

"What out?" She pressed her lips to his skin, a pressure building in her chest. "Alice?" he prompted.

"Why everything seems so strange."

Her thready whisper sounded very fragile in the yawning silence that followed.

For a moment, he didn't speak. Alice imagined he was trying to decode her feminine oddness in his rational male brain, and again experienced that twinge of discomfort. She was exposing too much of herself.

Dylan's hand opened at her back. He stroked her along her spine. She sensed a tension building in the air between them and regretted her momentary weakness.

"Aren't you going to ask me anything about the reports?" she asked.

"Did you actually get anything out of them? I thought you were too distracted," he murmured. She heard the humor in his voice and suppressed a sigh of relief. The tense moment had passed.

"I didn't attend to them a fraction as much as I could have, but I have a few preliminary observations."

"Okay. Let's hear them," he said, his firm, matter-of-fact tone reassuring her.

"That new marketing firm you hired for the Northwest region? You might want to consider hiring them globally for the VitaThirst campaign," she said, referring to a new and popular Durand energy drink. "That social media campaign they've designed has had a huge effect on sales for the eighteen- to twenty-four-year-old age group, and the cost of their campaign was a fraction of what other regions spent."

"Yeah. I noticed that. The Northwest was our test market, and that's where we hit the hardest."

"To good effect, obviously. But I'd warn against assuming that because you had such awesome results generally, that you'd spent your advertising dollars as wisely as you could have." She delved into her findings, hitting the statistical highlights of what she'd absorbed so far. She sensed Dylan's sharp focus on her the whole time, although he remained silent. "My quick and dirty cost-benefit analysis of the Northwest region campaign versus your more traditional campaigns in the other regions shows a fifteen-to-one payback, factoring in relative population of the region, age group disbursement, company costs and net sales," she finished.

"If that's true, then we also might need to make a correction in regard to our targeted market as well. We were going for the twenty-five- to thirty-nine-year-old health-obsessed urbanite," Dylan mused.

"That's exactly what I was thinking. The numbers suggest that the younger person in more sparsely populated, 'outdoorsy' regions might be just as prime for the product, if not more so, than your current target. Those commercials that little advertising firm came up with were hilarious. They went viral, you know," Alice said, yawning. It took her a few seconds to realize he didn't speak. "If you don't believe me, I can show you my numbers. I drilled it down. The spike in sales in that region *has* to be due to that advertising campaign." She started to get up from bed despite her exhaustion, determined to get her notebook and defend herself.

Dylan halted her. He pulled her back against him.

"I'm not doubting you. I'm amazed, that's all. You got all that, after looking at those reports—by your own admission distractedly—for a little over an hour?"

"I can do better with more time. I only got through the VitaThirst numbers."

He laughed. The low rough sound of his mirth made her stiffen.

"Relax, Alice," he said sternly, and she realized he'd sensed her bristling. He sighed and pushed at the back of her head, urging her back to her relaxing pose. She resisted a little, until her cheek touched his skin and she inhaled his addictive scent. He sank his fingers into her hair.

"I'm *impressed*, not doubting you," he added gruffly. Her pique evaporated at his sincerity. "Where do you think you got that head for numbers from?" he asked after a moment of her melting into him as he massaged her scalp. She closed her eyes, her flesh growing heavy and warm.

"Certainly not Sissy. She got confused counting change. In all fairness, though, she may have been a genius before meth turned her brain into Swiss cheese," she mumbled.

"You never mention your dad."

Her eyelids flew open. Had Dylan felt her eyelashes flick against his skin?

"You said he'd passed away. Did you know him?" he asked.

"No," she replied shortly. She couldn't stop herself from swallowing thickly, and thought Dylan might have felt the convulsion of her throat. She held her breath, worried she was revealing too much. His fingertips continued to move in circular, soothing motions on her scalp.

"Do you think you got your mathematical brilliance from him?" Dylan asked.

For several seconds, her lungs locked. Finally, they gave with a hitching inhale. "I sincerely doubt it," she said.

"Why do you doubt it? Alice?" he prompted when she didn't speak.

It struck her how gentle he sounded in those moments as he held her fast against him and stroked her. It only increased the swelling pressure in her chest. Was Dylan patronizing her? She lifted off him abruptly.

"Just how far back in my life did Durand go when they did that background check?" she blurted out.

"*What?*"

"Answer me, damn it. If you know something about my father from that stupid investigation Durand Enterprises did, just say so. Don't *play* with me."

"I didn't learn anything about your father," he replied in a hard tone that informed her he was insulted. "It was a standard report about criminal charges or any unusual circumstances you'd been involved in since you turned eighteen. What did you *think* I'd find out about your dad?"

"Nothing. I just wish you'd stop—" She cut herself off suddenly, unsure of what she wanted to say. "*Pushing* me," she finally hissed between clenched teeth. She turned over on her side and clamped her eyelids shut when she realized how tense and crazy she sounded. Mortification swelled inside her for a few awful seconds. The truth did, too. She had a practiced lie at the ready about her father dying in a car accident before she was born, but it wouldn't leave her throat for some reason. Not while she was with Dylan, it wouldn't.

She didn't know who her father was, but she knew *enough* to harbor shame. The probable truth was disgusting.

Wasn't she—Alice—disgusting, in turn?

Shame flooded her, anger fast on its heels. It was all *his* fault. She pulled out of Dylan's arms.

"I'm going," she said. The need to be alone suddenly over-whelmed her, that harsh mandate of a wounded animal. She jerked furiously when Dylan halted her with a firm grip on her upper arms.

"Alice, stop it," he said firmly.

"I don't know who my father is! There. Are you happy?" she spat.

The silence seemed to press on her eardrums and chest. She didn't know why she'd said it. Desperation? Irrational anger at Dylan for inspiring such a friction of feelings inside her? Maybe she wanted to let him in.

Maybe she just wanted to show him her ugliness, and get his inevitable dislike of her over with and done.

"I don't know who my father is, either."

He said it so evenly, so calmly, it took her a moment to soak in what he'd said. When it did, all the air rushed out of her lungs. *"What?"*

"My mother was a prostitute. My father could have been one of any number of assholes, one as worthless as the next."

She heard herself panting softly. "I don't believe that."

"It's the truth," he said, and this time, she heard the tiny edge of anger to his tone, the legacy of a defensiveness she understood all too well. It *was* true. That hint of vulnerability, a distant echo, given the man he'd become, was the stamp of the genuine. He really *was* akin to her, in a way.

The glimpse of his reality made her feel twice as naked, yet strangely . . . a little stronger, too.

He exhaled, and at the same time, slowly brought her back

against him. Her nipples brushed against the taut skin covering his ribs, and she relented, sinking against him. His hand spread again at the back of her skull. Those magical fingers . . .

"Why do you say you don't believe it?" he asked quietly after a full moment of silence.

"Because . . . of who you are," she whispered brokenly. "You're so . . ." *Brilliant. Special. Wonderful.*

He cradled her chin with his hand and lifted. She was glad for the cloak of darkness when she raised her face to his.

"Thanks. And so are you, Alice," he said as if he'd heard her thoughts. "We define who we are with our everyday lives. Not by our parents. Not by the circumstances to which we're born. You're living proof of that."

She gulped thickly, despised tears filling her eyes. "But what if . . ." She broke off because emotion was closing off her throat, and she sounded so weak. So helpless.

"What if *what*?" Dylan asked.

She closed her eyes. Tears spurted down her cheek. "Nothing," she managed thickly. She pulled away again, desperate that he not feel the wetness of her tears, the evidence of her weakness.

"Alice—"

"I'm not leaving. I'm just going to the bathroom," she reassured through a congested throat.

He let her go, but she felt his eyes on her as she moved through the darkness.

DYLAN had an overnight trip planned to New York on Friday. He instructed her—a little too sternly for Alice's liking—to return to her cabin on Friday night after her shift was finished and lock the door.

"Why are you so paranoid?" Alice demanded as they left the

darkened castle early on Friday morning, walking out into a humid predawn. "Did you find something out about that person following me in the woods?" she asked, recalling how he'd said he'd look into the matter.

"Not really," he said, taking her hand and leading her across the dewy side lawn toward the woods. "I asked the sheriff of Morgantown to come out and I reported the incident. I like to keep him apprised of what goes on here, especially when camp is in session. His name is Jim Sheridan. He's an old friend."

"What did he say?" Alice asked.

"That it was more than likely someone else taking an early morning jog, just like you."

"So why are you so worried about me being attacked or something?" she asked with amused puzzlement.

"Because I saw how afraid you were that morning," he replied simply.

She'd wanted to thank him for that—she *had* been terrified that morning—but didn't know how to without sounding stupid. She gave his hand a warm squeeze instead. He kept his gaze trained ahead on the shadow of the tree line, but she thought he'd understood when he squeezed her back.

FOR the last event before supper that night, the scheduled mandatory camp activity was a group discussion about trust along with an exercise. At the last moment, Kehoe announced that two assigned teams would participate in the event together. Alice didn't think it was chance that her campers got paired up with Brooke Seifert's Silver Team. She worried several of the Durand managers had noticed how the chill factor went to negative territory whenever Alice and Brooke were around each other.

Alice gritted her teeth and dove into the task.

The guided group discussion went all right, seeing how she and Brooke basically had only to follow a loosely structured script designed for group leaders. They didn't really have to interact personally with one another. The hitch came afterward, during the activity.

It was the standard organizational trust activity, where team members were asked to let go of control and fall backwards into a peer, trusting to be caught and kept from harm. Brooke and Alice demonstrated using members from their team how to safely catch, slowing the fall and gently guiding the person to the lawn. The kids practiced on members of their own team. Then, the circle of trust was widened to include less familiar members of the other team. They were nearing the end of the exercise, and dinnertime was drawing near, when Terrance Brown suddenly called out.

"Hey, Alice. You've got to do it now. Counselor to counselor, Red Team versus Silver Team, *Alice versus Brooke*," he said dramatically, putting up his hands into claws like he was announcing Godzilla versus Mothra. Alice glared at Terrance. Several of the kids laughed, but she didn't think they understood why entirely. Leave it to Terrance, the walking social barometer, to have picked up on the dislike between Brooke and Alice.

"Yeah," Judith said, tossing her long dark hair over her shoulder and smirking as she glanced between Alice and Brooke. "I'd like to see that."

I'll bet you would.

Judith's sneering contempt of Alice hadn't eased up a bit. Alice glanced at Brooke, who was watching her with bitchy wariness.

"Well?" Alice asked, shrugging and moving into position behind her. Might as well get this over with.

"Why do I have to go first?" Brooke hissed as the kids crowded around excitedly in a loose circle to watch. Their talking and laughing muted Brooke's and her conversation.

"Why do you care? Do you have some reason not to trust me?" Alice asked very quietly.

Brooke's gaze skittered anxiously off the surrounding faces and then back at Alice.

"I'm not going to drop you. *I'm* not that petty," Alice said through stiff lips, making a subtle reference to what Brooke had done on the zip-line platform.

Just as she suspected, her reassurance had the opposite effect on Brooke, who briefly looked even more nervous. Nevertheless, Brooke lifted her chin and turned around, a grim expression of determination falling over her face.

Alice had to hand it to her. She had courage, especially since Alice would have *loved* to see her fall on her ass in front of all the kids.

And Brooke knew it.

In the periphery of her vision, she saw Kehoe's head appear at the back of the crowd. Brooke stood stiff as a statue. She fell gracefully, and Alice caught her with ease. As she stood, Brooke's gaze glided over the crowd and landed on Kehoe. They switched places, and Brooke brought her gently to the grass.

Alice calmly ignored Terrance's and Judith's disappointed expressions at the lack of drama (in Terrance's case) or violence (in Judith's). Alice praised the kids for a job well done and dismissed them to wash up for dinner. Brooke took off toward the cabins, surrounded by her team. Alice did the same, herding her chattering campers. In the distance, Kehoe walked toward the main lodge alone.

She was *positive* Brooke hadn't seen Kehoe come to observe. Brook had been turned away from him when he'd quietly arrived at the back of the circle. Alice, on the other hand, had fallen knowing Brooke was aware of Kehoe by the time they'd switched places.

So why had Brooke trusted that Alice would catch her when she had no knowledge of Kehoe hovering? The question festered

like a splinter under her skin. Somehow, it meant Brooke had been
the bigger person. Brooke had excelled at the personal challenge,
choosing to trust even when she doubted . . .

While Alice had never really taken a risk like Brooke had. She'd
never trusted.

Alice had only played it safe.

THAT night after dinner and the evening activity, Alice sat with
three of the girls on the sectional couch in the common room. A
television show had got them casually talking about the highs and
lows of dating, and—much to Alice's shock—Judith had actually
drifted over from where she'd sat alone reading and listened in on
the conversation. Predictably, she remained standing, hovering
around the periphery, instead of totally entering their circle.

"You're giving him too much power over you," Judith said
abruptly as Darcy Givens, a talkative, anxious-to-please sixteen-
year-old, gushed and anguished over a guy in her neighborhood
back home. "He'll walk all over you with that attitude. You're like
a puppy begging to be petted. You'll get kicked instead."

Darcy looked stung.

"What are you hoping to achieve by talking to her like that,
Judith?" Alice wondered, irritated and genuinely curious at once.

Judith's expression turned truculent as she regarded Alice. "I'm
trying to give her some advice."

"*Really?*" Alice asked.

"Why else would I have bothered coming over here with you
losers?" Judith snapped. She started to turn away in a huff.

"If you really meant to help Darcy out, then sit down and *do*
it," Alice challenged. Judith's hair whipped around her shoulders.
She glared at Alice fiercely. Alice just arched her eyebrows in
pointed expectancy.

A few seconds later, Judith fell to the sofa, crossing her arms in a belligerent gesture. Alice inhaled slowly to calm herself.

"I believe you," Alice said, holding Judith's stare.

"You believe me about *what*?" Judith asked, sarcasm dripping like toxic ooze.

Alice silenced her own knee-jerk, aggressive response with gargantuan effort.

"I *believe* you wanted to help out Darcy. I've seen how good you are with Jill," Alice said pointedly, referring to Jill Sanchez, the young, vulnerable girl who worshipped Judith. In the distance, Jill looked up from where she was diligently drawing in her sketchbook. Art had proven to be Jill's strength and solace. Alice was keeping close tabs on her with the camp's talented art therapist, Miguel Cabrera. Jill was still drawing and painting comfortable landscapes versus working out some of her past domestic trauma through her art, but Miguel assured Alice she'd venture into more challenging topics when she felt more psychologically secure.

Presently, Judith noticed Jill's anxious expression, and forced the frown from her face. She smiled reassuringly at the girl. Looking reassured, Jill went back to her drawing. Alice nodded once at Judith in approval.

"When you come on so strong," Alice continued more softly, "it's really hard to take in what you're saying." Judith opened her mouth to retort. "A bitchy attitude gets through to people, Judith," Alice said before the girl could interrupt. "Just not in the way that you want it to. It hurts. It doesn't help. If you came over to give advice, then the arrow strayed way off target by the way you offered that help."

Judith just stared for a moment, her mouth falling open.

"Did you really mean to help me out?" Darcy asked shakily after a tense moment.

"Yeah," Judith mumbled irritably, staring at the carpet.

"Thanks," Darcy said.

Judith twitched slightly in a "no problem" gesture and Alice sensed the give in her armor.

"And to be honest, I think Judith had a point, Darcy," Alice said, trying to diffuse the girl's focus on Judith. "You're not acting like a slobbering puppy, I don't mean that. But this guy's attention isn't going to make your life perfect, and you're acting like it will."

"But he's so incredible," Darcy persisted.

"If you're so preoccupied with *his* incredibleness, he's never going to notice yours," Judith said.

Alice blinked, stunned by the girl's conciseness. "Now *that's* good advice," she said, a smile breaking free.

"Maybe you're right," Darcy acknowledged.

Judith looked at Alice warily from beneath a lowered brow. Hopefully. A rush of amazement went through Alice. She recognized Judith's expression.

Alice was the one usually wearing it.

"I'm here early," Crystal Dean called out, approaching them. It felt like the fragile moment among Alice and the girls fractured. "It's Friday night, Alice. Why don't you take off? I saw some of the other counselors out on the grounds, and they were talking about going into Morgantown to get something to eat. Maybe you can join them."

Judith abruptly got up.

"Judith," Alice called out, getting up from the couch as well. Judith flew out of the common room. Alice followed her down the girl's hallway, hoping to solidify the tenuous connection. Before she could reach her, however, Judith disappeared into her room and slammed the door behind her. Alice pulled up short and started to walk away.

Suddenly, she halted.

She recognized this particular gesture on Judith's part as well, and had responded to it instinctively by departing. Didn't Alice constantly retreat when her defenses were breached, eager to be alone so that she could lick her wounds and let the scar tissue build up once again?

She thought of last night, in bed with Dylan. She'd felt raw and exposed when he'd asked about her father. But Dylan hadn't let her run away. Not completely. He'd only let her retreat to the bathroom for a bit to gather herself.

When she'd reemerged and come back to the bed, he hadn't said another word. He'd just held and stroked her until she'd fallen asleep, his quiet acceptance and strong embrace speaking louder than words.

Well, she wasn't as skilled at this communication thing as Dylan. But she wasn't going to just give up, either. Alice hurried to the common room and found some paper and a pen. She wrote briskly, and then folded the note.

"Night, everybody," she called out to the kids. She smiled broadly at the loud chorus of good-byes. She was starting to really like her kids.

"Don't do anything I wouldn't do tonight, Alice!" Terrance called out slyly.

"Okay, so don't be silent and tactful?" she tossed off over her shoulder, giving the boy a fond but pointed glance. Terrance's brown eyes went wide. He and his friends roared with laughter. Alice paused, waiting for their amusement to quiet. "Remember what we're doing Monday before breakfast?" she asked Terrance.

Terrance rolled his eyes and groaned. "Ah, no. You *really* going to make me go jogging with you? And *that* early in the morning?"

"You lost the bet during football practice," Alice said, shrugging. "A deal is a deal. You go jogging with me at least three times a week. You afraid you can't keep up?"

"I'll keep up," Terrance insisted while his friends snickered.

"Can I go, too?" Justin Arun piped up.

"No, just me and Alice, fool," Terrance said, scowling forbiddingly at his friend.

Alice suppressed a grin. Terrance acted miffed about their deal, but she could tell he was secretly pleased to have been singled out for a little individual time with her. She prayed she could sell him on the benefits of exercise. She knew Terrance was strong physically from their football practices and various activities. He was just alarmingly obese, and had to deal with a chronic illness—diabetes—that most adults struggled with when it came to treatment compliance. Just today, the visiting physician had okayed Terrance for jogging. Alice had her work cut out for her.

On so many levels.

Before she left for the night, she slid the folded note under Judith's door.

THAT night, she thought a lot about her encounter with Judith, and her earlier experience with Dylan. Was Dylan as challenged by Alice's defensiveness and suspiciousness as Alice was by Judith's? The thought made her feel a little guilty.

It also made her feel a lot heartsore, because she couldn't make it up to him. Dylan was hundreds of miles away.

After she walked out of the Red Team cabin that night, her gaze was immediately drawn to the top of the tree line and the distant bluff. She couldn't see it because of the woods, but the castle was up there, empty as a shell without its master.

A sharp, poignant feeling rose in her chest. It took her a moment to recognize it as potent longing. She missed him. Like hell.

And she'd just seen him this morning.

A huge red warning flag unfurled in her mind's eye.

You are making the biggest mistake of your life, caring about him.

"Hey, Alice," Dave Epstein called out to the right of her, interrupting her self-lecture. She turned to see Dave and Kuvi walking toward her.

"Some of us are going into town to the Lakeside Tavern. They're supposed to have good pizza. Gina Sayre lives in Michigan, so she brought her car to camp," Kuvi said, referring to another counselor. "You up for it?"

Alice hesitated. Dylan had said he wanted her to stay in behind a locked door tonight. But surely he was overdoing his cautionary measures.

Besides, Dylan Fall didn't control her.

"Yeah, sounds good," Alice agreed, falling into step beside her friends.

Of course nothing sinister happened that night, and Alice managed to put her longing for a man that was way out of her league on the backburner—for a few hours, anyway—while she drank a few beers and socialized with her fellow counselors at a cute lakeside pizza place. She had a good time sitting on the back patio with her friends, even if she sensed Thad's gaze on her cheek way too often. She hoped the fact that she treated Thad exactly the same as her other friends sent a gentle message to him.

Well, nothing *majorly* sinister happened that night, anyway. Something odd *did*. The more Alice thought about it later, the more it bothered her.

She walked with Kuvi, Thad, Dave, and Gina to the car when their night came to an end. The parking lot was dimly lit. Alice was carrying a to-go pizza box, and the menu attached to it flew off, skittering away in the lake breeze. The others kept going, but Thad halted.

"Go ahead, I'll catch up," Alice assured him. The two of them hadn't really had a chance to rehash the conversation they'd started before Dylan interrupted them last night, and Alice wasn't really up for doing so at the moment. Thad looked a little disappointed, but nodded once before he jogged to catch up with the others.

Alice chased after the wind-tossed menu. After she'd caught it, she spotted a garbage can at the edge of the parking lot. As she turned away from disposing of the paper, her gaze glided past a parked car. A man was slumped behind the wheel. She recognized the averted profile. He turned to her suddenly, maybe sensing her attention on him. An uncomfortable jolt went through her as she briefly locked stares with Sal Rigo, one of the Durand managers.

She hurried across the dark parking lot, her skin tingling, eager to catch up with her friends.

Was Rigo following them? They'd been told several times by Sebastian Kehoe that their personal time was their own. But was that just a Durand ploy, in order to observe them when their guard was down?

As soon as they all got in the car and exited the parking lot, Alice told the other four about seeing Rigo. Everyone was surprised, but Dave got mad.

"Figures," Dave stated bitterly. "They're always spying on us."

"I saw Rigo following us when we left the beach this afternoon," Kuvi said to Thad and Alice. "He creeps me out. I've seen him lurking around our cabin, too."

"Really?" Alice asked Kuvi, who nodded.

"But Rigo was probably just waiting for someone after they ate at the Lakeside, right?" Gina reasoned. "It's a popular spot in Morgantown. Plus, as a Durand employee, Rigo probably lives around here. Over half the executives they employ do. He might be a regular at the Lakeside, for all we know."

"I didn't see him anywhere in that place. Did any of you?" Alice asked the others.

All of them shook their heads.

"Well he didn't come there to admire the view of the parking lot," Alice mumbled, staring blindly out the window.

What if the counselors *were* being followed?

What if the Durand managers—or Sebastian Kehoe himself—knew about her nocturnal meetings with Dylan Fall?

Did Dylan himself approve of this surveillance? If so . . . did that mean that the Durand employees were colluding with their boss's activities? Or was Dylan in the dark about the surveillance as well?

THIRTEEN

He returned home from his business trip at around noon and made it only as far as his in-home office. Without pause, Dylan plunged into a number of calls to the marketing division. He wanted to clear his slate before he met with Alice. Her concise, brilliant drill-down of the numbers followed by his meeting with Durand's northeastern region vice president yesterday had engineered the structure for a bold new marketing plan for VitaThirst utilizing the advertising firm Alice had recommended.

"Fall," he answered distractedly into the phone when it rang at around one thirty. He assumed it'd be one of the marketing managers getting back to him with the data he wanted.

"Dylan? It's Sidney."

Dylan blinked at hearing the name, trying to clear the number-strewn contents of his brain.

"Sidney? Is anything wrong?"

"I thought I was supposed to be the one asking you that," Sidney said. Dylan imagined the sharp amused glint in the eminent psychiatrist's eyes. Sidney had his own private practice in Morgantown, but he also did consulting work for Durand Enterprises on an international basis. It was easy for Dylan to call up an image of the doctor. When he'd been fourteen years old, he'd seen Sidney once a week in the summer months every year before he'd left for college. That, and an adult friendship, had made Sidney one of a handful of true confidants. He'd selected Sidney to be one of his

Durand advisors, and often sought his counsel, valuing his psychological acumen on issues ranging from staff motivation to complicated business negotiations.

"Nothing's wrong," Dylan said, dragging his glasses off his head and rubbing his burning eyes. He hadn't been getting much sleep lately, thanks to Alice. He planned to be getting little rest again tonight, and he was damn well looking forward to it.

"Any more nightmares?" Sidney asked.

"No. Nothing obvious. Or that she's told me about, anyway. But as I've said, she's far from being an open book. She does seem less anxious, though."

"And she and you are still—"

"*Yes.*"

He immediately regretted his sharpness. It was guilt that was making him so defensive with his old friend—a man he trusted at this point in his life more than anyone. And Sidney had looked *very* worried when Dylan had told him he and Alice were sleeping together. It had been an unexpected situation, Alice looking up at him in those stables with desperate, raw need blazing in her eyes.

It'd been an unexpected *complication*, one he hadn't been able to resist.

It was too late to go back now. He'd crossed the line. She wasn't something he was going to give up without a fight. She was worth too much.

Everything, in fact.

Sidney cleared his throat. "You sound worried."

"Is that a surprise?" Dylan asked gruffly.

"No. Of course not. I had thought, given the way things were progressing from the first, there might be more of these— *intrusions* on her part. The gong. Her fear in the woods. The vision in the hallway. Fascinating, all of it."

"She's not the subject of one of your academic journal articles."

"Of course not. At any rate, it seems her integration process has slowed. Anxiety isn't pleasant, but it can signal that something is trying to rise from the unconscious mind. It's undesirable to slow that process until it halts completely. A pressure is required, a subtle but firm one. Maybe it's time you stepped up the process, let a little more light into the darkness, so to speak. Maybe you should expose her to *more* potential triggers instead of less."

"Do you really think that's wise?" Dylan asked slowly. "I thought you said if we just dumped the truth on her, it could have unforeseen, potentially catastrophic results."

"I'm not suggesting we bludgeon her with the truth, perhaps just test her a little more intensely so that we can observe the results. I don't pretend to be an expert on the precise amount of pressure required."

"You're the best expert we have. You're one of the best in the world," Dylan said.

"Every human being is different, every mind's strengths and weaknesses impossible to tally given a specific stressor."

Dylan exhaled, but the tension remained in his muscles. "I'm starting to think we should just tell her. There are times when I look into her eyes, and she seems . . . so close."

"I still think it'd be best not to force the issue entirely. It's impossible to know precisely, just how much anxiety she's experiencing. Especially since, as you've reported, she disguises it so well. By all reports, she's functioning adequately at the camp."

"I told you not to rely on Kehoe's reports alone," Dylan said sternly. "He's taken a dislike to her. My more objective observers tell me she's *excelling* as a counselor. She's compassionate, smart, hardworking, not afraid to try new strategies, and the kids and staff love her."

"All the better for Durand Enterprises. You don't suppose Kehoe suspects—"

"No. I don't see how he could. He's just noticed my interest in her, that's all. He suspects it's about sex, but he knows that's not my typical MO—to show interest in a Durand recruit—so he's playing cautious. He's puzzled and pissed off about the whole thing, but there's nothing he can do without exposing his own slithering ways. He's got people sniffing around Alice, but he hasn't found the trail yet."

"Watch yourself there."

"I'm very aware of Kehoe. And I'm keeping a close eye on *her* around the clock."

"Good. We all knew this was an unavoidable risk. That's why I suggested this course of action. It was impossible to gauge her accurately without introducing her to the environment."

Dylan pressed his fingertips to his eyelids. "When she's with me, she's less confused. Less overwhelmed."

"She's got other things to occupy her," Sidney said wryly.

"You said yourself that might not be a bad thing," Dylan bit out. He took a moment to calm his flash of anger.

"I did say it was possible. The problem is, just about *anything* is possible in this situation."

"If you're so damn worried about the potential damage I'm doing her, why don't you come and see her yourself?"

"Dylan, I don't think you're damaging her. I only meant that we don't want sex to be *too* much of a Band-Aid. And yes, I'd like to meet her. Very much. How do we manage that?"

"You could stop by unexpectedly. She has Sundays off."

"And she'll be there, at the house with you." Again, that subtle, but stinging note of condemnation.

"Damn it, Sidney, you know the last thing I want to do is have this blow up in our faces. I wouldn't have taken things to this level if I didn't care so much."

"I know that. Perhaps that's the issue at hand."

"What's that supposed to mean?" Dylan demanded, immediately recognizing the other man's misleadingly mild tone for what it was.

Sidney sighed, sounding a little regretful that he'd broached the topic. "No one knows as well as I do how much guilt you harbored in regard to this girl. I know you care, but as your onetime psychiatrist, I can't help but feel that the majority of your emotional baggage in regard to her relates to a misplaced sense of responsibility and guilt for—"

"Cut the psycho-crap. I'm not your patient anymore, Sidney. You're not my doctor. And Alice and I are consenting adults. You aren't in my head. You don't know what this means to me, even if you're convinced you do."

Again, Sidney sighed. "You're right. I'm sorry. I'll stop by tomorrow."

"Good," Dylan said, stifling his anger.

"I *am* curious to see her," Sidney said thoughtfully after a pause. "I would imagine she's quite special, despite what you've told me about her history. There must be a glimmer of what *could* have been."

Dylan clenched his jaw hard. Sidney hadn't meant to sound patronizing. It was just that his scientific brain couldn't help but be fascinated by this unprecedented circumstance.

"Come by and meet her. I think you'll see a hell of a lot more than just a glimmer. She's a beacon."

"Or a boatload of fireworks with a cloud of sparks flying in every direction around it?" Sidney asked quietly.

Dylan firmly changed the subject to a safer one.

SHE and Dylan had agreed that he would wait for her at the tree line that Saturday after she'd finished work for the day. He'd suggested that they were going to spend the night together—the *full* night for once, since Alice had Saturday evenings and Sundays off. However, their parting on Friday morning had been hurried and furtive because they'd heard a cabin door opening and closing

through the trees. There hadn't been time for them to exchange
many details about what they'd be doing Saturday night.

Alice had mentioned in passing to Kuvi that she shouldn't be
surprised if Alice didn't return over the weekend. Kuvi's conspiratorial wink at hearing this made Alice's guilt swell. It was only a
matter of time before Kuvi and Dave figured out she wasn't stealing away at night to be with Thad. She'd just have to cross that
bridge when she got to it.

She wasn't sure if she should pack a bag or not. The idea of
showing up to meet Dylan carrying an overnight bag made her
feel too vulnerable, her expectations exposed. What if Dylan had
changed his mind about his plans in the interim? So she skipped
the bag. She'd deal with the need for a change of clothes if and
when the situation arose.

Since it was the first time they'd met secretly in broad daylight
and Alice now knew about the entrance to the woods leading to
the castle, Dylan had grudgingly agreed it would be safe for her
to approach alone. Besides, from his observation post at the edge
of the trees, Alice knew he could watch the majority of her solitary
walk toward him.

By the time she left for their assigned meeting at half past three
that afternoon, her nerves were jumping in anticipation of seeing him
again, no matter how much she told herself to relax. It seemed like
forever since they'd parted in the darkness early on Friday morning.

A lot had happened with her work since she'd last seen him.
Just an hour ago, she'd pulled Judith aside, and told her she'd liked
the way she'd turned around the situation with Darcy last night.
Presently, Alice recalled their conversation with a combination of
irritation and bemused satisfaction.

*"Is that what you wanted to talk to me about?" Judith had
asked stiffly, referring to the note Alice had left last night. Her
attitude wasn't quite as defensive as it had been last night, but it
wasn't exactly welcoming, either.*

"*Yeah, in part,*" *Alice agreed.* "*As you probably know, the counselors are expected to choose a student team leader this weekend.*"

"*So?*"

"*After watching you with Jill all week, and after seeing how you managed to get past your pride last night and say something meaningful to Darcy, I was considering making you team leader. The kids respect you, grudgingly at times, given your attitude, but they do. They'd follow you.*"

Alice might as well have dropped a bomb. Judith looked that stunned.

"*You're shitting me,*" *Judith stated flatly.*

"*No.*"

"*What about Noble D? Everyone says he's been team leader the past two years.*"

"*He's the obvious choice,*" *Alice said matter-of-factly.* "*You're the right one.*"

"*You think so?*" *Judith bristled.*

"*Yeah. I think so. And that's what counts,*" *Alice said with more confidence than she felt.* "*So, do you want the job or not?*"

Judith blinked and shook her head, half dazed and half cynically disbelieving. "*Me, lead this bunch of losers?*"

"*If you agree to do it, you'll have to stop calling them losers. They'll be yours, Judith. Yours to care about. Yours to protect.*"

"*Is that the real reason you're picking me?*" *Judith asked, her nasty attitude making a flaming reappearance.*

"*Maybe,*" *Alice replied edgily. She noticed Judith's extra-offended expression and exhaled, silently begging for patience.* "*I'm asking you to do it because I think you'd be fantastic at leading. If you can ever come off that damn pedestal and stop playing the lone bitch, that is.*"

"*Quit calling me a bitch, bitch,*" *Judith seethed, taking an angry step toward her, fists bunched tight. Alice stepped in just as aggressively.*

"*I'm not calling you a bitch. I'm saying you act like one some-times,*" Alice grated out, now *eye-to-eye with the girl.* "*I think you can do this, Judith. But you're going to have to sacrifice the ped-estal and show the kids the humanity I know you have. In spades. So what's it going to be? Are you going to take the easy route and back down from this? Or are you going to accept the challenge?*"

"*I'm not afraid. I'm not gonna back down.*"

"*Good. Then I'll make the announcement. You're the Red Team's student leader. Don't disappoint me, Judith,*" Alice warned with a pointed glare before she turned and walked away.

In reflection, it hardly seemed like the joyful event she'd first imagined when she'd heard about her role in bestowing the honor on a student. It'd been more like the prelude to a fistfight. Just the memory of the volatile exchange got Alice worked up all over again, her adrenaline pumping, primed for a fight.

Alice knew firsthand that warm, fuzzy expectations only earned her a slew of disappointment. In reality, things had gone *exactly* as they should have, given Judith's issues.

Given Alice's own.

As she walked through the sunny pasture and all these thoughts swam around in her head, she realized she was perhaps girding herself for her meeting with Dylan . . . defending herself against more rainbows and sunshine fantasies. There was nothing that created a stampede of wild anticipation and unrealistic expecta-tions than the topic of Dylan Fall.

After he'd told her about his mother being a prostitute, and how he didn't know the identity of his father, it was like another dimension had been added to how she felt about him. And how she felt about him was already complex enough as it was. No mat-ter how far he'd left that vulnerable boy behind to become the powerful man he was today, it couldn't have been easy for Dylan to admit that to her. She could only imagine the bravery it would take to speak something like that aloud.

She could only imagine, because Alice herself didn't possess the courage to speak of a shame like that.

Stepping into the shadow of the thick woods a moment later, she sighed in relief. It was a sunny, humid day. Peering around, she stole deeper into the canopied forest. She'd broken a sweat even during the relatively short walk from the camp. Wiping the moisture off her brow, she squinted, adjusting her eyes to the dimness.

At first, she thought he wasn't there. Disappointment flooded her. Then a flicker of movement caught her eye.

She started.

He leaned against a wide oak tree, completely still save that movement she'd caught—a lifting of a thumb on the hand that rested on his thigh. Had he made the movement to betray his camouflage and draw her attention? One long leg was bent, one booted foot and his ass resting against the bark of the tree. She went nearly as still as him, her gaze seeking him out in the shadows. Even her heart seemed to go motionless for a split second. She made out the glint of his eyes as he watched her.

"Let me guess," she said in a hushed tone as the tops of the trees sighed in a brisk lake breeze. "When you were here at Camp Durand, you excelled at woodcraft," she said wryly, taking a step toward him.

"Never underestimate the ability to take your enemy by surprise," he replied.

"Is that what I am? An enemy?" she asked provocatively, taking another step toward him. He remained unmoving, his narrowed gaze tracking her. He looked exceptionally good resting against that tree, his lean, powerful body seemingly relaxed, but in reality poised for action. Alice saw that he wore jeans and a plain cobalt-blue T-shirt. Dylan did incredible things to expensive European suits, but it struck her that he was born to wear jeans. They emphasized his ruggedness, his unconventionality, his origins. She realized it was one of the things she loved about him, the unique combination of power, street smarts, sophistication, and bold brute strength.

He shook his head ever so slightly and glanced at the sunny meadow where she'd just approached. "I was watching your face as you walked up just now. You're not my enemy, but you sure looked like you were spoiling for a fight."

Heat rushed into her cheeks when she realized he'd read her emotions so easily as she'd thought about her exchange with Judith . . . and her strong, bewildering feelings for him. She took another step toward him, coming within inches of his bent knee.

"Maybe I am," she said.

"Why? What happened?"

"I don't feel like talking about it right now. I don't feel like talking at all," she murmured, her gaze moving over him. He hadn't shaved this morning. His upper lip and lower face were shadowed with whiskers. He looked good enough to eat. She resented him a little, for creating this rabid longing in her.

His hand suddenly shot out to the top of her back. He pulled her to him at the same time he lowered his bent knee. Air popped out of her lungs as she thumped against his length. He caught her surprised reaction as his mouth seized hers. He kissed her roughly. Thoroughly. Alice moaned shakily into his mouth, tangling her tongue with his, her body going tense with wild excitement. Her hands encircled his waist and she pressed closer, rubbing against him, desperate to mount the friction.

Needy for release from this tension he always built in her.

He cupped her jaw with his hand and ripped his mouth from hers. She strained against him, grinding her breasts, belly, and sex against his hardness.

"You need something to work it out, don't you?" he rasped against her lips. "Do you want to fuck to get it out of your system?"

"I wish I could fuck to get *you* out of my system," she gasped before she could censor herself.

Again, he went completely still. She swallowed thickly at something she saw blaze into his hooded gaze. Why did she always forget she shouldn't rile him?

Or had riling him been exactly what she'd intended all along?

"I can't help you with that, Alice."

A tremor went through her—one of anxiety and lust—because she knew what he was saying. Every damn thing he did was designed to make her remember him until her dying day.

She went up on her toes, seeking his mouth again, begging for euphoric forgetfulness. His head moved back slightly, dodging her seeking lips. Irritation spiked through her, but she'd seen the muscle leap in his cheek and she felt his cock hardening against her. He wasn't as unaffected and insouciant as he'd have her believe.

"Fuck me here," she taunted, again pressing her body from sex to breasts tighter to him, rubbing her peaking nipples against his ribs. She was shameless in those moments. Sex was cut and dry, an acceptable, *delectable* way for her to display her need. "Fuck me in these woods against this tree."

His mouth shaped into a snarl. "I'm not going to have you out here in the open."

"Why?" she demanded edgily. "Are you having someone follow me?"

He blinked, his gaze going glacial. He gripped her upper arms. "Why would you say that?" he bit out.

"Are you having that manager, Sal Rigo, follow me or any of the other counselors? Because he was just sitting in the Lakeside's parking lot last night after we finished there. It looked like he was spying on us. Is that part of Durand's protocol for dealing with possible new hires?" she demanded.

"Of course not," he said, scowling fiercely.

She peered at his shadowed face closely. "Why do I feel like you're lying?"

She saw that glitter in his eyes that signaled danger. "I'm *not* lying. Your time is your own once you're off the clock for the day. Rigo is not *spying* on the counselors in their off time."

"He sure looked like he was," Alice said with a lofty air.

"I'll look into it and take care of it if there's something to be taken care of," he said, his mouth slanted in irritation. "But what's this about the Lakeside? The restaurant in Morgantown? I thought I asked you to stay in last night."

"You *asked* it," she said, her tone making it clear he could ask her to do any number of things. That didn't mean she'd *do* them.

"Careful, Alice," he warned softly.

A thrill of anxious excitement coursed down her spine. She really *was* in a volatile mood, about to either break or go up in flame at any moment.

"I don't *want* to be careful." She reached for his cock.

He caught her wrist lightning quick and jerked her hand away, lunging off the tree.

He pulled her after him through the wooded upgrade. Alice felt like a she was being towed by a tornado. She jogged to keep up with his long legs, twigs and brush snapping beneath her sandals. She spied the castle's sloping emerald-green lawn through the trees and began to regret her provocative behavior.

What the hell is wrong with you? You were so happy to see him. And all you could do was piss him off? What are you, some kind of social moron?

"Wait, Dylan, I didn't—"

It was like talking to a storm. She tried to interrupt his determined stride, but he didn't turn around, and she certainly didn't think he was listening. They broke the tree line. He hauled her in front of a neat, wooden shed at the edge of the woods. Alice had never noticed the secreted outbuilding before. He reached for the door. He pulled on her hand, drawing her over the threshold in front of him. As soon as she was inside, he dropped her hand. Alice spun around to see his tall shadow blocking the brilliant sunlight before he slammed the door shut with a bang. She glanced around the darkened room anxiously.

"What is this place?" she asked between pants for air.

"The gardener's shed. This isn't going to wait for us to make it to the house."

She heard the sound of a lock snick into place. Her heartbeat began to throb in her ears. She took a step back from Dylan's encroaching shadow. Light snuck in around the frame of the door, but otherwise it was dark.

"I don't want to do it in here," she said defiantly. "It's hot."

"It's air-conditioned."

"Not very well. And there are probably spiders."

"I agree. And mice. And sharp implements all over the place." She jumped when his arm snaked out and his hand opened on the back of her neck. "I wouldn't touch anything but what's necessary, if I were you. Now. Let's scratch that itch you have, Alice. Or should I say, let's blast that chip off your shoulder?" he asked sarcastically before his mouth covered hers.

She moaned as his arms went around her and his mouth single-mindedly consumed. His taste registered in her flustered brain, already so familiar. So delicious. It took only seconds before she was digging her fingertips into his T-shirt and lean waist, kissing him back angrily. Hungrily. It rose in her again like pressurized magma, her need alarming but undeniable.

His hands moved between them, unfastening her cotton blouse. With the last two buttons to go, he made an impatient, rough sound in his throat and tore open the shirt. Through the roar in her ears, Alice vaguely heard the sound of plastic buttons skittering across the tile floor. He broke their kiss and whipped the shirt down her arms and hands, her bra following almost immediately.

His hands slid along her naked sides, the slight calluses on them making her shiver despite the heat. His hands cradled her naked breasts, his fingertips pinching lightly at her nipples. Liquid heat rushed through her. She moaned shakily, dipping her knees and rubbing up against him, desperate for friction. His touch undid her, as always. The bulge of his cock behind his jeans drove her crazy. He molded her breasts to his big hands, massaging her tautly. His groan spiked her arousal. "I was going to pamper you tonight, but Princess Alice always gets what she wants, doesn't she?"

Princess Addie.

A frisson of anxiety swept through her as she heard the words in her head, like a memory . . . but not her own. Where had that inexplicable phrase come from?

"Princess?" she scoffed, forcing her mind onto the solidity of the moment . . . the vibrant reality of Dylan. She reached between his thighs. She found the rigid column of his cock and stroked it at the same time she ground their pelvises tighter, rolling her hips. "I'm no *princess.*"

"No," he agreed grimly, leaning over her and cradling one of her breasts in his hand. He pinched a nipple between thumb and forefinger. "You're a fucking dictator, the way you jerk my dick around."

He forced her back to arch. He sucked her nipple into his mouth and applied a hot, taut suction. Alice writhed against him. Her fingers ran the length of his turgid cock, pumping and pressing through his jeans. It made her crazy, feeling his shape and the strength of his arousal. She used her other hand to find his testicles, cupping them through the fabric. Her nipple popped out of his mouth. He found her wrists and pulled her hands away from his cock.

"I'm going to give you what you want this afternoon, little girl," he said, his voice rough and ominous sounding in the darkness. "But tonight, I'm going to make you show me some control."

She thought of demanding what he meant by that, but then he was unfastening her shorts and jerking her clothing down over her hips. It was like that day in the stables. Hot. Sweaty. *Definitely* out of control.

After a moment, she stood panting, wearing only her sandals. Dylan spun her in his arms. He hugged her to him, his greater height and weight forcing her to bend at the waist. She felt his hand between their bodies, working at the buttons of his jeans and hauling them down to his thighs.

"You know what to do," he said, his mouth near her ear. "Bend over. Let me at that hot little pussy. I'm going to give you what you need."

She clenched her eyelids shut at his illicit instructions, both agitated and aroused by his dirty talk. Her sex was wet and tingling, so needy for pressure. Relief.

She bent at the waist, sending her bare ass against his protruding sex. God, it felt good. He was so heavy and hard for her. Such a beautiful man; such a mouthwatering cock. She circled her bottom against him in a tempting gesture.

He popped her ass with his hand. The resulting sting ramped up her excitement.

"I'm going to fuck you raw. No condom. Do you hear me?" he asked angrily, because she'd resumed her gyrations and he'd cracked her bottom again in a reprimand.

"Yes. Yes, just *do* it," she pled between clenched teeth.

"Over further," he urged, one hand on her back. The smooth, hard head of his cock nudged her slick entry. He grunted. She whimpered at the relentless pressure as he pushed into her, both his hands holding her hips steady. It felt unbearable.

It felt *so* damn good.

Her whimper escalated to a whine. She bumped her hips back, trying to get him into her completely. Her thighs strained. She felt unsteady, despite his firm hold on her hips.

"Spread your thighs a little and plant your feet. Brace yourself. I'm going to fuck you hard," he said tensely from behind her. Alice did what he said and he slid deeper. His balls pressed tight against her outer sex. She was so full of him. So incendiary. "I need a better angle. Over further. Hold on to your ankles. Send up your tailbone."

She hesitated at that.

"Who do you think you've been teasing?" he bit out furiously. She blinked in surprise. He throbbed inside her. Oh God, who *had* she been teasing? "I'll hold you steady, but, you're going to have to take what you asked for," he bit out.

She clamped her eyelids shut and grasped her ankles, using the hold to tilt up her pelvis.

He withdrew and sank back into her to the hilt. She cried out in excitement. The angle of penetration was prime.

"You feel like sin straight up," he snarled. "I knew you would. So tight. So wet for me," he mumbled before he began to fuck her.

Hard.

Alice howled at the pressure, but he continued his wicked pace without mercy. Her eyes sprang wide. He was huge with need. Without a condom, she could better feel the shape of the swollen cockhead and steely shaft as he built a fire in her. He drove into her with long forceful strokes. Her body rocked at the impact of him crashing into her, but he held her hips and bottom steady for his pillaging cock. He cupped her ass cheeks and pulled up, plunging into her, circling his hips slightly before he withdrew and repeated the ruthless stroke again and again. His hips glided and charged like a well-oiled machine. The indirect pressure on her clit was fierce.

Fantastic.

God, the man knew how to fuck. She was going to explode. A scream rose in her throat as the friction built in her.

"Is this what you needed?" he rasped, his cock driving deep, the harsh tattoo of their slapping flesh mixing with the roar of her heartbeat. He landed a spank on her ass before he clutched her again, driving deep. She was at his mercy, bent over and exposed, a flammable substance about to ignite. A desperate cry popped out of her throat. "*Answer* me."

"*Yes,*" she cried out.

"A nice hard fuck," he said darkly, giving her just that without pause.

"I needed you," Alice said in a tiny, shaky voice.

He paused with his cock halfway in her. His harsh swear sounded strangely sweet in her ears. He reached between her legs. He rubbed her slick clit and drove into her.

She screamed as climax slammed into her. Dylan kept fucking her while she wailed and shudders of pleasure wracked her.

"Jesus, I can feel you coming," he muttered viciously. The next thing she knew, he was grabbing her shoulders and lifting her against him. He filled one hand with her right breast. He bent his knees and pressed her back against his straining rock-hard body. Holding her in place, he thrust into her with short precise strokes. She shuddered around him, helpless in the onslaught of violent pleasure.

"I'm going to come in you," he said tensely near her ear a moment later. "Nothing is going to separate us again."

"Yes," Alice agreed. She was too mindless with pleasure to notice how their primal, raw joining had somehow turned sublime.

He withdrew partially and then pulled her back on him, dipping his cock deep, her ass slapping against his tensed thighs.

"*Now* Alice. That's so damn good."

Her eyes flew wide at the sensation of him swelling in her. She felt his cock lurch and spasm. His powerful body shuddered behind her.

He held her fast against him as he came deep inside her. She'd remember his harsh, wild groan in her ear forever.

Slowly, their erratic pants for air slowed and evened. She leaned her head back against his chest. His hold on her loosened slightly, his fingers slowly rubbing her perspiration-damp belly. It felt wonderful.

Emotion expanded in her breast. She cherished the moments with him, and that was a truth she feared. It was hard not to face that fear, though, when they were joined like two halves of a whole and she breathed in his scent.

"Dylan?" she whispered cautiously.

"Yeah?" he replied. She loved the sound of his low, rough voice behind her. He pressed his mouth to her pulse.

"I'm sorry. I don't know why I was so edgy and . . ." *Difficult,* she finished silently. He'd been right, of course. She *had* been spoiling for something, and it wasn't a fight.

"It's okay," he rumbled, planting a kiss on her shoulder and lingering to taste her sweat with his tongue.

"It is?" she asked uncertainly. It was okay for her to taunt and tease him?

She felt him nod because his face was pressed between her neck and shoulder. "Yeah," he said gruffly, his lips moving in a sweet glide against her neck. She shivered and turned her chin. Their mouths touched, clung, and parted ever so slightly.

"I missed you like hell, too, Alice."

He caught her surprised gasp of pleasure at his admission with his mouth, and then he was kissing her again, deep and sound.

HALF an hour later, they dried off after a languorous shower in Dylan's luxurious bathroom. Alice wrapped the towel around her, securing it at her breasts, and watched him breathlessly. He arched his brows when he noticed her enthralled expression as he dried his hard hair-sprinkled thighs with a fluffy white towel. He'd washed her with soapy, sensuous hands minutes ago and brought her to climax with his slippery fingers. Their lazy, delicious shower play had hardened him again. His cock protruded from between his muscular thighs. He was so beautiful. He'd caught her admiring him, but for once, she didn't mind. Somehow, his saying what she'd been too afraid to tell him—*I missed you like hell*—had made her a little freer in showing her feelings.

"Wouldn't you like me to do something about that?" she asked, nodding at his cock. She'd tried to return the favor or orgasm in the shower, but he'd enigmatically told her they'd let it wait.

He smiled that sex-god smile. His cock tented the towel in the front when he wrapped it low on his hips. He reached for her and she went into the circle of his arms. She pressed her nose against his humid warm skin, her hunger mounting at the sensation of his cockhead poking at her lower belly through their towels.

"I want your mouth on me," he growled near her ear. She shivered in excitement and reached for him. He grasped her wrist and pushed it back to her side. "Soon. I'll tell you what I want when the time is right."

"Oh you will, will you?" she asked archly, both miffed and mystified. She wasn't irritated enough at his cocky reply to stop herself from kissing his chest, loving the contrast of wiry hair and smooth skin against her lips.

"Bet on it," he said, caressing her shoulders. His hand rose to her face, his thumbs hovering near her eyebrows. She obligingly closed her eyes. He caressed her eyelid with his fingertip. "You have the longest eyelashes I've ever seen. Your eyes are so beautiful."

"Thank you," she murmured, entranced by his low, rough voice and gentle touch.

"I hate that you darken your eyebrows," he murmured. "And you shouldn't put so much liner and mascara on your eyes."

Embarrassment fractured her lassitude. "You sound like Maggie," she said, referring to her graduate school advisor and landlord. "She's always reminding me that I'm a walking fashion mistake."

"She just doesn't like to see you hiding behind so much dark makeup or hair dye. You're stunning. Why should you hide it?"

She blinked her eyelids open at that, and he moved aside his finger. For a lung-burning moment, their gazes clung.

"Oh well," he said after a moment, still studying her closely. "Maybe it's best for now."

"What do you mean?" she said with a laugh, puzzled.

He just shook his head, as if to say it wasn't important. "I noticed you didn't bring a bag. You're planning on staying tonight, right?"

She nodded her head.

"I have some clothes for you, including some dresses."

"Are we dressing up?"

He nodded. "I'm taking you to dinner at a place that's an hour or so up the coast. But we're going somewhere else first."

Pleasure rushed through her at the idea of spending so much time alone with him. Another thought intruded.

"Where did you get the clothes?" she asked. He gave her a long-suffering, sardonic glance at her suspicious tone. "I mean . . . it's not clothing left by one of your old girlfriends or something, is it?"

"Do you think I'm not capable of purchasing something specifically for you?"

"You don't know my size, do you?"

"You're a size-six pants and dress, a size-eight shoe." He leaned down and spoke near her mouth. "Bra size: thirty-four C."

"How did you know that?" she demanded, heat flooding her cheeks because he'd cradled the weight of her left breast lightly in his hand as he spoke and was caressing her softly.

"By looking at you," he said as he straightened.

She gave him a look that told him she wasn't buying it. He laughed and ran his thumb over her peaking nipple through the towel. She shivered in pleasure. She felt his cock swell against her.

"Okay, I'll admit I checked your shoe size," he conceded. "I'm not much of a foot expert."

"Hmm. But you are a breast one." He merely looked down at

her, that small, enigmatic smile lingering. She bit her lip and studied him through lowered lashes, fighting an unwelcome feeling of shyness. "Have you been in lots of relationships?" she ventured, attempting a light, casual tone.

"There have been a lot of women," he said simply. "Few relationships."

"Why so few?"

His shrug brought her attention to his broad shoulders. She caressed the dense muscle there. He smelled like soap and man. The weight of his erection behind their towels was a mind-blowing tease.

"I tend to be kind of single-minded when it comes to Durand. Work consumes me. I'm not attentive enough to women's needs."

"Except the sexual variety?" she mused knowingly. She was sure Dylan had more than fulfilled his lover's sexual needs.

"You might say I'm selfish."

She peered up at him. "That's funny. You never seem overly focused on Durand when we're together."

"That's because I'm with you."

Pleasure flooded her at his matter-of-fact reply.

"I *am* single-minded a good portion of the time, though. My focus has been called an obsession by a lot of people."

"Why? Why are you so obsessed with Durand?"

"Presently? Mostly because the pride of knowing I've worked so hard for it, the pride of ownership."

"And in the past?"

His smile turned grim. "In the past, I felt like I owed it to the Durands."

"The original owners?"

He nodded. "Making Durand Enterprises one of the most successful companies in the world was my form of payback. Making it up to Alan and Lynn Durand."

Her forehead bunched in consternation. "Why would you have to make something up to them?"

He didn't reply for a moment, making Alice suspect he wouldn't answer the personal question at all.

"I owed them a lot, for their kindness to me. And I made a mistake once. I lost something of theirs."

"Did they forgive you?" Alice whispered. Something sharp pulled in her chest when she saw the shadow of anguish on his face freeze into impassivity.

"I'd like to think so."

Her mouth quivered as she looked up at him. There was so much about him she didn't understand.

"Dylan . . . what happened on April eighteenth?" she asked.

He started at her question. She felt it in the slight tensing of his muscles because she was touching him. She'd caught him off guard.

"*What?*"

"You mentioned the first night you brought me here that you hadn't been with a woman since April eighteenth. You said that exact date, like it was meaningful. *Was* it?"

He surprised her by closing his eyes for a brief moment. For some reason, her heart squeezed a little in anguish. For a split second, he looked like he carried the weight of the world on his shoulders.

"Yeah. Very," he said after a moment. "Something happened on that day that sort of monopolized all my energy. Come on, and I'll show you the clothes."

He grabbed her hand, and the moment vanished. Alice was left wondering if it had ever been there at all.

HE hadn't just bought her a dress. Not by a long shot.

Alice watched in wide-eyed amazement as he brought several bags out of his enormous walk-in closet. She sat on the edge of the bed and he piled them around her. Inside one bag, she found a pair of sophisticated black pumps, in another a sleek zippered bag filled with personal hygiene items.

"I thought you might like to keep a few things up here at the house," he said when she held up a toothbrush with a puzzled glance. He said it so matter-of-factly, she was forced to see his point. She'd been spending the nights with him. It'd be nice to brush her teeth properly or have something other than expensive men's shower gel and deodorant to clean up with, even if the spicy scents on her skin did remind her of Dylan.

There was also a cosmetic set filled with top-of-the-line makeup, and she experienced a pang of embarrassment at the memory of his mention of her liberal use of her cheap eyebrow pencil, eyeliner, and mascara. There was a fluffy robe. Next, she discovered an assortment of lingerie wrapped in tissue paper. She held up a black silk bra-and-panty set and met Dylan's stare.

"I suppose you have a thing for lingerie, too?" she asked dryly.

He arched his brows. "I have a feeling I'm going to have a big thing for *you* in lingerie," he replied without pause.

Her gaze dropped to the bulge at the front of his towel. She snorted with laughter. He smiled full-out at her reaction. Her mirth faded.

Dylan's smiles were really something to see.

Much to her amazement, he returned to his closet and brought out another armful of items.

"What did you *do*?" she demanded, distressed at the amount of shopping he'd done. Although more than likely, he'd had someone purchase the items for her. Still, he would have had to put some significant thought into the items. He placed two large glossy boxes one on top of the other in her lap. "I can't accept all this," she exclaimed, flustered.

"Sure you can," he said nonchalantly. "What else am I going to do with it?"

She'd never seen such gorgeous packages, let alone received any. Curious despite her protests, she flipped open the lid on the sleek top box. She stared down at a beautiful pair of brown boots made of supple smooth leather. He must have paid more money for them than she'd ever had in her checking account at one time, never mind the cost combined with all the other items surrounding her. Something caught her eye, and she pulled out a pair of soft leather gloves that matched the boots. "Are these *riding* boots and gloves?" she asked dazedly.

"Yes. There's something else for you in there." He stepped closer and moved aside some tissue paper. He lifted a brown leather crop from the box. The rod was thin and whippy, and there was a two-inch-square black leather slapper on the end.

She stared up at him, bewildered. "I don't ride."

He walked over to the bedside chest, opened a drawer and dropped the crop inside. "Actually, that stays here. The other things *are* for horseback riding, though."

She choked back incredulous laughter, her cheeks flushing at what had just occurred, even though she was still a little confused. "You're not listening. I don't ride," she repeated.

"I'm going to teach you. *Alice?*"

She blinked at the sound of him saying her name sharply. She'd felt a little disoriented there for a moment.

"I hate horses," she whispered.

"Why? What do you remember about them?"

She gave him an incredulous glance at his taut question. Wasn't that an odd thing to ask?

"*Remember* about them? Nothing. There's nothing to remember. We didn't exactly have equestrian lessons offered at Club Little Paradise," she laughed. "I just don't like horses."

"But why?"

She shook her head, suddenly feeling like she was under a spotlight. "They're too far off the ground." He just stared at her, his expression unfathomable. "I have a fear of heights," she explained. "Or more accurately, a fear of falling. Do you *really* want to take me horseback riding?"

He nodded and stepped toward her, digging in one of the bags. "Here are jeans, socks, a few shirts. We're going this evening, before dinner. There's a stable just down the road from the inn where we're having dinner. I've arranged a private meal there, and the owner has said we can use the facilities there to clean up after our ride."

She shook her head. "I don't know, Dylan," she said doubtfully, referring to the horseback riding.

He studied her closely for a moment, and then shrugged. "Okay. It was just a thought."

She swallowed thickly and stared down at the beautiful boots. She rubbed the soft leather with her fingertips. A longing welled up in her to go with him, but she was afraid, too.

"Do you think I could ride with you?" she asked, belatedly realizing how small her voice sounded. How weak. "I mean . . . on the same horse? Until I get more used to them?" she said more forcefully.

He surprised her by coming closer and cupping the side of her head with his hand. His thumb stroked her cheek when she looked up at him.

"Of course," he said. "All you had to do is ask."

She rolled her eyes, trying to diminish her vulnerability and the impact of what she saw in his eyes at that moment.

"Right. Ask and my every wish is granted," she joked. "Princess Addie and all."

His expression stiffened. A cascade of shivers ran down the length of her spine and coursed down her arms and legs.

"What did you say?"

She gave him a confused glance. She laughed uneasily, trying to rid herself of a strange sense of foreboding. "Princess Alice. That's what you called me. In the shed?" she reminded him, her cheeks heating when she recalled the surrounding circumstances. Had Dylan been so crazed with lust that he'd forgotten? And why was he looking at her so oddly? "I just thought it was funny when you said that. Only *you* would ever think to call me a princess," she scoffed.

"Yeah. Only me."

The silence stretched.

He moved aside the boots and opened the box below it. Slipping his fingers through the thin straps, he lifted a stunning dark blue backless silk dress.

"I thought it'd bring out the color of your eyes," he said quietly.

Alice gaped in awe, and the strangeness of the moment faded back into the shadows.

FOURTEEN

They left Morgantown and Castle Durand behind.

The stable where Dylan took her was just north of the beach town of Saugatuck. Alice enjoyed herself on the ride as Dylan drove the luxury sedan down state highways and rural routes and they chatted about whatever came to mind. Being in the car with him made her feel less self-conscious and more relaxed. Dylan himself seemed more approachable, wearing a pair of jeans, a simple black T-shirt, and sunglasses. She kept stealing covetous glances at his long legs or the succulent dense muscles of his upper arms peeking out just beneath his sleeves or the distracting vision of his large hands holding the leather wheel lightly.

When she wasn't leching over Dylan, she was admiring her sleek new boots and cute jeans and top. Her new clothing made her feel pleasantly pretty and feminine, but also transparent somehow. She was just starting to learn how natural it was for her to guard her sexuality, to diminish the impact of her femininity as a means of self-protection. It was an ingrained instinct, and going against it left her feeling vaguely uncomfortable.

It was a new experience for her, not to duck into the shadows. Dylan wasn't in the shadows. The temptation of him was so great, she'd been lured out of her place of safety. And there in that tempting, wonderful place of being with him, she fought her urge to cringe back and take cover.

Under Dylan's spell, she opened up to him more than she ever had in the past. He asked her on the drive about her experience as a counselor, and she had the impression he really wanted to hear what she said. She told him about some of her kids, the good, funny moments and the challenging ones. When she talked about the Red Team, she was surprised to hear the note of pride ringing in her voice.

She told him about Judith and their prickly interaction just hours earlier. Dylan listened without interrupting, his gaze steady on the road.

"Do you think I made the right decision in making Judith the student leader?" she asked him a while later.

"Yes," he said without hesitation. "She's strong. That's what you see in her. It's what others will see, too."

"It'll be hard," Alice said, staring out the windshield. The afternoon sun was starting to dip in the sky, making Lake Michigan sparkle brilliantly to the left of the car. "To trust her not to screw up, I mean."

"Hard. But worth it," Dylan said. "It's a big part of being a manager, you know. That's why we emphasize trust so much at Camp Durand. There's no quicker way to burn out and fail as an executive than taking on all the responsibility yourself because you can't trust anyone else to do the job. The ability to delegate is a must."

Alice listened with wary interest. She understood what Dylan meant. But she wasn't so certain it was smart to let go of *too* much control. Alice knew herself. She *knew* she could get a job done. She wasn't so sure anyone else could do it as well. That's why she was a workaholic. She'd take on extra work because she wanted it done *right*.

"There's the stable," he said, lifting two fingers off the wheel and pointing. Alice peered out the window, seeing long stretches of white picket fences in a golden green meadow. One black and two brown horses grazed in the pasture. In the distance, she saw a neat white building at the edge of some woods and a fenced-off corral.

"How long have you ridden?" she asked him, a feeling of excitement and nervousness going through her at the idea of crawling up on one of the large animal's backs.

"Since I was twelve."

She looked at his profile. "Did you first ride at Camp Durand?"

"Yeah. And I've been hooked ever since."

"Who taught you?"

"Alan Durand."

"Really?"

He nodded, keeping his eyes trained on the road. "Alan loved horses."

"So you knew him really well?" Alice queried, her curiosity on the subject making her heart race.

"Yeah. We became close," Dylan said. Something in his tone warned her that he wouldn't elaborate, so she was surprised when he continued after a moment. "I knew his wife, too. They didn't take a regular part in Camp Durand programming, although the camp was their baby—their favorite philanthropic project. It was Lynn Durand's pride and joy. She loved children. But they usually let the staff and the counselors handle things at the camp, with a few exceptions for special occasions."

"Like you do now," Alice filled in.

He nodded. "But since they both rode, I ran into them once in a while at the stables when I came to camp that first time. I got close to them my second summer."

"What were they like?"

"Nice. You've never met a warmer couple. Easy to talk to despite their classiness. Welcoming. Gracious."

"And they took to you?" Alice asked quietly. She'd been avidly curious about Dylan's association with the Durands, especially since it all seemed to be veiled in mystery.

"Yeah," he replied, turning the sedan onto a gravel road. "I took to them, too. After a bit. Or maybe a little more than a bit."

"What were *you* like then?"

"Me?"

"Yeah," she said, smiling because he sounded mildly surprised she'd want to know.

"You know how I described the Durands?"

"Uh-huh."

"Pretty much the opposite of that."

She laughed in understanding. Before she could follow up with a question, however, he stopped the car and put it into park. A smiling silver-haired man was approaching the car to greet them.

"There's Kevin Riley. He owns the stables. He's been around this area forever. He supplies us with a lot of the Durand horses and tack," Dylan said as they unbuckled their seat belts.

Kevin was down to earth and easy to talk to from the first. They walked together toward the stables, Kevin asking Dylan about the health of his horse, Kar Kalim, who, Alice discovered, had been purchased from Riley Stables. Kevin quickly picked up on Alice's wariness about horses, which was no surprise. She'd never been good at hiding suspiciousness.

"She'll go up this first time with me," Dylan said. "So we'll need a good-sized saddle and a steady mount."

"Quinn, do you think?" Kevin asked as he led them through a small corral to the entrance of the handsome stables.

"Yeah, that's what I was thinking, too," Dylan agreed. Kevin nodded, his gaze sliding off Dylan and sticking on Alice, who walked between them. Alice did a double take when she saw Kevin's expression turn perplexed as he stared at her profile.

"Sorry. It's the damnedest thing," Kevin said, shaking his head as if to clear it and smiling sheepishly. "I'm gawking at you because you look so much like—"

"She does look a little like Jamie, doesn't she?" Dylan interrupted.

Alice blinked when Dylan took her hand and pulled her up short. "Jamie is the stable hand here," he explained to Alice. "Too bad she's off today, or we could do a side-by-side comparison. Kevin, could you please bring Alice a helmet, as well?"

Kevin paused and glanced around. "Uh, sure . . . sure thing. Be back out with Quinn in a jiff," he said before he disappeared into the stable.

She peered at Dylan suspiciously. "*So*, is that why you're interested in me? Because I look like this Jamie girl?" she asked, mostly joking, but a little serious.

He snorted with laughter. Alice couldn't help but grin, his surprise at her question seemed so genuine.

"No. I've met Jamie all of three times, and only remembered her name because Kevin told me she wasn't working today earlier on the phone."

Dylan started to put on his riding gloves, snapping them at the wrist in a practiced gesture. She followed suit with her new ones. When they'd finished, she studied him from beneath lowered lashes. He looked very natural in this setting, rugged with a shadow of whiskers on his jaw and upper lip, his hair gleaming in the sunshine, his jeans, boots, and leather riding gloves all worn from use. She had a sudden urge to have those large gloved hands on her, reassuring her . . .

Making her forget her fear. Making her forget everything but the way he made her feel.

As if he'd read her mind, Dylan suddenly reached out and took her hand. She tried to smile, but ended up scowling worriedly instead. "Did you ask him about a helmet because you knew I might fall?"

"I asked him because I thought it'd make you feel more secure, not because I think you're going to fall. You'll be fine. You'll be with me," he said, his arched brows and firm tone sounding final and absolute. She nodded.

"Come on," he said, hitching his head toward the distant fence and the shimmering blue lake in the distance.

While Kevin saddled the horse, they admired the view. The earlier humidity and scattered clouds had cleared, leaving a warm clear summer's day. The setting was beautiful, and she was happy being there with Dylan. If only she weren't so prickly at the idea of getting on a horse's back . . .

She heard the sound of a horse's clopping hooves behind them and spun around. Her eyes went huge.

"Oh my God, he's *gigantic*," she exclaimed before she could stop herself, eyeing the approaching dark brown horse anxiously. "I thought we'd have something smaller for the first time."

"We don't want him too small, he's got to hold both of us." Dylan said, a smile pulling at his mouth. "Quinn is as steady as a rock. You'll see."

He took her hand, urging her toward Kevin and Quinn. Alice followed him reluctantly, hanging back. Kevin paused the horse in the shade of a maple tree and dropped what appeared to be a small wooden stepladder to the ground next to the horse.

"I'll just leave you all to get acquainted, if that's all right?" Kevin said, a hint of amusement in his tone. Alice was busy studying Quinn like she might a potential enemy. Kevin handed the reins to Dylan. "My accountant is due up at the house in a bit. With Jamie gone, you two will be on your own."

"No problem. I'll see to Quinn when we're finished," Dylan assured, shaking the older man's hand. "Thanks for taking the time out when I called at the last minute."

"Anytime, Dylan," Kevin assured, before he waved and strode toward the white house in the far distance.

Alice's gaze remained locked with Quinn's the whole time. The horse regarded her back with liquid brown eyes.

"He seems nice. Is he nice?"

"He's a real good guy, aren't you, Quinn?" Dylan assured in a deep even tone, reaching up and petting Quinn's nose. Quinn gently nuzzled Dylan, and Dylan fondly patted the side of his neck. "Do you want to pet him?" Dylan asked her. "His nose is like velvet."

Alice blinked and looked at Dylan's profile, startled. He noticed her abrupt movement, doing a double take.

"What?"

"Nothing," Alice whispered. "Déjà vu, I guess."

For a moment, it'd been like she'd heard someone say that exact thing before. *Do you want to pet him? His nose is like velvet.*

Not just someone. *Dylan.*

"Alice?" he prompted.

She shook her head slightly as if to clear it and put out her hand. She held her breath.

"He *is* soft," she said, smiling a moment later as she stroked the animal's nose. "I think he likes it," she added tentatively when Quinn's eyelids lowered slightly and he held still for her touch.

"I think he likes you," Dylan said, a smile in his voice. Encouraged, she stroked the side of the horse's head and neck, grinning wider when Quinn's ears twitched and he moved his head to be closer to her. While she made friends with the horse, Dylan put the riding helmet on her head and tightened the band beneath her chin.

"You ready?" he asked.

Her stomach lurched, but she nodded determinedly.

"Who's going up first, you or me?" she asked.

"You. I'll come up behind you once you're on," he said.

He kicked the stepladder, repositioning it.

"Easy, Quinn," Dylan steadied at the same time he urged Alice to the ladder. She rose to the top step directly beside Quinn, her breath growing choppy. What was wrong with her? This wasn't *that* far off the ground. She couldn't shake the feeling of being a frightened child. Her embarrassment approached cringing shame.

Dylan came up behind her on the first step of the stool. He placed his hands on the outside of her hips, and her nervousness fractured for a split second. Leave it to Dylan, to make her feel like a grown woman with just one touch.

"Take the reins with one hand. Put your hand on the pommel," he said, guiding her, "and this foot in the stirrup," he designated, sliding his hand down one hip to show her what he wanted. "Don't worry, Quinn will stay steady for you. He's extremely well trained."

Alice lunged into the stirrup and lifted her other leg. For a second, she felt awkwardly suspended, and knew a moment of fear. Then Dylan heaved gently on her ass and the back of her thigh, and the next thing she knew, she was straddling Quinn's back high up off the ground. She remained bent over, clutching the pommel for dear life, her face near Quinn's mane.

"You got it," Dylan praised, using his hands to reposition her hips on the saddle. "Straighten up, now," he urged. "Good girl." She heard the sound of him kicking the ladder away. "Take your foot out of the stirrup for a second."

He was making the requests verbally, but Alice was too dazed, staring at the grass far below her in fear, that she wasn't really responding. Dylan's hands maneuvered her more than her uncooperative muscles did. She unwillingly straightened at his urgings, not liking the fact that the ground grew even farther away. He swung up behind her without using the ladder, his show of easy strength distracting her for a few seconds. Before there was too much opportunity for her anxiety to mount, he was landing in the saddle behind her, his long legs bracketing hers. His arms came around her, too, his hands covering hers.

He remained like that, so that she could feel his motions. He flicked the reins, and Quinn lurched under her.

"Whoaaahh," erupted out of her throat involuntarily. Quinn was just walking slowly, but it'd felt like the earth had moved. The rocking sensation so far off the ground made her a little queasy.

"It's okay. I've got you," Dylan said quietly near her ear. He tapped her left thigh. "Both feet in the stirrups. Steady yourself. Find your center. That's right. Just relax and get used to Quinn's pace. *Alice*," he said with emphasis after a moment when she remained stiff and tense as a board. "Relax. Quinn's got you. So do I."

"I'm sorry," she moaned miserably, panic rising in her. "I told you I wouldn't be good at this. Dylan, I want to get off."

"I'm right here, baby. You're doing fantastic."

A terrible swooping sensation went through her stomach. "I'm afraid of falling," she blurted out uncontrollably.

"Look out at the lake. Don't look at the ground," he soothed. Alice jerked her gaze off the swaying, lurching ground and followed his instructions. Slowly, the feeling of panic receded.

"You're doing just fine," he assured, his rough, compelling voice in her ear tickling her. Mesmerizing her. "There's no way in hell you're going to fall with me holding on to you. Horses don't just go down for no reason. Quinn is steadier than a mountain, trust me. Just feel him. Absorb Quinn's movement. You feel my arms around you, don't you?" he murmured comfortingly near her ear.

Alice nodded, sinking back against him a little for reassurance. She exhaled in relief at the familiar solid feeling of his body. He transferred the reins into one hand and placed one opened gloved hand on her belly. It felt good. It grounded her.

Slowly, when nothing major happened, and Quinn's slow circle around the corral remained steady, the tension in her muscles began to uncoil.

"There you go." The side of her neck roughened at the impact of his voice so near her ear. "You're feeling Quinn's movement. You're letting your body roll with it a little." To demonstrate his point, he moved his hand on her belly in a subtle up and down, circular motion that matched the horse's cadence. Suddenly, she was far more focused on the pressure of his hand and the heavy warm feeling growing at her sex than she was on how far away the ground looked.

"Still nervous?" he asked, his lips brushing against her ear when they completed a circuit of the corral. She tingled with sexual awareness.

"No. Not too much, anyway," she added hesitantly.

He instructed her on use of the reins, guiding her with his hands.

"So if you loosen up on the reins, it's like letting up on a brake, right?" she asked a moment later.

"Right. You're giving him a free head . . . free rein. You control the speed by how much tension you put in the reins."

She nodded, understanding instinctively despite her anxiety.

"Do you want me to teach you how to post?" he asked when they'd circled the corral once.

"What's that?"

"When the horse trots, you have to bob your body up and down in rhythm with it," he said, his hand moving again in an erotic motion on her belly. His lips brushed against her sensitive ear. "It makes for an easier ride."

She shivered, tempted by his deep seductive tone and moving lips. Her nipples had tightened against her new bra at those words: *easier ride*. Yet—

"I'm not sure I want to go any faster," she said, twisting her head slightly to better feel his whiskers and lips against her ear and neck. She inhaled choppily when his warm mouth landed against the corner of her lips. His long fingers lowered on her belly. He pushed her back more firmly against him. She bit her lip, suppressing a soft moan at the feeling of his hard thighs and cock against her ass. "Can we just walk today?"

"Yes. We'll go at your pace. But I think you should push yourself a little."

"Why?" she asked breathlessly, because his first two fingers were rubbing the flap of her zipper directly over her mons.

"Because I think you can do this."

"Okay," she said, unable to disguise her trepidation.

"Tell you what," he said after a short pause. "We'll walk him on the straightaway toward the lake, and trot and post on the way back. Sound good?"

She frowned. They'd already traversed half the length of the corral toward the lake. They'd have to go faster *soon*. Too soon. Dylan must have sensed her hesitance, because his mouth nuzzled the side of her neck and his fingers lowered. Suddenly, he was applying a concise pressure on her fly just above her clit.

"And I'm going to touch you and make you feel good," he said quietly. "But *only* on the slow stretch."

Her mouth fell open, but nothing came out. His hand opened over her entire outer sex. He rubbed her firmly, applying an eye-crossing pressure and pushing her against him at the same time, making her highly aware of the fullness behind his jeans.

"Won't someone see?" she asked breathlessly.

"No. The view of the corral from Kevin's house is obstructed by trees, but even if someone did glimpse us, I'm only going to touch you while we face the lake. As you can see, there isn't a soul in sight. Okay?"

He was circling over her sex now, his motions subtle yet firm. The rolling cadence of the horse beneath them took on a new meaning, adding to the stimulation.

"Okay," she mumbled. She would have agreed to just about anything with Dylan's hand between her spread thighs and his cock growing distractedly hard and full against her ass. As if he agreed, he flexed his hips slightly, pressing her bottom tighter to his crotch.

He groaned.

"These new jeans make your ass look edible," he breathed out near her ear. Alice quaked and then melted at the sensation of his front teeth scraping her earlobe. "I noticed right away. But I hadn't considered the torture of being behind you on a horse."

"I'm so sorry to torture you," she muttered with distracted sarcasm.

"That's okay. I'll get you back. We're to the turn. Take the reins and tell Quinn what you want." Alice took the reins without thinking, doing what seemed natural to guide Quinn, tilting the reins in the direction she wanted to go. The animal followed her lead without hesitation. She gave a little triumphant laugh, but it segued to a little cry of displeasure when Dylan's hand moved off her sex.

"Only on the approach toward the lake," he reminded her. She frowned at the hint of laughter in his deep voice. "Okay, straighten Quinn out. Good girl." He put his hand over hers again as Quinn came around the bend, taking control of the reins. His arm circled her waist. "Now we're going to go faster and post. I want you to move with me on the trot, do what I do."

Panic leapt in her belly. "I need more instructions than *that*!"

"No, you don't. I know how you move with me. You're perfect."

"But—"

He dropped the reins and made a chirruping sound. Quinn bolted forward. She choked off a gasp. It was a slow trot, nothing more. It *felt* like freefalling through space. Her body went stiff in fear, her hands grasping the pommel, her thighs squeezing the saddle hard.

Dylan's arm tightened around her.

"I've got you. Everything's fine. We're moving, but there's control, Alice. Move with me. Don't fight it."

It took a moment for her anxiety to subside enough to really absorb what he was saying. As keyed in to him as she always was, her body began to match the cadence of his instinctively. She realized that when she matched both his and the horse's rhythm, the jolting, jostling, out-of-control feeling subsided.

A spike of exhilaration pierced her anxiety.

"That's it," Dylan murmured behind her warmly, sensing her body joining with his. "See how well you move with me?" he said near her ear.

No sooner had she matched his and the horse's stride than they had reached the length of the corral, and Dylan was pulling up on the reins. A combination of relief and disappointment went through her as Quinn slowed. Her heart was racing like mad, but she was grinning.

"That wasn't so bad, was it?" Dylan asked.

"No. It was amazing. Scary, but amazing."

"Just like life, huh?" he teased darkly.

Just like being with you. Her broad smile faltered slightly at that incendiary thought.

"Here, take the reins," he said. "Hold them nice and firm so he knows to keep it slow, but don't jerk or pull on his head too hard. Gentle, but firm. That's right."

No sooner had Quinn straightened and started the slow walk toward the lake than Dylan's fingers were deftly unfastening the buttons on her jeans.

"What are you doing?" she asked shakily.

"What do you think? Keep the reins firm. Don't let them go slack," he rasped. She watched wide-eyed in mounting excitement as he flicked the leather tab on the glove of his right hand, unfastening the snap. He peeled off the glove.

"Oh," Alice said shakily when he shoved his ungloved hand into the opening of her jeans. His deft fingers rubbed her tingling labia. Alice stared blindly at the glimmering lake between the distant trees, every nerve in her body focused on Dylan's hand between her thighs.

"I'm addicted to your pussy," he told her gruffly, nuzzling her neck. It was hot beneath the summer sun, but the wave of heat that swept through her had nothing to do with the outdoor temperature. He burrowed his finger deeper, parting the lips. Alice gasped loudly as he dipped into the cleft and agitated her clit. He grunted and kissed her ear. "You may be scared, Alice, but you're turned on, too," he said, sounding gratified. "Things are nice and warm and wet down here."

"You're so dirty," she accused.

His hand moved faster between her thighs. Her clit burned deliciously beneath the firm, lubricated glide of his fingertip. He pressed back on her with his palm, grinding his erection against her ass. Alice cried out shakily. "And you love it," he told her hotly, nipping her earlobe. "Don't you?"

"*Yes.*"

He chuckled at her begrudging, dazed admission. His hand slid out from between her fly.

"Hey—"

"Time to trot," he reminded her, sliding his leather glove back on. He kissed her ear when she made a sound of disgust. "The quicker we take this part of the trip, the sooner we'll be walking again."

Alice scowled, her cheeks going hot. He had a point.

He tugged on the end of her T-shirt, effectively covering her opened fly. Suddenly, Quinn had turned, and Dylan was putting his hand on top of hers, again demonstrating the movement required for a trot.

This time, it took her less time to diminish her anxiety and match Dylan and Quinn's movement. This time, she became hyperaware of moving in tandem with him while his thighs surrounded her and her ass rose and fell in rhythm with his cock.

His jeans must be getting pretty tight, given the size of his erection.

She was actually disappointed when he pulled up on the reins, and Quinn slowed. Their movement on the trot excited her as much as his hand between her thighs on the walk. Her breath was coming short and choppy from anxious excitement. She held the pommel and wiggled her bottom against the stiff column of his cock.

She jumped when he landed a spank on the outer curve of her hip and ass.

"Careful, Alice," he warned. She shivered. As Quinn circled

onto the straightaway, she sensed Dylan's focused attention on her. "Take off my glove," he told her thickly.

Her clit twinged. Somehow, he'd known that instructing her to peel off his leather glove would excite her, and he'd been *so* right. She exposed his hand, peeling off the glove. How could the vision of his *hand* make her ripple with sexual anticipation?

"Take the reins," he instructed shortly.

Alice complied, her breath stuck in her lungs. He lifted her shirt, and his bare hand again slid into the opening of her jeans. This time, he wrapped her waist with his left hand like he did on the trot, while he stirred her pussy with his right hand. He pulled her tighter against him when she moaned shakily. His cock throbbed against her ass, spiking her excitement.

"Do you feel that?" he breathed out near her ear. Since almost her entire awareness was on his cock at that moment, she answered with that in mind.

"Yes," she said in a strangled voice. He was making her burn so *good*. She shifted her hips forward slightly against the pressure of his hand and then back with her ass against his cock, undecided as to which sensation she craved more.

"Do you like to suck cock, Alice?"

Her lips fell open. She couldn't think with him stirring her sex so precisely.

"I think I'll like sucking yours," she gasped sincerely.

He reached up with the still gloved hand and palmed her chin and jaw firmly. The feeling of the leather against her sensitive skin was delicious. Holding her in place, he spoke in her ear below the helmet. "I'm going to take you into those stables and you're going to take me in your mouth and suck me off. You've been killing me on this damn horse. Your mouth has been killing me for a hell of a lot longer than that."

Alice's hips writhed in excitement. His hand moved faster between her thighs. The burn in her clit mounted to a sizzle.

"Alice?"

"Yes," she moaned mindlessly. She was in a fever. The idea of him in her mouth maddened her. "I'm going to suck your cock. Whatever you want."

"What I want right now is for you to come." He took the reins from her. He lifted the hand between her legs and popped her labia. It was a tap, really, but a taut, precise one. Alice gasped, her body clenching tight at his unexpected action. He plunged his forefinger back into the juicy cleft, rubbing briskly. A startled cry left her throat as she shuddered in orgasm.

"That's right," he said behind her, his tone lust-bitten. He worked her through a hot delicious climax, his hand moving demandingly at her sex.

Alice opened her eyelids a moment later when Dylan's hand slid out of her button fly, leaving a trail of warm juices along her pelvis and lower belly.

"Riding lessons are over," he rasped.

"They went a lot better than I expected," she replied dazedly.

She loved his sharp bark of laughter. He hastily pulled her shirt down to cover her opened jeans. He pulled on the reins, and Quinn turned sharply.

"How should we get to the stables?" he asked pointedly.

"Fast," Alice panted without a trace of hesitation.

Dylan flicked the reins and moved his legs, and Quinn was speeding them to the stables.

THE dim cool interior of the stables was a delight to her hot skin and sun-dazed eyes. She followed Dylan as he led Quinn to a fenced-off paddock that was separate from the individual horse stables in the distance. She watched as he quickly and efficiently loosened the girth and removed the bridle. He tied off Quinn a moment later and turned to where she was waiting in the corner near some bales of hay. The lighting was very dim in here, but she could see his lustrous eyes gleam as his gaze dipped over her.

"We didn't work Quinn hard, but it's hot out. I need to unsaddle and brush him down before I stable him. He shouldn't wait. I don't want him to be uncomfortable."

"Okay," she said.

He nodded once, but he didn't turn. The air between them seemed to crackle with electricity. He just kept staring at her with a hard inscrutable look on his shadowed face. Her gaze dropped over him as if of its own will, skimming his lean hard torso and lingering on his full crotch.

"Fuck," he muttered tensely, stepping toward her at the same time he ripped at his button fly. Alice's heart jumped when he jerked his jeans and a pair of white boxer briefs down to his thighs. He reached for her shoulders. "Just give me a taste before I stable him," he rasped, his bold face looking fierce as he stared down at her.

"You're sure no one will come in?" she whispered, her gaze latched onto the temptation of his cock where it poked out lewdly beneath the hem of his T-shirt.

"Not likely. Kevin, if anyone, and if he did, we'd have a few seconds of warning before he reached us."

She nodded and sank down to her knees. The smooth head of his cock brushed against her cheek. Her breath caught. She worked desperately at her gloves while she turned her head, letting the flaring crown brush across her sensitive lips. He grunted softly. Impatiently.

He slid his hand along the shaft, cradling his weight. "Open those beautiful lips, Alice." She looked up at him, her fingers freezing on the snap of her glove. She parted her lips. Their gazes held as he pushed his cock into her mouth. The crown slid onto her tongue. The thick shaft stretched her lips tight. He paused, his eyes glittering as he stared down at her. Alice swirled her tongue around the flaring cockhead. His rigid cheek muscle twitched. He withdrew and plunged back into her, groaning harshly.

"Ah, Jesus. What a hot little mouth," he muttered tensely, pulsing between her lips for a moment. His hand moved to the back of her head.

Behind them, Quinn whickered. Dylan blinked and cursed. He drew out of her mouth, a snarl shaping his lips. For a moment, his slick erection bobbed in front of her face, heavy and mouthwatering.

"Let me take care of Quinn. Just a minute," he said, his jaw clenched very hard. Alice nodded, understanding, but also excited.

Hungry.

Dylan helped her to her feet. He turned away, fastening his jeans in a cursory manner, his haste obvious. Alice, too, fastened her button fly with clumsy fingers—she hadn't fastened them since she'd climaxed in the corral—and sat on a bale of hay. He rapidly unsaddled Quinn. She loved watching him, admiring his sure action and flexing muscles, captured by the brisk yet somehow sensual movements as he toweled off and brushed the horse's sleek coat. He didn't look around at her as he led Quinn out of the paddock to stable him, but she knew he was highly aware of her. She felt his attention on her like a mild current on every inch of her skin.

Her anticipation bordered on anxiety waiting for him to return. She wanted to please him. She just plain wanted *him*.

But surely he's been with more skilled, knowledgeable lovers than you.

Alice wasn't sure that her clawing hunger for him was enough to please him.

She heard the sound of his boot steps coming closer. Her breath caught at the sight of his tall form. He approached, watching her from beneath a lowered brow, peeling off his remaining glove as he entered the paddock. He walked over to where she sat and tossed the glove on the hay behind her. For a moment, their gazes locked. Something she read in his lustrous dark eyes made everything but her desire fade.

Wordlessly, Alice reached for his waistband and unbuttoned his jeans. He helped her get his clothing over his swollen erection and down to his thighs.

"I'm going to be coming in no time," he said.

Her heart paused at his stark confession of boiling need. It was *exactly* what she required at that moment.

She ran her hand along the underside of his thrusting erection, overwhelmed by the weight of his arousal. No *wonder* he said he'd be coming soon. He was stretched tight with lust. His need sparked her own flame high. She lifted the succulent cockhead to her lips. He hissed between clenched teeth and cupped the back of her head with his palm.

She knew instinctively Dylan would like it fierce and forceful. Why wouldn't he, when those two words described the essence of his character? She sucked him into her mouth, clamping her lips hard. Her entire awareness narrowed to the feeling of him filling her mouth.

Overfilling.

She bobbed her head and moaned, sinking him as deep as she dared. He was so warm and alive, so hard and teeming with raw lust. His fingers tightened at the hair at her nape, and he groaned deep and rough. It thrilled her to touch his most sensitive flesh so intimately, to control his pleasure so completely.

She cupped his balls in her hand and bobbed her head over him, sucking hungrily, clamping him so hard her jaw ached.

"God, Alice," he grated out, pushing her head slightly against him as she worked him farther and farther into her mouth with each pass. "Yeah, that's good. I knew you'd be hungry, baby." Spurred on by his rough praise, she pulled her head back. The fat cockhead popped out of her lips. She batted at the jutting staff with her hand, loving his turgid weight. She grasped the stalk and plunged him almost immediately between her lips again.

He growled in surprised ferocity and gripped the hair at her nape. "I'm going to pay you back for that."

His erotic threat only fevered her more. His cock thrust farther into her mouth than ever, brushing her throat. Alice gagged, and he immediately withdrew. She grabbed a dense, smooth buttock and pulled him back to her. Breathing through her nose, and willing her throat to relax, she plunged him deep and sure. His harsh grunt was her reward. His hand on her head grew more forceful as she bobbed forward and back, but Alice wanted it. He was guiding her in his pleasure, and she didn't expect the journey to be gentle.

"Aw, yeah. Fuck *yeah* . . . Oh, Jesus, that's so good," he muttered, sounding fierce even as he abandoned himself. She lost herself a little, too, in those tense, desperate moments, sacrificing herself to his pleasure. She became distantly aware of him pulling gently on the hair on her nape. Opening her eyes, she looked up at him in surprise as he pulled her down the length of his cock. He popped out of the ring of her lips, the glistening, plump cockhead bumping against her swollen, sensitive mouth.

"I want to see your eyes," he bit out. "Look at me while you use your tongue. Lick it all over. *Yeah*, that's right," he rasped as she followed his instructions, holding his cock at the base and laving her tongue along the cockhead and distended staff. She pressed tight, tracing a swollen vein with the tip of her tongue. A muscle jumped in his rigid cheek, and a thrill coursed through her. He watched her with a tight, feral focus. When she'd tongued him everywhere, she closed her eyes and lowered her head, licking his round, full testicles.

He groaned roughly above her and tugged on her hair, gentle but firm. She glanced up at him as he used his hand to guide his cock back between her lips. "I'm going to come in your mouth," he said as he pushed the flaring cockhead between her lips and thrust along her tongue. "Do you understand?"

Alice held his stare and nodded, making his cock bob in the air. The tight, wild pleasure on his face at that moment held her spellbound.

His buttocks bunched tight in her hand as he thrust into her again and again, and she kept pace with him, straining not to break rhythm. For a moment, they existed together at the core of unbridled lust, and Alice let him have free rein. It excited her, to engage in that race with him, to let him use her for his pleasure, to be the source of the taut friction that would shatter into his bliss.

Her eyes sprang wide when he thrust and swelled huge in her mouth. She pumped the lower portion of his shaft with her hand and sank him deep, craving her due.

LATER, after they pulled themselves together and walked out to the car, sex-flushed and satisfied, Alice wondered with a rush of embarrassment if Kevin and his accountant had heard Dylan's harsh roar as he came in her mouth minutes ago.

But in those moments when he'd clutched her to him desperately and she'd had her first taste of Dylan's pleasure, her sole mandate had been to drink deeper.

FIFTEEN

The place where Dylan had made reservations for them for dinner was called the Twelve Oaks Inn. It stood majestically on the peak of a massive sand dune overlooking Lake Michigan. The moment Alice saw it in the distance, she gasped in awe.

"It looks like Castle Durand, but smaller," she said as they coasted down the country road toward the solitary inn. The sun was starting to dip toward the glistening Great Lake ahead of them.

"It was designed by the same architect and built within two years of the Durand home. It's owned by a nice lady named Deanna Shrevecraft. She used to work in Durand Enterprise's human resources department. She and her husband bought it a few years back," he said as he pulled into a small parking lot. "She should have everything ready for us so that we can clean up and change."

Dylan glanced over at her as he unfastened his seat belt and did a double take. He went still. Alice was already feeling like a cake left out in the scalding sun, her perspiration just drying from her first riding lesson and intense, raunchy sex. Dylan's slow smile made her melt even more, especially when he reached out and smoothed her short hair behind her ears and skimmed his fingertip gently across her flushed cheek.

"Are you blushing or is this from before?" he murmured, referring to their heated trysts at the stables.

"It's from before, I guess."

She noticed his arched brows and silent query. He knew she wasn't being entirely honest. "It's just . . . isn't it kind of unusual, for an innkeeper to agree to let us use the facilities to shower and change before dinner?"

"No," he said without pause. "I'm paying for two rooms for the entire night."

"But we're not going to actually sleep here?" Alice asked, confused.

"I'd rather we slept at home tonight. I don't want to waste part of your day off driving around."

Alice's mouth fell open. His matter-of-fact statement flustered and pleased her.

"What's really wrong?" he asked, his fingertip trailing along her neck, making her skin prickle in awareness. "Alice?" he prompted when she hesitated.

"Do you do this a lot?" she couldn't stop herself from asking, no matter how hard she tried. "Bring women here? I mean . . . it's very romantic, isn't it?" He blinked, his caressing finger stilling. She glanced uneasily out the window, feeling undone for some reason as she stared at the idyllic setting of the lovely country inn perched on the white dune and the sun setting in the sea-like lake behind it.

She swallowed thickly, realizing how stupid she sounded. "Never mind, it doesn't matter," she said gruffly, turning to open her car door. He halted her by grasping her shoulder. She turned to him uneasily.

"Are you asking me if you're like other women I've been with? Is that what you want to know?"

She swallowed thickly. *Yes*, that's what she meant. But it felt unbearable in that moment, to want that answer so much. So needy and pitiful. She ducked her head to hide her shame, but Dylan caught her chin. Gently, he urged her to look at him.

She could have brushed him off and gotten out of the door. She *wanted* to do that, very much.

Unfortunately, she wanted something else more.

One look into his dark lustrous eyes and his starkly handsome face, and she couldn't look away.

"You must realize you're special. Don't you?" he asked quietly.

"I'm not special," fell past her lips before she could censor herself. "That's why I can't figure out *why* . . . any of this . . . why you—"

Her blundering came to a halt when he leaned forward and kissed her, firm and questing, a simmering, unhurried seduction. A charge tingled through her, and she opened her mouth to increase their contact. Their lips nibbled and molded and slid together in sublime carnality.

"That's why," he said huskily against her lips a moment later. "Because of that."

Dylan's kisses scrambled her brain. It took her a moment for her to piece the topic together again. "Because of sex? Because we're so attracted to each other?"

He put his hand at her nape and pushed her forward slightly so that their foreheads touched. His low mirthless laugh made goose bumps rise beneath his warm hand at her neck.

"Is that all you felt in that kiss?" he demanded.

She pushed her head back, wild to read his expression. He'd sobered. He looked fierce, but she couldn't interpret *why* exactly. It took her a moment to realize he was waiting for her answer.

"I don't know," she admitted, cornered into honesty. "I mean . . . It was . . . I've never had anything like this happen before."

"Neither have I."

"Oh," she muttered tremulously, warmth rushing through her.

His hand moved on her neck, his fingertips caressing her. "Let's just say this for now: I haven't had a peaceful, complete night's rest since I knew of your existence." Her cheeks turned hotter . . . if that was possible. "And as far as your original question?"

She met his stare with wary hopefulness.

"I knew about Deanna and her husband opening this inn for years. This is the first time I've been here, though. I'm glad you think it's a romantic spot, because I don't usually do romance, Alice. At least not with any degree of expertise," he added dryly.

Alice couldn't help but snort with relieved laughter. His lips tilted with humor.

"Okay?" he asked, still stroking her neck. Alice nodded, feeling both vastly pleased and reassured by his answer, but also still unsettled by her need to hear it in order to calm her doubts . . .

To silence her fears.

DEANNA Shrevecraft herself opened the front door to Twelve Oaks for them, her anxious, eager face telling Alice loud and clear that she considered the CEO of Durand Enterprises' presence at her establishment a major coup. She was a pretty, thin woman in her early forties who wore her clothes in the carelessly elegant fashion Alice admired, but knew she could never hope to replicate. Deanna and Dylan conversed comfortably as their hostess led them through the attractive inn. Alice trailed behind, her new hygiene bag clutched in one hand, glancing all around with wary admiration at the interior of the beautiful inn.

"Here we are," Deanna said breathlessly as she paused on the second floor before an antique table with a magnificent fresh flower arrangement. "Mr. Fall, I have this room over here equipped with everything you might need, and Ms. Reed, you'll be in the Sunset Suite, our finest set of rooms," she said, waving gracefully from right to left. "Mr. Fall has asked me to make sure your dress is fresh after your trip, so I'll bring it up in a half hour or so?"

Alice nodded, uncomfortable being the object of such gracious attendance. "Wonderful," Deanna said, clapping her hands together. "Champagne will be served out on the terrace at eight thirty, with dinner to follow at nine. You two are going to have a lovely night for it. The sunset will be breathtaking," Deanna said, beaming at them before she hurried down the hall.

"Why do we have separate rooms?" she whispered to Dylan, very aware of Deanna's footsteps on the stairs behind them.

His dark brows went up. "Would you rather come shower with me? You're more than welcome."

Heat rushed into her cheeks. "No, it just seems strange, to take rooms in an expensive place like this when you don't even plan to sleep in them. And not even one room, but *two*."

"So you're worried about the money," he clarified, deadpan.

"That's not what I mean," she said, scowling. She was lying a little. In truth, she felt awkward in this luxurious setting, unsure of what to expect. She wasn't used to such opulent surroundings or careless spending. Castle Durand was the height of luxury and good taste, but when she was there, it was just Dylan and her. The heat between them always eclipsed her sense of awkwardness.

Dylan stepped into her and brushed his smile against her heated cheek. "I reserved two rooms so that I wouldn't be in your way while you got ready for the evening. I thought you might appreciate a little space. But maybe you're right," he murmured, his firm moving lips on her skin distracting her. "You can come shower with me if you do one thing."

"What?" she asked, turning and lifting her face upward, her lips seeking him like a hardwired instinct.

"I'm getting a little tired of having to interpret what you want, Alice. So tell me you *want* to shower with me, and you will," he told her quietly, his lips brushing hers.

Alice opened her mouth to do just that, but hesitated at the last second. Their fierce, sweet sexual exchanges out at the stables and

Dylan's enigmatic but powerful declaration in the car just now had left her overwhelmed. She could use a little space from him, to gather her thoughts, to solidify a willpower that always turned to melted goo in his presence.

"Well, you've already gotten the rooms." He kissed her on the mouth softly. "And Deanna *did* say she'd bring the dress to the room she gave me," Alice backpedaled lamely.

"Fine," Dylan said as he kissed her one more time, this time dipping his tongue between her lips in a fleeting, electrifying caress. Her sex prickled. He stepped back. "I'll see you out on the terrace at eight thirty?"

"All right," Alice agreed.

She hastened to her room, feeling some strange combination of anticipation, doubtful triumph, and breathless pleasure from Dylan's kiss.

ALICE had finished her shower and was laying out some of her new cosmetics when she heard a soft tap on the door. She rushed through the suite, which seemed obscenely large and luxurious when its sole purpose for the night was for Alice to shower and put on a dress. Deanna stood in the hallway, holding the garment bag.

"Your dress looks perfect. It's unbelievable, by the way. May I come in and hang it for you?" Deanna asked.

"Sure," Alice said, because she sensed it would be rude to say the obvious. *I'm capable of hanging a dress in the closet, thank you.*

Deanna hurried into the room and opened the closet door near the bathroom. Quickly and efficiently, she removed the dress from the bag and hung it on the hook on the inside door over a mirror. She studied the garment closely, using her hand to smooth the flowing fabric.

"Beautiful. You're going to be a knockout in that dress." Deanna

set the garment bag down on a dresser in the large closet and turned
to Alice. Her gaze caught on the opened door to the bathroom and
she did a double take. "You use Dior cosmetics?" Alice realized
she'd seen her new makeup kit opened on the vanity. "That's a great
line of makeup. I have some of the eye shadows, and they're amazing," Deanna said as she walked toward Alice. Not for the first time
since meeting her, Alice studied the older woman's pretty brown
eyes and her subtle, skillful makeup application.

"I just got that makeup," Alice admitted awkwardly. Deanna
was too elegant and polite to ever show an ounce of nosiness in
regard to the nature of Alice's relationship to Dylan, but she knew
the polished woman wasn't stupid. Dylan had ordered a romantic
lakeside dinner for two and hadn't bothered to hide the nature of
their relationship from Deanna, despite the separate rooms.
Deanna must suspect Alice herself could never have afforded that
silk dress or the luxurious makeup. "It was a gift. The truth is . . .
I never usually wear eye shadow."

"You should, with those eyes," Deanna stated unequivocally.

"Thanks," Alice murmured. "I'll give it my best shot."

Deanna tilted her head, smiling. "I don't suppose you'd let me
do your makeup? Before I went to work in human resources at
Durand, I worked at a cosmetics counter in a department store
during summer breaks from college. I used to love it."

"That must be why your makeup is so good," Alice said.

"Thanks. I kind of miss it, to be honest. Well?" Deanna asked
mischievously, tilting her head toward the bathroom. "Will you
let me experiment on you?"

Alice hesitated. "That's okay, I'm sure you're busy."

"Come on," Deanna grinned gamely. "With your face, that
gorgeous skin, and that dream makeup kit in there? I'll be in sev-
enth heaven."

"Are you *sure*?"

"Oh my gosh, I'll be like a kid in a candy store," Deanna

insisted, coming and taking Alice's hand. She led her to the bathroom. "Now you just sit down right there," she said, urging Alice to one of two stools pulled up before a large vanity. She spun Alice so that she faced away from the large mirror and began scrutinizing the contents of the makeup kit on the counter. She picked up a small tub of powder and selected a brush.

"Okay, let's make some magic."

Alice was wary and bemused at first, but soon relaxed under the influence of Deanna's warm banter. Watching the older woman, she grew fascinated. She liked observing Deanna's graceful hands as she wielded wands, brushes, and blending sponges so expertly. She'd never really had anyone dote on her before, or touch her with soft warm fingertips.

Like a mother would fuss over a daughter.

Besides, Alice could understand why Deanna had gone into the hospitality business. She was very easy to talk to. Topics that could be potentially uncomfortable—such as Alice's relationship with Dylan Fall, or how they knew one another—just never seemed to come up. Alice understood it wasn't because Deanna was stupid, but just the opposite. Deanna skillfully and subtly wove their conversation, avoiding uncomfortable topics.

"Do you ever miss working at Durand?" Alice wondered as Deanna blended her blush with a silky soft brush.

"Once in a while. Not enough to want to ever go back. I love being my own boss."

A thought occurred to Alice. "You worked in human resources, right? I don't suppose Sebastian Kehoe was there when you were there?"

"Of course. Kehoe has been at Durand for ages. He's the top man in human resources globally. He had his thirtieth anniversary at Durand just before I left, and that was over three years ago," Deanna said as she exchanged some powder for some eye shadow. "Eyelids closed, please."

Deanna began applying the shadow. "He doesn't really look old enough to have been there that long," Alice mused.

"Kehoe? He's held up well, but he's probably fifty-seven, fifty-eight? He rose up the ranks at a young age and has held mighty sway ever since. Of course, he's an exercise- and health-aholic. Completely rigid about his daily routine. No," Deanna said firmly as she transferred her attentions to Alice's other eyelid. "I *definitely* don't miss having a boss."

Perhaps Deanna hadn't intended to allow the wry, sharp edge into her tone, because she fluidly changed the subject as she picked up some mascara.

"Look down at the floor," she directed. "Did Mr. Fall tell you that Twelve Oaks and Castle Durand were designed by the same man?" she asked as she whisked the mascara wand over Alice's lashes.

"Yes. Twelve Oaks is like a miniature version of it, almost," Alice said.

"Alike in nearly every way. Okay, look up now," Deanna said with the air of someone concentrating on a task. "The castle and Twelve Oaks are alike down to the crown moldings, the type of marble used for the fireplaces and secret cubbyholes."

"You've been to the castle before?" Alice asked.

"I have," Deanna said as she began applying the mascara to Alice's other eye. She straightened after a moment and picked up a tube of lipstick. "I wasn't a Camp Durand manager," she said, referring to the class of elite managers culled from the Camp Durand experience. "But I *was* invited to the castle for a human resources retreat when Mr. Fall first took residence there. He knew my husband and I had bought Twelve Oaks and about the houses' common history, so he was kind enough to let me explore to my heart's content. Okay, blot," she directed as she held a tissue up to Alice's lips. Alice was confused at first, but then pressed her lips gently to the tissue to mute the cosmetic.

"All finished," Deanna said with an air of satisfaction as she regarded Alice. She spun her on the stool.

Alice stared into the mirror. She blinked, her brow crinkling slightly in confusion. Who *was* that woman? Her skin looked flawless and glowing, her lips pouting and sensual, the rich berry color making them appear as full and ripe as summer fruit.

And her *eyes*. Alice was stunned. She'd had no idea that they were so large, or that rich brown and subtle peach shadows could make the midnight-blue shade of the irises so stunning by contrast. Everything Deanna had done with the cosmetics had been to subtly accentuate her features, to highlight them.

While all Alice had ever used cosmetics for was to obfuscate.

"You're beautiful," Deanna said smugly. "Absolutely gorgeous." She picked up a comb from the vanity and brushed back Alice's short hair behind her ears. It'd almost dried since her shower. When Alice combed her hair in a similar manner, it looked merely convenient and shorts-and-T-shirt-ready. When Deanna did it, she looked polished and sophisticated.

Her. *Alice*.

"You're naturally a redhead, aren't you?"

Alice blinked in surprise at Deanna's question. She peered closer in the mirror. "Can you see my roots?"

"No, it's not that. They aren't too bad. It's your eyebrows. I see you have an eyebrow pencil there. Would you like me to darken your brows?" Deanna asked matter-of-factly.

"Yeah, okay."

"It's a unique color," Deanna murmured a moment later as she brushed the pencil over Alice's brow. "Eyebrows are usually darker than the hair on your head. Are you a light auburn?"

"Yeah, reddish blond, maybe. I don't really know anymore. It hasn't been that color in a long time, and I'm not sure what it'd look like if it ever grew out completely. Maybe it's darkened," she confessed uncomfortably.

Alice saw the concerned question in Deanna's kind eyes in the reflection in the mirror. But then she noticed Alice's attention, and she smiled, quashing her curiosity.

"How about if I help you with your dress?" Deanna enthused, stepping back.

"This has all been so nice of you. Thank you. But you really don't have to—"

Deanna pulled a humorous, fake-wounded expression. "After all I've done, you're aren't going to let me see the grand result?"

Alice laughed. "If you *really* want to," Alice said dubiously.

"I do. I haven't had a project this rewarding in a while. I can't *wait* to see Mr. Fall's expression when he gets an eyeful of you."

SIXTEEN

Alice looked around the outdoor terrace admiringly. Deanna and her staff had turned it into a romantic dream setting, including a candlelit table, set with low bowls of white hydrangeas, crystal goblets, and white and silver china. She noticed a waist-high machine near the table, and realized as she stepped closer that it was an air cooler. It worked, because the temperature felt comfortable next to her exposed arms and back, despite the warm summer night. Soft music was being piped onto the terrace, too, subtle notes drifting about on the gentle breeze. A metal frame had been set up around the lovely table, and white linen curtains had been attached. Each of the curtains had been caught back to the frame to grant a full view of the sun beginning to descend into the pale blue Great Lake.

Dylan didn't see her as she approached because of one obscuring curtain. He stood outside of the metal structure. She could just make out his dark pant legs and his forearm resting on the balustrade. He wore a black suit and held a highball glass in one hand.

Alice approached the opening between the swooping curtains and paused. She opened her mouth to speak, but an uncustomary feeling of shyness swept through her, silencing her tongue. She felt beautiful in her new clothing, but also foolish, like the chambermaid parading around in her employer's finery.

Dylan looked over his shoulder, perhaps sensing her there. His expression stiffened. At first he didn't move his body. Only his gaze descended slowly over her, lingering on her breasts. Her nipples tightened. Because of the cut of the dress and the open back, she couldn't wear a bra with it. His stare lowered and then trailed up to her face again, taking his time.

He turned slowly, and she saw that he looked devastating in a black suit, white shirt, and thin black tie.

"Aren't you going to say anything?" she asked, her voice sounding congested with anxiety.

"What should I say?"

Alice exhaled, feeling a little let down by his flat reply. A trace of something—was it dissatisfaction?—flickered across his bold features. He stepped toward her, coming within several inches of her. She looked up at him uncertainly.

"I just meant that words don't suffice. You're a vision."

A smile curved her lips as heat curled in her lower belly. "Deanna helped me," she admitted, her gaze skittering away, as if his stare was too scorching to remain locked with it for long. "With my makeup and making sure the dress was on right and everything."

"It's most definitely on *right*," he said, peering down at her. "I'll have to remember to thank Deanna personally," he murmured. He ran one forefinger softly beneath her chin and she looked up.

"This is the real you, Alice."

She blinked. "If this is the real me, then why do I feel like such a fake?" she asked him. His smile was a sexual caress.

"Maybe the real you is a lot bigger than you thought. You just need time, to familiarize yourself with all the parts." His head dipped. Her breath hitched. "To discover all the mysteries," he added quietly.

His mouth brushed very gently against hers. Alice's eyes fluttered closed. The moment felt sublime. The setting sun was warm on her cheek, the waves hitting the shore below sounding like a soughing sigh.

Dylan was right. Some things *were* mysteries. And maybe

sometimes, you just had to accept the beauty of the unfolding moment. Because if you did what Alice usually did—doubt, question, and refuse to trust—if you grasped *too* hard to understand, you risked rupturing that fragile, ephemeral reality.

DINNER with Dylan was a feast for the senses, every bite of the exquisitely prepared meal a delight, each sip of the cool, dry champagne elevating her euphoric mood. But the man seated across the table from her was the vision on which she feasted most. She couldn't get enough of him, so devastatingly handsome in his suit, his lustrous dark eyes capturing the candlelight as the sun slowly faded. He couldn't seem to take his eyes off her, either, and that had only added to the intoxication of the night. He found her beautiful. Desirable.

Special.

Alice had never come closer to accepting that unlikely reality as she did on that sunset-gilded terrace.

"Would you like more of the cake?" Dylan asked her, and Alice glanced up sharply, hearing the humor and fondness in his deep voice. Night had fallen. Candlelight didn't soften his bold features, but it did make them all that much more compelling. The five-course meal had been incredible, but still she'd found room for dessert—a delectable chocolate molten lava cake. She guiltily stuck her forefinger in her mouth, licking away the last evidence of her greed.

"Sorry," she murmured, realizing she'd been highly focused on her cake for the past few minutes. Meanwhile, Dylan hadn't touched his. He sat back in his chair, a cup of coffee steaming in front of him, watching her while she stuffed her face. "I sort of have a thing for chocolate," she admitted.

"I noticed."

Alice set down her silver fork with a clinking sound. Dylan's smile widened.

"Don't take offense because I noticed. Most men *would* notice you eating chocolate. And not just that example, either," he said, nodding at her spotless plate. "When you came to the house with the others on that first night, you ate all of your chocolate cheese-cake in addition to the serving belonging to that young woman sitting next to you. You flattened that package of Jingdots the other night in seconds."

"You noticed that?" Alice asked with amazed embarrassment. He'd taken note of her eating habits, even that first night at the castle?

Dylan smiled and poured a dollop of cream into his coffee. She watched him stir it with a silver spoon, entranced by the sensual-ity of his movements. He picked up the cup. "I notice a lot of things about you," he said before he took a sip. "And there's no reason to ever apologize for liking your dessert. I liked watching you eat it." Her eyebrows arched in surprised curiosity. "*A lot*," he added significantly.

Alice laughed softly, warmth suffusing her when he joined her.

"Would you like to dance?" he asked after their laughter quieted.

Her mirth evaporated. She shook her head resolutely. "I don't dance."

"You said you didn't ride, either."

"I'm not sure I'd call what we did today *riding*," she mumbled dubiously.

He looked amused, but determined. He stood and put out his hand for her. Alice sighed and reached for him.

"It's not just that I can't dance," she explained when he took her into his arms a moment later and the music swirled around them. "It's these shoes. I'm not used to wearing heels," she explained, looking down at her feet as she began to move with Dylan's body.

"Alice. Look at me, not your feet," he ordered.

She did. His dark eyes shone in the candlelight. His brows quirked into a sardonic, knowing expression.

"There. I told you we move well together."

She realized she'd been gliding in smooth harmony with his body, too enraptured by his eyes to worry about her stumbling feet. The tips of her breasts tingled as they skimmed against his lapel and jacket. She wanted to press closer to his long, hard length. She relished the teasing brush of their clothing, too, however, the elusive hint of his body just as potent as her craving to crush against him greedily.

"I think you take advantage of how attracted I am to you," she said.

His brows went up. "To what end, do you suppose?"

"To get me to do all sorts of things I normally would refuse to do."

He seemed to consider what she said soberly as they swayed to the music. "Maybe you're right. Is that such a bad thing?"

"Maybe not," she admitted. A smile twitched his lips.

"Good," he murmured, dipping his head and brushing his mouth against her temple. She shivered in pleasure. He moved his mouth near her ear. "Because I'm going to take you back to the house and ask you to do a few more things you normally don't do. Not because I *can*." He kissed the shell of her ear, and she trembled. "Because I want to. Because you're the most beautiful thing I've ever seen, and I have to have you completely. I don't want you to hold back. I won't allow it. Do you understand?" he asked quietly, moving his head back and examining her face.

Alice nodded, her stare swallowed by his.

"I want you to trust me, Alice."

"I do," she whispered through lips that felt numb before Dylan lowered his head, and his mouth heated and softened them.

SHE was so keyed up from the magical night, she was a little surprised that she drifted off to sleep on the ride home. She awoke to the sound of the driver's side door opening and closing. Her eyelids opened sluggishly. The passenger door opened, and she peered up at Dylan's hard features softened by amusement . . . and some other emotion that made her just stare up at him dazedly.

"Can you walk?" he asked.

"'Course I can," she muttered. No sooner had she alighted than she stumbled. Dylan steadied her, and then he was lifting her in his arms. She startled at the sound of the passenger door slamming, and suddenly she was flying across the large garage.

"Stupid shoes," she mumbled, her voice thick with sleep. He shifted her in his arms to deactivate the security alarm, and she wrapped her arms around his shoulders, thrilling anew at how big and solid and male he was beneath his suit coat. When she became aware of how good he felt to her, how much she loved being in his arms, guilt wriggled into her awareness at her growing dependence on him . . . her helpless addiction.

"Put me down now," she said as he opened the door.

He gave her a hard, dry glance as he stepped over the threshold and kicked the door closed.

"You're fine where you are. I don't want any broken ankles," he said as he reactivated the security.

She sighed and rested her cheek against his suit jacket. She was too tired to argue.

Or she just didn't want to.

Before she knew it, he was sweeping her into his bedroom and kicking the door closed.

"Lock it, Alice," he said.

She recalled him saying something similar that first night they had sex here together. Excitement rippled through her as she recalled what he'd said to her during their dance. She was suddenly wide-awake, her skin prickly with awareness.

He carried her over to the bed once she'd secured the lock. He set her on the edge and immediately whipped off her new pumps.

"We'll get you flats from now on."

"I'll never get used to wearing heels then," she protested.

"You want to get used to them?"

"I don't know. Maybe," she said. He urged her to stand in her bare feet. "Don't men think high heels are sexy?"

"You'd learn to wear them for that?" he asked as he took her loosely into his arms. She'd grown used to wearing the heels for the past few hours and was struck anew at how tall he was, and how small she felt next to him.

"Maybe," she hedged again, glancing up into his face. "Maybe . . . if you thought they were sexy."

He cradled her chin, his thumb brushing against her jawline. "I think *that's* sexy."

"What? Wearing heels?" she asked, confused.

"That you'd do it if you thought I liked it. But don't worry. I'd think you were sexy in ratty old slippers."

"Right."

He laughed, low and rough, then sobered as he watched himself trace the line of her jaw and then her ear. "There *is* something I'd like to see you in."

"What?" she asked, because she'd felt the increase in tension of his body as he asked the question.

"Cuffs, both on your ankles and wrists. And not a stitch else."

She quickened in excitement. "You want to restrain me again?"

He met her stare. "I told you what I wanted at the Twelve Oaks. I don't want you to hold anything back. I want your trust."

"Sexually?"

"It's a start."

She studied him warily.

"I'll tell you exactly what I'd like to do, and you can decide if you want to proceed," he said, stepping out of her arms. She watched, puzzled, when he went over to the seating area of the suite and reached beneath a long console table behind the couch. He withdrew a stool of sorts. It was very low to the floor, thus the reason it fit beneath the table. She'd noticed it in passing, but never paid much attention to it in the past. She'd thought vaguely it must be some kind of artwork that could pass as furniture. It had a sleek, modern design. There were usually several leather and suede pillows on it.

She looked at it fully for the first time as he carried it toward where she stood. She saw that the seat wasn't really a traditional seat, but instead two wide pieces of supple leather with about a two-and-a-half-inch-wide empty space between them. The leather strips were suspended about nine inches off the floor by a frame. The frame was on both sides, but the center portion of the stool was open. Dylan set the stool on the rug before her, and the front of it bounced ever so lightly, indicating there was a spring to the structure. Alice had thought the frame was made of wood before, but now she realized it was metal painted to match the brown of the leather.

She stared up at Dylan bemusedly.

"It's designed to be used for sex," he stated bluntly. "I'm going to have you sit on it and restrain you."

Alice blinked. "And then what?"

He shrugged, his sexy smile lingering. "What else? I'm going to make love to you."

"You mean you're going to torture me, don't you?" she asked suspiciously, even though her breath had grown choppy with excitement.

"I'm going to have you at my mercy," he corrected quietly as he reached around her back and began to lower her zipper. The dipping of his hand coincided with the delicious sinking sensation of arousal in her belly and sex. "I'm going to punish you a little. I'm going to ask you to trust me enough to give me control, and I'm going to make you feel very good. Does that sound like torture to you?"

He swept the thin straps of her dress over her shoulders and the fabric fell to her waist. Dylan moved his hands along the side of her rib cage, making her skin roughen and her nipples tighten. He cradled her breasts and whisked his thumbs over her nipples, watching his actions the whole time.

"God, you're beautiful. I've been waiting to do that all night," he said, a slight snarl shaping his mouth as he stared at her breasts in his hands. He pinched her nipples lightly. She tightened her thighs to ease the sudden sharp ache that flared at her sex. "Answer me, Alice," he insisted, because her lungs had frozen at his touch. "Does my plan sound like torture?"

"Maybe a little," she admitted. He continued to play with her breasts, and she shivered in pleasure. She trusted being in *his* hands. She loved it. "But for the most part, it sounds really dirty. And potentially extremely nice," she added very quietly.

His gaze zoomed to meet hers. She gave a dubious shrug, and he smiled, the flash of white teeth against his face breathtaking and a little dangerous. Her heart leapt beneath his stroking, knowing fingers, but then he was dropping his hands.

"Take off your dress and panties then," he directed. He waited for her to follow his instruction, his gaze unwavering.

She swept the dress down and off in an instant. It'd been exciting to be nearly naked beneath the sensual, soft fabric all night, but it was exponentially more thrilling to take it off while Dylan watched her like a hawk. She laid the dress on the upholstered bench at the foot of his bed and turned back to him. He glanced down pointedly at her silk briefs, and she obligingly drew the panties down and stepped out of them, tossing them on top of her dress. When she turned back to Dylan, he hadn't moved. Alice felt her heart expanding until it felt like it was pressing against her rib cage, his stare on her was so hot.

So possessive.

Surely he was about to throw her down on the bed and ravish her.

Instead, he blinked once and turned away.

From inside a bedside chest of drawers, he withdrew several cuffs. As he walked toward Alice, she saw that they were different than the ones he'd put on her the other night to restrain her arms to the bed. First of all, there were four of them. They each contained a padded leather wristlet or anklet portion attached to an adjustable strap. Alice eyed them with mounting anxious excitement as Dylan placed the restraints on the bed and swiftly removed his suit jacket, tossing it aside. He glanced over at her as he began to remove his cuff links from his shirt.

"Come here," he said.

He seemed very stern all of a sudden, and Alice experienced a flash of shyness walking toward him naked. It escalated her arousal. Everything felt very exposed and vulnerable, her thighs and belly and breasts. Her mind. Her nipples tightened in a rush, resulting in a slight pinching sensation. She paused a foot away from him, watching warily as he loosened his tie. She wished he'd look at her with that amused, warm gleam in his eyes that she often saw mixing with his raw lust. But he was different tonight, his authority and seriousness somehow just as natural and exciting as his fondness and undisguised lust as he'd sexually guided her in the past.

He dragged his gaze off her and turned away. He withdrew something else from that forbidden treasure chest next to the bed and slammed the drawer shut.

Alice's eyes widened when he placed her new crop on the bed next to the restraints. Arousal shot through her like a jolt of adrenaline mainlined into her blood. It had embarrassed her, how wild she'd become when he spanked her the other night, how she'd transformed into a hedonistic wild thing she barely recognized.

Just the vision of the crop brought it all back in a rush. *This* was more serious, though. It looked like it'd sting. She resisted an urge to touch her ass. The nerves already seemed to prickle, as if in anticipation of what was to come.

"So that you know what's going to happen before you agree to let me restrain you," Dylan said, nodding pointedly at the crop. He unfastened his shirt and whipped it off his shoulders with a distracting flex of bulging muscle and gleam of smooth skin. The truth struck her full force. He was strong—much more powerful than her. He could subdue her anytime he chose. Instead, Dylan was asking her to give him the reins of her own free will, to trust him enough to submit, to understand he would keep her safe while she did.

The idea made her anxious, but aroused her almost unbearably as well.

She ate up the vision of his naked torso while her pulse began to throb at her throat. He reached for one of the restraints and held it up expectantly, his dark, sleek brows arched in a silent question.

Alice licked her lower lip nervously, eyeing the crop, and held out her wrist.

SEVENTEEN

The cuffs were made of padded leather, supple and strong. There were silver loops and hook fasteners on them. Dylan stood after attaching the last two to her ankles, his hooded gaze moving slowly over her as she stood there wearing only the four cuffs. She almost said something joking to lighten the intensity of the moment, but then saw his jaw clench with tension. Her ability for sarcastic flippancy evaporated. He took her hand and led her over to the stool.

He'd said it was designed for sex, but she only understood dimly what that entailed. "Sit down on the front part," he said, and Alice realized she was about to find out.

She lowered with Dylan's guidance, her knees bent in front of her, her butt coming to rest on the leather seat. The thick leather straps were taut but springy, suspended as they were between the flexible metal frame. Dylan knelt before her, his knees on the carpet.

"Spread your thighs," he murmured, and she realized his stare was on her pussy. She obliged, opening herself further. He put his hands on her hips and urged her sideways on the seat slightly.

"*Oh,*" she muttered in surprised understanding, because her pussy had just slid between the two leather straps, exposing it from below. Her body weight on the taut straps spread her sex wide.

Dylan gave a small, knowing smile at her exclamation. He

drew her wrists behind her to her lower back. Her spine arched slightly, her breasts thrusting forward. She felt him fasten the cuffs together, restraining her hands behind her.

"Comfortable?" he asked.

"Yes."

"Put your feet to the side of the stool." He gently maneuvered her left leg so that her knee was bent and the top of her foot rested on the soft carpet, the inside pressing against the metal frame of the stool. She heard a metallic clicking sound. She pulled on her foot experimentally. It was bound.

"You restrained me to this stool? Like *this*?" she asked, referring to her splayed, wholly vulnerable position.

"I told you," he said gruffly, standing, "I want you at my mercy." He walked to the other side of her. He must have noticed her anxious expression because he paused and touched her cheek. "Do you want to stop?"

Alice swallowed thickly and shook her head. Staring into his eyes, seeing whatever mysterious but nevertheless *incredible* thing she saw there, pushed away her anxiety. He just nodded and knelt, restraining her other ankle to the metal frame.

When he'd finished and stood, she perched on the stool, her legs spread as wide as possible and restrained, her sex and buttocks parted and suspended in the gap between the leather straps, her naked breasts thrust forward and heaving slightly as she panted shallowly in mounting excitement.

By the time he rose and came around to the front of her, she was staring at him in wide-eyed amazement. Her position was blatantly lewd, and suggestive of any number of sexual possibilities, each one dirtier than the next.

"Are you comfortable?" he asked.

"*Comfortable?*" she repeated, stunned. She was way too aroused and anxious to call her state remotely *comfortable*.

"I mean are you in any pain or discomfort," he said, caressing her shoulder. Her nerves tingled beneath his touch. Her nipples pinched tight.

"No," Alice said honestly.

He nodded. She met his steady stare, her heart starting to throb faster, the sensation amplified because of her stretched, exposed torso.

"You have to tell me at any time if your joints start to get uncomfortable, or if you cramp up, *anything*."

Alice just stared at him, speechless.

"Alice?" She blinked. "I mean it. At the slightest twinge, call out. Do you understand me?" he repeated fiercely. "I don't want you to suffer a pulled muscle or something. Agree to it, that you'll speak up if you get uncomfortable or have any pain from the restraint, no matter what's happening. I'm trusting you to do that, as much as you're trusting me in this." He nodded at her bound body. "Do you understand?"

"Okay," she agreed.

His rigid expression relaxed slightly. He walked over to the bed and picked up the crop. Alice's already escalated heartbeat seemed to redouble. A protest flew to her throat, but she stifled it at the last minute as Dylan walked toward her, the crop hanging by his side. Yes, she was unbearably exposed and vulnerable, but he was so commanding in that moment, so beautiful and exciting. He still wore his suit trousers, but nothing else. She could tell by the bulge at his crotch he'd become aroused by restraining her to the stool.

But it was the hot, possessive gleam in his eyes as he stepped toward her that silenced her protest most effectively.

"Don't be afraid," he said quietly, and Alice realized he'd read her anxiety despite the quashing of her misgivings. "I told you I'd keep you safe." He lifted her new crop and ran the leather slapper down the side of her ribs to her waist, and then back up again. Alice gasped and shivered. The leather was cool and soft, the feeling of it on her sensitive skin exciting. Dylan had stepped closer as he rubbed the slapper against the curve of her hip and the expanse of her belly. She watched his progress, spellbound, but then he slid the crop to her lower back. She lifted her head, only to stare directly at his crotch just inches away. He stood close. She could see the column of his cock as it slanted upward and at a diagonal to the left, trapped between his body and briefs. Longing overwhelmed her. She craned forward instinctively.

Pop.

"Ouch," she exclaimed, stunned. He'd lifted the crop and slapped the top of her right buttock.

"Don't stretch forward. I don't want you to hurt yourself, since your hands are bound," he said, now using the leather slapper to rub the stinging spot on her ass.

"Fine," she muttered, throwing him a miffed glance. He smiled.

"You know I'm going to use this crop on you. Why are you acting mad because I did?"

"Because I don't need to be lectured while you're doing it," Alice mumbled distractedly, because he was running the slapper all over the tops of her buttocks now, even dipping it into the spread crevice of her ass. Meanwhile, his taut abdomen and crotch took up almost her entire field of vision. She could only look, not touch.

"I won't lecture you if you do as I say," he growled. He ran the slapper up the side of her body, sending a ripple of excitement through her. She moaned when he slid it over the globe of her breast. He covered her nipple with the leather slapper, pressed, and circled very subtly.

Liquid warmth rushed through her. She bit off a moan. It felt forbidden, but the vision of him holding that crop and pressing it against her nipple was downright dirty. Exciting.

"You like your new crop," he said warmly, swishing the leather between the valley of her heaving breasts and stimulating her other nipple. Her nipples pinched tight, making her grit her teeth.

"Who says?" she grated out.

"You do," he replied, using the leather to flick slightly at her left nipple. She moaned uncontrollably. She knew what he meant. He was making her nipples tight and hard. They hurt for stimulation. He lifted the slapper and tapped it against her right nipple. Air hissed between her teeth. Dylan made a deep rough sound of gratification.

"So sensitive. You're going to break in this crop with a fury, aren't you?"

"You're the one doing that," she said in a choked voice.

He laughed softly. "You're right," he agreed, before he continued to play with her breasts using the slapper, lifting and caressing the globes, rubbing the aching nipples, and every once in a while, erotically slapping the sides. Alice grew so aroused by the forced stimulation, a scream built in her throat.

He stepped closer, one foot between her splayed thighs, his crotch now just inches from her face. She could make out the shape of his succulent cockhead where it pressed against his pants. She craved the hard pressure of it against her parted lips, could imagine exactly how it would feel. Dylan had something else in mind, though.

"Lean into me a little. I've got you," he said, his opened palm on her shoulder a steady support. She tilted toward him an inch, her hips rolling on the leather straps. The position exposed more of the tops of her buttocks, she realized with a sense of trepidation and excitement. He lifted the crop to her bare back and swished it up and down the length in a rhythmic motion. Down, up, down.

Pop.

He'd slapped the top of her buttock, but no sooner had he done it, then the crop was gliding back up her back. She tensed when he slid it down her spine again, but he only glided it back up to her shoulder blade. Then down to her ass and . . .

Smack.

Her body jolted in excitement. Her bottom tingled. She suddenly damned the stool very much, because she was left with no way to apply pressure against her wet pussy, suspended as it was between the leather straps. She shifted her hips in restless arousal.

"Keep still," Dylan ordered tensely, never breaking his stride. He swished the slapper up and down her back, up and down, *pop*. He slapped her bottom. The steady rhythm, the sure knowledge that she'd be spanked on the second downstroke, drove her wild with aroused anticipation. Her clit pinched very tight. The air tickled at her wet, spread sex. Her entire awareness focused down to the movement of that evil, gliding little slapper and its cadence: up, down, up, down, *slap*; up, down, up, down, *pop*.

The tops of her buttocks started to burn. She knew that Dylan would protest if she shifted her hips too strenuously, but she instinctively pressed down with her pelvis, almost as if she thought the mere air could give the friction against her pussy she needed. It didn't work. A frustrated, furious cry flew from her throat.

Dylan broke his wicked rhythm and rubbed the crop against her hip softly.

"What?" he murmured.

"My . . . There's nothing to . . ." Alice paused in her desperate, flustered explanation for what she needed. Dylan had slid the crop to the front of her hip and now whisked it across her belly. He pressed up on it slightly, mounting the heavy, thick feeling of congestion at her sex.

"Alice?" he coaxed.

"What?"

"Just ask."

She closed her eyes at the two words. Why did he have to make her say it? Both her ass and her pussy burned in tandem. Her clit sizzled. She bit off her plea and flexed her hips, whimpering when she couldn't get the pressure she needed.

Required.

She clamped her eyes shut. A tiny bead of sweat rolled down the valley between her breasts.

"Put it between my legs like you did on my breast," she whispered weakly.

He gently pushed back on her shoulder, straightening her. He lowered the slapper to her mons. She moaned as he pressed upward suggestively.

"Open your beautiful eyes and look at me," she heard him say, his stern tone cutting through her increasingly mindless state. Slowly, she pried open her eyelids and peered up at him. His face looked fierce and rigid, but there was compassion mixing with the blaze in his eyes. "Say it out loud, Alice. What do you want?"

Her sex clenched tight, so hungry for pressure.

"Put the slapper on my pussy. Make me come," she requested tremulously.

Savage triumph passed across his handsome face. Then he was lowering the leather slapper to her spread outer sex. Alice cried out shakily when he pressed up on her labia and clit. The rod moved back and forth in a taut rhythm as he stimulated her. It was lewd and divine in equal measure. He stirred her perfectly with that little slapper.

She shuddered as climax hit her.

"That's right," she heard him say through her keening. It took her a moment to realize it was *her* making all that noise. The scream that had been building in her throat had erupted as she came. She bit her lip, trying to stifle her rampant pleasure, but Dylan rubbed her pussy with the slapper more strenuously.

"Oh God" broke out of her throat as the shudders of pleasure amplified.

"This is your crop now. Get it nice and wet with your juices."

She shook helplessly, her bliss spiking up yet again at his illicit words.

A delicious, stretched moment later, Dylan removed the crop

from between her legs, halting her stimulation. She sagged, panting for air. Vaguely, she realized he had stepped way from her. It took a few seconds for curiosity about what he was doing to seep into her awareness. She opened her eyes sluggishly, forcing her focus onto Dylan as he walked across the room with a long-legged stride and tossed the crop onto the bed. Then he was coming toward her, his blazing expression making her blink. Her brain struggled to recover from her explosive climax.

He knelt before her, and much to her surprise, lowered to a supine position on the floor.

"What are you . . . *doing*?" she asked brokenly when he slid his head beneath the stool and reached up to grasp her hips.

"I could hear that crop moving in your pussy. You're soaking wet," she heard him grate out from beneath her. "What do you think I'm going to do?"

He ran his tongue between her labia, gathering her juices. Alice quaked. The tip of his tongue laved her clit with a hard pressure, and she cried out in harshly reawakened pleasure.

He pushed down on the tops of her thighs, bouncing her body on the leather straps and his tongue. The stool squeaked as she bobbed subtly against his mouth and probing tongue, up and down, up and down. She screamed. She'd wanted pressure, and he gave it to her now in spades.

He ate her with savage abandon, his focused hunger stunning. Alice was trapped . . . both at the mercy of her swamping pleasure and Dylan. She was his willing victim. She had no choice but to sit there while he tongued her clit ruthlessly and applied an eye-crossing suction, bouncing her against him the entire time. He wouldn't let *her* bob her body, but instead insisted on controlling the rhythm. Her entire world became the pulse of her sex against him, the illicit sound of the squeaking bouncing frame and her heartbeat roaring in her ears. Her body was stretched tight on a rack of pleasure. Time collapsed . . .

And then exploded violently.

He made her come not once, but twice, pausing to slide his tongue high into her channel following each climax, drinking deeply of the fruits of his labor.

Alice slumped in the restraints following her second climax, feeling dazed and thoroughly wrung out by pleasure. Dylan's mouth was still moving on her sex, sending post-climactic spasms through her flesh. Her pussy seemed to be charged in a way she'd never known it to be, his continued, focused stimulation oversensitizing her nerves to the point where she experienced almost a constant low-grade orgasm. Dylan lay on his back in front of her, his nude, ripped torso stunning to behold. Her gaze fixed on the large bulge behind his black trousers. She moaned, riding the edge between satiation and hunger.

It was unbearable.

"Dylan, stop, please," she said, her voice quaking. She couldn't stand it anymore, having what she wanted so acutely paraded in front of her while she was helpless to touch.

He slicked his tongue between her labia one last time, and then nuzzled her gently with his nose.

"Have you had enough?"

"No," she said miserably, because the lack of his firm, lashing tongue was a blow. "It's just that I can't take it anymore."

He caressed her thighs, and her muscles tightened beneath him.

"What is it that you want?" he asked. She shivered at the sensation of his warm breath against her hyper-aroused tissues.

"You."

She shut her eyes, the single word, her naked plea, echoing around her skull. His hands slipped off her. She clamped her eyes tight, as if she could deny her need by doing so. Then she felt his hand cradling her jaw, his thumb whisking over her scalding-hot cheek.

"So beautiful," he said. "Open your eyes, Alice."

She blinked up at him. He stood before her. He'd wiped his mouth while he stood, but his lips and chin still glistened from her juices. She wanted to close her eyes again, because he looked so beautiful to her in that moment, it was a like a small, sharp pain. His dark eyes willed her not to look away, though.

"You trusted me. I felt it," he rasped.

She nodded. It must be true. Alice would never have considered in a million years letting another person have the control over her that she'd just granted Dylan. She'd not only granted it. She'd loved every second of it.

Holding her stare, he began to unfasten his pants. He jerked his boxer briefs down over his erection along with his trousers. His cock sprung free. She held her breath, enthralled by the vision. Not only his size made her aroused; he was so beautifully shaped, the shaft thick and straight where it rose from his shaved, round balls. The cockhead was a succulence that made her salivate.

He stepped forward, his hand sliding to the back of her head.

"Don't, Alice," he said sharply when she strained for him. "It'll pull your shoulder muscles. I'm going to give it to you. Do you understand?"

She looked up at him, her lips parted. His jaw looked very tight.

"I'm going to fuck your mouth. I don't want you to move. Do you trust me to do that?"

A ripple of something went through her. Was it trepidation? Or excitement? Talk about being at his mercy. He could hurt her. *Dylan wouldn't.*

"Yes," she whispered.

He studied her face closely, and then stepped closer. The smooth dense surface of his cockhead brushed against her mouth. A thin stream of pre-ejaculate spread on her lower lip. Her heart leapt in her chest when he cupped the shaft from below.

"Open your lips," he said.

She parted for him willingly. She'd breathed in the scent of his arousal, caught the hint of it on her tongue. Her fears evaporated under the spell of her hunger. He paused, only the fat tapered head penetrating her mouth.

"Polish it with your tongue," he demanded.

She followed his instruction eagerly, his taste penetrating her awareness.

"That's right. Nice and firm," he praised, and she felt his focus on her from above, the attention thrilling her.

His hand tightened at the back of her head, steadying her.

"I'm only going to subject you to this for a minute or two," he said thickly. "I'm going to explode in your pussy." Her eyes sprang wide at that. She tried to look up at his face to read his expression, but couldn't see him, given their positioning.

Subject her to this?

It sounded like he planned on having his way with her.

A thrill of anxious excitement went through her.

He bent his knees slightly, parting his thighs to steady himself and finding the right angle.

His cock slid across her tongue. She sucked hungrily.

He grunted. "God, your mouth. I've been thinking about doing this since the second you squeezed me dry in the stables this afternoon," he said. His other hand rose to her head, this one cradling her jaw to give her support. He started to pulse in and out of her mouth.

It was horribly exciting. She couldn't do anything, but be a receptacle of his desire. She was restrained to the stool, and he held her head so that it was unmovable. All she could do to show her desire was form her lips into a tight, clutching ring, massage the bottom of his thrusting cock with her tongue, and suck.

So she sucked for all she was worth.

"Aw Jesus, you really want it, don't you?" he growled, sounding almost angry. He took his pleasure, flexing his hips and pumping his cock in and out of her mouth. He wasn't gentle, but he didn't abuse the situation, either. He penetrated her fast and firm, but shallowly, sparing her throat.

"That's so fucking good," he moaned raggedly. "I want to come in your hot mouth again. I want to fuck your sweet little pussy raw, too. Damn you, Alice. I want you everywhere. All the time," he added darkly, pumping more strenuously.

She found herself wishing he'd go deeper. There was something about him using her for his pleasure that excited her. Maybe because it clearly excited him. His need was naked and raw. She strained against his hold, craning to duck deeper down over his thrusting shaft. She gained a fraction of an inch and felt him thrust into her throat.

He made a wild, rough sound. His hips pulled back, and his swollen cock popped out of the ring of her lips.

"What?" she mumbled dazedly, blinking her eyes open. Her lips felt numb and swollen from squeezing him so relentlessly, but nevertheless, she craved that hard pressure again. Dylan was no longer standing in front of her. She tried to look around to see what he was doing, but then she felt the give on her right foot, and realized he was releasing her from the restraint on the stool. Her left foot gave as well.

"Put your feet back to the front of the stool," he directed, sounding grim. She felt the tension in her arms lessen. He pulled her arms around to the front. Stepping in front and to the side of her, he massaged her shoulders briskly. She realized she'd winced in pain upon being released from the restraint. The position hadn't hurt when she'd held it and been drugged by lust, but she felt discomfort once the tension was released. Dylan's warm, massaging hands quickly loosened the tight muscles.

"Okay?" he asked.

"Yes," Alice assured.

"Good. Then come here," he said.

He helped her to stand, keeping his hands on her shoulders to steady her. When she stood on shaky legs again, her gaze dropped downward. He'd shucked off his pants and briefs at some point while releasing her restraints. His cock jutted forward from his body, huge and a little intimidating. He made a rough sound in his throat, and she realized he'd seen her staring at him.

He took her hand and pulled her over to the bed.

"I don't mean to be crude, but you're driving me crazy. I just want to explode in you."

"Okay," Alice agreed, wide-eyed. She loved a lot of things about Dylan, but she thought she liked him best when his control started to crumble.

"Bend over the bed."

She hastened to take the position, all too glad to put an end to his suffering, craving his release perhaps as much as him. He'd brought her to climax again and again, so unselfish in giving her pleasure. She wanted nothing more than to give him a small measure of what he'd given her.

She leaned over, putting her hands on the bed. His hands glided across her hips, pushing slightly so that her pelvis curved around the edge of the mattress. He pressed gently on her back, and her breasts and then her cheek dropped to the soft duvet.

"Spread your legs," he directed, and she felt his cock nudging her pussy. "This isn't going to take long. And this is for *me*. You've been a trial, Alice. This is what you've driven me to."

A spasm of excitement went through her. He's said it fondly, but with that edge of steel that excited her. *This is for me*. She bit her lip to keep from crying out when he squeezed one buttock, holding her in place, and drove his cock into her.

"Fuck," he muttered viciously. He was enormous with need, stretching even her satiated flesh. He paused when he was fully sheathed, his cock throbbing high inside her. She started when he grasped one of her wrists.

"Place it at your back," he said thickly.

Even though he told her what to do, he guided her. He held her wrist firmly at her lower back, his other hand cupping one of her ass cheeks.

She braced herself for being fucked hard, but he surpassed her expectations.

It was like being taken by a storm. She quaked on the bed, rattled and shaken by his stark possession. The way he held her wrist at her lower back excited her, as did his hold on her ass. She was his to do with as he pleased. He knew it, and that knowledge aroused him, she could tell.

It aroused her, too.

His seemingly aggressive hold on her as he took his pleasure wasn't what it seemed. It made her feel so secure. Beautiful, because she was the sole focus of his monumental desire, and that was an undeniable truth.

A moment later, she felt his cock lurch inside her, making her cry out in anguished excitement. She felt a great shudder go through him and instinctively tightened around him. His shout as he came was harsh, ripping straight to the heart of her.

Alice lay there, panting and undone, feeling Dylan convulsing inside her and his warm semen filling her, and wondered how the hell she'd gotten to this inexplicable, beautiful moment.

EIGHTEEN

I t was her day off. Even though she didn't have to wake up before dawn today, Alice cursed the fact that she did anyway. She awoke slightly chilled on the front of her body, but warm and toasty on her backside. The suite was cloaked in the darkest shadows of the night. The sheet and comforter had slid off her, but Dylan's long body was curved around her protectively. She drew up the covers, careful not to wake him.

For a few seconds, she just absorbed how good it felt, to wake up in the circle of his body, his arm draped around her. It was sublime. In the past, she'd had a couple of boyfriends who wanted to hold her while they'd slept. Alice had always eased away in the bed, feeling suffocated by the weight of another human body pressing on her while she tried to succumb to sleep.

When Dylan held her, it felt different. It grounded her; it was also a pleasure to her senses. When he sought her out in the darkness, it seemed like a natural pull of their bodies, as if when they were close together, they were meant to touch. Alice had the strange, vague idea that he felt reassured by having her against him, as if it eased him to know she was present. It was a fuzzy concept that made no sense now that she considered it lying there in the darkness.

He was probably worried she was going to sleepwalk again, like she had that first night when she slept at the castle.

She shivered involuntarily recalling that night. Surely it had all been a product of her imagination. Either that, or she really had been walking around while in that realm between sleep and wake-fulness.

Fear slinked into her awareness.

Don't think about that night. You're going to spook yourself.

Since she'd told herself not to recall the details of that night, that's precisely what her brain decided to do, of course. She could hear that eerie woman's call replay in her memory. Her eyes opened in the darkness, searching out familiar landmarks in the large suite. Her ears, too, went on high alert, as if on a search mission.

And she heard precisely what she dreaded hearing.

Aaa—eee!

Alice started. It was like the voice from her memory had jumped out of her head and into the house. It was indistinct, and she couldn't quite make it out, but she had the single horrifying thought that the voice had been calling her name.

"You okay?"

"*What?*" Alice asked in a high-pitched voice, Dylan's deep, sleep-roughened voice ringing in her ears. His hand opened on her naked hip and followed the curve up to her waist. It took her a moment to realize she'd awakened him when she jumped. She waited, anxious for the woman to call again so that Dylan could confirm it. Silence pressed on her ears.

"Alice?"

"Uh . . . yeah, I was dreaming. Sorry I woke you."

His warm hand coasted down her thigh. "It must have been a nightmare. You're covered in goose bumps. What were you dream-ing about?"

"That woman . . ." she muttered.

"What woman?"

She swallowed thickly. "Nothing. It's fading," she evaded. "I don't remember."

He didn't reply, but his warm hand kept moving, soothing her roughened, tingling skin. She was positive she hadn't convinced him.

As the seconds passed, however, she realized she was being ridiculous. There was no way Dylan could have possibly understood that strange, atavistic fear that had swept through her just now. She sensed him lifting his head, and realized he was glancing at the clock.

"It's the time we usually wake up," he said. She snuggled deeper into his hold, taking solace in it.

"I know. Bad luck."

"Maybe not."

She turned her chin toward him and felt his nose and lips nuzzle her ear. "What do you mean?"

"We could take advantage instead of going back to sleep right away," he said, making her shiver in pleasure as his lips moved against her ear.

"What'd you have in mind?" she asked, wiggling her ass against him. He grunted softly and spread his large hand over her naked hip.

"*That*, for certain," he said dryly, sinking his fingers into her buttock suggestively. "But maybe we can go up and catch the sunrise first?"

She turned onto her other hip hastily. "Really?"

"Yeah. Why not?"

"For someone who claims he doesn't do romance, you certainly get some pretty romantic ideas."

"Are you complaining? Because if you are, you're going to cut off my attempts just as I'm getting started," he said dryly, whipping the sheet and comforter off them.

She jumped and laughed when he swatted her butt playfully. "No complaints, I promise."

"Then on your feet, you romance-slacker."

TEN minutes later, Dylan led her from the kitchen to the backstairs they'd taken that first evening of the party, when he'd found her alone in the dining room. Dylan had quickly and efficiently made them cups of coffee using the Keurig machine in the large kitchen. They both clutched steaming mugs now as Alice followed him up to the second, third, and then a fourth level of the stairs.

"Where are we going?" she whispered. Dylan had turned on a dim light to illuminate the narrow set of stairs, but Alice realized that their spontaneous little activity in the darkness had a furtive, exciting feeling to it, similar to how a lot of things felt in this grand old house.

Just like a lot of things felt with Dylan.

"There's an east-facing balcony. This area is known for our sunsets over the lake, but if you can see over the tree line, the sunrises are nice, too. The view is good up here."

"You sound like you watch the sunrise there a lot," Alice said, stepping through a door on the fourth floor when Dylan opened it.

"Not a lot, but I've told you I'm not the best of sleepers."

Alice didn't respond, because they were on an even narrower staircase now, going from the third to the fourth floor, the wooden steps squeaking loudly beneath their bare feet. She opened the door at the top of the stairs and they walked into the inky-black, warm night. The light from the opened doors allowed her to navigate across a long twelve-foot-deep terrace.

"A swing," she exclaimed, ignoring several Adirondack chairs and making a beeline for a large wooden porch swing suspended from the eaves. She plopped down on the swing, careful not to spill her coffee. She caught Dylan's small smile as he came to sit next to her.

"Little girls always love a swing," he said, pushing with his feet so that they swayed gently.

"This big girl does, anyway," Alice said, grinning. The ropes squeaked in the hooks above them, the sound cozy and somehow relaxing as it resounded into the darkness of predawn. "It's old," she observed, running her fingertips along the worn wood.

"Yeah. I've been meaning to have it repainted," Dylan said, his arm going around her. Alice snuggled up next to him, her cheek pressing against his T-shirt-covered chest. She still felt a little sleepy, but also very content.

"White," Alice said quietly, the sound of the squeaking swing lulling her.

"Hmmm?" Dylan asked, his hand cupping her shoulder. Alice noticed distractedly that although his query sounded casual, he'd halted taking a sip of his coffee mid-motion.

"You should paint the porch swing white," Alice clarified. "And put pots of flowers along there," she said, waving her coffee cup along the white posts of the balcony. She took a sip of her coffee. "That's how it should be."

"I see," Dylan said before he lifted his coffee cup to his lips. Even though he sounded very sober, Alice was sure he was humoring her dozy flight of fancy.

"The sky is starting to lighten a little," Alice murmured a moment later, her gaze on the tree line. The birds had started their predawn chatter. "I think I'll call Maggie later today."

One long finger reached and caressed her neck. "What made you think of Maggie?"

"I don't know," she mumbled, turning her face into his T-shirt and inhaling the delicious scent of clean cotton and Dylan. "I guess it's because this has been the longest I haven't talked to her since I moved into her place a few years ago."

"You guys talk regularly?"

"Yeah. We talked at school, of course, in Maggie's lab. But we usually had dinner together at her house, and we'd watch TV and stuff." She kissed his chest before taking another sip of coffee. "I miss Doby," she reflected after a moment.

"Doby, the flea-ridden dog who hates the vet?"

She looked up into his face, beaming. "You remember I told you that?"

He shrugged. "Apparently," he said with a small smile. Their gazes held. "Maggie sounds like she's family to you," he said, stroking the shell of her ear.

Alice thought about that for a moment.

"She is, I guess. She's been very good to me. If it weren't for her, I don't think I could have gotten through graduate school. You'd think she won a spot as a Camp Durand counselor herself, as proud as she's been about me getting in here."

"She's almost like a mother."

Alice blinked. "Maybe. Sort of. Certainly more of a mother than I've ever had," she laughed shortly. "What about you?" she asked tentatively after a moment, taking a sip of coffee and straightening.

"You *better* not be thinking I'm like a mother figure."

She laughed at that. *As if.* "No, I mean . . . do you ever see your mom? You never talk about family."

"That's because I don't have any."

"None? You don't have brothers or sisters?"

He shook his head. "Not that I know of."

She nodded, recalling all too well what he'd told her about his mother.

"I know you never knew your father," she said in a rush, as if to get it over with. "But your mom? Is she still alive?"

"No. She died of liver disease five years ago."

"I'm sorry," Alice whispered, peering into her coffee cup. She didn't like it. She didn't like it at all, thinking of Dylan being so alone in the world. "Was she"—she swallowed thickly—"proud of you? For all you'd accomplished in your life? I hope she was, because you're an incredible success story."

She looked into his face when he didn't respond immediately. "No."

"Oh," Alice said, her shoulders slumping despondently.

He grimaced. "It's not like that. I never *expected* her to be proud. My mother never wanted me to begin with. I was a burden to her from day one," he said in a hard tone. "Why should she care what I was doing with my life? I'm not even entirely sure she knew what I *did* for a living, let alone had the wherewithal to be proud. It's not a tragedy, though. I had someone, like you had Maggie."

"Alan Durand?"

He nodded. For several seconds, both of them sat silently and stared out at the coming dawn. Alice could clearly make out the shape of the tops of the trees now against the backdrop of a pinkish gold sky.

"Was your mother an alcoholic? Or a drug abuser?" Alice asked softly, thinking of what he'd said about his mother dying of liver disease.

"Alcohol was her poison."

Alice nodded in understanding. "I'm waiting for Sissy's liver to give out any day now. It's a miracle that woman keeps walking, the things she does to her body . . ."

The hand on her shoulder rose to her chin when she faded off. He nudged her slightly and Alice looked at his face.

"Do you love her?" he asked.

"My mother?"

"Sissy."

Alice just stared for a moment. "I don't *want* to love her. Most of me hates her."

Her blunt words only seemed to highlight the *other* part. Alice wished like hell she didn't cringe every time she witnessed or thought of Sissy destroying herself bit by bit every day, knowing there wasn't a damn thing she could do to stop it. A fiery glow bathed Dylan's rigid features now.

"What about you? Did you love your mother?"

His mouth tightened. "I didn't *want* to love her," he repeated her words after a pause.

A small spasm of emotion coursed through her. She brought

her feet up next to her on the swing and curled into him, her cheek pressed to his chest, her hand on his abdomen. He cupped her shoulder, bringing her closer against him.

Together, they watched the burning dawn in a full, compassionate silence.

AFTER the orange ball of the sun had risen over the tree line, Dylan stood and wordlessly took her hand. She wasn't exactly sure why, but Alice's chest felt tight and achy as he led her through the house to his bedroom. There, he began to undress her, his actions deliberate and unhurried. When she finally stood before him, trembling and naked, he whisked both of his hands down her sides, cupping her hips.

"You're a living miracle," he said quietly. Something in his somber stare made her throat ache, making speech impossible. Was it reverence? Gratefulness? How could that *be*?

How could *any* of this be?

It was, though. There was no denying it, no matter how much she might want to try. Emotion swelled in her, uncomfortable and unstoppable. The truth hurt. It erupted in her, tore at her, like the Alice she'd been wasn't big enough to hold it anymore. Is this why people rejected or sabotaged love, because they knew it would destroy what they were, that it'd shatter that old shell of identity and force them into being something different, insist that they transform?

She was falling for him. So hard.

Dylan held her stare as she lay on her back on the bed a moment later and entered her. The monumental fullness overwhelmed her. It broke through her brittle, hard-won armor.

She'd *already* fallen for him, and there was no going back.

"Shhh," Dylan whispered, leaning down to kiss the tears that had spilled on her cheeks. She stared up at him as he began to move, knowing he saw her for what she was, vulnerable and naked, but unable to look away. Unable to protect herself. Sensation and emotion crashed together violently. Fused.

He should have been a near stranger to her, but he wasn't.

Dylan braced himself on his arms and leaned down to touch her mouth with his.

LATE that morning, Alice heard the sound of dishes rattling in the distant kitchen. She grabbed Dylan's hand, and he came to a halt, turning to where she'd stopped in the hallway.

"Is that Marie in there?" Alice asked him anxiously.

Dylan nodded. "Yeah. She usually makes a big breakfast on Sundays if I'm here, even though I tell her not to," he replied quietly.

"Aren't you worried about her seeing me?"

He came closer and lowered his head, brushing his lips against her temple. Alice shivered and stepped into him. They'd fallen asleep after they'd made love and when they'd wakened, shared a shower. Dylan hadn't shaved afterward, and there was a scruff on his jaw and around his mouth. He looked delectable, wearing a pair of jeans and a dark blue T-shirt, his feet bare, his thick lustrous hair still a little damp. He smelled even better, Alice acknowledged as she lifted her face and nuzzled his whiskered jaw. They hadn't spoken about that rush of violent emotion she'd experienced while they made love, but somehow, those moments were present, like a delicate, newly born energy that seemed to pulse between them. She swore Dylan felt it, too, because he couldn't seem to stop touching her. Maybe she was being stupid, but she felt wonder in his searching, pleasure-giving hands and lips.

"No," he answered against her lips a moment later. Alice

blinked, straining to recall the topic. "Why shouldn't Marie see you? She has no problem speaking her mind with Louise or me, but she's discreet. This is her domain as much as mine," he added wryly as they resumed down the hallway. "And the queen keeps the secrets of her castle safe."

"You make it sound like there are lots of secrets to keep up here," Alice observed wryly as they descended the back stairs.

"I'm sure Marie knows about more of them than I do," Dylan replied. They crossed into the kitchen. Alice inhaled a delicious aroma.

"What are you saying behind my back?" Marie called out from where she stood behind a large granite-topped kitchen island. She was a middle-aged woman with a square jaw and short honey-colored hair. Her heft suggested that she appreciated her own cooking as much as anyone, and wasn't afraid to admit it. She held an egg-dripping whisk over a mixing bowl while she regarded Alice with a frankly curious stare.

"Just the usual praise," Dylan replied smoothly, leading Alice toward the cook. Marie's doubtful smirk said she wasn't buying it, and Dylan's reciprocated one indicated he didn't expect her to. Marie nodded when Dylan introduced them and resumed beating her eggs.

"Nice to meet you, Alice. There's coffee ready, and I'm making omelets for you both. We've got muffins in the oven. I set the table for two on the terrace."

"How did you know I was here?" Alice asked, bemused. This was the first time she'd ever shared Dylan's bed and awakened with his staff there. *God, what if Marie or Louise had heard them making love?*

"I saw the two Keurig containers, and figured Dylan had a guest," she said, referring to the discarded cups they used to make their coffee early that morning. "There's no need to look like that," Marie told Alice bluntly as she poured the egg mixture into a sizzling skillet. "He doesn't usually have them stick around to serve them coffee. I figured we were due an exception, and made breakfast for two."

Alice gave a bark of stunned laughter at the cook's statement. Marie must have clearly read Alice's flash of concern as she'd watched Louise's preparations. *Does Dylan regularly have female companions for his Sunday brunch?*

Dylan cleared his throat to break the awkward silence. "Tactful to the last," he muttered under his breath. Marie gave him an arch look. He just shook his head and rolled his eyes as he opened a cabinet. "Coffee, Alice?"

Suppressing a grin, Alice nodded.

"It's so beautiful out here," Alice said a while later before she popped her last bite of succulent apple cinnamon muffin into her mouth. The day was shiny and golden, and Alice didn't *think* that was just because of her euphoric mood. "So this is your normal Sunday routine?"

"No."

"What is, may I ask?" Alice asked with amused sarcasm over his brevity. He smiled.

"The same routine as every day of the week."

"Work, you mean?" Alice replied knowingly.

"If I'm here, I usually take my omelet in the den," he said, pointing his fork toward a window in the house. He took a swift bite of fluffy egg, watching her steadily, and swallowed. "But I'm traveling half the time. If I am here, I often skip breakfast altogether and go into the office. This is nicer," he said after he took a swig of some juice.

"You make me feel special," she said airily, smiling and looking around the sun-dappled and shaded terrace while a gentle lake breeze tickled her cheek.

"What did I tell you yesterday?"

She blinked at the sudden steel in his tone.

"That I was?" she asked, laughing because she was surprised at his sudden seriousness.

He reached under their small breakfast table and put his hand just above her knee. He squeezed.

"You *are* special to me. Don't make light of it."

Alice opened her mouth to reply, but the blaze of heat in his eyes left her tongue-tied. His phone started to ring. He held her stare, his expression hard, while he took it from his pocket. He glanced at the number and frowned. "Would you mind if I took this?" he asked her. "I wouldn't if it weren't important."

"No problem," Alice assured. "I'll just take our plates in and you can have privacy out here."

"Thanks," Dylan said, hitting a button on his phone.

Inside, Alice chatted with Marie as she helped her put their dishes in the washer. She thought of that intense moment with Dylan just now. He'd been irritated by her flippancy in regard to his feelings for her. He'd been telling her loud and clear that she might minimize *her* feelings because she was scared, but she'd *better* not do the same for his.

"How long have you worked here?" she asked Marie.

"Ever since Dylan came to live, six years ago," Marie replied, handing Alice the last plate. Alice put the plate in and closed the dishwasher, wiping off her hands with a towel. "I see you're used to working for yourself instead of being waited on," Marie observed as she transferred the omelet skillet to the sink. "Another good thing about you."

Alice grinned and leaned against the counter. "What was the first thing?"

Marie nodded pointedly through the window over the sink. Outside it, she caught a glimpse of Dylan pacing distractedly while he spoke on the phone.

"You made him smile," Marie said.

Alice flushed with pleasure at the brisk, potent compliment.

She glanced around the kitchen. Despite its luxury and expensive appliances, the room was stamped with Marie's character: warm and comfortable yet spotlessly clean and utilitarian. This room belonged to Marie, and there was no doubt about it.

"Where is the gong?" Alice asked impulsively, searching the countertops.

"*Gong?*" Marie repeated blankly as she rinsed out the skillet.

"The one you use to get the caterers' and servers' attention? Dylan told me how you found it here in the house. He said it was an antique. It sounded interesting. I was hoping to see it," Alice explained, remembering how she'd heard the clear, sweet, mysterious sound on that first night she'd entered the castle.

"You'll have to ask Dylan, honey, because I haven't got any idea what you're talking about. Maybe he keeps this gong in his den or something. Do you want another muffin before I put them away?" Marie asked, picking up the muffin tin.

"Uh . . . no, but thank you. They were delicious. Everything was," Alice said distractedly, her brows knitted as she stared out the back window at Dylan. A chill went through her. Why had he told her that story about the gong? It didn't make any sense.

Just like so much else doesn't.

"Will you let Dylan know I went upstairs to make a phone call?"

"You got it," Marie said.

She flew up the back stairs, her heart starting to race. She didn't have much time. Dylan might finish his call any second, although he did look quite intent from what she'd glimpsed through the window just now. The back stairs led to a place that was farther down the hallway than the main staircase. When Alice emerged, she was only fifteen feet away from that branch of the hallway where Dylan had found her that strange night . . .

From that portion of the hallway where she'd seen that phantom figure.

A few seconds later, she stood in front of the carved wood door, her breath coming in erratic puffs. The soft roar in her ears grew louder, becoming a rushing wind.

Don't just stand here, stupid. There isn't much time. Do *it.*

In one swift, desperate motion, she twisted the knob and threw open the door. She blinked. Bright sunlight flooded out into the dim hallway, bathing her face and bare arms and legs.

Her lungs burning, she stepped across the threshold.

"THERE you are," Dylan said when he saw Alice standing at the window in his bedroom suite. She had the blind up and the curtains open, and her back was to him. "Sorry about taking so long. Did you already make your call to Maggie?"

He paused in the process of walking across the room toward her. She stood stock-still. It was like he hadn't spoken at all. Sunlight flooded around her. He had the random, distracted thought that the sunlight illuminated the golden-reddish roots of her hair, giving the impression of a corona around her head.

"Alice?"

He ate up the distance between them when she still didn't respond. He thought she'd jump when he touched her upper arm—she seemed lost in her thoughts—but she turned around without flinching. She met his stare.

"Why are you lying to me?"

A chill passed through him—not just because of her flat, calm query, but the strange, masklike quality of her expression.

"Lying to you? What are you talking about?"

She pointed wordlessly out the window, watching his face the whole time.

"So?" he asked, seeing nothing out of the ordinary through the pane of glass. *Outside* everything looked normal. *She* was another story. "Alice, what's wrong?" he demanded tensely.

"The *driveway*?" she asked, and despite his bewilderment, he was glad to hear the familiar biting sarcasm and anger in her tone. He much preferred it over the marble-like Alice he'd just seen. "You had a magnificent lake view in that other room. Why did you move in here, where you have a view of the driveway?"

"What the hell are you talking about?"

"I went in there!" She pointed, her eyes blazing. "I went into that room just now. The one you wouldn't let me go into that night because there was a *damaged floorboard*. There was no damaged floorboard! It's *your* old room. The one you used to occupy before you moved into this bedroom. It looks like it's the master suite of this whole damn palace. Some of your old things are still in there."

Shit.

"Alice—" he began, alarm making the hair on his forearms stand on end.

"You told me when I first came here that you liked the view better in this suite, and that's why you moved!" She pointed again out the window. "You liked the view of the *driveway* better than the most amazing, stunning lake view I've seen yet in this house? You liked this room versus what looks to be some kind of fantasy suite?" she asked, her voice high-pitched with disbelief. He put his hands on her upper arms and turned her to face him.

"I can explain about that."

"*Really?*" she asked, her expression wild. She lurched past him, breaking his hold on her. She seemed to think again and spun around, panting. "All right. Go ahead. And while you're at it, explain why you told me there was a hole in the floorboard in that room in order to keep me out of it. Face it, Dylan. You're a *liar*. You lied so that I wouldn't go in that room. You lied about why you moved over into this one! You lied about that gong. Marie had no idea what I was talking about when I mentioned that gong I heard my first day here. I can't figure out *why* you're lying, because they seem like completely stupid things to lie about, but you *are* doing it! *I'm* not going crazy," she yelled, panting heavier now. "It's *you. You're* lying!"

He put up a cautionary hand and approached her, holding her stare. "I'm not denying it, Alice. Let me explain."

"I've thought this whole thing between us was too good to be true from the beginning. I knew there had to be some kind of a catch. I knew you were lying," she said under her breath.

"Jesus," he grated out, because he saw she was shaking. He grasped her shoulders, refusing to let go even when she flinched. "Listen to me. It's true," he said. "I have been lying about a few things. But I only did it because I was worried about you."

She looked up at him, her broken, stunned expression cutting him to the quick.

"You were worried about *me*? You made me feel like I was going nuts, when it's you that's crazy. How could my knowing about some stupid room alleviate your *worry* about me?" She broke frantically from his hold and stumbled. He caught her in time to keep her from falling. He brought her closer to his body.

"Look at me," he demanded. Her frantic, skittering gaze caught on his stare. "I will explain, but you have to calm down, Alice."

"Let. Go. Of me," she grated out succinctly.

He immediately released her and stepped back. They regarded each other warily from a distance of several feet, both of their breathing erratic. She jumped when someone knocked on the door.

"*What?*" he bellowed, keeping his gaze fixed on Alice's pale face.

"Dylan? It's me," a woman said hesitantly, her voice weak and muffled because of the thickness of the door.

"Not now, Louise," he shouted.

"I'm sorry. It's just that Sidney Gates is here. Should I tell him you're not available?"

Alice looked like a wild animal backed into a corner. He wouldn't have been surprised if she flew at him in that minute, teeth bared. *Fuck*. He'd thought he'd known the meaning of help-lessness, but this was a whole new level of the definition. He raked his fingers through his hair and closed his eyes briefly.

"No. Tell Sidney Alice and I will meet him in my den," he called to Louise, sounding much more calm than he felt.

He met Alice's suspicious stare, and took a slow, steady inhale to brace himself for the unknowable.

For the worst.

ALICE swallowed, attempting desperately to slow her choppy breathing. "I don't want to go meet with some stranger. I want the truth!" she told Dylan.

"That's what I'm planning to give you. Sidney can help. He knew Alan Durand."

"Why should I care about that?" she asked, her amazed disbelief amplifying. "Stop bullshitting me and—"

"Alice," Dylan said sharply, interrupting her hissing demand. She blinked, her words freezing on her tongue. "Sidney knew your father."

Her mouth fell open.

"He knew my father?" she asked incredulously. This couldn't be happening. *Why* was this happening? Shivers of dread crawled beneath her skin. Dylan put out his hand, as if to escort her out of the room, but she stepped back, avoiding his touch.

"Just lead the way," she managed coldly.

It felt like a pair of hands clutched her throat, squeezing until only the tiniest air hole remained.

SHE sensed Dylan's stare on her as he held the door open for her once they were downstairs. Alice marched into the masculine, handsome den, chin up, defiant.

Numb.

It hadn't changed much. Book-filled shelves lined three walls, and the fourth had a row of windows that looked out on the gardens and lake. The enormous carved desk—a good hiding spot—had been moved to a new position to the right of the room.

You've never been in here before!

Dizziness assailed her at the thought. Her legs forgot their purpose. She plopped down on a deep blue velvet couch before they could give out beneath her.

"Alice?"

It took a moment for her vision to resolve. There was a tall distinguished-looking man with silver hair looking down at her with concerned gray eyes. She stared up at him dazedly. Dylan entered her narrowing field of vision.

"Things have changed," she heard him say quietly to the other man. "She's realized some of the things I've told her about the house don't make sense, and it's . . . upset her," Dylan finished tensely.

For a few seconds, she was looking into Dylan's lustrous dark eyes and she was falling . . .

Falling.

What is wrong with me? I'm strong. I need to get out of here. This place is making me so weak. This house—this whole damn estate—is like my personal Kryptonite . . .

Panic sent fingers tighter around her throat. "Dylan," she managed.

"It's okay, Alice," he said, and he grasped her hands. Had she stretched her arms out toward him, reaching like a little child? God, what was wrong? There was a strange ringing in her ears. "Everything's going to be okay, baby." He came down on the couch next to her and put his arm around her. Alice clutched at his free hand like a lifesaver.

"Something's wrong," she whispered. *Something is horribly wrong.*

"Sidney, *do* something," Dylan rasped.

The sunlight streaming through the windows seemed to be blinding her. All she could do was hold on to Dylan, her safety. Her anchor. Her . . .

"Knight in shining armor," she whispered through numb lips.

"What's that, Alice?" Someone was blocking the sunlight. "Here. Drink this." The man with the gray eyes said. He was kneeling in front of her and handing her a glass. The man smiled kindly. "It's all right. It's just water," he assured. "You've had a dizzy spell. Take a sip, and then take a few deep breaths."

She nodded. She wanted to take the water, but she was afraid to let go of Dylan for some reason. Then the edge of the glass was pressing against her lower lip, and she drank thirstily. It helped, the familiar sensation of the cool liquid slipping down her throat clearing her fog a little. The glass moved away. Dylan handed it to the gray-haired man, who stood and set the glass on the desk. Then he pulled an armchair in front of her.

"Better?" he asked.

Alice nodded.

"I'm Sidney Gates. I'm a friend of Dylan's," he explained gently. "What was that you were saying about a knight in shining armor?"

"Dylan," she whispered. His arm tightened around her. The man named Sidney smiled.

"Dylan is your knight in shining armor?"

"Like the knight knocker," she mumbled.

Sidney glanced at Dylan, a question in his eyes.

"The door knocker. On the front door. She used to like it." Alice turned her chin and stared at Dylan in amazement. It was like he'd just taken form in front of her eyes, and she was seeing him for the first time. Different. Familiar.

"I think I'm gonna be sick," she said.

Dylan nodded, his expression very grim. "Come on. I'll take

you to the bathroom." He gently helped her to her feet. Alice swayed. Everything went foggy and then black.

"Dylan," the man said sharply.

"I've got her," Dylan said.

She couldn't see him anymore. But sure enough, Dylan's arms were right there when she sank into them.

WHEN she awoke, she again could hear Dylan, even if she couldn't see him. It reassured her. She was lying on her back. She blinked her eyes open heavily, and saw she was still in the sunlit den. Not much time had passed, if the quality of the sunlight was any indication. She was stretched out on the velvet couch.

"We should take her to a doctor," Dylan was saying.

"*I'm* a doctor."

"She should be in a hospital."

"She's not physically ill, Dylan. She's in shock. This is what shock looks like. It's not as if a pill is going to make her fine. I'll know better what to do when she wakes up. Don't say anything until we see how much she remembers about the past hour or so. I need to determine how much she's integrating."

She didn't know what that man meant. It was like he was speaking English, but in a garbled, inexplicable manner that her brain couldn't quite interpret. Alice blinked and saw the two men standing just feet away. She immediately recognized Dylan's tall, formidable form. She recalled his casual clothing—jeans and a dark blue T-shirt from this morning. It'd been what he'd put on after they showered.

After they'd made love.

Everything was muzzy, but the memory of their soulful, fiery lovemaking early this morning possessed a crystalline clarity. Other memories pressed at the edge of her consciousness. The pressure of them made nausea rise in her belly and her throat to tighten. She willfully pressed the intruding thoughts down.

One thing, she definitely recalled all too well.

Sidney knew your father.

The memory of Dylan saying that with a rigid expression had been burned into her brain, surviving even the fog.

"Dylan," she croaked.

Both men glanced around sharply.

"I'm here," he said gruffly, sitting on the edge of the couch, his hip pressing against her waist. He took her hand. "You okay? Do you want some more water?"

She shook her head and swallowed. "No. I'm all right." She started to get up.

"Not yet," Dylan said firmly, halting her with a hand on her shoulder.

"It's okay," she said, meeting his stare. "I want to talk to this man. The one you said knows my father."

I want to get this over with.

"Let her sit up, Dylan," the man said. Dylan hesitated, but when she again tried to sit up, he didn't stop her. "Nice and slow," the man urged. Alice swung her legs to the floor and came to a sitting position next to Dylan.

"That was so weird. I've never passed out before," she mumbled, rubbing her eyes. She'd been afraid and filled with dread, because of what she suspected they'd say to her. It was time she faced the truth, no matter how ugly it was. The gray-haired man sat in the chair in front of the couch. She forced herself to focus on him, grasping for his name. "You said your name was Sidney Gates?"

"Yes," the man replied.

She swallowed thickly. She felt very strange, like an exposed, quivering nerve, hypersensitive and numb at once. "Dylan said you knew my father?" she asked hollowly.

Sidney nodded. She found his gray eyes comforting, soft and yet steely strong at once.

Alice glanced up at Dylan. Her heart squeezed a little when she realized how pinched his expression was, how fierce his eyes. "You said you didn't use a private investigator to find out who my father was, but you *did*, didn't you?" she asked resignedly. Why had he done that? Why was he so intent on seeing her exposed and vulnerable?

And *why*, despite the feeling of betrayal she experienced at that thought, did she still desperately seek Dylan out for comfort in her disorientation?

She closed her eyes when her voice played back in her head, and she recognized it shook. She took a deep breath. "What did you find out?" she demanded. "Is he . . ." Nausea rose in her. She fought it back. "Is my father one of Sissy's brothers?"

A ringing silence. "What?" Dylan's harsh query shattered it.

"*Is it?*" she demanded, looking from Dylan to Sidney.

"*No,*" Dylan said heatedly, grabbing her hands. "Why would you *think* that?"

"It's what I've always thought. Worried about. Suspected," she mumbled the last, staring blindly at her knee.

"You thought one of your uncles was your father?" Dylan asked.

Shame wriggled its way in, even through her thick state of shock. "They were the most likely candidates, yeah," she said a little defensively. It'd been the first time in her life she'd spoken aloud this deeply mortifying suspicion. Despite Dylan's adamant denial, she felt no relief. Shame swelled in her like a living creature coming to life and writhing in her belly. "Are you *sure*?" she asked in a cracking voice.

"Alice, look at me," Dylan said.

She recognized that steely tone. She fought her shame and stared up into his face, her mortification making eye contact difficult. Their gazes locked. She'd never seen him look so fierce.

"*Dylan . . .*" Sidney Gates said warningly.

"I won't have her continuing to believe something so poison-ous, not if I can stop it," Dylan bit out, glaring defiantly at Sidney. He turned back to Alice. "I'm *very* sure. I knew your father."

"*You* did?" she asked, amazed.

He nodded. "And he wasn't one of the Reed brothers. Not by a long shot. He was a wonderful, brilliant, caring man. I knew your mother, too. And she was *no* Sissy Reed," he said forcefully, tightening his grip on her hands. A muscle leapt in his cheek. "I know this may seem incredible, but I'll try to explain—"

"Dylan, as a psychiatrist, I don't advise this—

"Alice, your mother and father were Alan and Lynn Durand," Dylan said.

NINETEEN

Both men stared at her like they expected her to transform into an alien right before their eyes. Strangely, Dylan's ludicrous statement and their tangible anxiety served to steady her by contrast. She took a deep, even breath of air and smiled.

"Ha-ha," she said with weary sarcasm. She noticed her discarded water glass on a side table. She stretched, reaching for it, and prepared to stand. Dylan caught her with his hand on her upper arm.

"Alice."

She looked at his face. It struck her in that moment. The hint of some weight, of some intense pressure or burden, had always been cast over his handsome features. She only noticed it now because it was there in full force, undisguised. She read it in his eyes.

A spasm of some unnamable emotion went through her.

"I don't believe you," she muttered. "You're crazy."

"No," he said emphatically, an apology softening his rocklike expression slightly.

Alice glanced up at Sidney Gates, not because she trusted him more than Dylan, but because he was an outsider. Surely he could offer some objectivity to these bizarre unfolding events.

"It's true, Alice," Sidney said gently instead. "Your real name is Adelaide Lynn Durand. You're the daughter of Alan and Lynn Durand, and you were the center of their world. They absolutely adored you."

"I don't understand what you're saying," she said incredulously, turning to Dylan. It stunned her, to realize he would play this cruel joke on her. "Why are you two doing this to me?"

Dylan gave Sidney a flickering glance before he grasped her hands. He squeezed, and as always, she felt that sense of a center. Grounded by his touch . . . even when she shouldn't be, given this bizarre situation.

"Alice, this isn't some kind of a trick. I've never been more serious, but I know it must be overwhelming. Do you need to go lie down for a bit? Or do you want to know more now?" Dylan asked simply.

She gave a bark of mirthless laughter. "You can't say something like that and then expect I'm going to drift off to sleep. You've *got* to tell me now, preferably the punch line of this joke."

"It's the opposite of a joke," Dylan said grimly. He gave her hands one more squeeze and then stood. He crossed the room and opened one of the cabinet doors of the built-in bookcase. From her place on the couch, she caught a glimpse of several photo frames, stacked and laid on their sides on a shelf. Bewildered, she glanced at the many shelves in the room. There wasn't one photo on them. Someone had removed the framed photos and put them in the cabinet, she realized dazedly.

Dylan removed a dark red leather box and grabbed the top frame. On the way back to his seat next to Alice on the couch, he snagged a small table with one hand. Sidney moved his chair aside to make room for the table, and Dylan plopped it down in front of Alice. Both men sat, Dylan next to her on the couch.

"I can only imagine how strange this all sounds to you," Dylan said after he'd set down the box on the table. "But the fact of the matter is, I knew you a long time before our meeting at your interview." He handed her the framed photo. The sunlight cast a glare on it, and Alice squinted to see.

The image resolved before her eyes.

It was a photo of a tiny girl sitting on the back of a shiny black pony. She wore khaki-colored riding breeches, a white blouse, black boots, and a little black riding helmet that was strapped under her chin. Two strawberry-blond wavy pigtails fell from beneath the helmet. She looked at the camera, her smile the most unguarded, innocent, blissful one Alice thought she'd ever seen in her life.

Standing next to the little pony and the girl stood a tall, thin, rangy young man who wore jeans, a T-shirt, and dusty boots. He looked like he might be fourteen or fifteen years old. His longish brown hair gleamed in the bright sunshine. His stance was a little stiff. Not awkward, necessarily. Wary, Alice recognized. He gave a half grin to the camera, a glint of amusement or even happiness shining through his guard. One hand was on the girl's saddle, the gesture somehow joining the boy and little girl in the photo.

That . . . and the glow of pride on both of their youthful faces.

Alice couldn't pull her stare off the boy.

"That's you," she whispered to Dylan.

"And you," Dylan said.

The two words seemed to bounce right off her. She stared up at Dylan's face. She could see the similarities to the photo. Both boy and man were beautiful, but in different ways. The boy's innocence was still evident, despite his wariness. Despite his wounds. The man was everything the boy had promised to be, and more.

She swallowed thickly. "What happened?" she asked blankly.

He briefly closed his eyes. "You were kidnapped when you were four," he said heavily. "Taken from the Durand estate. Taken from me."

"From you?" Alice asked, hearing him, but not really absorbing what he was saying.

"You know how I told you that I met Alan and Lynn during the first summer I came here when I was twelve? They taught me to ride that summer, and we became friends. Alan saw how much I loved the horses, and he requested that the camp manager make a special assignment for me as an assistant to the stable manager. Late that next summer, I met you. Your dad would bring you down to the stables. You were three, and you loved the horses," he said gruffly.

"You loved Dylan."

Dylan stared down at the floor at Sidney's interruption, his expression wooden. Alice blinked, her trance broken by Sidney's voice. "Your father told me about it several times, before he died. You idolized Dylan. The two of you had a special bond. I remember Alan saying fondly many times that his daughter was usually a Sweet Adelaide, but occasionally she would be a Sour Citrus," Sidney smiled, naming two iconic Durand Enterprises candies Alice recognized. "You could be headstrong, but you listened to Dylan. And Dylan came out of his shell a little, around you—a tiny, innocent girl who saw the world as fresh and beautiful as the first day it was minted. Seeing how much his little girl loved horses—and the boy at the stables—Alan purchased a gentle pony for you that following summer. That pony right there," Sidney said, nodding at the framed photo she still clutched in her hand. "Both Alan and Dylan were there when you first mounted her."

"Angelfire," she said slowly, deliberately, as if attempting a foreign language. The name lingered on her tongue, strange and beautiful.

Dylan's head jerked up. "Yes. That was your pony's name. Do you remember anything else, Alice?"

Alice shook her head. On the contrary, her mind felt strangely blank. "No. It just came to me . . . like a shot in the dark."

"Are you all right?" Dylan asked.

"Yes. I'm fine. Better than before, actually," she said honestly. "Please go on with your story."

"It's your story," Dylan said stiffly. "And it's not a *story*. It's your life, Alice." He flipped off the lid on the dark red box and withdrew some folded newspapers. "On August second, almost twenty years ago, Camp Durand was in session. I was fourteen years old, and you were four. Alan and I were teaching you to ride Angelfire, and you were coming along." He opened the newspaper. "Alan had been letting me take you out for short, early morning rides."

"Alan trusted Dylan to the task," Sidney said.

"*Sidney,*" Dylan growled ominously. Sidney seemed quelled.

Alice's brow quirked at that tense exchange. Sidney had said the words with some weight, and Alice didn't understand either his gravity or Dylan's warning. Anxiety flickered in her belly. Not anxiety for her—because the story being told to her didn't feel personal. It definitely felt a hell of a lot more distant than her long-held fear and shame about being a child of Sissy and one of her uncles. No, the nervousness she felt was for Dylan. She recognized that boy in the photo in some vague sense, certainly more than she identified with that glowing little girl. That girl was cherished and loved, the center of a radiant world that spun happily around her. She was entirely unfamiliar to Alice.

Dylan, though—she experienced a mysterious, charged tendril of connection to that wary, beautiful boy.

"One early morning, I was leading you and Angelfire on a path in the woods. Two men attacked us," Dylan explained, his tone flat. Terse. He handed the newspaper to her and Alice's fingers closed around the pages instinctively.

The first thing she saw was a color photo of a tall, handsome man with dark blonde hair and a receding hairline sitting beside a striking woman with shoulder-length auburn hair, large eyes, and a very pretty, delicate face. The couple held the same little girl between them who had been on the pony. They all looked so happy. So blessed.

The headline was a jarring counterpoint to the photo of the handsome family.

DURAND HEIRESS KIDNAPPED
MASSIVE HUNT UNDERWAY

Alice didn't read the front-page article from the *Morgantown Gazette*. Her gaze stuck on the cuff bracelet the woman wore. It was made of exquisite filigreed metal depicting interlaced vines and leaves. She searched the woman's face.

She abruptly handed the newspaper back to Dylan.

"Just tell me what happened to *you* when these men attacked you in the woods," she said through a dry throat. "I want to hear *your* story."

From the periphery of her vision, she saw Dylan sharply look at Sidney. Sidney nodded.

"That's a good idea. Alice knows best," Sidney said enigmatically. "Tell her *your* story, Dylan. That's a good place to start."

DYLAN examined Alice once again, at a loss. She was very pale still, but her large eyes looked clearer than before when she'd passed out. It worried him that he had no idea what she was experiencing on the inside. It was driving him to distraction that he had no ruler, no barometer to gauge what a "healthy" reaction to this situation would be.

Wasn't a revelation like this by nature a huge blow to the psyche? How could it be *healthy*?

Even Sidney was cautious, he could tell. He was worried about Dylan telling her the truth. Dylan had reacted purely on instinct, however, when he'd witnessed firsthand the weight of Alice's shame and anxiety, believing herself to be the child of incest. She'd been *cringing*, for Christ's sake. Maybe it'd been wrong of him to tell her at that moment, but Dylan didn't think so. The idea of Alice believing something so heinous about her origins for so many years didn't sit well with him.

It didn't sit well at all.

Still, he'd understood the psychiatrist's reference just now, and was willing to play along. Sidney was guiding Dylan to follow Alice's lead. She wasn't ready to hear Addie Durand and herself referred to as the same person. But she *was* saying she wanted to learn about him—Dylan's experience. It was safer for her, perhaps, to hear it from his point of view, to absorb it slowly as if from a distance.

"That stretch of path between the lake and the stables used to be a horse trail," Dylan began, the words strange on his tongue. He hadn't spoken much about that life-altering day since he'd been in therapy, and he'd stopped seeing Sidney sixteen years ago. "That was where we were when it happened. You were on Angelfire, and I was leading her. I had you on the lunge, still getting you used to the saddle. Alan and Lynn had talked to my counselor, and they'd all agreed to allow me to teach you after they'd watched us together for a week or so. The kidnappers must have been watching us from the woods for days, maybe weeks beforehand, waiting for their chance."

"Did you want to do it?" Alice asked. He looked at her bemusedly at her change of topic. "Did you want to teach that little girl how to ride her pony?"

He opened his mouth, but only exhaled at first. He spread his hands, trying to find the words, struggling.

"I was a refugee in this paradise, an outsider. And then one day, I met Alan Durand. I came to respect him more than any other man I'd ever known. He might as well have been a different species than the other people I'd known in my life. He was warm. Wise. His kindness went so deep. Same with Lynn. Both Alan and Lynn treated me like an equal from the first minute I met them. I didn't get *why*. But when their attitude held up over three summers—when their trust in me only seemed to grow—I started to believe in it. I started to believe in myself." He paused, ironing the tension out of his forehead with his fingertips. "One day, Alan trusted me with nothing less than his universe." He heard Sidney clear his throat and rustle in his chair. He met Alice's stare. "There were two charges Alan gave me in his life that stand out as life-changing: when he asked me to run his company, and when he trusted me with his little girl. To answer your question? *Of course* I wanted to teach Addie Durand to ride."

He saw her throat convulse as she swallowed. She nodded, as if signaling him to continue. For a split second, the memory of that day came back to him in a vivid flash of confused, horrific movement.

"I had my head turned and was instructing Addie and they hit me from behind. I went down, but I wasn't completely knocked unconscious. I saw them. One of them went to grab Addie off the horse, but she panicked and struggled. She kicked the guy in the face with her riding boot," Dylan said, a bitter smile tilting his lips at the memory—one impression of grim triumph interspersed with thousands of terrifying images. "He lost hold of her for a second, and Addie fell off Angelfire on the opposite side. I heard her hit the ground, saw she wasn't moving."

Dylan saw no spark of memory in Alice's sapphire eyes when their stares met, but her gaze didn't skitter away, either. At least she wasn't afraid, which was something. "One of the kidnappers held Angelfire. As the other guy started to go around the horse to get Addie, I tackled his legs and brought him down. We fought."

"What happened?" Alice asked.

I failed.

It was a voice from his past, a child's voice resurfacing, one he thought he'd silenced forever. The circumstances had unearthed it again.

"The other man stabbed Dylan," Sidney said when Dylan didn't immediately respond. "He's lucky he wasn't killed."

He felt Alice's anxious stare on his profile. "I woke up in a hospital bed the next afternoon," Dylan said gruffly.

"How bad were the injuries?" Alice asked.

He shrugged. "Pretty bad. But I was fourteen, and healthy, and I healed fast enough."

"That's where you got those scars," Alice said, glancing down to the side of his torso. He nodded.

"I was afraid to ask you about them. Why *didn't* I before?" she said almost to herself, shaking her head slightly. His concern mounted.

"Are you okay?" he asked her pointedly. She nodded and cleared her throat.

"Do you want some more water?" he asked.

"No," she said distractedly. "Did you see them? The kidnappers?"

"They were wearing masks and hats. All I could give the police and the FBI was my best guess on their heights and weights and their clothing descriptions."

"And a description of the damage you managed to give the man you tackled with your fist," Sidney added dryly.

"It wasn't enough," Dylan said.

"It was more than most grown men could have done, being attacked like that unexpectedly by men willing to kill to accomplish their crime. You were only a boy, Dylan."

A flash of irritation went through him at Sidney's familiar litany. It'd been Alan's regular speech as well.

"So the kidnappers were never caught or found?" Alice asked.

"Dylan found them," Sidney said. "Just recently. One of them was dying, and the other was already dead. *Both* of them are dead now. They died in two different Michigan penitentiaries."

"But I thought you said they weren't caught."

"Do you really want to hear this part now?" Dylan asked her doubtfully.

She nodded. Damn it, he was having trouble reading her. He looked at Sidney, who nodded once. He sighed and continued.

"One of the men was brought in to a Detroit police station for a serious assault charge ten months after Addie Durand was kidnapped. He had multiple arrests on his record, but none, including this arrest, had anything to do with the Durand case. The FBI's investigation into the Durand kidnapping had been cooling fast as the weeks passed by, and then months. The expected ransom note never came. Leads to Addie or her kidnappers never panned out."

A weariness hit him as he said the words. Maybe it was a remembered pain of all those months and years of waiting as hope slowly faded until it was nothing but an aching, cruel memory. Or maybe that pain lived in his bones still, and had knitted to the very fabric of them.

As if to fortify himself, he looked at Alice's face.

"This man's name was Jim Stout, and when they brought him in to the police station, he was intoxicated. He was put into a holding cell so that he could sober up before he was interrogated. But while he was still drunk, he confessed to the kidnapping of Addie Durand to one of the arresting officers. Apparently, he confessed because he was under the mistaken impression the Durand kidnapping was why he was being arrested. He wanted to make it clear that while he was one of the kidnappers, he'd never murdered the girl."

"Murdered?" Alice asked. She looked blank with shock.

"According to Stout, Addie Durand had died when his partner, a man by the name of Avery Cunningham, had accidentally administered a lethal dose of the sedative they'd planned to use to keep her under control following the kidnapping. Stout was blabbing, panicked, and drunk to boot, because he didn't want to have the charge of child murderer pinned on him. He soon passed out in the cell. When he woke up, and was confronted with his confession, everything was different. He must have realized how stupid he'd been to confess such a thing when he didn't understand his current charges or have a lawyer present to protect him. He recanted, and no matter how much they pushed and pried, neither the police, the district attorney, nor the FBI could get him to open up ever again about a hint of Addie Durand."

"I don't understand," Alice said, and Dylan once again heard that hollow shock in her tone. He glanced at Sidney doubtfully, but the doctor was studying Alice's face closely. Feeling highly uneasy, he placed his hand above Alice's knee and squeezed slightly. She was wearing shorts. It was good to touch her, skin to skin. "What about the other man?" she asked. "The one Stout said killed that little girl?"

"Cunningham was already in prison on a separate murder charge," Dylan said. "He'd killed a man a few months before when he'd been whacked out on amphetamines. Cunningham denied everything Stout had referred to during his drunk confession. To make a very long story short, a trail could never be picked up that provided sufficient evidence to make a formal charge against the two men. The FBI and police were convinced, however, that these two *were* the kidnappers of Adelaide Durand. And they believed they were also responsible for her murder."

Beneath his hand, he felt Alice's skin roughen.

"They just got away with it?" she croaked.

"It wasn't like they went scot-free," Sidney said. "Cunningham already had a life term. Stout's assault charge was for a beating that had nearly been fatal. Given his past arrest record and the general suspicion that he was likely one of Adelaide Durand's kidnappers and an accomplice to her murderer . . . well, let's just say the judge made it certain that Stout wasn't ever going to walk outside a prison's walls."

"And neither of them did, right?" Alice asked Dylan.

"No. Small satisfaction, given what they should have been nailed for," he said grimly.

"You brought the truth to light, Dylan," Sidney said quietly.

"Who else would have had the determination and patience to chip away at an ice-cold case after so many years . . . after so much hopelessness."

AGAIN, Dylan averted his face. Alice wondered what he was shielding from her.

It was like her consciousness crouched at the center of a swirl of confusing thoughts and feelings, like she existed at the still eye of the storm. She felt calm and clear enough, but chaos swirled all around her. She was so overwhelmed, she wasn't sure *what* she was feeling. She did know one thing. When Dylan looked away like he was right now, she didn't like it. It made the storm of confusion whirl closer.

"How did you find out the truth, Dylan?" she asked, damning the tremor in her voice.

She saw his jaw working subtly, but he didn't answer.

"He never gave up hope," Sidney said after a pause. "He's had an investigator on retainer for the last eleven years, searching around on a trail that had long ago been swept clean. Most importantly, he insisted upon visiting Avery Cunningham twice a year for ten years. It looked as if it wasn't going to pay off. Cunningham maintained he knew nothing about the Durand kidnapping. Until this past April."

A shiver tore through her.

"Dylan . . . what happened on April eighteenth?"

Another shudder went through her when she recalled the heaviness of Dylan's expression when she'd asked him that. Some part of her must have guessed that date was crucial.

"Are you all right?" Dylan asked, glancing around. He must have noticed her shivers. His dark brows slanted as he stared at her.

"What happened on April eighteenth?" Alice repeated her earlier question numbly.

She read a fierce misery in his dark eyes.

"Dylan?" she prodded.

"We'll talk about it later," he said. "You've heard enough for now."

"I disagree," she said vehemently. "What happened on April eighteenth?"

"Alice—"

"Tell me."

"Avery Cunningham confessed," Dylan said through a tight jaw. "Every year when I made those visits to the prison, he was adamant about one thing: He swore he'd never killed a child in his life. Strangely, it was one of the few things he ever said that I believed. Most people thought it was just the standard denial of the guilty, but for me . . . Cunningham's claim had a ring of truth to it."

"That's what kept you going," Sidney said. "And as it turned out, you were right."

"Cunningham was dying of prostate cancer, and he had nothing to lose," Dylan continued. "He finally confessed to the Durand kidnapping, along with Jim Stout, after years of denying it. He also insisted he hadn't killed Addie Durand. Stout had truly believed her to be dead. But Addie was still alive when Cunningham had last seen her. Addie Durand was still alive," he repeated, his hand tightening on Alice's knee. "And I *found* her."

SHE held Dylan's stare, her lungs burning, as his voice echoed all around her head.

"Take a deep breath of air, Alice." She blinked and inhaled with a hitch of her lungs. Sidney must have realized she was holding her breath.

"What are you thinking?" Sidney asked her, his manner intent and concerned as he leaned forward in his chair, resting his elbows on his knees.

"I'm thinking it's too incredible to believe," she said. She glanced at Dylan uneasily. "But if you believe it," she said. "It must be true. And that's hard to comprehend, let alone accept."

"It's true, Alice," Dylan said.

Her lungs jerked involuntarily, making her breath hitch. "Well . . . then I'm thinking that I'm sorry you went through all of that."

Dylan opened his mouth to speak, but seemed to stop himself at the last minute. "The important thing is that it's done. Addie Durand has come home."

Alice shook her head in denial. Suddenly, she felt very tired. "I don't know what that really means."

"It will take a good deal of time before you do. You shouldn't press yourself. Dylan and I are both here, to answer any questions you might have over the next hours and days, weeks, and months. Years, if necessary," Sidney said.

"Do you have any questions now?" Dylan asked.

She had a million questions. There were so many, but they were all caught up in the spinning maelstrom of her mind. She couldn't extricate them, couldn't focus.

"Not now," she said. She put her hand on Dylan's hard jean-covered thigh, and before he could stop her, she stood. Dizziness assailed her. Dylan flew up next to her, his hands gripping her upper arms. She focused with all of her will, and his chest solidified before her eyes.

"I'm really tired all of a sudden," she said. Her throat felt raw, like it'd been scraped.

"I think a rest might be just what's called for," Sidney said pointedly.

Dylan nodded. "I'll take her up," he said to Sidney, putting his arm around Alice. "Are you going to stay?"

Sidney shook his head. "Call me just as soon as she wakes up. If need be, I can come back. Do you think you might need any medication?" he asked Alice.

"For what?" Alice asked, confused.

"You're in shock," Sidney said.

Alice shook her head. "No. I'm just tired. I don't need any medicine."

She saw Sidney and Dylan share a glance.

"This is going to take time, Alice. You know that you're safe here, in the meantime?" Sidney asked kindly. "Dylan really is your champion knight. He always has been."

Alice looked at Dylan's face. He was right there, solid and beautiful. He steadied her, as always. What would she do if he wasn't here?

She wouldn't *be* here, if it weren't for him, she realized with numb disbelief. She pushed the impossible thought from her brain. Once again, fatigue pressed on her. She hadn't thought it was possible, to be so tired when she'd just slept a few hours ago.

"Lie down with me?" she asked Dylan.

He nodded soberly. "I'm not going anywhere else."

THROUGH her oppressive exhaustion, Alice recognized that Louise had straightened Dylan's suite in their absence. She'd closed the drapes Alice had opened earlier, and the room was dim and cool. She and Dylan paused next to the great bed, and he drew down the duvet and sheet. He turned her to face him and began unfastening her shorts.

"You'll be more comfortable out of them," he said gruffly a moment later as her shirt joined her shorts on the carpet.

She curled into the opening of the bedclothes wearing just her bra and underwear. The cool sheets felt wonderful on her tingling skin. Dylan came in behind her, his front to her back. He hadn't undressed. She wished he had. She shut her eyes tight, overwhelmed when his arms came around her. He pulled her against him. She gripped at his hands where they joined around her waist. Perhaps he felt her spasm of emotion.

"Alice? Are you all right?" he asked.

"Yes," she gasped softly. "Just . . ."

"What?" he asked when she faded off.

"Hold me tighter," she whispered.

SHE came back to consciousness to the sensation of him still embracing her, his presence the first thing onto which her consciousness latched, as if she'd awakened on a tossing sea and grasped for a solid hold. How long had she slept? she wondered muzzily. She squinted at the light glowing around the drawn drapes. There was a rosy quality to it. Her fingers moved on Dylan's knuckles, and he turned his palm, her hand sliding into his.

"How long did I sleep?" she asked in a muffled voice.

"It's almost eight o'clock."

"At night?" she murmured, confused. It must have been no later than two o'clock when they'd got into bed. She tried to turn over in the circle of his arms. He loosened his hold, and she flipped over onto her other hip, facing him. His whiskers had deepened into a sexy scruff that highlighted his mouth. He nodded, his face shadowed and unreadable in the dim room.

"Did you sleep?" she asked, reaching to touch his jaw with her fingertips.

He just shook his head. When he did, she saw the gleam of his lustrous eyes. She'd been asleep for over six hours. They were in the exact same position they'd been in when they first got into bed. If he hadn't slept, he must be so uncomfortable, lying there without moving.

She must have been so out of it. The memories of what had happened in the den seemed clear, but not as *close* somehow. They didn't crowd her as much. Sleep had served to distance her from the bizarre events of this afternoon. Her body and mind had shut down to give her space.

"I'm sorry," she said softly, the thought of him enduring all those hours of discomfort so that she could have uninterrupted rest made emotion pierce her. "You must be so stiff," she said, rubbing his shoulder and dense upper arm muscles. He felt so good.

"*I'm* okay. Are *you?*" he asked, and again she experienced his wary watchfulness. She couldn't even begin to imagine the weight he experienced at that moment; what he'd been thinking while he lay there awake, holding her for hours. Every time she considered the burden he'd carried since he was a fourteen-year-old boy, it threatened to make emotion spill out of her like an erupting volcano.

She met his stare squarely, still rubbing his muscles. "*I'm* going to be fine. It's not like what you're thinking."

Something flickered across his shadowed features. "What do you mean?" he rumbled.

"I'm not the one with the memories, Dylan. You are."

Her soft reply seemed to hang in the hushed air between them.

She swallowed thickly, her throat congested with emotion. "I know I should thank you, but it just seems so"—she paused, several words popping into her head: *lame, trite, hollow*—"inadequate to say it," she finished.

"You have nothing to thank me for."

Her thumb found its way into the cleft on his chin. She rubbed it distractedly, loving the feel of his whiskers, his skin.

"I disagree." She opened one hand over his chest, needing to feel his strength in order to ask the question.

"Dylan? Why did Jim Stout think Addie Durand was dead?"

He opened his hand on her hip. She was highly aware of his touch.

"Because at one point, she stopped breathing," he said gruffly. "According to Cunningham's confession last April, they both thought she was dead. That's why a ransom demand was never made. They'd sedated her too strongly on the morning after she was kidnapped."

She caressed his chest, absorbing the feeling of him. "Go on," she whispered.

"Cunningham took her in the car just before dawn. The plan was to dispose of her body in a nearby creek in the country," Dylan said woodenly.

Alice held her breath and kept stroking him.

"Do you really want to hear this?" Dylan asked.

"Yes," she gasped.

For a few seconds, they just touched and stroked one another in the grave silence.

"There's a train trestle that runs over a creek, about fifty miles from here. It's at a desolate place in the country."

She leaned back and looked into his face. "You've been there?"

He nodded. An image flashed into her head of him making that solitary mission after hearing Cunningham's confession last April. Her chest ached.

She sensed his hesitation. "Dylan?" she prodded.

"Cunningham took her onto the trestle planning to throw her into the creek," he said rapidly with the air of someone grimly ripping a stuck bandage from a wound. "But just as he started to let go, he saw Addie's eyelids flicker open, and at the last second, he realized she was still alive."

Shivers coursed through her. "So he didn't throw her into the creek?"

His face looked like a death mask.

"He didn't stop himself in time. Just as he saw the little girl's eyelids flicker, he let go. It's about a twenty-five-foot drop, depending on how high the water was at the time."

Alice stared at him openmouthed, her caressing fingers stilling. Primal, atavistic fear sliced through her.

"What happened?" she managed after a moment.

"Alice, are you sure you want to—"

"I want to hear. You said I could ask you questions."

He grimaced.

"Cunningham ran down to the creek bed and followed her body, finally wading in and pulling Addie out of the creek. Her head was injured, and she was bleeding and unconscious. But she was breathing," Dylan said grimly.

She reached and smoothed her fingertips over his clenched jaw.

"It's okay," she whispered. He grasped her stroking hand with his.

"*No*, it's not, Alice," he said, his deep rough voice cracking slightly.

"Yes. It is. Or it will be," she assured. "Why do you think Cunningham did it? Saved her after he'd—" She experienced a swooping sensation that stole her breath momentarily. Was *this* why she was so deathly afraid of heights?

No, that little girl wasn't me. She couldn't have been.

Don't think about it now!

It took her breath away, to consider that adorable little girl and herself as the same person.

"—he'd dropped Addie into the creek?" she finished.

"I think that's obvious," Dylan said bitterly. "She was only worth something to them alive. Of course, that's not the reason Cunningham claimed before he died."

"What reason did he give?" Alice asked, her hand stroking lower, over Dylan's ribs and taut abdomen.

"He said it was her eyes."

Her glance jumped to his face. "What about her eyes?"

"He said they were huge and dark blue. Unlike anything he'd ever seen," Dylan said gruffly, their stares holding. "He said her eyes haunted him, until his dying day. According to him, that's why he agreed to see me every year while he was in prison. He regularly flirted with the idea of confessing, but Cunningham was a coward at heart," he said, his lip curling in disdain. "He couldn't bring himself to do the right thing until death was close." His hand tightening on her hip. "Even though I despised him, I thought of Addie when Cunningham told me that. I've thought to myself since then: *Damn*. I could almost believe that worthless son of a bitch meant it."

The silence swelled.

Slowly, determinedly, she began to move Dylan's T-shirt up over his torso. He caught her hand at his waist.

"What are you doing?" he demanded.

"I want to make love," she said.

"Now? After all this?" he asked, sounding stunned.

She pushed her hand away from his restraining one and shoved it up under his shirt. His skin felt warm and smooth, the hair on his chest springy, a sensual delight beneath her seeking fingertips. She found a nipple and rubbed the disc with her fingertip.

"*Especially* after all this. You're the realest thing in the world to me right now. I need to feel more of you, not less," she said huskily, feeling his nipple harden at her ministrations. She craned up for him, seeking his mouth. Like that first time in the stables, he didn't kiss her back at first, but she felt the give in his firm lips. "*Please,*" she whispered against his mouth.

And just like that other time, he came to her, gifting her with his heat and his strength.

He rolled partially on top of her, his mouth seizing hers, his tongue piercing her lips. Like always, he owned her in those moments. He swept aside everything else. His scent and taste inundated. Intoxicated. Alice delved her fingers into his thick hair, gripping him to her. God, she needed him *so* much. The complexity of her feelings for him, a depth of emotion that made no logical sense to her in the past, rushed through her at that moment. Just a glimpse of what he meant to her, and how their lives had been mysteriously entwined, swelled large in her spirit and flesh, threatening to explode.

She couldn't understand all of those things. She couldn't assimilate them.

But Dylan, she could absorb wholeheartedly.

His hands opened on the side of her ribs, his fingers curving around her back. He embraced her heart. His fingers moved, and her bra snapped open. His hands moved beneath the fabric, cupping her breasts tenderly.

"Alice," he whispered tensely, his mouth moving along her throat. His fingertips plucked gently at her nipples. Heat rushed through her, hardening the flesh Dylan touched, softening her sex. He leaned up slightly, and drew her bra off her arms. She could see the gleam in his dark eyes as he looked down at her a moment later.

"You're a miracle to me. I wanted to tell you the second I saw you. So much," he bit off. "But I couldn't."

His lips trailed over her skin, both soothing and mounting the ache in her chest and between her thighs. He kissed a breast, his mouth closing over a nipple, and Alice gasped and trembled. There was hunger and possession in his touch, but it was twined with a reverence that nearly overwhelmed her.

She felt herself falling again, and she felt the familiar breathless struggle. His mouth blazed across her ribs and belly. His tongue slipped beneath the elastic of her panties, and she found herself reaching for him, trusting him to catch her when she fell.

TWENTY

After they made love, Dylan insisted that she eat something. He got up from bed to go to the kitchen. Alice watched him pull up his jeans over his smooth, muscular ass and scurried out of bed.

"Get back in," he said, eyebrows slanting. "I'll bring it to you."

She shook her head and grabbed her shirt from the carpet. "I'm not an invalid."

"Alice—"

"I want to go with you," she interrupted with a fierce glance.

She didn't want to lie there in that bed alone, waiting in dread while the swirl of emotion and confusion grew nearer and nearer.

He studied her closely, and then nodded once. "Put on the robe I got you, then," he instructed gruffly. "There's no call for you getting dressed again. Louise and Marie are gone by now."

Down in the kitchen, Dylan opened a can of soup and put it on the stove to heat, while Alice chose the ingredients for some sandwiches.

"Do you mind if I call Sidney?" Dylan asked her as she laid out bread on two plates.

"No. You told him you'd call," Alice said neutrally, finding the drawer that held silverware. "I heard him say he was a doctor. What kind of a doctor is he?"

"A psychiatrist. One of the best there is. He consults for

Durand Enterprises, and has an office in Morgantown. He'll want to know how you're doing."

She nodded with forced casualness, finding a paring knife to cut a tomato.

"Alice?"

"Yeah?" she asked, looking up from her task.

"How are you doing?"

She blinked and laughed. "I'm okay."

He nodded slowly, and Alice knew he didn't believe her. But what could she say? She wasn't anywhere near as bad off as she'd been in the den, when she'd been convinced due to a lifetime fear that it was about to be revealed that she was the daughter of Sissy and one of her uncles. How stupid could she be? Why would Dylan bother to find out about *that*? As unlikely as that scenario was, it seemed far less bizarre than what he'd told her instead.

She picked up the top slice of the tomato and popped it into her mouth. "Just tell him I'm in a holding pattern," she said as she chewed. She raised her eyebrows when Dylan didn't move. "It's a pretty good place to be for now, don't you think?" she asked him dryly. "Rome wasn't built in a day."

He grunted softly, clearly only partially convinced, and turned to dial his phone.

AFTER Dylan had spoken to Sidney and they'd eaten their dinner from a tray in Dylan's suite, Alice asked if they could watch television. Dylan must have sensed she was coping by distracting herself, but he made no comment about it. He merely got up and moved the console doors on a large armoire, revealing a television and entertainment system. It soothed her, like a calm before the storm, to lie on the pillows with Dylan spooning her, willing her mind to go blank as they watched the end of a comedy on one of the movie channels.

She yawned as the credits began to roll at the end, and turned toward Dylan.

"I should go to sleep. I have a big day tomorrow," she said.

His expression stiffened. "What do you mean?"

"Marco Fernandez is doing his public speaking presentation at eleven. He's demonstrating how to cook chili, and I'm supposed to help him prep and be moral support. *Oh*, and I'm trying to get Terrance hooked into jogging, and we're going out together early. I haven't told you much about him, but he's this really bright kid, a jokester, and he's got no one at home who has really looked out for his health. He's diabetic and dangerously overweight. I really want to teach him some basic self-care. I bet Terrance about a play in football. When I won, I challenged him to—"

"Alice," Dylan said, halting her rambling.

"What?" she asked, surprised by his abrupt tone.

"You act like you plan on going back to the camp tomorrow, back to being a counselor," he said.

"That's because I do. What else would I plan on doing tomorrow?"

He leaned up slowly on his elbow, spearing her with his stare. "Do you remember what happened in the den? What we talked about up here?"

She realized he thought she'd repressed everything, because she was so traumatized or something. "I remember it all, Dylan."

"Then why would you think you'd go back to being a counselor? Hiring you was only a scheme Sidney and I came up with to get you back into these surroundings without forcing things on you, to try to figure out how much you remembered . . . if anything."

She pressed her hand against her heart, as if to alleviate the pinch of sudden pressure. It felt like ice water spilled down her spine. "Oh my God. You mean . . . you really *didn't* think I was good enough to be here?" she asked, horrified. She hadn't even considered this angle. "I kept thinking it was a mistake. I should have known! I think lots of people—like Kehoe—are wondering what the hell I'm doing here. It couldn't be any clearer I don't belong—"

He sat up abruptly and clutched at her shoulders, bringing her to a sitting position next to him. She gasped at his firm action, halting her pressured speech.

"Alice, stop it. You're *more* than qualified to be here. And how can you say you don't belong here? *Here* is you. This house. Durand Enterprises. *Everything.* I didn't get a chance to mention the trust that's was set up by Alan—"

"No, *don't,* stop!" she blurted out, sounding frantic and stupid to her own ears. "They're *Addie Durand's,*" she said in a choked voice.

Dylan's mouth clamped shut. His eyes looked wild. "I'm Alice," she continued shakily. "And Alice Reed is a counselor at Camp Durand. I have a million things to do tomorrow, including announce to the kids that I've elected Judith their team leader and put out any fires that might be associated with that. And, oh right—and there's the big campfire on the beach tomorrow after dinner! It's the first time we get to hear the team point tallies so far."

He shook his head, clearly stunned. Speechless. Her heart squeezed.

She put her hand on his jaw. "You have to let me do what *I* came here to do," she said.

"It's not right," he said. "I won't let you do it."

"Are you saying you're going to fire me as a counselor?"

"*No.* I can't let you go down there and pretend like today didn't happen!" he bellowed.

"I'm not pretending anything," she exclaimed. "I remember what happened to *you,* Dylan. God, I'll never forget," she added feelingly. "I remember what happened to Addie. It's going to take

a while for me to figure out what it all means, and in the meantime, I'm going to live my life. *My* life."

He grunted in disbelief, and glanced around the room as if
searching for some tool in order to convince her. Her fingers dug
into his hair, her fingertips rubbing his scalp. She hated seeing that
tense, desperate look on his face.

"I'm not convinced you're safe down at the camp," he said
suddenly, as if he'd landed on his weapon of choice and brandished
it now.

She shut her eyes and shook her head. "I'm perfectly fine.
Besides," she added wearily, "it's not like you're not having me
followed constantly, right?"

His gaze narrowed dangerously on her. She didn't know why
the thought had come to her all of a sudden, but his reaction
informed her that her impulsive statement had been dead-on.

"Sal Rigo? That Durand manager? You *have* been having him
follow me," she said, anger entering her tone. "Why did you lie to
me?" she paused and made a disgusted sound. "Right. Stupid
question. You've made it your business to lie to me ever since I
walked into that interview last May."

"I only lied to you when it was necessary. You've been telling
me yourself that you're only ready to hear so much," he said, and
Alice could tell by his tight jaw she'd pricked his temper with her
last comment. Well, she couldn't help that. "Besides, I didn't lie to
you about Rigo. He and one other manager are from Durand's
security department. They've been brought in on a confidential
basis, arranged solely by me, to keep an eye on you. It has nothing
to do with the Durand executive selection process."

Alice shook her head, incredulous at his admission. She vaguely
recalled Kehoe mentioning on that first day she'd arrived that there
were two more Durand managers there this summer than was
usual. *Dylan strikes again.*

"None of the other Durand managers know the reason Rigo and Peterson are here, including Kehoe," Dylan continued. "Our security division doesn't usually attend the camp, and I told Kehoe at the last minute I thought their managers should be included. He couldn't refuse. It's not a bad idea. As for my lying to you, you asked me if Rigo was watching all the Durand counselors after hours, and I said no. Which is true," he said with a sideways glare before he got up off the bed. "They were only hired to watch you."

She sprung up off the bed as well and followed him to where he stood in front of a dresser, taking his phone out of his jeans pocket.

"Jesus. It was Rigo or Peterson that was following me in the woods that morning. Wasn't it? By the stables?" she demanded.

A trace of annoyance crossed his handsome face. "I spoke to Peterson about it. Idiot. You'd think he'd never tailed anyone in his life. And then Rigo went and screwed up as well, letting you see him in the parking lot."

Alice's mouth fell open in disbelief. Hurt and embarrassment followed fast. "How could you not have said anything in the stables? How could you let me go on being that afraid when you knew who it was all along?"

He dropped the phone on the dresser with a thump and turned to her. "Damn it, what did you expect me to do?" he asked, his eyes ablaze. "You were scared out of your mind, and it wasn't because a man was behind you on the path in those woods—or at least not completely. Peterson only triggered something in you, that's all. A buried memory of something that happened a long time ago, a genuine fear for your life that happened in that exact same spot! You were in a panic, Alice. Are you forgetting where I said that kidnapping took place?"

"I don't want to talk about that right now," she nearly shouted.

"So what do you expect me to do?" he replied just as fiercely. "Let you walk around like a lit fuse down there at the camp? Go to work at my office in town and pretend you couldn't blow at any second back here, that something traumatic couldn't happen to you?"

"I'm not that fragile!"

"Yes. You *are*," he grated out, grasping her shoulders for emphasis. His deep voice rang in her ears like a struck gong.

She looked into his eyes and unwillingly saw his desperation. She couldn't imagine what this was like for him. How *could* she imagine, really, when she couldn't fully grasp what had happened to her in the past twelve hours of her life?

The last twelve hours? Every day, every minute of her entire life suddenly seemed inexplicable. She was mentally grasping for a sense of the familiar. Knowable.

She swallowed thickly. "I disagree," she said more quietly. "But I'm trying to see your point of view."

"Thank you," he said, his hands tightening and then gentling on her shoulders.

She met his stare. "I'm still going to go back to work tomorrow at the camp."

"Alice—"

"Nothing will have changed, Dylan. The men you brought here to look out for me will keep doing their job."

"Everything's changed."

"If you don't agree to this, then you're going to have to fire me as a counselor. Because otherwise, I'm going back to the camp tomorrow." Regret spiked through her at her unintended harshness. She reached, touching his whiskered jaw, trying to ease some of the anger and tension she saw there.

"You can't just let this go on indefinitely," he said.

"I won't," she whispered heatedly. "I just need time. Isn't that a reasonable request? The camp, the kids—all of it is important to me. It's familiar. Comfortable."

A spasm went through his stiff features. "There's so much you haven't let me explain, Alice. I feel like I'd be sending you out into the world completely vulnerable. You're even more at risk than you were before."

She stepped closer to him, her arms going around his neck. He lowered his head slowly when she pressed gently at the back of his neck. She pressed her lips to his rigid ones. "I'm not a child. Not anymore. I'm going to be okay. Dylan?" she whispered when he didn't respond, and his lips remained stiff.

"I want to speak to Sidney about it to get his opinion," he said after a pause.

"Okay," Alice agreed. She had a feeling from some of the things Sidney had said that he would agree more readily than Dylan. Hadn't he told Dylan they should follow her lead? His arms went around her waist and he pulled her against him. She pressed her face against his chest.

"And you'll keep spending the nights and Sundays with me. Otherwise I won't agree to it."

Alice smiled against a dense pectoral muscle and hugged him tighter. "I didn't want that part to change. If it weren't for you, I think I'd be going stark raving mad right about now," she mumbled.

Should she be angrier at Dylan for his lies and manipulation? Maybe. All Alice knew was that she couldn't muster outrage at that moment. Perhaps to be angry at him would imply that she took it all personally, which she didn't.

Addie Durand wasn't *her*—Alice.

As if to willfully contradict her forceful thought, a vision of that woman in the hallway, the one wearing that filigreed gold bracelet popped into her mind's eye. She clamped her eyelids shut against Dylan's chest as a powerful emotion surged through her, and she desperately stifled it. She didn't want Dylan to sense her piercing angst.

She knew who that woman was now.

It'd been Addie Durand's mother, Lynn. She'd been calling out to her daughter. It'd been like little Addie's memories had been transplanted into Alice's head, or at least that's what it felt like.

She held on to Dylan tighter, willing the agonizing moment to pass.

THE next day, she submersed herself in her work. Every time she started to feel fuzzy and disconnected, like she was watching herself in some kind of detached fashion from a perspective about two feet above her head, she reached out to Kuvi, Thad, Dave, or one of her kids, forcing herself to concentrate on the conversation and the moment.

All in all, it was a pretty decent day, despite everything. Again, she was reminded that she was a good actress under pressure. She and Terrance completed their exercise, Terrance complaining, puffing for air and joking the whole time, until Alice got a stitch from their slow-paced jog and laughing nonstop. Marco was extremely nervous for his public speaking demonstration, but came through with flying colors while Alice stood close by and played both support person and kitchen assistant.

Her team had been quietly amazed when she'd made the announcement that Judith would be their student team leader. Clearly, they'd been expecting that Noble D would be chosen. But when Noble was the first to clap and shout out an encouraging word to Judith, the rest of the team began to join him. Their cheer started subdued and escalated to enthusiastic as Judith stood to go and stand next to Alice, trying to hide her grin. Alice realized she'd never seen the girl smile without a trace of sarcasm or bitterness. Her happiness transformed her.

During the last activity before dinner, she and Dave Epstein were leading an archery activity. The numbers of interested campers had increased to twice the size of what they'd had earlier in the week, and many of the new attendees were novices. As a result, Alice wasn't too surprised that arrows were being released haphazardly and going far afield.

"I'll make this run, you did the last," Alice told Dave resignedly when yet another camper's arrow zinged into the woods. She and Dave allowed a half a dozen or so to go before they'd make a retrieval run.

"I'll switch them off this target," Dave called, meaning he'd stop the kids from shooting in Alice's direction as she scurried toward the edge of the woods. She cautiously moved past the tree line, avoiding the high grass and peering around the dim woods. She recovered five of the arrows, but had to hunt for the sixth. After several seconds, she spotted the orange arrow in the dirt between two oaks. Picking through the brush, she recovered it and turned to leave.

". . . why you can't just tell me what's going on."

Alice paused upon hearing the female voice in the near distance. The tone had been a little irritated and tense. Cautiously, she looked around the trunk of an oak tree. She saw Thad and Brooke standing in a secluded clearing around twenty feet away.

"Do you think I should have refused?" Thad asked.

"No, of course not. But why all the interest in *her*? It doesn't make any sense, " Brooke said, and Alice heard desperation in her tone.

"I'm not going to defend myself on that score again. I haven't lied to you about anything."

Brooke stepped into him. Thad's face hovered over her upturned one.

"What do you think it's like for me?" Brooke asked him in a choked voice. "Knowing that practically everyone in this damn camp thinks you're crazy for her?"

"I can't help what they think. She doesn't feel the same way, so what difference does it make?"

"It makes all the difference in the world," Brooke said miserably.

"Then why are you here with me?" Thad asked quietly, his hand bracketing her jaw. His golden head dipped. Their mouths fused.

Alice slowly, carefully fled the scene.

WHILE she and Kuvi partnered to get the bonfire on the beach ready, Alice had time to think about what she'd seen in the woods. In many ways, it was comforting for her, to have something so concrete and thought provoking to distract her. True, it worried and confused her, what she'd seen and heard, but at least it was better than focusing on everything she'd learned yesterday in Dylan's den.

She was pretty certain that she—Alice—was the person to whom Brooke referred. Alice couldn't think of anyone else that other people at the camp might suspect Thad was interested in romantically. He certainly never gave the impression he was partial to Brooke. Alice had thought Brooke's interest in him entirely one-sided. Clearly, she'd been wrong. It disturbed her, to think of Thad purposefully misleading her.

"Do you ever see Thad and Brooke together?" Alice asked Kuvi as they laid some thick logs in a ring on the beach to serve as an outer limit for the beach bonfire.

"Sure," Kuvi said, frowning and straightening from a kneeling position. She dusted off her hands. "She follows him around like she's an addict and he's her favorite drug."

"Well I know *that*," Alice said. "I just mean . . . do you ever see him reciprocate the interest?"

Kuvi's eyes went wide. She suddenly looked very uneasy. "Do you have some reason to think he's cheating on you?" she hissed.

"Cheating on me? No, Kuvi, you're all wrong about Thad and me—"

"Really?" she squeaked. She seemed surprised, and then

relieved. "Good, because I've been on hot coals trying to figure out whether or not I should tell you."

"Tell me what?" Alice asked, dropping a log on the beach.

"You said you were going to be busy this weekend, so I thought—you know—you and Thad were going to go away together or something for your night off. But then I saw him on Sunday night with Brooke past dark out on the dock. They looked a little chummy from what I could see. In fact, I made a fool of myself and called out your name. I thought that's who Thad was with."

Alice shook her head. "It wasn't me. Thad and I aren't together."

Kuvi's eyebrows knitted together. "*Hey*—then where have you been going all these nights?"

"I've been wanting to talk to you about that," she began, knowing it was time to at least come clean about her affair with Dylan Fall to her roommate, if not the other bewildering stuff she'd learned yesterday. Alice couldn't begin to imagine trying to explain *that* story to another person.

Someone called out. Three other counselors approached, carrying armfuls of wood.

"I'll explain it to you the first chance we get," Alice promised hurriedly. "But Kuvi? You've got to promise not to tell a soul when I do."

Kuvi nodded earnestly, her gaze concerned. The other counselors approached, halting their conversation.

THAT night, they got the bonfire going at dusk, and the campers and staff all gathered together on the beach, lounging, sipping sodas, talking, and roasting marshmallows for s'mores. The night staff was already there. They'd go later tonight, because of the bonfire. At the end, the night staff would take over immediate supervision of the kids. She'd already explained to Dylan that she'd be later tonight than usual.

As the colorful, gorgeous sunset faded, Alice saw heat lightning flickering in the western sky. It only added to the excited ambience of the night. The crowd was anxious to hear about the team point totals. Everyone was directed to take a seat on the beach. Alice and Judith organized the Red Team around them. Sebastian Kehoe himself was going to be announcing the team point count after a week of camp. There was a lot of anticipation in the air.

As Kehoe talked in a booming voice from where he stood near the roaring bonfire, darkness fell around them. Alice and her kids were seated near the outer edge of the ring, facing the lake and the bonfire, their backs to the woods. The reach of the bonfire light was weaker where they sat huddled together. Lightning lit up the southwestern sky again, illuminating the outline of huge thunderheads. Electricity seemed to charge the air, making her forearms prickle.

Kehoe began to announce the point counts for each team, but Alice was distracted. The back of her neck prickled. She glanced around, peering at the dark tree line in the distance. A shiver tore through her. Those were *the* woods. They weren't far from the spot where Addie Durand had been taken.

Where Dylan had been stabbed.

She shuddered.

"You okay?"

She blinked, focusing on Judith's face cast in dim firelight.

"Yeah. Just caught a chill," Alice replied softly. "What do you think? Do we stand a chance?" she asked, nodding toward Kehoe.

"It's going to be rough," Judith said. "Thad's team is miles ahead of everyone else's so far."

"I don't know. It might be close," Alice whispered.

"You're right. The Red Team's got a good chance," Judith muttered intently, sitting up taller and craning to hear Kehoe. Alice repressed a smile. It was the first peaceful conversation she'd ever had with the girl. It was nice, hearing Judith take ownership of the Red Team.

Despite her thoughts, she again was distracted by the woods behind her. She stared over her shoulder, trying to tease the shadows apart. Thunder rumbled in the distance.

"God, he saved us for last," Judith said miserably a moment later, biting at a thumbnail.

"The Red Team," Kehoe called out. "Team counselor Alice Reed and team leader Judith Arnold: a grand total for week one of six hundred and forty-seven points."

Alice startled at the explosion of shrieks and shouts of triumph coming from all of her kids. They'd beat Thad's Orange Team by two points!

Maybe I got here under suspicious circumstances, but I'm not doing half bad.

She couldn't believe it. Laughing, she shared an impulsive hug with Darcy and then Judith.

"Not losers now, huh?" she said quietly near Judith's ear. Judith gave her a sharp glance when they parted, but her happiness was clearly too big for cattiness at that moment. She grinned full-out instead.

"Who ever said we were?" she asked with fake innocence.

"No one, of course," Alice replied, clapping and whooping for her kids.

AFTER everyone had settled down, one of the Kehoe managers stood and said it was a tradition at the bonfires to tell ghost stories. She announced that the kids could earn public speaking points for their team if they volunteered.

"And we've got a good night for it," the manager said, waving significantly at the southwestern sky where lightning smoldered among the clouds. "Any volunteers?"

Matt Dinorio, who sat next to Judith, raised his hand and waved it strenuously. The manager called his name. A prickle of trepidation went through Alice. Suddenly, the little details of Matt's ghost story leaped out at her, taking on new life and meaning.

I can tell you one ghost story about Camp Durand that's real . . . that one about the mother who haunts the woods and the castle because her baby was killed in there, and she wanders around looking for her . . . I'm telling you, it's true! . . . I told one of my teachers about it after I heard the story last year, and Mr. Glyer said he did *remember something about that happening years ago, right* here *at Camp Durand. It was all over the news.*

Oh no.

She'd been so preoccupied with what she'd learned yesterday, she hadn't put together the pieces in her mind. Matt's tale had been a bastardized version of Addie Durand's story, some lingering ghost of the event that must have rocked Morgantown and the surrounding area twenty years ago. Crystal must have known. That's why the night supervisor had been so adamant about denying the truth of the story. And in fact, Crystal hadn't lied. It *hadn't* been a camper who had been kidnapped. Crystal just hadn't wanted to frighten the kids, and so had quashed the story. Alice wondered if Camp Durand employees hadn't been doing something similar for years, even if they couldn't entirely erase the Durand kidnapping from the public's consciousness.

"Matt," Alice said tensely as the boy started to stand. "Not the story about the kid being snatched at Camp Durand."

"I've got it all figured out," Matt told her excitedly in a hushed tone, wiping the sand off his cargo shorts. "Crystal was mad the other night because I said it happened *here*. She thought that's what scared the little kids the most. I'm going to make it generic, and say it happened near some woods around here, not at Camp Durand," he hissed before he lunged through the crowd.

He was gone like a shot arrow, beyond the reach of Alice's voice unless she wanted to yell at him and make a scene. She listened uneasily as Matt began his story, adding more details and drama here at the bonfire than he had in the Red Team common room a few nights ago.

". . . this man and woman—the parents," Matt was saying, "loved their little girl so much. She was their whole world, and everything was so great for them and they were all so happy. But that all changed one dark, stormy summer night . . . a night a lot like this one," Matt said, his eyes moving theatrically over his audience, pulling them into the story. "On that night, the mom had taken a walk and visited some friends. She stayed later than she'd intended. A storm had moved in fast, and it made the night darker earlier than it normally would have been. She had her little girl with her, and the little girl had fallen asleep during the visit. So the mom had to carry the girl into a path in the dark woods in order to get to their house. She was really nervous, and she couldn't shake the feeling that she was being watched.

"And she *was* being watched from the cover of the trees. There were these kidnappers in the woods, waiting, and they snatched the little girl right from her mother's arms. One second, her daughter was there, and the next, the mother was alone and screaming for her baby . . . screams you can still hear echoing in those woods today."

Shivers rippled across Alice's skin. She rubbed her arms, trying to diminish the goose bumps that had popped up on her flesh. She glanced behind her to the woods uneasily. Had the bonfire started to dim, because the shadows seemed closer now . . .

"Well, these men killed the little girl; murdered her in cold blood," Matt said solemnly, and he had the campers' full attention now. Even Alice, who was highly unsettled by the story, was listening while her lungs burned as she held her breath. "And when the mother heard about her little girl being murdered, she went crazy.

She didn't want to live, with her daughter being taken right out of her arms like that and murdered. She was out of her head with grief. So one night, the mother—"

"Excuse me, I'm sorry to interrupt," a man said loudly.

Alice gasped and jumped when someone touched her arm. She stared up at Dylan's face, shocked. His fingertips brushed lightly across the back of her shoulder, as if in a furtive gesture of reassurance, before he straightened.

"Excuse me," he said again, his gaze meeting hers ever so briefly. "Can I get through? I have an announcement to make to everyone."

Alice moved, as did the other kids in front of her, parting the way so Dylan could walk through the crowd. His commanding, dark figure seemed to blaze along the outline with the light from the bonfire. Sebastian Kehoe stood to meet him when he reached the center of the ring of people. Alice watched anxiously as the two men conferred in subdued voices. Everyone started chattering in the interim, curious and interested as to the reason for the interruption.

Dylan turned and held up a hand. Everyone's chattering silenced.

"I'm afraid I'm going to have to ask everyone to return to their cabins," he called out loudly. "There's a bad storm on the way. If the night staff can quickly organize their teams, please? Everyone should get inside as fast as possible."

Alice stood with everyone else, bemused and unsettled by the interruption.

EVEN though her assigned meeting with Dylan wasn't for another fifteen minutes, Alice left her cabin and entered the woods. The storm had come closer, and she somehow knew he'd be waiting for her now, before the storm broke. The air seemed to crackle with electricity and thunder rumbled ominously overhead.

Suddenly, she felt his hand brush her forearm and she turned to him in the darkness. She opened her mouth to say something—she wasn't sure what, because she was too anxious to ask him if he'd interrupted Matt's "story" at that particular point on purpose—but then his mouth was covering hers, hot and possessive, and her thoughts scattered beneath his heat.

Thunder rolled through the sky, louder this time.

"Come on," Dylan said urgently next to her lips. "The storm is about to break."

She followed him in the pitch black, no longer as hesitant as she had been on the first night, trusting him to guide her unerringly. When they reached the edge of the woods past the stables, she moved behind him, her arms around his waist. He led her into the woods, and she shivered despite the warm, humid air. The trees thrashed and groaned around them. A shocking flash of lightning made the woods go iridescent for a moment, leaving the impression of Dylan's head and broad shoulders burned behind her eyelids. The hair on her forearms stood on end, and it felt like every inch of her skin tingled with electricity.

Rain started to spatter her skin as they reached the castle grounds.

"Come on. It's going to unload on us," Dylan said, urging her to run up the grass slope. Wind and rain buffeted her as they made their way to the back terrace. Thunder boomed, and Dylan was herding her up the back steps for cover beneath the eave. He unlocked the door, prodding her with his touch to go before him into the unlit media room. She waited, panting, while he locked the door and keyed in the code to the alarm system. By the time he turned to her, the air conditioning had caused her wet skin to roughen. Outside in the yard, the wind bent the trees and whipped the branches like they were made of rubber instead of bark.

"It really *is* a bad storm," she said quietly when he faced her.

"Did you think I made the whole thing up?" he asked, stalking toward her. Without breaking her stare, he dropped his keys onto a nearby table, causing a loud jangle of metal against wood. Despite the reference he'd made last night to going into the office in Morgantown, she wondered if he hadn't worked at home today instead. He wore jeans and a blue and white plaid button down. He hadn't shaved yet again. With that thickening scruff shadowing his lower face and upper lip, he really had his pirate-look going on. He looked a little dangerous.

Sexy as hell.

"No, it's not that. It's just *when* you chose to interrupt the campfire. Dylan, that story Matt was telling, was that a"—she swallowed thickly, rubbing her chilled arms—"a sort of urban legend about Addie? It was, wasn't it?" she whispered when he didn't immediately reply, and his expression remained masklike. He took her into his arms, his hands opening at the back of her hips.

"I told you how it really happened. I was there. Who knows better? That was just a campfire story that's been embroidered over the years."

"About a ghost of a woman who haunts these woods?" Alice said, studying his hovering, handsome face intently while her heart beat a tattoo in her ears. "The mother of the little girl—"

"Now's not the time," Dylan cut her off. He stepped closer, and she could feel his body heat penetrate her T-shirt and the fullness behind his fly. She pressed against him, stifling a whimper as need roared into her awareness.

"What's it time for?" she asked. He dipped his head and she lifted her chin. Her provocative question was a cover for the sudden stab of fear that went though her. Dylan was right. She *didn't* want to talk about Lynn Durand right now.

"I think you know," he said, the slant of his mouth grim. His hands lowered to her short-covered ass. He cupped her buttocks. He shifted her, bending his knees, sliding his cock between the juncture of her thighs. "I worried about you all day."

"I'm sorry. I was fine," she whispered after a peal of thunder had quieted. The shine of his eyes in the darkened room was making her shiver, but this time not in fear. He moved his hands, cradling her jaw. It sent a thrill through her when he did that, his large hands holding her securely. He lifted her face further.

"Prove it to me, Alice. Prove to me you're fine," he rasped before he seized her mouth with his.

Her hands rose to his head, her fingers digging into his hair. Her hunger sprung at her with fierce claws, powerful and rampant. Had it really only been a matter of hours since she'd last held him in her arms?

He began to undress her a moment later, even as they continued to crane for each other, their kiss voracious. They only broke apart reluctantly after he'd removed her shirt and bra, and shoved her shorts down over her hips. Alice stepped out of her sandals, and helped Dylan get the garments down her legs. No sooner had she freed herself of her clothes than he was reaching for her, his mouth hard and slanted with arousal.

"Come here," he mumbled gruffly, turning her firmly in his arms. He pressed her against him, her naked body to his clothed one, her back to his front. His hands moved over her belly and hips, pushing her closer. Despite the rush of heat that went through her, her skin pebbled in the cool, air-conditioned room and beneath his hot touch. His hands moved greedily, sliding against her overly sensitive skin, molding her hips, waist, and breasts into the curve of his palms. She sensed his barely controlled hunger, a simmering sexual desire that was spiked with a dark, glorious intensity of emotion Alice could feel, even if she couldn't fathom entirely. His mouth pressed against her neck. She shivered uncontrollably as rain began to crash against the terrace and eave outside and lightning lit up the dark room. His long body curved around her, his cock pressing against the tops of her buttocks and lower back. One hand cupped a breast, the other slid along her pelvis and thigh. He bit at her shoulder.

"Dylan," she moaned shakily, trying to turn in his arms, seeking the mindless rapture of his kiss. The hand on her thigh held her in place, however, and then opened between her thighs. She gasped at this new restraint. He covered her entire sex, applying a sweet pressure at the same time he ground his cock against her.

"I don't like you being down at that camp, Alice. I can't control what happens to you," he said near her ear, his voice a low, rich seduction.

"You can't control what happens every second of my day," she whimpered, because he was kissing and nibbling at her ear, molding her breast to his palm, and applying an eye-crossing pressure to her sex, and it all felt so hot and delicious.

"Maybe not," he rasped. "But right now I can."

He shifted his hand slightly, sending the ridge of his forefinger between her labia. He grunted and kissed her ear more forcefully as he rubbed her slick clit. She cried out shakily at the burn.

"That's so good, baby, so hot and wet," he hissed in her ear. "Come over here." He backed up, and she followed his lead. He fell onto the couch, pulling her with him. A surprised yelp flew out of her mouth when she plopped down into his lap. Before she'd recovered from the drop, he put his hands on her naked hips and began circling her against his cock.

Alice moaned, surrendering to the moment. She arched her back and let him grind her against him, joining in the subtle, erotic dance. Lightning lit up the room and thunder rent the night sky. Electricity zipped through her veins and tingled her skin. Dylan's large hands cupped her ass and he groaned roughly.

"Stand up for just a second," she heard him say through the pounding rain. She slid between his spread thighs at his urging, her feet finding the carpet. She sensed him rustling behind her, and knew he was unfastening his jeans.

"No, stay still. Keep your feet on the floor," he bit out when she started to straighten and turn toward him. And then his hands were on her hips again, and he was pulling her back toward his lap. "Sit back on me," he directed tensely. He wrapped his arm around her waist and slid forward on the couch. Then she felt his hand moving between their bodies and the brush of his cockhead against her sex.

She whimpered shakily as he lowered her on him, and his cock slowly carved its way into her pussy. When she finally sat in his lap, his cock throbbing high inside of her, he tightened his hold on her, his lips and teeth moving along her shoulder blade, firing her already prickling nerves.

"Now I can control you, Alice," she heard him say darkly through the roar of the rain.

And it was true, she thought through a haze of thick desire. He could do whatever he wanted to her, in that moment, and she would have begged him for more.

He slid one hand along her lower spine, urging her to bend forward. The feeling of fullness and pressure only amplified. She placed her hands on his hard thighs to steady herself. At his urging, she started to move. He lifted her and pushed her back on his cock with his strong arms, but Alice was an equal, eager participant. She'd never made love in this position before, but instinctively understood the necessary motion. She stood on the floor, her knees bent, flexing her thighs for an up-and-down motion over his lap.

It felt exciting and lewd, her vulnerability and nakedness high-lighted by the position and the frequent illumination of the room from the lightning. Dylan held her hips possessively, plunging her forcefully onto his cock. His rough groan entwined with the thunder and rain, and the sound of their bodies crashing together in a primal tempo. The friction was intense. Ideal. She burned every-where: the tips of her heaving breasts, beneath Dylan's forceful hands, along her flexing, straining thighs . . . all around his thrust-ing, demanding cock.

She craved release. She reached for it, the crash of their bodies and roar of the rain a wild cacophony in her ears. The burn in her rapidly flexing thighs segued to an almost unbearable pain. She let out a desperate cry at the discomfort, but never ceased her hopping in his lap, too drunk from the pleasure.

He must have heard her pain, however, because he slammed her down onto his cock and kept her in place in his lap.

"Shhh," he growled when she made a mewling, desperate sound. His hand reached between her thighs. He found her clit, rubbing and tapping at the sensitive flesh.

She lit up like a Roman candle, pleasure shuddering through her.

She came back to herself with the sensation of him lifting and lowering her tensely in his lap, piercing her with short, sharp jabs. It didn't take him long. He plunged her onto his lap, his fingers delving in her hips and buttocks.

"*This* is where I want you, Alice," he grated out. Her eyes sprang wide as she felt his cock swell huge in her. "I'm never going to be happy when you wander too far away."

She stared out onto the storm-tossed terrace and yard, not really seeing. Only feeling as his cock twitched inside her, and she felt his warm semen filling her. His rough groans of pleasure filled her ears. But in her head, she kept hearing his words echo again and again, like they'd been scored into her spirit.

AFTER the monumental tension had left his body, and he sagged back on the couch, Alice rose over him. She stood and turned, and he reached for her.

She curled into his lap, her knees against his heaving ribs, her cheek against his chest. He cupped her head with one hand, his fingertips massaging her scalp. His other arm encircled her waist, shielding her nakedness from the chill of the air-conditioning.

The roar of the rain turned to a gentle hum, and the thunder to a rumble. Alice felt like she was melting into him.

"The storm is letting up," she murmured.

"Hmmm," he acknowledged, sounding satiated.

Distracted.

She lifted her hips, making out his bold features in a flash of lightning.

"What?" he asked quietly, his knowing fingertips transferring to the back of her neck. She closed her eyes briefly in pleasure as he massaged tense muscle.

"Are you really that worried?" she asked. She opened her eyes. "There's no reason to be."

Given his soft grunt, he remained unconvinced. She bit her lip. Despite all her confusion and trouble absorbing the events of the past few days, there was one question that refused to be suppressed or put on the back burner.

"Dylan?"

"Yeah," he muttered.

"Can I ask you something?"

His massaging fingers stilled. "About Addie's mother?" he asked warily.

Her throat tightened. "No," she whispered. "I think . . . I think I don't want to get into that tonight."

His fingertips resumed their massaging motion. "I agree. There's so much you still have to learn. So much to take in. Everything about . . . Addie's parents . . . about her mother, that can wait," he said grimly. "So what was your question, then?" he rumbled.

"Why did you first make love to me?"

He didn't respond immediately. A flash of lightning—dimmer than it had been during the full force of the storm—allowed her to see his face. Was it her imagination, or did he look stunned by her question.

"What do you mean?"

"I mean . . ." She broke off suddenly. What *did* she mean?

Everything felt so new and foreign to her, and it was so strange to try to assimilate everything that had happened to her since she first walked into the office and saw Dylan Fall last May, the barrage of bizarre information she'd received yesterday. . .

And now sitting here, curled up in his protective embrace after the fierce storm of their lovemaking. Such large, mind-blowing leaps and changes had occurred.

"Did you do it, so that you could have more control over me?" She realized how baldly negative that sounded, and hurried to smooth things over. "I mean so that there was a good excuse to have me with you during the nights, and . . . just a better idea of what was happening with me at Camp Durand? Dylan?" she asked uneasily after a pause, because he'd stopped his relaxing massaging motions on her neck and didn't reply.

"You don't know why I first made love to you?" he asked. She heard the blank incredulity of his tone, but didn't register its meaning.

"No. Should I?" she asked bemusedly.

He slid his hands along the side of her neck, the movement making her hyperaware of the congested feeling in her throat. He cupped her jaw with both hands, the gesture tender.

Prizing.

"I made love to you because I've never wanted anything so much as I did you there in those stables, and every time since then."

"Because of everything you went through," she asked shakily. "Because of Addie . . ."

"Not because of Addie," he cut her off. "Because of Alice."

Lightning illuminated him for a brief moment. She wondered at what she saw in his expression. She touched his face in awe, like she thought she could capture what she'd seen with her fingertips, imprint it on her soul.

"I knew I would care about you," he said gruffly when she touched his lips. "I had no idea I'd fall in love with you."

Her breath hitched with emotion. "It was an unexpected complication?" she asked with a soft bark of laughter.

His thumbs caressed her cheek, and the tightness in her throat
transferred to her chest. "That's what I thought at first," he said,
his arms going around her. Alice laid her head on his chest, secure
and awed in the cocoon of his arms. "Now it feels more like fate.
Or a blessing," she heard him rumble against her pressing ear.

Intense emotion rushed through her.

What he was telling her was nothing short of a miracle.

Had she—Alice—reached a point where she could trust in
miracles? She didn't know. It was just that there, in that moment,
the swelling ache she held inside her for Dylan was bigger than the
black hole of doubt and cynicism.

"The next few weeks or months are going to be hard sometimes. Challenging," Dylan said. "You still have so much to take
in, so much to learn. But I want you to remember what I just said,
through it all. Alice? Promise me."

He cupped the back of her head. Alice turned her nose into his
chest, inhaling his scent, letting it wash away the residue of her
insecurities and anxiety. When she was with Dylan, her fears and
distrust grew so small.

One doubt, however, seemed to grip at her very heart at that
moment.

She lifted her face, seeking out his lips in the darkness. "I
promise," she said. Their mouths fused. She couldn't stop the
shudder of emotion that went through her; she couldn't disguise
it from him.

"Alice?" he prodded, his brows slanting.

She pressed her forehead to his.

"I'm afraid," she admitted through a choked throat.

His arms tightened around her. "I know. I can't imagine what
these last few days have been like for—"

"*Not* of that. That's not what I'm afraid of. At least not right this second," she said.

"What, then?"

She gasped softly against his lips, the truth cutting at her. "I'm afraid because I would promise you almost anything."

Keep reading for an excerpt from
the next book by Beth Kery

GLOW

Available December 2015 from Berkley Books

t was the second time in a week that Dylan awoke in the dark room to find his arms empty. Instinct told him that it was still too early for him to escort Alice to the camp, a clandestine ritual they went through every morning before dawn. Neither of them wanted the Durand managers to know that Alice, who was a candidate to become a Durand executive, had taken up with the CEO of the company. What was between Alice and him was complicated, and it was their business alone.

At least for now it was. Dylan wasn't sure how long he could keep Alice and Durand Enterprises in separate spheres. For all intents and purposes, Alice *was* Durand Enterprises. She just didn't want to—or couldn't—accept that reality as of yet.

He reached blindly, finding his cell phone on the bedside table. He squinted at the time. No, he'd been correct. It was only a few minutes past two in the morning, way too early for Alice to be up and preparing to return to the camp.

He rose from the bed with just as much haste and alarm as that first time, but on this occasion with more certainty that he knew where to find her. The knowledge didn't quiet his worry any. He flipped on a bedside lamp and hauled on some jeans.

On that other night, he'd found a half-wild, disoriented Alice blindly seeking in the pitch darkness of the west hallway. When he'd flipped on the hall light, he'd cringed at the vision of her searching hands, pale face, and huge haunted eyes. The ghosts of the past could come so close to her at times—even leap from the deepest recesses of her unconscious mind until they seemingly took form in front of her. Alice had said she'd seen a woman in that hallway on that night, a woman that Dylan knew for a fact had died nearly two decades before.

The human mind was as mysterious and vast as the night sky.

That night, Alice had seen her biological mother. It was as if her long-buried, resurging memories were too foreign to process in her everyday consciousness. Instead, those memories had been projected into her nightmares and even into the solid reality of her surroundings, like a weird unconscious hologram effect or a ghost taking shape. Or at least that's how psychiatrist Sidney Gates had tried to explain it Dylan.

Presently, he found Alice standing square in the middle of the large empty bedroom suite in the west hall. Her long, toned legs were naked. They looked especially vulnerable in the bright glow of the overhead chandelier.

Tension coiled tight in his muscles. It was so hard at times, not knowing what to expect from her from one moment to the next. Sometimes he felt like he could only be certain of her when he was making love to her, and he felt her to be entirely present in the moment with him, abandoning herself wholesale to pleasure.

To him.

"Do you remember to whom this room belonged now?" he asked from behind her, his voice echoing off the bare walls in the mostly empty room. She'd accused him of manipulation and lying when she'd realized he'd purposefully kept her from entering this room. That was before he'd told her the truth of her identity.

He was glad when she started slightly and turned her head, meeting his stare. Since Alice had come to Castle Durand, there were a few times when she'd go utterly still in his presence, and he'd seen the ghosts of her past flicker eerily in the depths of her eyes.

Is that what *he* was to her? A ghost?

"Was it Addie Durand's room?" she asked slowly, her low, hoarse voice causing his skin to roughen.

His heart knocked uncomfortably against his sternum, even though he knew his appearance remained calm. No matter how hard he was trying—no matter how much he understood—he couldn't entirely adjust to Alice's distant, disconnected attitude about what he'd told her about Adelaide Durand.

He nodded and stepped toward her. "It was originally Addie's nursery, and it had just been remodeled for her before she was taken. Are you remembering?" he asked her again cautiously.

She shook her head adamantly. Her short, dark hair was growing some. Her spiky bangs fell into her eyes. She stuck out her bottom lip and blew up on them to clear her vision. The uncontrived, potently sexy gesture distracted him.

Just like almost everything about Alice did.

"I don't remember anything," she said.

Despite her quick, firm denial, he wasn't entirely sure he believed her. "Then why did you come here?"

"I was curious," she replied, her eyebrows arched in response to his quiet challenge.

"And how did you guess this was Addie's room?"

She shrugged. "You tried to keep me from it. And it's the most ideally situated in the house, so large and airy . . ." She faded off, glancing around at the ornate crown molding, the bluish-silver silk wallpaper and the enormous bay window with a built-in, curving cushioned bench that looked down on the gardens, and the sharp drop-off of the dune to Lake Michigan. Because it was night, only their reflections and that of the chandelier's glowed in the black glass. The room was nearly empty, only a few of his personal items remaining from his recent occupancy. He saw Alice's neck convulse as she swallowed. "You and Sidney had suggested how the Durands prized Addie so much, always giving her the best. I just guessed it'd belonged to her. And to you. Alan Durand prized you, as well," she added, once again meeting his stare.

Slowly, she spun to face him. She wore only the fitted T-shirt she'd had on last night during the storm and a semi-transparent pair of white cotton panties. Instinctively, his gaze dropped over her, trailing along her elegantly sloping shoulders, the full, thrusting breasts that stood in such erotic contrast to her slender limbs and narrow waist and hips. His gaze lingered between her thighs. Alice dyed the hair on her head to an obscuring, near-black color, but her true shade was a dark red-gold, a combination of her father's blond and her mother's auburn. He was reminded of that yet again as he spied the triangle of light brownish-red pubic hair visible beneath her thin panties. Despite the tension of the moment, he felt his sex flicker in arousal. There was something about the contrast of Alice's tough-girl strength and her potent vulnerability that lit a fire in him, something elemental and strong. The paradox was singularly powerful.

He dragged his gaze to her face.

"It must be strange for you, thinking of me living in Addie's room. Here. In the Durand's house," he added, taking another step toward her. It struck him that he was often approaching Alice like he might a half-wild animal forced into some domestic confine, highly aware that she might bolt at any moment.

He was determined to catch her, no matter what move she made.

She shook her head. She wore not a trace of makeup. Without the heavy eyeliner and mascara she often wore to obfuscate or intimidate—or both—her dark blue eyes looked enormous in her delicate face. Jesus, what he'd experienced when she'd walked into that office last May, so awkward and yet so defiant in her inexpensive new interview suit. The truth had slammed home, jarring him, rattling him to the center of his bones, even though he'd taken great pains to hide it. He had seen those eyes before.

But even if it *had* been the first time Dylan had ever seen her, he suspected he might have been nearly as shaken. No wonder she'd been drawn to the eye-goop. Her eyes would draw men with the noblest intentions.

And the foulest.

"No, it doesn't seem strange to me at all. I can see you in this room." Her chin tilted and her eyes sparked in that familiar defiant gesture. "You moved out of it because of me, didn't you?"

"I didn't know what to expect. Sidney thought we should cautiously expose you to the surroundings," he admitted. Sidney was familiar with Adelaide Durand's history and had been friends with Alan and Lynn. He'd brought his psychological expertise to bear on Alice's unique situation, once Dylan had finally tracked her down after nearly two decades of searching. It was Sidney who had suggested bringing her to the estate under the pretense of hiring her as a Camp Durand counselor. In that scenario, Dylan could keep an eye on what she recalled and how she would react, monitor her for signs of trauma. If not him personally, then the two Durand security employees Dylan had hired to watch her could do the job.

"I was familiar with Addie Durand's habits," he began slowly. "There are a few rooms that I worried might be more likely to trigger something . . . undesirable. This one. Alan and Lynn's suite. The den, the original living room . . . and the dining room. With few exceptions, the entry hall, the kitchen, the terrace gardens, and the media room have been extensively renovated, so I didn't worry as much about that. Most of the other rooms here weren't used much—either by the Durands or by me, so they weren't of any concern." He hesitated.

"I never imagined you'd inadvertently find your way into the dining room that first night you arrived here at the castle. Or the woods and stables the next day," Dylan told her, choosing his words carefully. Alice had made it very clear to him that while she would discuss the details of Addie Durand, her kidnapping, and Dylan's part in the tragedy, she wouldn't talk about Addie and herself as if they were the same person. The recent revelation still seemed too overwhelming for her to assimilate. Currently, they were treading on dangerous ground.

Her eyelids narrowed slightly, and he knew he'd made some kind of misstep, despite his caution. "You suspected I was going to be in your bedroom, even before I came here? And so you moved suites, in order not to trigger any . . ." She faded off uncertainly, aware she was skimming close to the fire. Her defiant expression made a quick resurgence. "I thought you said that you hadn't planned for anything sexual between us . . . that it just *happened* that morning in the stables?"

"That's true. And since you seem to need a reminder, *you're* the one who seduced *me*, Alice," he said with a hard, pointed glance meant to quash her suspicion immediately. It didn't work. He mentally damned her defensive posture and angry expression and closed the space between them. Satisfaction went through him when he took her into his arms, and she pressed her front against him.

"If that's what you want to call the first three seconds of our being together. It was all you after that, baby," she grumbled under her breath.

"I didn't hear you complaining."

Her eyes flashed up at him defiantly.

"I'm telling you the truth, Alice. I didn't plan for us to be together in the stables that morning. How could I have? I didn't know you'd show up there. I *didn't* plan for us to get involved that way when you came here."

"Then why would you worry about me being *here* . . . in this room? Why did you pack up most of your things and decorate a whole new suite if you didn't *plan* on us sleeping together from the first? Why else would I be in Dylan Fall's bedroom if not for sex?" she demanded.

Dylan suppressed a sigh. Despite the fact that she grasped his waist and lightly pressed her breasts and belly against him in a tempting gesture, her trademark wary expression remained as she stared up at him.

"I didn't move out because I had plans to seduce you," he told her with an air of finality, mapping her elegant, supple spine and the tight curve of her hips with his hands. He felt his need for her mount. How would all of this have played out if this powerful attraction hadn't been there? It was so hard to say, but he would have contrived something to bring her closer to him.

"*Why*, then?" she insisted, undaunted by a tone that Dylan used regularly to subdue some of the most tried and hard-boiled executives in the world. Of course it didn't faze Alice. He closed his eyes briefly. Dammit, she could be impossible.

"Dylan?"

"I felt like an interloper, being in here . . . knowing you were about to come to the Durand Estate."

"You felt like an *interloper*?" she asked slowly, looking slightly dazed by his reluctant confession. "Because this was Alan Durand's house? Because of your history with him?"

"Because it was no longer my room. No longer my home. Not since you came. Period." Regret sliced through him at his harsh tone when he saw her lush lower lip quiver.

"I'm sorry," he said, frustrated. "It's just that sometimes you keep pressing. And it's hard to know when you want the truth and when you don't."

"I know," she said quickly. She, too, looked regretful. "And it's not true, what you said. Of course Castle Durand is your home. You own it, don't you? You bought it?"

"Yes, but only because Alan Durand offered the house to me as part of the special contract he created to make it possible for me to purchase Durand shares when he made me CEO. I wouldn't have been able to afford it at that time in my life if he hadn't offered me certain concessions." He exhaled as the memory of their negotiations for his taking over Durand entered his brain. Alan had been so stubborn. So insistent. So *generous* in contriving a way to set terms that would allow Dylan to smoothly and completely take the helm of Durand Enterprises. "In the olden days, a lord's title was tied to the land. That's what Alan explained to me once," he recalled with fond, wry amusement. "Alan loved his European history. He insisted that I'd be taken more seriously as the head of Durand Enterprises if I was master of the company's symbolic domain."

"The castle," Alice said, a small smile flickering across her lips. She sobered. "And you *are* the master, Dylan."

"No. Not entirely."

He cupped her jaw, trying to ease her sudden troubled expression . . . her abrupt fragility. She looked up at him through her spiky bangs, her glance reminding him again of that of a cautious, wild thing.

"It's just so impossible to believe, Dylan," she said in a rush, and he knew instinctively she meant his revelation that she was the true daughter of Alan and Lynn Durand. "I mean, it's not that I think you're lying. Why *would* you? It's just . . ." Her expression grew a little desperate as she seemingly searched for words to explain. "You can't just start thinking of the world as round in a second when you've thought it was flat for your whole life." She gave a sharp bark of laughter, as if she'd just absorbed the meaning of her words only upon hearing them. "It's not a bad analogy, really," she mumbled to herself. "I sort of feel like I might fall straight off the earth into nothingness every time I think about what you told me." She looked up at him entreatingly. "Please understand."

"I *do*," he assured quietly, his fingers delving into her thick, short hair. He cupped her head. It was hard to be the rational executive when it came to Alice. It was hard to be clearheaded in this situation, period. But he had to try. So much was at stake.

"What do you think would help you most to make it real, Alice?"

She shook her head. "I don't know for sure. Just time, I guess."

He nodded, lowering his head until her upturned face was just inches from his. "Do you think it might help to see tangible proof?"

She blinked. "Like what? More photos?"

He pulled her tighter against him. Her T-shirt felt cool and slightly damp against the naked skin of his torso. Despite the chill of the fabric, it was the sensation of her full breasts pressing against his ribs that made his skin roughen. Her erect nipples were a fierce distraction. He forced his mind to focus.

"Not just photos. You've said yourself you don't experience any connection to photos of Adelaide Durand."

"What, then?" she asked in a hushed tone.

"Alan and Lynn Durand's physician still practices at Morgantown Memorial. He still possesses some of their genetic material. They will be able to tell you without a doubt who your parents were."

She stared up at him blankly. "You want me to go for genetic testing?"

"Only if you're up for it. It doesn't have to be now," he said, caressing her neck. He'd learned from experience in the past week that his touch helped to ground her. Soothe her. Distract her from her phantoms. He wasn't above using that fact proactively to help her through this process.

He wasn't above using *anything*, in that cause.

"You mean . . . it doesn't have to be *now*, but it does have to be *sometime*."

He strained to keep his expression impassive, very much aware that he was once again walking through a minefield.

"*I* don't need any proof that what I told you is one hundred percent true," he said firmly, holding her stare.

"But there will be those who will demand it," Alice added warily.

An imagined vision of a roomful of somber, suspicous Durand executives and attorneys—all the potential doubters and naysayers—flew into his mind's eye. "There will be plenty who eventually demand it." He repeated the obvious as calmly as possible.

She bit her lip and glanced aside. Aside from all these bizarre circumstances she found herself in, Dylan knew Alice Reed was typically a practical, down-to-earth young woman with a brilliant brain for mathematics and business. Never let it be said that genes weren't telling. Alan Durand had possessed one of the finest business minds he'd ever known, and Lynn had been an outstanding scholar. She'd been an assistant professor of mathematics at the University of Michigan when Alan had first met her.

Dylan was glad to experience Alice's sudden, intense focus on the issue at hand.

"I don't want anything of Addie Durand's, so why should it matter?"

"You don't know that yet."

"I know what I want and don't want, Dylan."

"Then do it for yourself," he suggested without pause. He'd been prepared for her response. He'd been prepared for her stubbornness.

"Myself?"

He nodded. "That's what I meant before. *You* need tangible proof. Not just my word. You need evidence you can hold in your hand. It'll be something solid to grasp on to."

"A start," she whispered.

"A start," Dylan agreed, relief sweeping through him because he'd seen something click in her eyes, and knew she'd go for the genetic testing. He needed that tangible proof for what was surely to come.

He leaned down and brushed his mouth against hers. His kiss was meant to be gentle and reassuring, but Alice was having none of it. She put her hand on the back of his head, pushing him further down to her and going up on her tiptoes. He responded to her invitation as always: wholesale.

Their kiss deepened. His lust flamed higher on the fuel of her reciprocated need.

So sweet.

So Alice-like, to be suspicious and doubting one moment, and then taking him to the center of the flames within two seconds flat. He would have to have her again tonight, experience her melting beneath his touch, laid bare and submitting to the bond between them. He needed it for Alice's sake.

He required it for his own.

ABOUT THE AUTHOR

Beth Kery lives in Chicago where she juggles the demands of her career, her love of the city and the arts, and a busy family life. Her writing today reflects her passion for all of the above. She is the *New York Times* and *USA Today* bestselling author of *Because You Are Mine*. Find out more about Beth and her books at Beth Kery.com or Facebook.com/Beth.Kery.